Praise for *Everything Good Will Come*

Winner of the Wole Soyinka Prize for African Literature

Finalist, Multicultural Fiction, Independent Publisher Book Awards

Foreword Magazine Book of the Year Award Honorable Mention

"A literary masterpiece... Everything Good Will Come *put me into a spell from the first page to the very last... It portrays the complicated society and history of Nigeria through... brilliant prose."*

—World Literature Today

"Skillful ... impressive debut novel...Thematically, her work is wide-ranging and yet powerfully focused, the different areas of concern drawn together so that they inform each other... Again and again Atta's writing tugs at the heart, at the conscience."

—The Sunday Independent (Lesotho, Africa)

"Sefi Atta's first novel is a beautifully paced stroll in the shoes of a woman growing up in a country struggling to find its post-Independence identity... The main characters are well realized, and the supporting cast—campaigning journalist, put-upon mother-in-law, co-wives in a polygamous marriage, stroppy secretary—avoid caricature. The relaxed tempo of the narrative allows for proper character development. Everything Good Will Come *depicts the struggles women face in a conservative society. This is convincing; more remarkable is what the novel has to say about the need to speak out when all around is falling apart."*

—Times Literary Supplement (London)

"...an original, witty coming-of-age tale: Tom Sawyer meets Jane Eyre, with Nigerian girls. Reading Everything Good....*you can feel the dust and the sun... an iridescent introduction to a fascinating nation."*

—The Observer Magazine (London)

"Atta's distinctive coming-of-age novel... will appeal to all readers interested in contemporary women's stories and/or African culture. Recommended..."

—Choice

Everything Good Will Come

A NOVEL

Sefi Atta

Interlink Books

An imprint of Interlink Publishing Group, Inc.
Northampton, Massachusetts

For my dearest, Gboyega, and our sweetest, Temi

First paperback edition published in 2008 by

INTERLINK BOOKS
An imprint of Interlink Publishing Group, Inc.
46 Crosby Street, Northampton, Massachusetts 01060
www.interlinkbooks.com

Copyright © Sefi Atta, 2005, 2008

Library of Congress Cataloging-in-Publication Data

Atta, Sefi.
Everything good will come / by Sefi Atta.
p. cm.
Includes bibliographical references and index.
ISBN 978-1-56656-570-7 (hard-cover); ISBN 978-1-56656-704-6 (pb)
1. Female friendship—Fiction. 2. Women—Nigeria—Fiction.
3. Social classes—Fiction. 4. Nigeria—Fiction. I. Title.
PS3601.T78I5 2004

2004012437

Printed and bound in the United States of America

1971

From the beginning I believed whatever I was told, downright lies even, about how best to behave, although I had my own inclinations. At an age when other Nigerian girls were masters at ten-ten, the game in which we stamped our feet in rhythm and tried to outwit partners with sudden knee jerks, my favorite moments were spent sitting on a jetty pretending to fish. My worst was to hear my mother's shout from her kitchen window: "Enitan, come and help in here."

I'd run back to the house. We lived by Lagos Lagoon. Our yard stretched over an acre and was surrounded by a high wooden fence that could drive splinters into careless fingers. I played, carelessly, on the West side because the East side bordered the mangroves of Ikoyi Park and I'd once seen a water snake slither past. Hot, hot were the days as I remember them, with runny-egg sunshine and brief breezes. The early afternoons were for eat and sleep breaks: eat a heavy lunch, sleep like a drunk. The late afternoons, after homework, I spent on our jetty, a short wooden promenade I could walk in three steps, if I took long enough strides to strain the muscles between my thighs.

I would sit on its cockle-plastered edge and wait for the water to lap at my feet, fling my fishing rod, which was made from tree branch, string, and a cork from one of my father's discarded wine bottles. Sometimes fishermen came close, rowing in a rhythm that pleased me more than chewing on fried tripe; their skins charred, almost gray from sun-dried sea salt. They spoke in the warble of island people, yodeling across their canoes. I was never tempted to jump into the lagoon as they did. It gave off the smell of raw fish and was the kind of dirty brown I knew would taste like vinegar. Plus, everyone knew about the currents that could drag a person away. Bodies usually showed up days later, bloated, stiff and rotten. True.

It wasn't that I had big dreams of catching fish. They wriggled too much and I couldn't imagine watching another living being suffocate. But my parents had occupied everywhere else with their fallings out; their trespasses unforgivable. Walls could not save me from the shouting. A pillow, if I stuffed my head under it, could not save me. My hands could not, if I clamped them over my ears and stuffed my head under a pillow. So there it was, the jetty, my protectorate, until the day my mother decided it was to be demolished.

The priest in her church had a vision of fishermen breaking into our house: They would come at night, *labalaba*. They would come unarmed, *yimiyimi*. They would steal valuables, *tolotolo*.

The very next day, three workmen replaced our jetty with a barbed wire fence and my mother kept watch over them; the same way she watched our neighbors; the same way she checked our windows for evil spirits outside at night; the same way she glared at our front door long after my father had walked out. I knew he would be furious. He was away on a law conference and when he returned and saw her new fence, he ran outside shouting like a crazed man. Nothing, nothing, would stop my mother, he said, until she'd destroyed everything in our house, because of that church of hers. What kind of woman was she? What kind of selfish, uncaring, woman was she?

He enjoyed that view. Warm, breezy evenings on the veranda overlooking it is how I remember him, easy as the cane chair in which he sat. He was usually there in the dry season, which lasted most of the year; scarcely in the chilly harmattan, which straddled Christmas and New Year, and never in the swampy rainy season that made our veranda floor slippery over the summer vacation. I would sit on the steps and watch him and his two friends: Uncle Alex, a sculptor, who smoked a pipe that smelled like melted coconut, and Uncle Fatai, who made me laugh because his name fitted his roly-poly face. He too was a lawyer like my father and they had all been at Cambridge together. Three musketeers in the heart of darkness, they called themselves there; they stuck together and hardly anyone spoke to them. Sometimes they frightened me with their stories of western Nigeria (which my father called the Wild West), where people threw car tires over other people and set them on fire because they belonged to different political factions. Uncle Alex blamed the British for the fighting: "Them and their bloody empire. Come here and divide our country like one of their bloody tea cakes. Driving on the left side of the bloody road... "

The day the Civil War broke out, he delivered the news. Uncle Fatai arrived soon afterward and they bent heads as if in prayer to listen to the radio. Through the years, from their arguments about federalists, secessionists, and bloody British, I'd amassed as much knowledge about the events in my country as any seven-year-old could. I knew that our first Prime Minister was killed by a Major General, that the Major General was soon killed, and that we had another Major General heading our country. For a while the palaver had stopped, and now it seemed the Biafrans were trying to split our country in two.

Uncle Fatai broke the silence. "Hope our boys finish them off."

"What the hell are you talking about?" Uncle Alex asked.

"They want a fight," Uncle Fatai said. "We'll give them a fight."

Uncle Alex prodded his chest, almost toppling him over. "Can you fight? Can you?" My father tried to intervene but he warned, "Keep out of this, Sunny."

My father eventually asked Uncle Alex to leave. He patted my head as he left and we never saw him in our house again.

Over the next months, I would listen to radio bulletins on how our troops were faring against the Biafrans. I would hear the slogan: "To keep Nigeria one is a task that must be done."

My father would ask me to hide under my bed whenever we had bomb raid alerts. Sometimes I heard him talking about Uncle Alex; how he'd known beforehand there was going to be a civil war; how he'd joined the Biafrans and died fighting for them even though he hated guns.

I loved my uncle Alex; thought that if I had to marry a man, it would be a man like him, an artist, who cared too much or not at all.

He gave my father the nickname Sunny, though my father's real name was Bandele Sunday Taiwo. Now, everyone called my father Sunny, like they called my mother Mama Enitan, after me, though her real name was Arin. I was their first child, their only child now, since my brother died. He lived his life between sickle cell crises. My mother joined a church to cure him, renounced Anglicanism and herself, it seemed, because one day, my brother had another crisis and she took him there for healing. He died, three years old. I was five.

In my mother's church they wore white gowns. They walked around on bare feet, and danced to drums. They were baptized in a stream of holy water and drank from it to cleanse their spirits. They believed in spirits; evil ones sent by other people to wreak havoc, and reborn spirits, which would not stay long on earth. Their incantations, tireless worship and praise. I could bear even the sight of my mother throwing her hands up and acting as I'd never seen her act in an Anglican church. But I was sure that if the priest came before me and rolled his eyeballs back as he did when he was about to have a vision, that would be the end of me.

He had a bump on his forehead, an expression as if he were sniffing something bad. He pronounced his visions between chants that sounded like the Yoruba words for butterfly, dung beetle, and turkey: *labalaba, yimiyimi, tolotolo.* He smelled of incense. The day he stood before me, I kept my eyes on the hem of his cassock. I was a reborn spirit, he said, like my brother, and my mother would have to bring me for cleansing. I was too young, she said. My time would soon come, he said. Turkey, turkey, turkey.

The rest of the day I walked around with the dignity of the aged and troubled, held my stomach in until I developed cramps. Death would hurt, I knew, and I did not want to see my brother like that, as a ghost. My father only had to ask how I was feeling, when I collapsed before him. "I'm going to die," I said.

He asked for an explanation.

"You're not going back there again," he said.

Sundays after that, I spent at home. My mother would go off to church, and my father would leave the house, too. Then Bisi, our house girl, would sneak next door to see Akanni, the driver who blared his juju music, or he'd come to see her and they would both go off to the servants' quarters, leaving me with Baba, our gardener, who worked on Sundays.

At least, during the Civil War, Bisi would sometimes invite me over to hear Akanni's stories about the war front far away. How Biafran soldiers stepped on land mines that blew up their legs like crushed tomatoes; how Biafran children ate lizard flesh to stay alive. The Black Scorpion was one of Nigeria's hero soldiers. He wore a string of charms around his neck and bullets ricocheted off his chest. I was old enough to listen to such tales without being frightened, but was still too young to be anything but thrilled by them. When the war ended three years later, I missed them.

Television in those days didn't come on until six o'clock in the evening. The first hour was news and I never watched the news, except that special day when the Apollo landed on the moon. After that, children in school said you could get Apollo, a form of conjunctivitis, by staring at an eclipse too long. Tarzan, Zorro, Little John, and the entire Cartwright family on *Bonanza* were there, with their sweet and righteous retaliations, to tell me any other fact I needed to know about the world. And oblivious to any biased messages I was receiving, I sympathized with Tarzan (those awful natives!), thought Indians were terrible people and memorized the happy jingles of foreign multinational companies: "Mobil keeps your engine—Beep, beep, king of the road." If Alfred Hitchcock came on, I knew it was time to go to bed. Or if it was Doris Day. I couldn't bear her song, "Que Sera."

I approached adolescence with an extraordinary number of body aches, finished my final year of primary school, and began the long wait for secondary school. Secondary school didn't start until early October, so the summer vacation stretched longer than normal. The rains poured, dried up, and each day passed like the one before unless something special happened, like the afternoon Baba found iguana eggs, or the morning a rabid dog bit our night watchman, or the evening Bisi and Akanni fought. I heard them shouting and rushed to the servants' quarters to watch.

Akanni must have thought he was Muhammad Ali. He was shadow boxing around Bisi. "What's my name? What's my name?" Bisi lunged forward and slapped his face. He reached for her collar and ripped her blouse. "My bress? My bress?" She spat in his face and grabbed the gold chain around his neck. They both crashed into the dust and didn't stop kicking till Baba lay flat out on the ground. "No more," he said. "No more, I beg of you."

Most days were not that exciting. And I was beginning to get bored of the wait when, two weeks to the end of the vacation, everything changed. It was the third Sunday of September 1971, late in the afternoon. I was playing with my catapult when I mistakenly struck Baba as he was trimming the lawn. He chased after me with his machete and I ran into the barbed wire fence, snagging my sleeve. Yoruba tradition has us believe that Nature heralds the beginning of a person's transition: to life, adulthood, and death. A rooster's crow, sudden rainfall, a full moon, seasonal changes. I had no such salutations as I remember it.

"Serves you right," came a girl's voice.

A nose appeared between the wide gap in the fence, followed by a brown eye. I freed my sleeve from the barbed wire fence and rubbed my elbow.

"For running around like that," she said. "With no head or tail. It serves you right that you got chooked."

She looked nothing like the Bakare children who lived next door. I'd seen them through the wide gap in our fence and they were as dark as me; younger, too. Their father had two wives who organized outdoor cooking jamborees. They always looked pregnant, and so did he in his flowing robes. He was known as Engineer Bakare. He was Uncle Fatai's friend and Uncle Fatai called him Alhaji Bakare, because he'd been on pilgrimage to Mecca. To us he was Chief Bakare. He threw a huge party after his chieftancy ceremony last year and no one could sleep that night for the sound of his juju band badabooming through our walls. Typical Lagos people, my father said. They made merry till they dropped, or until their neighbors did.

"I'm Sheri,"she said, as if I'd asked for her name.

"I've never seen you before," I said.

"So?"

She had a sharp mouth, I thought, as she burst into giggles.

"Can I come to your house?" she asked.

I glanced around the yard, because my mother didn't want me playing with the Bakare children.

"Come."

I was bored. I waited by the barbed wire fence, forgot about my torn sleeve, even about Baba who had chased me. He, apparently, had forgotten me too, because he was cutting grass by the other fence. Minutes later, she walked in. Just as I thought, she was a half-caste. She wore a pink skirt and her white top ended just above her navel. With her short afro, her face looked like a sunflower. I noticed she wore pink lipstick.

"How old are you?" I accused.

"Eleven," she said.

"Me too."

"Eh? Small girl like you?" she said.

At least I was a decent eleven-year-old. She barely reached my shoulders, even in her high heel shoes. I told her my birthday was next January, but she said I was still her junior. Her birthday was two months earlier, in November. "I'm older, I'm senior. Don't you know? That's how it is. My younger brothers and sisters call me Sister Sheri at home."

"I don't believe you."

"It's true," she said.

Breeze rustled through the hibiscus patch. She eyed me up and down.

"Did you see the executions on television last night?"

"What executions?"

"The armed robbers."

"No."

I was not allowed to watch; my father was against capital punishment.

She smiled. "Ah, it was good. They shot them on the beach. Tied them, covered their eyes. One, two, three."

"Dead?"

"*Pafuka*," she said and dropped her head to one side. I imagined the scene on the beach where public executions were held. The photographs usually showed up in the newspapers a day later.

"Where is your mother from?" I asked.

"England."

"Does she live there?"

"She's dead."

She spoke as if telling the time: three o'clock sharp, four

o'clock dead. Didn't she care? I felt ashamed about my brother's death, as if I had a bad leg that people could tease me about.

"*Yei*," she exclaimed. She'd spotted a circus of flying fish on the lagoon. I, too, watched them flipping over and diving in. They rarely surfaced from the water. They disappeared and the water was still again.

"Do you have brothers and sisters?" she asked.

"Nope."

"You must be spoiled rotten."

"No, I'm not."

"Yes, you are. Yes, you are. I can see it in your face."

She spun around and began to boast. She was the oldest of the Bakare children. She had seven brothers and sisters. She would be starting boarding school in two weeks, in another city, and she...

"I got into Royal College," I said, to shut her up.

"Eyack! It's all girls!"

"It's still the best school in Lagos."

"All girls is boring."

"Depends how you look at it," I said, quoting my father.

Through the fence we heard Akanni's juju music. Sheri stuck her bottom out and began to wriggle. She dived lower and wormed up.

"You like juju music?" I asked.

"Yep. Me and my grandma, we dance to it."

"You dance with your grandma?"

"I live with her."

The only grandparent I'd known was my father's mother, who was now dead, and she scared me because of the grayish-white films across her pupils. My mother said she got them from her wickedness. The music stopped.

"These flowers are nice," Sheri said, contemplating them as she might an array of chocolates. She plucked one of them and planted it behind her ear.

"Is it pretty?"

I nodded. She looked for more and began to pick them one by one. Soon she had five hibiscus in her hair. She picked her sixth as we heard a cry from across the yard. Baba was charging toward us with his machete in the air. "You! Get away from there!"

Sheri caught sight of him and screamed. We ran round the side of the house and hobbled over the gravel on the front drive.

"Who was that?" Sheri asked, rubbing her chest.

I took short breaths. "Our gardener."

"I'm afraid of him."

"Baba can't do anything. He likes to scare people."

She sucked her teeth. "Look at his legs crooked as crab's, his lips red as a monkey's bottom."

We rolled around the gravel. The hibiscus toppled out of Sheri's afro and she kicked her legs about, relishing her laughter and prolonging mine. She recovered first and wiped her eyes with her fingers.

"Do you have a best friend?" she asked.

"No."

"Then, I will be your best friend." She patted her chest. "Every day, until we go to school."

"I can only play on Sundays," I said.

My mother would drive her out if she ever saw her.

She shrugged. "Next Sunday then. Come to my house if you like."

"All right," I said.

Who would know? She was funny, and she was also rude, but that was probably because she had no home training.

She yelled from our gates. "I'll call you *aburo*, little sister, from now on. And I'll beat you at ten-ten, wait and see."

It's a stupid game, I was about to say, but she'd disappeared behind the cement column. Didn't anyone tell her she couldn't wear high heels? Lipstick? Any of that?

Where was her respect for an old man like Baba? She was the spoiled one. Sharp mouth and all.

～

Baba was raking the grass when I returned to the back yard.

"I'm going to tell your mother about her," he said.

I stamped my foot in frustration. "But she's my friend."

"How can she be your friend? You've just met her, and your mother does not know her."

"She doesn't have to know her."

I'd known him all my life. How could he tell? He made a face as if the memory of Sheri had left a bad taste in his mouth. "Your mother will not like that one."

"Please, don't tell. Please."

I knelt and pressed my palms together. It was my best trick ever to wear him out.

"All right," he said. "But I must not see you or her anywhere near those flowers again."

"Never," I said, scrambling to my feet. "See? I'm going inside. You won't find me near them."

I walked backward into the house. Baba's legs really were like crab's, I thought, scurrying through the living room. Then I bumped my shin on the corner of a chair and hopped the rest of the way to my bedroom. God was already punishing me.

My suitcase was under my bed. It was a fake leather one, large enough to accommodate me if I curled up tight, but now it was full. I dragged it out. I had two weeks to go before leaving home, and had started packing the contents a month early: a mosquito net, bed sheets, flip-flops, a flashlight. The props for my make-believe television adverts: bathing soap, toothpaste, a bag of sanitary towels. I wondered what I would do with those.

As I stood before my mirror, I traced the grooves around my plaits. Sheri's afro was so fluffy, it moved as she talked. I grabbed a comb from my table and began to undo my plaits. My arms ached by the time I finished and my hair flopped over my face. From my top drawer, I took a red marker and painted my lips. At least my cheeks were smooth, unlike hers. She had a spray of rashes and was so fair-skinned. People her color got called "Yellow Pawpaw" or "Yellow Banana" in school.

In school you were teased for being yellow or fat; for being Moslem or for being dumb; for stuttering or wearing a bra and for being Igbo, because it meant that you were Biafran or knew people who were. I was painting my finger nails with the marker pen, recalling other teasable offenses, when my mother walked in. She was wearing her white church gown.

"You're here?" she said.

"Yes," I said.

In her church gowns I always thought my mother resembled a column. She stood tall and squared her shoulders, even as a child, she said. She would not play rough, or slump around, so why did I? Her question often prompted me to walk with my back straight until I forgot.

"I thought you would be outside," she said.

I patted my hair down. Her own hair was in two neat cornrows and she narrowed her eyes as if there were sunlight in my room.

"Ah-ah? What is this? You're wearing lipstick?"

I placed my pen down, more embarrassed than scared.

She beckoned. "Let me see."

Her voice softened when she saw the red ink. "You shouldn't be coloring your mouth at your age. I see you're also packing your suitcase again. Maybe you're ready to leave this house."

My gaze reached the ceiling.

"Where is your father?"

"I don't know."

"Did he say when he will be back?"

"No."

She surveyed the rest of my room. "Clean this place up."

"Yes, Mummy."

"And come and help me in the kitchen afterward. I want to speak to you later on tonight. Make sure you wash your mouth before you come."

I pretended to be preoccupied with the contents of my dressing table until she left. Using a pair of scissors, I scraped the red ink from my nails. What did she want to speak to me about? Baba couldn't have told.

My mother never had a conversation with me; she talked and knew that I was listening. I always was. The mere sound of her footsteps made me breathe faster. She hardly raised a hand to me, unlike most mothers I knew, who beat their children with tree branches, but she didn't have to. I'd been caned before, for daydreaming in class, with the side of a ruler, on my knuckles, and wondered if it wasn't an easier punishment than having my mother look at me as if she'd caught me playing with my own poop. Her looks were hard to forget. At least caning welts eventually disappeared.

Holy people had to be unhappy or strict, or a mixture of both, I'd decided. My mother and her church friends, their priest with his expression as if he was sniffing something bad. There wasn't a choir mistress I'd seen with a friendly face, and even in our old Anglican church people had generally looked miserable as they prayed. I'd come to terms with these people as I'd come to terms with my own natural sinfulness. How many mornings had I got up vowing to be holy, only to succumb to happiness by midday, laughing and running helter-skelter? I wanted to be holy; I just couldn't remember.

I was frying plantains in the kitchen with my mother that evening, when oil popped from the frying pan and struck my wrist.

"Watch what you're doing," she said.

"Sorry," Bisi said, peeping up from the pots she was washing.

Bisi often said sorry for no reason. I lifted the fried plantains from the pan and smacked them down with my spatula. Oil spitting, chopping knives. Onions. Kitchen work was ugly. When I was older I would starve myself so I wouldn't have to cook. That was my main plan.

A noise outside startled me. It was my father coming through the back door.

"I knock on my front door these days and no one will answer," he muttered.

The door creaked open and snapped shut behind him. Bisi rushed to take his briefcase and he shooed her away. I smiled at my father. He was always miserable after work, especially when he returned from court. He was skinny with a voice that cracked and I pitied him whenever he complained: "I'm working all day, to put clothes on your back, food in your stomach, pay your school fees. All I ask is for peace when I get home. Instead you give me *wahala*. Daddy can I buy ice-cream. Daddy can I buy Enid Blyton. Daddy my jeans are torn. Daddy, Daddy, Daddy. You want me dead?"

He loosened his tie. "I see your mother is making you understudy her again."

I took another plantain and sliced its belly open, hoping for more of his sympathy. My mother shook a pot of stew on the stove and lifted its lid to inspect the contents.

"It won't harm her to be in here," she said.

I eased the plantain out and began to slice it into circles.

My father opened the refrigerator and pulled out a bottle of beer. Again Bisi rushed to his aid, and this time he allowed her to open the bottle.

"You should tell her young girls don't do this anymore," he said.

"Who said?" my mother asked.

"And if she asks where you learned such nonsense, tell her from your father and he's for the liberation of women."

He stood at attention and saluted. My father was not a serious man, I thought.

"All women except your wife," my mother said.

Bisi handed him his glass of beer. I thought he hadn't heard because he began to drink. He lowered the glass. "I've never asked you to be in here cooking for me."

"Ah, well," she said, wiping her hands with a dish cloth. "But you never ask me not to either."

He nodded in agreement. "It is hard to compete with your quest for martyrdom."

My mother made a show of inspecting the fried plantains. She pointed to the pan and I emptied too many plantain pieces into it. The oil hissed and fumes filled the air.

Whenever my father spoke good English like that, I knew he was angry. I didn't understand what he meant most times. This time, he placed his empty glass on the table and grabbed his briefcase.

"Don't wait up for me."

My mother followed him. As they left the kitchen, I crept to the door to spy on them. Bisi turned off the tap to hear their conversation and I rounded on her with all the rage a whisper could manage: "Stop listening to people's private conversations! You're always listening to people's private conversations!"

She snapped her fingers at me, and I snapped mine back and edged toward the door hinge.

My parent's quarrels were becoming more senseless; not

more frequent or more loud. One wrong word from my father could bring on my mother's rage. He was a wicked man. He had always been a wicked man. She would shout Bible passages at him. He would remain calm. At times like this, I could pity my mother, if only for my father's expression. It was the same as the boys in school who lifted your skirt and ran. They looked just as confused once the teacher got hold of their ears.

My mother rapped the dining table. "Sunny, whatever you're doing out there, God is watching you. You can walk out of that door, but you cannot escape His judgment."

My father fixed his gaze on the table. "I can't speak for Him, but I remember He will not be mocked. You want to use the Bible as a shield against everyone? Use it. One day we will both meet our maker. I will tell him all I have done. Then you can tell him what you have done."

He walked away in the direction of their bedroom. My mother returned to the kitchen. I thought she might scold me after she found my plantains burning, but she didn't. I hurried over and flipped them.

～

A frown may have chewed her face up, but one time my mother had smiled. I'd seen black and white photographs of her, her hair pressed and curled and her eyebrows penciled into arches. She was a chartered secretary and my father was in his final year of university when they met. Many men tried to chase her. Many, he said, until he wrote her one love letter. One, he boasted, and the rest didn't stand a chance. "Your mother was the best dancer around. The best dressed girl ever. The tiniest waist, I'm telling you. The tiniest. I could get my hand around it, like this, before you came along and spoiled it."

He would simulate how he struggled to hug her. My mother was not as big as he claimed. She was plump, in the way mothers were plump; her arms shook like jelly. My father no longer told the joke and I was left to imagine that it was true that she had once showed him affection. If she didn't anymore it was because it was there in the Bible: God got jealous.

After dinner I went to their bedroom to wait. I still had no idea what my mother wanted to speak to me about. My father had left the air-conditioner on and it blew remnants of mosquito repellent and cologne into my face. Their mosquito net hung over me and I inspected my shin which had developed a bump since my collision with the sofa.

My mother walked in. Already I felt like crying. Could Baba have told? If so, he was responsible for the trouble I was in.

My mother sat opposite me. "Do you remember, when you used to come to church with me, that some of the sisters would miss church for a week?"

"Yes, Mummy."

"Do you know why they missed church?"

"No."

"Because they were unclean," she said.

Immediately I looked at the air-conditioner. My mother began to speak in Yoruba. She told me the most awful thing about blood and babies and why it was a secret.

"I will not marry," I said.

"You will," she said.

"I will not have children."

"Yes, you will. All women want children."

Sex was a filthy act, she said, and I must always wash myself afterward. Tears filled my eyes. The prospect of dying young seemed better now.

"Why are you crying?" she asked.

"I don't know."

"Come here," she said. "I have prayed for you and nothing bad will come your way."

She patted my back. I wanted to ask, what if the bleeding started during morning assembly? What if I needed to pee during sex? Before this, I'd had blurred images of a man lying on top of a woman. Now that the images had been brought into focus, I was no longer sure of what came in and went out of where. My mother grabbed my shoulders and stood me up.

"What are you thinking?" she asked.

"Nothing," I said.

"Go and wash your face," she said tapping me toward the door.

In the bathroom mirror I checked my face for changes. I tugged at the skin below my eyes, stretched my lips, stuck my tongue out. Nothing.

There was a time I couldn't wait to be grown because of my mother's wardrobe. She had buckled, strapped, and beaded shoes. I would slip my feet into them, hoping for the gap behind my heels to close, and run my hands through her dresses and wrappers of silver and gold embroidery. Caftans were fashionable, though they really were a slimmer version of the *agbadas* women in our country had been wearing for years. I liked one red velvet caftan she had in particular, with small circular mirrors that sparkled like chandeliers. The first time my mother wore it was on my father's birthday. I was heady that night from the smell of tobacco, whiskey, perfume, and curry. I carried a small silver tray of meat balls on sticks and served it to guests. I was wearing a pink polyester babushka. Uncle Alex had just shown me how to light a pipe. My mother was late getting changed because she was busy cooking. When she walked into the living room, everyone cheered. My father accepted congratulations for spoiling his wife. "My money goes to her," he said.

On nights like this I watched my mother style her hair from start to finish. She straightened it with a hot comb that crackled through her hair and sent up pomade fumes. She complained about the process. It took too long and hurt her arms. Sometimes, the hot comb burnt her scalp. She preferred to wear her hair in two cornrows, and on the days my brother fell ill, her hair could be just as it was when she woke up. "It's my house," she would say. "If anybody doesn't like it they can leave."

It was easy to tell she wanted to embarrass my father. People thought a child couldn't understand, but I'd quarreled with friends in school before, and I wouldn't speak to them until they apologized, or at least until I'd forgotten that they hadn't. I understood, well enough to protect my parent's vision of my innocence. My mother needed quiet, my father would say. "I know," I would say. My father was always out, my mother would complain. I wouldn't say a word.

⁓

All week I looked forward to going to Sheri's house. Sometimes I went to the hibiscus patch, hoping she would appear. I never stayed there long enough. I'd forgotten about sex, even about the bump on my shin which had flattened to a purple bruise. This week, my parents were arguing about particulars.

My father had lost his driver's license and car insurance certificate. He said my mother had hidden them. "I did not hide your particulars," she said. He asked if I'd seen them. I had not seen his particulars, I said. I finally joined in his search for the lost particulars and was beginning to imagine I was responsible for them when he found them. "Where I already looked," he said. "See?"

I was tired of them. Sunday morning, after my parents left, I visited the house next door for the first time—against my mother's orders, but it was worth knowing a girl my age in the neighborhood. The place was full of boys, four who lived across the road. They laughed whenever they saw me and pretended to vomit. Next to them was an English boy who played fetch games with his Alsatian, Ranger. Sometimes he had rowdy bicycle races with the four across the road; other times he sent Ranger after them when they teased him for being white and unable to stomach hot peppers: "*Oyinbo* pepper, if you eat-ee pepper, you go yellow more-more!" Two boys lived further down the road and their mother had filled half the teeth of my classmates. They were much older.

With boys there always had to be noise and trouble. They caught frogs and grasshoppers, threw stones at windows, set off fireworks. There was Bisi at home, who really was a girl, because she was not old enough to be married, but she was just as rough. She watched whenever Baba beheaded chickens for cooking, flattened the daddy-long-legs in my bathtub with slaps. She threatened me most days, with snapped fingers. Then she pretended in front of my mother, shaking and speaking in a high voice. I kicked a stone thinking of her. She was a pretender.

Most houses on our quiet residential road were similar to ours, with servants' quarters and lawns. We didn't have the uniformity of nearby government neighborhoods, built by the Public Works Department. Our house was a bungalow covered in golden trumpets and bougainvillea. The Bakare's was an enormous one-story with aquamarine glass shutters, so square-shaped, I thought it resembled a castle. Except for a low hedge of dried up pitanga cherries lining the driveway and a mango tree by the house, the entire yard was cement.

I walked down the driveway, conscious of my shoes crunching the gravel. One half-eaten mango on the tree caught my eye. Birds must have nibbled it and now ants were finishing it up. The way they scrambled over the orange flesh reminded me of a beggar I'd seen outside my mother's church, except his sore was pink and pus oozed out. No one would go near him, not even to give him money which they threw on a dirty potato sack before him.

A young woman with two pert facial marks on her cheeks answered the door.

"Yesch?"

"Is Sheri in?" I asked.

"Is schleeping."

In the living room, the curtains were drawn and the furniture sat around like mute shadows. The Bakares had the same chairs as most people I knew, fake Louis XIV, my father called them. There wasn't a sound and it was eleven o'clock in the morning. At first I thought the 'sch' woman was going to turn me away, then she stepped aside. I followed her up the narrow wooden stairway, through a quiet corridor, past two doors until we reached a third. "Scheree?" she called out.

Someone whined. I knew it was Sheri. She opened her door wearing a yellow night gown. The 'sch' woman dragged her feet down the corridor.

"Why are you still sleeping?" I asked Sheri.

In my house that would be considered laziness. She'd been out last night, at her uncle's fortieth birthday. She danced throughout. Her voice did not yet sound like hers. There were clothes on the floor: white lace blouses, colorful wrappers, and head ties. She'd been sleeping on a cloth spread over a bare mattress, and another cloth was what she used to cover herself at night. A picture of apples and pears hung above her bed and on her bedside table was a framed photograph of a woman in traditional dress. In the corner, some dusty shoes spilled out of a wooden cupboard. The door dropped from a broken hinge and the mirror inside was stained brown. A table fan perched on a desk worried the clothes on the floor from time to time.

"Is this your room?" I asked.

"Anyone's," she said, clearing her throat noisily. She drew the curtains and sunlight flooded the room. She pointed to a wad of notes stashed by the photograph: the total amount she received for dancing.

"I got the most in the family," she said.

"Where is everyone?" I asked.

She scratched her hair. "My stepmothers are sleeping. My brothers and sisters are still sleeping. My father, I don't know where he is."

She reached for her behind.

I screwed up my nose. "I think you'd better have a bath."

One o'clock and the entire house was awake. Sheri's stepmothers had prepared *akara*, fried bean cakes, for everyone to eat. We knelt before them to say good morning, they patted our heads in appreciation. "Both knees," one of them ordered. I found myself looking at two women who resembled each other, pretty with watery eyes and chiffon scarves wrapped around their heads. I noted the gold tooth in the smile of the one who had ordered me to kneel.

In the veranda, the other children sat on chairs with bowls of *akara* on their laps. The girls wore dresses; the boys were in short-sleeved shirts and shorts. Sheri had changed into a tangerine-colored maxi length dress and was strutting around ordering them to be quiet. "Stop fighting." "Gani, will you sit down?" "Didn't I tell you to wash your hands?" "Kudi? What is wrong with you this morning?" She separated a squabble here, wiped a dripping nose. I watched in amazement as they called her Sister Sheri. The women were called Mama Gani and Mama Kudi after their firstborns.

"How many children will you have?" Sheri asked, thrusting a baby boy into my arms. I kept my mouth still for fear of dropping him. He wriggled and felt as fragile as a crystal glass.

"One," I said.

"Why not half, if you like?" Sheri asked.

I was not offended. Her rudeness had been curtailed by nature. Whenever she sucked her teeth, her lips didn't quite curl, and her dirty looks flashed through lashes as thick as moth wings. She knew all the rude sayings: mouth like a duck, dumb as a zero with a dot in it. If I said "so?" she said, "Sew your button on your shirt." When I asked "why?" she answered, "Z your head to Zambia." But she was far too funny to be successfully surly. Her full name was Sherifat, but she didn't like it. "Am not fat," she explained, as we sat down to eat. I had already had breakfast, but seeing the *akara* made me hungry. I took a bite and the peppers inside made my eyes water. My legs trembled in appreciation. "When we finish," Sheri said. "I will take you to the balcony upstairs." She chewed with her mouth open and had enough on her plate to fill a man.

~⌒

The balcony upstairs resembled an empty swimming pool. Past rains had left mildew in its corners. It was higher than my house and standing there, we could see the whole of her yard and mine. I pointed out the plants in my yard as Sheri walked toward the view of the lagoon.

"It leads to the Atlantic," she said.

"I know," I said, trying not to lose my concentration. "Bougainvillea, golden trumpets... "

"You know where that leads?"

"Yes. Almond tree, banana tree... "

"Paris," she said.

I gave up counting plants. Downstairs, two of the children ran through the washing lines. They were playing a Civil War game: Halt. Who goes there? Advance to be recognized. Boom! You're dead.

"I want to go to Paris," Sheri said.

"How will you get there?"

"My jet plane," she said.

I laughed. "How will you get a jet plane?"

"I'll be an actress," she said, turning to me. In the sunlight, her pupils were like the underside of mushrooms.

"Actor-ess," I said.

"Yes, and when I arrive, I'll be wearing a red negligée."

"Em, Paris is cold."

"Eh?"

"Paris is cold. My father told me. It's cold and it rains."

"I'll have a fur coat, then."

"What else?" I asked.

"High, high heels."

"And?"

"Dark sunglasses."

"What kind?"

"Cressun Door," she said, smiling.

I shut my eyes, imagining. "You'll need fans. All actresses have fans."

"Oh, they'll be there," she said. "And they'll be running around, shouting, 'Sheri. *Voulez-vous. Bonsoir. Mercredi.*' But I won't mind them."

"Why not?"

"Because I'll get into my car and drive away fast."

I opened my eyes. "What kind of car?"

"Sports," she said.

I sighed. "I want to be something like... like president."

"Eh? Women are not presidents."

"Why not?"

"Our men won't stand for it. Who will cook for your husband?"

"He will cook for himself."

"What if he refuses?"

"I'll drive him away."

"You can't," she said.

"Yes I can. Who wants to marry him anyway?"

"What if they kill you in a coup?"

"I'll kill them back."

"What kind of dream is that?"

"Mine." I smirked.

"Oh, women aren't presidents," she said.

Someone downstairs was calling her. We looked over the balcony to see Akanni. He was wearing heart-shaped sunshades, like mirrors.

"What?" Sheri answered.

Akanni looked up. "Isn't that my good friend, Enitan, from next door?"

"None of your business," Sheri said. "Now, what do you want from me?"

I smiled at Akanni. His sunshades were funny and his war stories were fantastic.

"My good friend," he said to me in Yoruba. "At least you're nice to me, unlike this trouble maker, Sheri. Where is my money, Sheri?"

"I don't have your money," she said.

"You promised we would share the proceeds from last night. I stayed up till five this morning, now you're trying to cheat me. Country is hard for a poor man, you know."

"Who asked you?"

Akanni snapped his fingers. "Next time you'll see who will drive you around."

"Fine," Sheri said, then she turned to me. "Oaf. Look at his face, flat as a church clock. Come on, let's go back inside. The sun is beating my head."

"Now?" I asked.

She pressed her hair down. "Can't you see I'm a half-caste?"

I didn't know whether to laugh or feel sorry for her.

"I don't mind," she said. "Only my ears I mind and I cover them up, because they're big like theirs."

"Whose?" I asked.

"White people's," she said. "Now, come on."

I followed her. She did have huge ears and her afro did not hide them.

"You know that foolish Akanni?" she asked as we ran down the stairs.

"He comes to our house."

"To do what?"

"Visit our house girl, Bisi."

Sheri began to laugh. "He's doing her!"

I covered my mouth.

"Sex," she said. "Banana into tomato. Don't you know about it?"

My hand dropped.

"Oh, close your mouth before a fly enters," she said.

I ran to catch up with her.

⁓

"My grandma told me," she said.

We were sitting on her bed. Sheri tucked her tangerine dress between her legs. I wondered if she knew more than me.

"When you... " I asked. "I mean, with your husband. Where does it go? Because I don't... " I was pointing everywhere, even at the ceiling.

Sheri's eyes were wide. "You haven't seen it? I've seen mine. Many times." She stood up and retrieved a cracked mirror from a drawer. "Look and see."

"I can't."

"Look," she said, handing me the mirror.

"Lock the door."

"Okay," she said, heading there.

I dragged my panties down, placed the mirror between my legs. It looked like a big, fat slug. I squealed as Sheri began to laugh. We heard loud knocks on the door and I almost dropped the mirror. "Who's that?" I whispered.

"Me," she said.

I hobbled to her bed. "You horrible... "

She rocked back and forth. "You're so funny, *aburo*!"

"You horrible girl," I hissed.

She stopped laughing. "Why?"

"I don't think it's funny. What did you do that for?"

"I'm sorry."

"Well, sorry is not enough."

I pulled my panties up, wondering whether I was angry with her, or what I'd seen between my legs. Sheri barricaded the door. "You're not going anywhere."

At first I thought I'd push her aside and walk out, but the sight of her standing there like a star tickled me.

"All right," I said. "But this is your last chance, Sherifat, I'm warning you."

"Am not fat," she yelled.

I laughed until I thought my heart would pop. That was her insecurity: her full name, and her big ears.

"Don't go," she said. "I like you. You're very English. You know, high faluting."

⁓

The woman in the photograph by her bedside table was her grandmother.

"Alhaja," Sheri said. "She's beautiful."

Alhaja had an enormous gap between her front teeth and her cheeks were so plump her eyes were barely visible. There were many Alhajas in Lagos. This one wasn't the first woman to go on *hajj* to Mecca, but for women like her, who were powerful within their families and communities, the title became their name.

Sheri did not know her own mother. She died when Sheri was a baby and Alhaja raised her from then on, even after her father remarried. She pressed the picture to her chest and told me of her life in downtown Lagos. She lived in a house opposite her Alhaja's fabric store. She went to a school where children didn't care to speak English. After school, she helped Alhaja in her store and knew how to measure cloth. I listened, mindful that my life didn't extend beyond Ikoyi Park. What would it be like to know downtown as Sheri did, haggle with customers, buy fried yams and roasted plantains from street hawkers, curse Area Boys and taxi cabs who drove too close to the curb.

My only trips downtown were to visit the large foreign-owned stores, like Kelwarams and Leventis, or the crowded markets with my mother. The streets were crammed with vehicles, and there were too many people: people buying food from street hawkers, bumping shoulders, quarreling and crossing streets. Sometimes masqueraders came out for Christmas or for some other festival, dancing in their raffia gowns and ghoulish masks. Sheri knew them all: the ones who stood on stilts, the ones who looked like stretched out accordions and flattened to pancakes. It was juju, she said, but she was not scared. Not even of the *eyo* who dressed in white sheets like spirits of the day and whipped women who didn't cover their heads.

Sheri was a Moslem and she didn't know much about Christianity, except that there was a book in the Bible and if you read it, you could go mad. I asked why Moslems didn't eat pork. "It's a filthy beast," she said, scratching her hair. I told her about my own life, how my brother died and my mother was strict.

"That church sounds scary," she said.

"I'm telling you, if my mother ever catches you in our house, she'll send you home."

"Why?"

I pointed at her pink mouth. "It's bad, you know."

She sucked her teeth. "It's not bad. Anyway, you think my father allows me to wear lipstick? I wait until he's gone out and put it on."

"What happens when he comes back?"

"I rub it off. Simple. You want some?"

I didn't hesitate. As I rubbed the lipstick on my lips I mumbled, "Your stepmothers, won't they tell?"

"I kneel for them, help them in the kitchen. They won't tell."

"What about the one with the gold tooth?"

"She's wicked, but she's nice."

I showed her my lips. "Does it fit?"

"It fits," she said. "And guess what?"

"What?"

"You've just kissed me."

I slapped my forehead. She was forward, this girl, and the way she acted with the other children. She really didn't do much, except to make sure she was noticed. I was impressed by the way she'd conned Akanni into staying up late for her uncle's party. Sheri got away with whatever she did and said. Even when she insulted someone, her stepmothers would barely scold her. "Ah, this one. She's such a terrible one."

They summoned her to act as a disc jockey. She changed the records as if she was handling dirty plates: The Beatles, Sunny Adé, Jackson Five, James Brown. Most of the records were scratched. Akanni arrived during, "Say it loud, I'm black and proud." He skidded from one end of the room to the other and fell on the floor overcome as the real James Brown. We placed a hand towel on his back and coaxed him up. By the time "If I had the wings of a dove" came on, I was singing out loud myself, and was almost tearful from the words.

As a parting gift Sheri gave me a romance novel titled *Jacaranda Cove*. The picture was barely visible and most of the pages were dog-eared. "Take this and read," she said. I slipped it under my arm and wiped my lips clean. My one thought was to return home before my mother arrived. I'd disobeyed her too much. If she found out, I would be punished for life.

Our house seemed darker when I arrived, though the curtains in the living room were not drawn. My father once explained the darkness was due to the position of the windows to the sun. Our living room reminded me of an empty hotel lounge. The curtains were made of a gold damask, and the chairs were a deep red velvet. A piano stood by the sliding doors to the veranda.

The house was designed by two Englishmen with the help of an architect my father knew. They lived together for years, and everyone knew about them, he said. Then they moved to Nairobi and he bought the house from them. The two men living together; the Bakare house full of children; grandparents, parents, teachers, now Akanni, and of all people, Bisi. The whole world was full of sex, I thought, running away from my footsteps. In my bedroom, I read the first page of Sheri's book, then the last. It described a man and woman kissing and how their hearts beat faster. I read it again and searched the book for more passages like that, then I marked each of them to read later.

My father arrived soon afterward and challenged me to a game of *ayo*. He always won, but today he explained the secret of the game. "You'd better listen, because I'm tired of defeating you. First, you choose which bowl you want to land in. Then you choose which bowl will get you there."

He shook the beads in his fist and plopped them, one by one, into the six bowls carved into the wooden slate. I'd always thought the trick was to pick the fullest bowl.

"Work it out backward?" I asked.

"Exactly," he said, scooping beads from the bowl.

"Daddy," I said. "I wasn't watching."

He slapped the table. "Next time you will."

"Cheater."

We were on our fifth round when my mother returned from church. I waved to her as she walked through the front door. I didn't get up to greet her as I normally would. I was winning the game and thought that if I moved, I would lose my good fortune.

"Heh, heh, I'm beating you," I said, wriggling in my chair.

"Only because I let you," my father said.

I scooped the beads from a bowl and raised my hand. My mother walked through the veranda door.

"Enitan? Who gave this to you?"

She grabbed my ear and shoved Sheri's book under my nose.

"Who? Answer me now."

"For God's sake," my father said.

Her fingers were like iron clamps. The *ayo* beads tumbled out of my hand, down to the floor. Sheri from next door, I said. My mother pulled me to my feet by my ear as I explained. Sheri handed it to me through the fence. The wide gap in the fence. Yes, it was wide enough. I had not read the book.

"Let me see," my father said.

My mother flung the book on the table. "I go to her suitcase, find this... this... If I ever catch you talking to that girl again, there will be trouble in this house, you hear me?"

She released my ear. I dropped back into my seat. My ear was hot, and heavy.

My father slammed the book down. "What is this? She can't make friends anymore?"

My mother rounded on him. "You continue to divide this child and me."

"You're her mother, not her juror."

"I am not raising a delinquent. You look for evil and you will find it."

My father shook his head. "Arin, you can quote the whole Bible if you want."

"I am not here to discuss myself."

"Sleep in that church of yours."

"I am not here to discuss myself."

"It will not give you peace of mind."

"Get up when I'm talking to you, Enitan," my mother said. "Up. Up."

"Sit," my father said.

"Up," my mother said.

"Sit," my father said.

My mother patted her chest. "She will listen to me."

I shut my eyes and imagined I was on the balcony with Sheri. We were laughing and the sun had warmed my ear. Their voices faded. I heard only one voice; it was my father's. "Don't mind her," he said. "It's that church of hers. They've turned her head."

He shook my shoulders. I kept my eyes shut. I was tired, enough to sleep.

"Come on," he said. "Let's play."

"No," I said.

"You're leading."

"I don't care."

Soon I heard his footsteps on the veranda. I stayed there until my ear stopped throbbing.

I spoke to neither parent for the rest of that evening. My father knocked on my door before I went to bed.

"You're still sulking?" he asked.

"I'm not sulking," I said.

"When I was a boy, I had no room to lock myself in."

"You had no door."

"Yes, I did. What are you saying?"

"You lived in a village."

"Town," he said.

I shrugged. It was village life outside Lagos, where he grew up. He got up early in the mornings to fetch water from a well, walked to school and studied by oil lamp. My father said his growth was stunted because food never got to him. If a Baptist priest hadn't converted his mother to Christianity and taken him as a ward, I would never have been born thinking the world owed me something.

He pointed. "Is this the famous suitcase?"

He was pretending that nothing had happened.

"Yes."

"I have something for it."

He retrieved a rectangular case from his pocket and handed it to me.

"A pen?"

"Yours."

It was a fat navy pen. I pulled the cap off.

"Thank you, Daddy."

My father reached into his pocket again. He pulled a watch out and dangled it. I collapsed. It was a Timex. My father promised he would never buy me another watch again, after I broke the first and lost the second. This one had a round face the width of my wrist. Red straps. I rocked it.

"Thank you," I said, strapping it on.

He was sitting on my bed. Both feet were on it, and he still had his socks on. I sat on the floor by them. He rubbed my shoulder.

"Looking forward to going to school?"

"Yes."

"You won't be sad when you get there."

"I'll make friends."

"Friends who make you laugh."

I thought of Sheri. I would have to avoid girls like her in school, otherwise I might end up expelled.

"Anyone who bullies you, beat them up," my father said.

I rolled my eyes. Who could I fight?

"And join the debating society, not the girl guides. Girl guides are nothing but kitchen martyrs in the making."

"What is that?"

"What you don't want to be. You want to be a lawyer?"

Going to work was too remote to contemplate.

He laughed. "Tell me now, so I can take back my gifts."

"I'm too young to know."

"Too young indeed. Who will run my practice when I'm gone. And another thing, these romance books you're reading. No chasing boys when you get there."

"I don't like boys."

"Good," he said. "Because you're not going there to study boy-ology."

"Daddy," I said.

He was the one I would miss. The one I would write to. I settled to write a poem after he left, using words that rhymed with sad: bad, dad, glad, had. I was on my third verse when I heard raps on my window. I peeped outside to find Sheri standing with a sheet of paper in her hand. Her face appeared like a tiny moon. She was crouching.

"Open up," she said.

"What are you doing here?" I whispered.

"I came to get your school address."

Wasn't she afraid? It was as dark as indigo outside.

"On your own?"

"With Akanni. He's in your quarters, with his girlfriend."

She pulled a pencil from her pocket. She was like an imp who had come to tempt me. I couldn't get rid of her.

"Eni-Tan," she spelled.

"Yes," I said.

"Your school address," she said. "Or are you deaf?"

1975

Had I listened to my mother, that would have been the end of Sheri and I, and the misfortune that would bind us. But my mother had more hope of squeezing me up her womb than stopping our friendship. Sheri had led me to the gap between parental consent and disapproval. I would learn how to bridge it with deception, wearing a face as pious as a church sister before my mother and altering steadily behind her. There was a name my mother had for children like Sheri. They were *omo-ita*, street children. If they had homes, they didn't like staying in them. What they liked, instead, was to go around fighting and cursing, and getting up to mischief.

Away from my own home, my days in boarding school were like a balm. I lived with five hundred other girls and shared a dormitory with about twenty. At night we let down our mosquito nets and during the day we patched them up if they got ripped. If a girl had malaria, we covered her with blankets to sweat out her fever. I held girls through asthma attacks, shoved a teaspoon down the mouth of a girl who was convulsing, burst boils. It was a wonder we survived the spirit of samaritanism, or communal living. The toilets stunk like sewers and sometimes excrement piled up days high. I had to cover my nose to use them and when girls were menstruating, they flung their soiled sanitary towels into open buckets. Still, I preferred boarding school to home.

Royal College girls came from mixed backgrounds. In our dormitory alone we had a farmer's daughter and a diplomat's daughter. The farmer's daughter had never been to a city before she came to Lagos; the diplomat's daughter had been to garden parties at Kensington palace. There were girls from homes like mine, girls from less privileged homes, so a boarder might come back from class to find her locker had been broken into. Since she knew she'd never see her missing belongings again, the next step was to put a hex on the thief by shouting out curses like, "May you have everlasting diarrhea." "May you menstruate forever." If the thief were caught, she would be jostled down the hallways.

I met Moslem girls: Zeinat, Alima, Aisha who rose early to salute Mecca. Some covered their heads with scarves after school, and during Ramadan, they shunned food and water from dawn till dusk. I met Catholic girls: Grace, Agnes, Mary, who sported gray crosses on their foreheads on Ash Wednesday. There were Anglican girls, Methodist girls. One girl, Sangita, was Hindu and we loved to tug on her long plait. The daughter of our math teacher and the only foreign student in our school, she had such a resounding, "Leave me alone!" she sent the best of us running.

I met girls born with sickle cell anemia like my brother. Some were sick almost every other month, others hardly ever. We called them sicklers. They called themselves sicklers. One thought it excused her from all ills: untidiness, lateness, rudeness. I learned from her that I carried the sickle cell trait, which meant I would never be sick, but my child could be, if my husband also carried the trait.

I learned also about women in my country, from Zaria, Katsina, Kaduna who decorated their skin with henna dye and lived in *purdah*; women from Calabar who were fed and anointed in fattening houses before their weddings; women who were circumcised. I heard about towns in western Nigeria where every family had twins because the women ate a lot of yams, and other towns in northern Nigeria, where every other family had a crippled child because women married their first cousins. None of the women seemed real. They were like mammy-water, sirens of the Niger Delta who rose from the creeks to lure unsuspecting men to death by drowning.

Uncle Alex had always said our country was not meant to be one. The British had drawn a circle on the map of West Africa and called it a country. Now I understood what he meant. The girls I met at Royal College were so different. I could tell a girl's ethnicity even before she opened her mouth. Hausa girls had softer hair because of their Arab heritage. Yoruba girls like me usually had heart-shaped faces and many Igbo girls were fair-skinned; we called them Igbo Yellow. We spoke English, but our native tongues were as different as French and Chinese. So, we mispronounced names and spoke English with different accents. Some Hausa girls could not "fronounce" the letter P. Some Yoruba girls might call these girls "Ausas," and eggs might be "heggs." Then there was that business with the middle-belters who mixed up their L's and R's. If they said a word like lorry, there was no telling what my bowels would release, from laughing.

It all provided jokes. So did the stereotypes. Yoruba girls were considered quarrelsome; Hausa girls, pretty but dumb; Igbo girls, intelligent, but well, they were muscular. Most girls had parents of the same origin, but there was some intermingling and we had a few girls, like Sheri, who had one parent from a foreign country. Half-castes we called them, without malice or implications. Half because they claimed both sides of their heritage. There was no caste system in our country.

Often at Royal College, we shared family stories while fetching water from a tap in the yard. I learned that my mother's behavior wasn't typical. I also learned that every other girl had an odd family story to tell: Afi's grandmother was killed when a bicycle knocked her down in the village; Yemisi's mother worked till her water broke; Mfon's cousin smoked hemp and brought shame on the family; Ibinabo's father stripped her down, whipped her, and made her say "thank-you" afterward.

In the mornings, we congregated in the assembly hall to sing our national anthem and took a few minutes to appreciate Beethoven or some other European composer. At meal-times we packed into our dining hall and sang:

Some have food but cannot eat,
Some can eat but have no food,
We have food and we can eat,
Glory be to God, Amen.

After school, we drummed on our desks and sang. We sang a lot, through the transformations in our country; when we began to drive on the right side of the road; when we switched from pounds, shillings, and pence to naira and kobo. Outside our school walls, oil leaked from the drilling fields of the Niger Delta into people's Swiss bank accounts. There was bribery and corruption, but none of it concerned me, particularly in June 1975. It was as vague as the end of Vietnam. I was just glad our fourth-year exams were over. For those sleepless weeks, I joined my classmates, studying through the night and spreading bitter coffee granules on my tongue. In a class of thirty odd girls, I was neither a bright star Booker T. Washington or dim-wit Dundee United. I enjoyed history, English literature, Bible studies because of the parables. I enjoyed music lessons because of the songs our black American teacher taught us, spirituals and jazz melodies that haunted me until I began to dream about churches and smoky clubs I'd never seen. I was captain of our junior debating society, though I longed to be one of those girls chosen for our annual beauty pageants instead. But my arms were like twisted vines and my forehead like sandpaper. Those cranky nodules behind my nipples didn't amount to breasts and my calf muscles had refused to develop. The girls in my class called me *Panla*, after a dry, stinky fish imported from Norway. Girls overseas could starve themselves on leaves and salad oil if they wanted. In our country, women were hailed for having huge buttocks. I wanted to be fatter, fatter, fatter, with a pretty face, and I wanted boys to like me.

Damola Ajayi had spoken like an orator, as good as any I'd heard. He was skinny with big hands that punched the air as he spoke. Warm hands. We almost collided on the stairs leading to the stage and I held his hands to steady myself. I turned to the Concord Academy debating team as he joined them. Their entire bench sat upright with the same serious expression. They were dressed, like him, in white jackets and blue striped ties. On the bench, next to them, our team slumped forward in green pinafores and checked blouses. Behind them were Saint Catherine girls in their red skirts and white blouses. The hall was a show of uniforms from all the schools in Lagos.

Here, we played net ball and badminton games; staged plays and hosted beauty pageants. Sometimes we had films shows and school dances. We never used the gymnastic equipment because no one had explained what it was for. By the back wall, a few boys draped themselves over two pommel horses, studying girls. Debating was the only way to socialize during school terms and if students had strict parents, it was the only way to socialize all year. We came together for tournaments, bearing our different school identities. Concord was gentlemanly but boring. Saint Catherine's was snobbish and loose. Owen Memorial boys and girls belonged in juvenile detention homes and their worst students smoked hemp. We at Royal, we were smart, but our school was crowded and filthy.

"Thanks to our co-hosts," I said. "And thanks to everyone else for participating."

Few people clapped. The crowd was getting restless. Yawns spread across the rows and students keeled over. Our own team looked as if their mouths had dried up from talking. It was time to end my speech.

"I would like to invite questions, comments from the audience?"

A Saint Patrick's boy raised his hand.

"Yes sir, at the back?"

The boy stood up, and pulled his brown khaki jacket down. There was a low rumble from the crowd as he strained forward: "Mr. Chairman, s-s-sir. W-when c-can we start the social acker-acker-acker-tivities?"

The crowd roared as he took bows. I raised my arm to silence them, but no one paid attention. Soon the noise trickled to a few laughs. Someone switched on the stereo. I came down from the stage and people began to clear their chairs for the dance.

Our final debate had lasted longer than I expected. We lost to Concord's team because of their captain. Damola was one of the best in the league, and he delivered his "with all due respects" to cheers. I couldn't compete. He was also the lead singer of a band called the Stingrays, who had caused a stir by appearing on television one Christmas. Parents said they wouldn't pass their school certificate exams carrying on that way. We wondered how they could dare form a band, in this place, where parents only ever thought about passing exams. What kind of homes did they come from? A girl on our debating team had answers, at least about Damola: "Cousin lives on the same street as him. Parents allow him to do what he wants. Drives a car. Smokes."

His hand tapped my elbow. "Well done."

"You too," I said.

He already had traces of mustache on his upper lip, and his eyes were heavy with lashes. "You're a good debater," he said.

I smiled. Normally, I could not accept verbal defeat. Arguments sent my heart rate up, and blood rushing to my temples. Outside the debating society, I annoyed my friends with words they couldn't understand, gagged class bullies with retorts until their lips trembled. "You have a bad mouth, Enitan Taiwo," one recently said. "Just wait and see. It will catch up with you."

I had nothing to say to Damola. As captains of our teams we had to start the dance. We walked to the center of the hall. People flooded the floor, pushing us closer. Damola danced as if his jacket were tight and I avoided looking at his feet to keep my rhythm. We ended up under a ceiling fan and the lyrics of the song amused me after a while: rock the boat one minute, don't rock it the next.

The song ended and we found two empty chairs. Damola was not an enigma, I'd told my friends, who were searching for the right word for nobody-knows-what's-inside-his-mind. Enigmas would have more to hide than their shyness. I counted from ten down.

"I've heard your song," I said.

"Which one?"

"No time for a psalm."

I'd memorized the words from television. "I reach for a star, it pierces my palm, burns a hole through my life line... "

My father said it was teenage self-indulgence and the boys needed to learn to play their instruments properly. They did screech a little, but at least they attempted to express themselves. Who cared about what we thought at our age? Between childhood and adulthood there was no space to grow laterally, and whatever our natural instincts, our parents were determined to clip off any disobedience: "Stop moping around." "Face your studies." "You want to disgrace us?" At least the boys were saying something different.

"Who wrote it?" I asked.

I already knew. I crossed my legs to look casual, then uncrossed them, so as not to be typical.

"Me," he said.

"What is it about?"

"Disillusionment."

Damola had a slight hook nose and from the side he almost resembled a bird. He wasn't one of the fine boys that girls talked about; the boring boys who ignored me.

"Are you disillusioned?" I asked.

"Sometimes."

"Me too," I said.

We would get married as soon as we finished school, I thought. From then on we would avoid other people. People our age clung together unnecessarily anyway. It was a sign of not thinking, like being constantly happy. Really, there was no need to reach as high as the stars. Around us was enough proof that optimism was dangerous, and some of us had discovered this before.

Outside it looked like it was about to rain. It was late afternoon but the sky was as dark as early evening because of the rainy season. Mosquitoes flew indoors. They buzzed around my legs and I bent to slap them. The stereo began to play a slow number, "That's the Way of the World" by Earth, Wind, and Fire. I hoped Damola would ask me to dance, but he didn't.

I tapped my foot under the end of that record. Afterward, our vice principal came into the hall to turn the stereo off. She thanked the boys and girls for coming and announced that their school buses were waiting outside. I'd spent most of the dance sitting next to Damola who nodded from time to time as though he were above it all. Together, we walked to the gates and I stopped by the last travelers palm beyond which boarders weren't allowed to pass.

"Have a nice summer," I said.

"You too," he said.

A group of classmates hurried over. They circled me and stuck their chins out: "What did he say?" "Do you like him?" "Does he like you?"

Normally, we were friends. We fetched water and bathed together; studied in pairs and shared scrapbooks details. Damola was another excuse for a group giggle. I wasn't going to tell them. One of them congratulated me on my wedding. I asked her not to be silly.

"What's scratching you?" she asked.

The others waited for an answer. I managed a smile to appease them, then I walked on. In the twilight, students shifted in groups back to the dormitory blocks.

The structure of our blocks, three adjacent buildings, each three floors high with long balconies, made me imagine I was living in a prison. Walking those balconies, I'd discovered they weren't straight. Some parts dipped and other parts rose a little and whenever I was anxious, because of an examination or a punishment, I dreamed they had turned to waves and I was trying to ride them. Sometimes I'd fall off the balconies in my dreams, fall, and never reach the bottom.

Friday after school, I received a letter from Sheri. I was sitting in class. It was raining again. Lightning flashed, followed by a crash of thunder. About thirty girls sat behind and on top of wooden desks indoors. School hour rules no longer applicable, we wore mufti and spoke vernacular freely. Outside, a group of girls scurried across the quadrangle with buckets over their heads. One placed hers on the ground to collect rain water. The wind changed direction. "Shut the windows," someone said. A few girls jumped up to secure them.

Over the years, Sheri and I exchanged letters, sharing our thoughts on sheets torn from exercise books, ending them "love and peace, your trusted friend." Sheri was always in trouble. Someone called her loose, someone punished her, someone tried to beat her up. It was always girls. She seemed to get along with boys. Occasionally I saw her when she came to stay with her father. She sneaked to my room, rapped on my window and frightened me almost to death. Her brows were plucked thin, her hair pulled back in a bun. She wore red lipstick and said *"Ciao."* She was way too advanced for me, but I enjoyed seeing her anyway.

She had had the best misadventures: parties that ended in brawls, cinemas where audiences talked back to the screen. Once, she hitched a ride from a friend who borrowed his parents' car. They pushed the car down the driveway, while his parents were sleeping, and an hour later they pushed it up again. She was a bold-face, unlike me. I worried about breaking school rules, failing exams. I even worried about being skinny, and for a while I worried that I might be a hermaphrodite, like an earthworm, because my periods hadn't started. Then they did and my mother killed a fowl to secure my fertility.

In her usual curvy writing, Sheri had written on the back of the envelope: *de-liver, de-letter, de-sooner, de-better*. And addressed it to: *Miss Enitan Taiwo Esquire, Royal College, Yaba, Lagos, Nigeria, West Africa, Africa, The Universe*. Her writing was overly curly, and her letter had been opened by my class teacher who checked our letters. If they came from boys she ripped them up.

June 27, 1975.

Aburo,

I'm sorry I haven't written for so long. I've been studying for my exams and I'm sure you have too. How were yours? This term has been tough for me. I've worked hard, but my father still says I'm not trying enough. He wants me to be a doctor. How can I be a doctor when I hate sciences? Now I have to stay with him over the summer and take lessons in Phi, Chem and Bi. I think I will go mad...

Someone switched the lights on as the sky darkened. The rain drummed faster on our roof and the girls began to sing a Yoruba folk song:

The banana tree
in my father's farm
bears fruit every year.

May I not be barren
but be fruitful and blessed
with the gift of children.

A fat mosquito landed on my ankle, heavy and slow. I slapped it off.

I can't wait to get away and see your face. I don't want to stay in my father's house though. It's too crowded. Can I come and stay in yours? I'm sure your mother will love that—ha, ha...

Sheri was not afraid of my mother. If she sneaked to my window, who would find out? she asked. But I knew she would not last a day in my house, loving food as much as she did. On my last vacation food had become a weapon in our house. My mother cooked meals and locked them up in the freezer so my father couldn't eat when he returned from work. I had to eat with her, before he returned, whether or not I was hungry. One morning, she took the sugar cubes my father used for coffee and hid them. He threatened to stop her food allowance. The sugar cubes came out, the other food remained locked in the freezer. I could not tell anyone this was happening in our house.

As the rain turned to drizzle, I finished reading Sheri's letter. Girls opened the windows and the wind brought in the smell of wet grass. My classmates were singing another song now, this one a jazz standard and I joined them, thinking only of Damola.

Always get that mood indigo
Since my baby said goodbye...

～〰

Summer vacation began and the smell of wet grass was everywhere. I'd seen fifteen rainy seasons and was finding this one predictable: palm trees bowing and shivering shrubs. The sky darkened fast; the lagoon, too, and its surface looked like the water was scurrying from the wind. The rain advanced in a wall across the water and lightning ripped the sky in two: *Boom!* As a child, I clutched my chest and searched for the destruction outside. The thunder often caught me by my window, hands over my head and recoiling. These days I found the noise tedious, especially the frogs.

Sunday afternoon, when I hoped it had stopped raining for the day, Sheri appeared at my window, startling me so much, I accidentally banged my head on the wall.

"When did you arrive?" I asked, rubbing my sore spot.

"Yesterday," she said.

Her teeth were as small and white as milk teeth. She stuck her head inside.

"What are you doing inside, Mrs. Morose?"

"I'm not morose," I said.

"Yes, you are. You're always indoors."

I laughed. "That is not morose."

Outside the grass squeaked and wet my shoes; mud splattered on the back of my legs and dried. Inside, I had my own record player, albeit one with a nervous needle. I also had a small collection of Motown records, a Stevie Wonder poster on my wall, a library of books like *Little Women*. I enjoyed being on my own in my room. My parents, too, mistook my behavior for sulking.

This vacation I found them repentant. They did not argue, but they were hardly at home either and I was glad for the silence. My father stayed at work; my mother in her church. I thought of Damola. Once or twice, I crossed out the common letters in my name and his to find out what we would be: friends, lovers, enemies, married. We were lovers.

"This house is like a graveyard," Sheri said.

"My parents are out," I said.

"Ah-ah? Let's go then."

"Where?"

"Anywhere. I want to get out of here. I hate my lessons and I hate my lesson teacher. He spits."

"Tell your father."

"He won't listen. All he talks about is doctor this and doctor that. *Abi*, can you see me as a doctor?"

"No."

She would misdiagnose her patients and boss them around.

"Let's go," she said.

"Walk-about," I teased.

She flung her hand up. "You see? You're morose."

I thought she was going home so I ran to the front door to stop her. She said she wasn't angry, but why did I never want to do anything? I pushed her up the drive.

"I'll get into trouble, Sheri."

"If your parents find out."

"They'll find out."

"If you let them."

Sheri already had a boyfriend in school. They had kissed before and it was like chewing gum, but she wasn't serious because he wasn't. I told her about Damola.

"You sat there not talking?" she asked.

"We communicated by mind."

"What does that mean?"

"We didn't have to talk."

"You and your boyfriend, *sha*."

I poked her shoulder. "He is not my boyfriend."

She forced me to call him. I recited his number which we found in the telephone book and my heart thumped so hard it reached my temples. Sheri handed the receiver to me. "Hello?" came a high-pitched voice, and I promptly gave the phone back to Sheri.

"Em, yes, helleu," she said, faking a poor English accent. "Is Damola in please?"

"What's she saying?" I whispered.

Sheri raised a finger to silence me. Unable to sustain her accent, she slammed the phone down.

"What happened?" I asked.

She clutched her belly.

"What did she say, Sheri?"

"He's not... in."

I snorted. That was it? My jaw locked watching her kick. She threatened to make another phone call, just to hear the woman's voice again. I told her if she did, I'd rip the phone from its socket. I too was laughing, from her silliness. My stomach ached. I thought I would suffocate.

"Stop."

"I can't."

"You have to go home, Sheri."

"Wh-why?"

"My mother hates you."

"S-so?"

We slapped each other's cheeks to stop.

"Don't worry," she said. "We won't phone your boyfriend again. You can communicate with him, unless his mind is otherwise occupied."

She went home with mascara tears and said it was my fault. The following Sunday, she appeared at my bedroom window again. This time, Baba was burning leaves and the smell nauseated me. I leaned over to shut my window and Sheri's head popped up: "*Aburo!*"

I jumped at least a foot high. "What is wrong with you? Can't you use the door?"

"Oh, don't be so morose," she said.

"Sheri," I said. "I don't think you know the meaning of that word."

She was dressed in a black skirt and strapless top. Sheri was no longer a yellow banana. She could easily win any of the beauty contests in my school, but her demeanor needed to be toned down. She was *gragra*. Girls who won were demure.

"You look nice," I said.

She also had the latest fashions: Oliver Twist caps, wedge heels and flares. Her grandmother knew traders in Quayside by the Lagos Marina, who imported clothes and shoes from Europe.

She blinked through her mascara. "Are your parents in?"

"Out."

"They're always out."

"I prefer it."

"Let's go then."

"No. Where?"

"A picnic. At Ikoyi Park. Your boyfriend will be there."

I smiled. "What boyfriend, Sheri?"

"Your boyfriend, Damola. I found out he'll be there."

Tears filled my eyes. "You rotten little... "

I resisted the urge to hug her. As she tried to explain her connection to him, I lost track. I wore a black T-shirt and white dungarees. In the mirror, I checked my hair, which was pulled into two puffs and fingered the Fulani choker around my neck. I picked a ring from my dressing table and slipped it on my toe.

"Boogie on Reggae Woman," Stevie Wonder was singing. Sheri snapped her fingers and muddled up the lyrics between grunts and whines. I studied her leg movements. No one knew where this latest dance came from. America, a classmate had said, but where in that country, and how it crossed an ocean to reach ours, she couldn't explain. Six months later the dance would be as fashionable as our grandmothers. Then we would be learning another.

"Aren't you wearing makeup?" she asked.

"No," I said, letting my bangles tumble down my arm.

"You can't come looking like that," she said.

"Yes, I can."

"Morose."

I was, she insisted. I wore no makeup, didn't go out, and I had no boyfriend. I tried to retaliate. "Just because I'm not juvenile like the rest of you, following the crowd and getting infatuated with... "

"Oh hush, your grammar is too much," she said.

On the road to the park we kept to the sandy sidewalk. I planned to stay at the picnic until six-thirty if the rain didn't unleash. My mother was at a vigil, and my father wouldn't be back until late, he said. The sun was mild and a light breeze cooled our faces. Along the way, I noticed that a few drivers slowed as they passed us and kept my face down in case the next car was my father's. Sheri shouted out insults in Yoruba meanwhile: "What are you looking at? Yes you. Nothing good will come to you, too. Come on, come on. I'm waiting for you."

By the time we reached the park, my eyes were streaming with tears.

"That's enough," she ordered.

I bit my lips and straightened up. We were beautiful, powerful, and having more fun than anyone else in Lagos. The sun was above us and the grass, under our feet.

The grass became sea sand and I heard music playing. Ikoyi Park was an alternative spot for picnics. Unlike the open, crowded beaches, most of it was shaded by trees which gave it a secluded air. There were palm trees and casuarinas. I saw a group gathered behind a row of cars. I was so busy looking ahead I tripped over a twig. My sandal slipped off. Sheri carried on. She approached two boys who were standing by a white Volkswagen Kombi van. One of them was Damola, the other wore a black cap. A portly boy walked over and they circled her. I hurried to catch up with them as my heart seemed to punch through my chest wall.

"We had to walk," Sheri was saying.

"You walked?" Damola asked.

"Hello," I said.

Damola gave a quick smile, as if he had not recognized me. The other boys turned their backs on me. My heartbeat was now in my ears.

Sheri wiggled. "How come no one is dancing?"

"Would you like to?" Damola asked.

I hugged myself as they walked off, to make use of my arms. The rest of my body trembled.

"How long have you been here?" I asked the portly boy.

The boys glanced at each other as if they hadn't understood.

"I mean, at the party," I explained.

The portly boy reached for his breast pocket and pulled out a packet of cigarettes.

"Long enough," he said.

I moved away. These boys didn't look like they answered to their parents anyway. The portly one had plaits in his hair and the boy with the cap wasn't even wearing a shirt under his dungarees. Damola, too, looked different out of school uniform. He had cut-off sleeves and his arms dangled out of them. He was smaller than I'd dreamed; a little duller, but I'd given him light, enough to blind myself. I pretended to be intrigued by the table where a picnic had been laid. The egg sandwich tasted sweet and salty. I liked the combination and gobbled it up. Then I poured myself a glass from the punch bowl. I spat it back into the cup. It was full of alcohol.

The music stopped and started again. Sheri continued to dance with Damola. Then with the boy in the cap, then with the portly boy. It was no wonder other girls didn't like her. She was not loyal. I was her only girl friend, she once wrote in a letter. Girls were nasty and they spread rumors about her, and pretended to be innocent. I watched her play wrestle with the portly boy after their dance. He grabbed her waist and the other two laughed as she struggled. If she preferred boys, she was free to. She would eventually learn. It was obvious, these days, that most of them preferred girls like Sheri. Whenever I noticed this, it bothered me. I was sure it would bother me even if I was on the receiving end of their admiration. Who were they to judge us by skin shades?

I walked toward the lagoon where the sand was moist and firm, and sat on a large tree root. Crabs dashed in and out of holes and mud-skippers flopped across the water. I searched for my home. The shore line curved for miles and from where I sat I could not see it.

"Hi," someone said.

He stood on the bank. His trouser legs were rolled up to his ankles and he wore bookish black rim glasses.

"Hello," I said.

"Why aren't you dancing?" he asked.

He was too short for me, and his voice wavered, as if he were on the verge of crying.

"I don't want to."

"So why come to a party if you don't want to dance?"

I resisted the urge to frown. That was the standard retort girls expected from boys and he hadn't given me the chance to turn him down.

He smiled. "Your friend Sheri seems to be enjoying herself. She's hanging around some wild characters over there."

That wasn't his business, I wanted to say.

He pushed his glasses back. "At least tell me your name."

"Enitan."

"I have a cousin called Enitan."

He would have to leave soon. He hadn't told me his own name.

"Would you like to dance?" he asked.

"No, thanks."

"Please," he said, placing his hands together.

I swished my feet around the water. I could and then go home.

"All right," I said.

I remembered that I sat on my sandals. Reaching underneath to pull them out, I noticed a red stain on my dungarees.

"What?" he asked.

"I'm sorry. I don't want to dance."

"Why not?"

"I just don't."

"But you said... "

"Not anymore."

He stood there. "That's the problem with you. All of you. You're not happy until someone treats you badly, then you complain."

He walked away with a lopsided gait and I knew he'd had polio. I considered calling after him. Then I wondered why I had needed to be asked to dance in the first place. I checked the stain on my dungarees instead.

It was blood. I was dead. From then on I watched people arrive and leave. More were dancing and their movements had become lively. Some stopped by the bank to look at me. I tried to reason that they would eventually leave. The day could not last forever. For a while a strange combination of rain and sunset occurred, and it seemed as if I was viewing the world through a yellow-stained glass. I imagined celestial beings descending and frightened myself into thinking that was about to happen today. My feet became wrinkled and swollen. I checked my watch; it was almost six o'clock. The music was still playing, and the picnic table had been cleared. Only Sheri, Damola, and his two friends remained. They stood by a Peugeot, saying goodbye to a group who were about to leave. I was planning exactly what to say to Sheri, constructing the exact words and facial expression to use, when she approached me.

"Why are you sitting here on your own?" she asked.

"Go back to your friends," I said.

She mimicked my expression and I noticed her eyes were red. She was barefooted and about to scramble up a tree, or fall face down on the bank; I wasn't sure which.

"Are you drunk?" I asked.

"What if I am?"

The air smelled sweet. I looked beyond her. The Peugeot had gone. Damola and his friends were huddled in a semi-circle by the Kombi van. Damola was in the middle, smoking what looked like an enormous cigarette. I'd never seen one before, never smelled the fumes, but I knew: it reddened your eyes, made you crazy. People who smoked it, their lives would amount to nothing.

"What are they doing?" I asked.

Sheri lifted her arms and her top plummeted.

"We have to go," I said.

She danced away and waved over her shoulder. When she reached the boys, she snatched the hemp from Damola. She coughed as she inhaled. The boys laughed. I stamped my feet in the water. I would give them ten minutes. If they hadn't gone, I would risk the disgrace and walk away. I heard Sheri cry out, but didn't bother to look.

I got up when I no longer heard voices, walked toward the van. From the angle I approached it, I could see nothing behind the windscreen. As I came closer, I spotted the head of the boy with a cap bent over by the window. I edged toward the side door. Sheri was lying on the seat. Her knees were spread apart. The boy in the cap was pinning her arms down. The portly boy was on top of her. His hands were clamped over her mouth. Damola was leaning against the door, in a daze. It was a silent moment; a peaceful moment. A funny moment, too. I didn't know why, except my mouth stretched into the semblance of a laugh before my hands came up, then tears filled my eyes.

The boy in the cap saw me first. He let go of Sheri's arms and she pushed the portly boy. He fell backward out of the van. Sheri screamed. I covered my ears. She ran toward me, clutching her top to her chest. There was lipstick across her mouth, black patches around her eyes. The portly boy fumbled with his trousers.

Sheri slammed into me. I shook her shoulders.

"Sheri!"

She buried her face in my dungarees. Spit dribbled out of her mouth. She beat the sand with her fists. Her arms were covered in sand and so were mine. I tried to hold her still, but she pushed me away and threw her head back as the van started.

"N-nm," she moaned.

I dressed her, saw the red bruises and scratches on her skin, her wrists, around her mouth, on her hips. She stunk of cigarettes, alcohol, sweat. There was blood on her pubic hairs, thick spit running down her legs. Semen. I used sand grains to clean her, pulled her panties up. We began to walk home. The palm trees shrunk to bamboo shoots, the headlights of oncoming cars were like fire-flies. Everything seemed that small. I wondered if the ground was firm enough to support us, or if our journey would last and never end.

She looked tiny. Tiny. There were red dots at the top of her back, pale lines along her lower back where fingers had tugged her skin. She hugged herself as I ran warm water into a bucket. I helped her into my bathtub. I began to wash her back, then I poured a bowl of water over her. She winced.

"Too hot?" I asked.

"Cold," she said.

The water felt warm. I added hot water. The hot water trickled out reluctantly.

"My hair," she said.

I washed it with bathing soap. Her hair was tangled, but it turned curly and settled on her cheeks. I washed her arms, then her legs.

The water dribbling down the drain, I wanted it to be clear. Once it was clear, we would have survived. Instead it remained pink and grainy, with hair strands and soap suds. The sand grains settled and the scum stayed.

"You have to wash the rest," I said.

She shook her head. "No."

"You have to," I said.

She turned her face away. I could tell her chin was crumbling.

"Please," I said. "Just try."

I placed my book on the table. It was her fourth donut since we'd been sitting on the veranda and it was hard to concentrate with the gulping sounds she was making. Biscuits, coconut candy, now donuts. Sheri brought food to my house each time she visited and she had not said a word about what happened.

"Where are you going?" she asked when I stood up.

"Toilet," I snapped.

How could she eat so much? After I bathed her, I had to teach myself how to breathe again. Breathing out wasn't the problem, breathing in was. If I didn't prompt myself, I simply forgot. Then when I wasn't thinking, the rhythm came back. I realized I hadn't felt hungry in days. I didn't even feel thirsty. I imagined my stomach like a shriveled palm kernel. At night, I had visions of fishermen breaking into my room. I dreamed of Sheri running toward me with her face made up like a masquerader. She slammed into me and I fell out of my bed. I held my head and sobbed.

I sat on the toilet and waited for the urge to pee. What I wished was for my parents to come home. Sheri was making me angry enough to punch walls. I came out without washing my hands. She was eating another donut.

"You're going to be sick," I said, grabbing my book.

"Why?" she asked.

"If you keep eating and eating like that."

She wiped grease from her mouth. "I don't eat that much."

I used the book to cover my face. "Eating and eating," I said to provoke her.

"I don't... "

She stood up and let out a cry. My book slid off my face, just as she lurched. Her vomit splattered over the table, hitting my face. I tasted it in on my tongue; it was sweet and slimy. She lunged forward and another mound of vomit plopped on the veranda floor. I managed to grab her shoulders.

"Sorry," I said. "You hear me?"

Tears ran down her face. I sat her in the chair and went to the kitchen to get a bucket and brush. The water gushed into the bucket and I wondered why I was so angry with her. Holding my breath, I delved deeper and the fist in my stomach exploded. Yes. I blamed her. If she hadn't smoked hemp it would never have happened. If she hadn't stayed as long as she did at the party, it would certainly not have happened. Bad girls got raped. We all knew. Loose girls, forward girls, raw, advanced girls. Laughing with boys, following them around, thinking she was one of them. Now, I could smell their semen on her, and it was making me sick. It was her fault.

The foam poured over the edge of the bucket. I struggled with the handle. The water wet my dress as I hobbled through the living room. I remembered the moment Sheri came to my window. Why did we go? I could have said no. She wouldn't have gone without me. One word. I should have said no. Damola and his friends, they would suffer for what they did. They would remember us, our faces. They would never forget us.

I reached the veranda and she stood up.

"I'll do it," I said.

She shut her eyes. "Maybe I should go home."

"Yes," I said.

She'd eaten the last donut.

She didn't come back to my house, and I didn't visit her either because I hoped that if we pretended long enough the whole incident might vanish. As if the picnic hadn't done enough damage that summer, as if the rains hadn't added to our misery, there was a military coup. Our head of state was overthrown. I watched as our new ruler made his first announcement on television. "I, Brigadier..."

The rest of his words marched away. I was trying to imagine the vacation starting over, Sheri coming to my window. I would order her to go home.

My father fumed throughout the announcement. "What is happening? These army boys think they can pass us from one hand to the other. How long will this regime last before there's another?"

"Let us hear what the man is saying," my mother said.

The brigadier was retiring government officials with immediate effect. He was setting up councils to investigate corruption in the civil service. My father talked as if he were carrying on a personal argument with him.

"What qualification do you have to reorganize the government?"

"I beg you," my mother said. "Let us hear what he is saying."

I noticed how she smirked. My mother was always pleased when my father was angry.

"You fought on a battle front doesn't make you an administrator," he said. "What do you know about reorganizing the government?"

"Let us give him a chance," she said. "He might improve things."

My father turned to her. "They fight their wars and they retire to their barracks. That is what they do. The army have no place in government."

"Ah, well," she said. "Still let us hear."

They followed the latest news about the coup; I imagined the summer as I wished it had started. That was how it was in our house over the next few days. There was a dusk to dawn curfew in Lagos and I wanted it to end so I could have the house to myself. I was not interested in the political overhaul in our country. Any voices, most of all my parents' animated voices, jarred on my ears, so when Uncle Fatai came by a week later, I went to my bedroom to avoid hearing about the coup again.

I thought they would all talk for a while. Instead, my father knocked on my door moments later. "Enitan, will you come out?"

I'd been lying on my bed, staring at my ceiling. I dragged myself out. My mother was sitting in the living room. Uncle Fatai had gone.

"Yes, Daddy?"

"I want you to tell me the truth," my father said.

He touched my shoulder and I forgot how to breathe again.

"Yes, Daddy... "

"Uncle Fatai tells us a friend of yours is in trouble."

My mother stood up. "Stop protecting her. You're always protecting her. Don't take her to church, don't do this, don't do that. Now look."

"Your friend is in hospital," my father said.

"Your friend is pregnant," my mother said. "She stuck a hanger up herself and nearly killed herself. Now she's telling everyone she was raped. Telling everyone my daughter was involved in this." She patted her chest.

"Let me handle this," my father said. "Were you there?"

"I didn't do anything," I said, stepping back.

"Enitan, were you there?"

I fled to my room. My father followed me to the doorway and watched my shifting feet. "You were there, weren't you," he said.

I kept moving. If I stopped, I would confess.

"I didn't do anything."

"You knew this happened and yet you stayed in this house, saying nothing."

"I told her not to go."

"Look at you," he said, "involved in a mess like this. I won't punish you this time. It's your mother that will punish you. I guarantee."

He left. I shut my door quietly and climbed into bed.

She was at my window. It was night outside.

"Let's go."

Our yard was water. The water had no end.

"Let's go."

I struggled to pull her through my window. She was slipping into the water. I knew she was going to drown.

"They're waiting for you," I said. "At the bottom."

Three slaps aroused me. My mother was standing over me.

"Out of bed," she said. "And get yourself ready. We're going to church."

It was morning. I scrambled out of my bed. I had not been to my mother's church in years, but my memory of the place was clear: a white building with a dome. Behind it, there were banana and palm trees; behind them a stream. In the front yard there was red soil, and the walls of the building seemed to suck it up. People buried curses in that soil, tied their children to the palm trees and prayed for their spirits. They brought them in for cleansing. More than anything else, I was embarrassed my mother would belong to such a church—incense, white gowns, bare feet and drumming. People dipping themselves in a stream and drinking from it.

Along the way, road blocks had been set up, as they always were after a military coup. Cars slowed as they approached them and pedestrians moved quietly. A truck load of soldiers drove past, sounding a siren. The soldiers jeered and lashed at cars with horsewhips. We pulled over to let them pass. A driver pulled over too late. Half the soldiers jumped down from the truck and dragged him out of his car. They started slapping him. The driver's hands went up to plead for mercy. They flogged him with horsewhips and left him there, whimpering by the door of his car.

At first the shouting scared me. I flinched from the first few slaps to the driver's head, heard my mother whisper, "They're going to kill him." Then, I watched the beating feeling some assurance that our world was uniformly terrible. I remembered my own fate again, and Sheri's, and became cross-eyed from that moment on. The driver blended in with the rest of the landscape: a row of rusty-roofed houses; old people with sparrow-like eyes; barefooted children; mothers with flaccid breasts; a bill board saying "Keep Lagos clean." A breadfruit tree; a public tap; its base was embedded in a cement square.

I had no idea what part of the city we were in.

My mother's priest was quiet as she explained what had happened. He had the same expression I remembered, his nose turned up as though he was sniffing something bad. She was to give me holy water to drink, since my father would not allow me to stay for cleansing. Then he produced a bottle of it, green and slimy. I recognized the spirogyra I'd seen in biology classes. I had to drink the water in the churchyard, and make myself sick afterward. None of it was to remain in me. Outside my mother handed the bottle to me. I gagged on every drop.

"Stick your finger down your throat," she said, when I finished.

Two attempts brought the entire contents of my stomach onto the ground, but I continued to retch. My eyes filled with tears. Some of the water had come through my nose.

"Good," my mother said.

I thought of stamping on her feet, squeezing her hand to regain my sense of balance.

"You should never have followed that girl," she said. "Look at me. If anything had happened to you, what would I have done? Look at me."

My gaze slipped from hers.

"The bottle," she said. "Give me the bottle, Enitan."

I handed it to her. It could have been a baton. My mother was hollow, I thought. There was nothing in her. Like a drum, she could seize my heart beat, but that was all. I would not say another word to her, only when I had to, and even then I would speak without feeling: "Good morning, good afternoon, good evening. Good night."

We arrived home and I walked to the back yard, by the fence where the scarlet hibiscus grew. Sheri had gotten pregnant from the rape. Didn't a womb know which baby to reject? And now that the baby had been forced out, how did it look? The color of the hibiscus? I placed one by my ear and listened.

1985

M uffled rage stalks like the wind, sudden and invisible. People don't fear the wind until it fells a tree. Then, they say it's too much.

The first person to tell me my virginity belonged to me was the boy who took it. Before this, I'd thought my virginity belonged to Jesus Christ, my mother, society at large. Anyone but me. My boyfriend, a first-year pharmacy student at London University, assured me that it was mine, to give to him. In those brief seconds between owning and giving up my virginity, he licked the walls of my mouth clean. After I thought he pierced my bowels, I burst into tears.

"What's wrong with you?" he asked.

"I'm sorry," I said. "I have to wash."

It was his semen. I couldn't bear the thought of it leaking out of me and rolling down my thighs. But each time I opened my mouth to tell him, about Sheri and me that awful summer, I thought my voice would blast my ribs apart, flatten him, flatten the bed, toss my sheets around like the wind, so I said nothing.

The next time around my boyfriend strummed me like a guitar. "I don't know what's going on," he said. "Maybe you're frigid." Frigidity was a form of mental illness, he said. We would eventually separate one night, when he complained that I was just like other Nigerian women in bed. "You just lie there," he said. "Like dead women."

I escorted him to my door.

I was in England for nine years, coming home only for vacations. My parents sent me to a boarding school there after that summer, as was the fashion in the seventies, and for the first time I would have to explain why I washed my hair once a week and put grease straight back in. My new school friends were surprised that I didn't live in a hut in Africa, that I'd never seen a lion except in the London zoo. Some confessed their parents didn't like black people. Only one had decided that she didn't either and I ignored her, the way I ignored another who said "hey man" and did all sorts of silly dances whenever she saw me.

I'd always thought English people didn't wash regularly. I expected them to behave like characters from an Enid Blyton book. My best friend, Robin, thought this was absolutely *wuh*-diculous. We became close because she, too, thought Bob Marley was a prophet, and she loved to abhor her parent's values. Dear Robin, she couldn't pronounce her R's. "Wound and wound the wound-about," the other girls teased her. "Wound and wound the wound-about the wabid wascal wan Wobin Wichardson."

Twagic. Altogether I thought it was easier being black in that school, but Robin wouldn't say the word: black. Her parents had taught her that it was rude. So, I was her friend with the afro, you know, The-Brown-One. I told her that black was what I was, not an insult. I wasn't even proud of it, because I'd never been ashamed of it, so there. I forced her to say it one night: Black. Bu-lack. Buh-lee-yack. She burst into tears and called me awogant. The day she finally plucked up the courage, I took offense. I didn't like the inflection in her voice. "Flipping heck," she said. "There's no pleasing you."

Robin was the laziest and smartest fourteen-year-old I knew, and she beat me in class tests every time. She was the first person to tell me that nothing a woman does justifies rape. "Some girls encourage it," I said. "Who taught you that cwap?" she asked. I couldn't remember, but bad girls got raped was all I'd heard before, and of the bad girls I knew, not one had taken her matter to court. For Sheri, justice came when Damola Ajayi was admitted into a mental institution where drug addicts in Lagos ended up: therapy included regular beatings. I wasn't even sure she knew about his demise. Her family moved out of our neighborhood and I lost contact with her. Robin assured me that justice was not much fairer in her country. The motto of the Old Bailey should read, "Pwotect the wich and punish the Iwish."

My parents separated while I was in school in England. My father delivered the news to me and I remember feeling like I'd mistakenly swallowed a worm in a glass of water; I wanted to throw up. I wondered if the trouble I'd caused hadn't divided them further. My father explained that my mother would take his duplex in another suburb of Lagos, and she would live in one unit while collecting rent from the next. There were no phone lines in the area, so I couldn't call her. I was to stay with him.

A squabble began between them, over ownership of property and over me. My mother vowed to have my father disbarred. Instead she developed hypertension and said my father had caused it. I spent vacations with her, and she spent most of them complaining about him; how he ignored her in public; how he insinuated something or the other. My mother clung to details while my father seemed confused: "I don't know what she's talking about. I haven't done anything to her." Soon I began to spend vacations in London, working as a shop assistant in department stores to supplement my allowance to avoid staying with either of them.

I studied law at London University and became part of the Nigerian student community, who, like the English community in Lagos, clung to each other, grappling with weather conditions and sharing news from home. We had had two military governments since the summer of 1975. The first ended with the assassination of our head of state; the second, in a transition to civilian rule. Still the news from home had not improved: "Ah, these civilians, they are worse than the military." "Ah, these politicians. Don't you know? They're nothing but thieves." I heard about Sheri again during this time. She had won the Miss Nigeria pageant, after taking her university title, and would be representing our country in the Miss World contest in England. I was curious to see her. I watched the contest that night with two fellow law students, Suzanne and Rola. Rola was Nigerian and Jamaican, and rooting for both Misses, Suzanne was from Hong Kong and rooting for no one. "I can't believe we're sitting here watching this," she kept mumbling. Rola, as usual, was ready to analyze. "I mean, she is pretty, but nothing special. Just pretty-pretty. I mean, she couldn't catwalk or anything. Maybe face model, but not even that. I mean, she definitely can't model-model... "

I was too busy smiling. It wasn't Paris, Sheri wasn't wearing a red negligee, but it was good enough. I regretted judging her; regretted my ignorance at age fourteen. Sheri didn't make it past the first round of the Miss World contest. None of our girls ever did. Later, I heard she'd become part of the sugar daddy circuit in Lagos, hanging around senators, and going on shopping sprees abroad. She was given all the titles that came with that.

1981, I graduated from university and joined a firm of solicitors in London. 1983, there was another military coup in my country. This time, I was recovering from a failed relationship, having discovered the boy I'd been dating half the year was dating someone else. It was out of respect for me that he lied to me, he said. He knew I wasn't the sort of girl to like two-timing. Still, he called to invite me to a vigil.

"Vigil for what?" I asked.

"Democracy," he said.

At the Nigerian High Commission. Would I come? I almost checked the ear-piece. When did he ever do such a thing? We called him Stringfellow, after the night club. And wasn't he the one who, whenever we passed the South African embassy in Trafalgar square, would say about the English people protesting against apartheid, "There they go again. Always fighting for blacks who live far away, never the blacks they have to live with."

I thought of standing on Fleet street where our High Commission was, in the cold, with a candle in my hand, all night long, for any cause. I thought of this boy who had lied from the minute I set eyes on him.

"Stringfellow," I said. "Never call me again."

People talked about the influence of Western culture as though Western culture were the same throughout the West, and never changed. But our parents had graduated in the dawn of sixties England, and we were to graduate in the material eighties. Like any generation defined by the economics of their childhood, we were children of the oil boom, and furthermore, we were the children who had benefited from the oil boom. Politics in England played out on a continuum from left to right wing. Politics in our country was a scuffle between the military and politicians. Both were conservative and so were we. Now our greatest contribution to our society was that we were more traditional than the people who had given birth to us.

A boy loved a girl and he called her his wife. A girl loved a boy and she stayed at home on weekends to cook for him, while he went out with some other girl. We were going out and staying in. Any talk of political protest was the talk of mad English people, or Nigerians who were trying to be like them. We didn't spare a thought for those who were finding it difficult to pay their school fees, now that the oil boom in our country had become a recession. We rebelled and used our pocket money to buy leather jackets, or unusual shoes. That was what we did.

I looked at the small stack of books in my room long after I hung up on Stringfellow. I'd acquired them after I stopped reading stories I could predict, or stories that had nothing to do with my life. Stringfellow would say they were written by women who really ought to straighten their dreadlocks and stop complaining.

"Bloody wolly," I said.

All lines to Lagos were busy. I didn't get through to my father until late the next evening and by then, had established my opinions. Our civilian government had begged for the coup. Never had there been a more debauched democracy: champagne parties, embezzlements. My father explained that our constitution had also been suspended, a development I couldn't fathom with my head full of English text-books. "Can they really do that?" I asked. "They can do whatever they want," he explained. "The power of a constitution comes from the respect people give it. If they don't, then it is words on paper. Nothing else."

He was wary of the new military government, and their promise to wage war against indiscipline. I thought that it wasn't such a bad idea, in a country where you still couldn't expect electricity for a full week. Then the reports started coming in: floggings for jumping bus queues; squats for government workers who came late to work; a compulsory sanitation day to stay home and dust; military tribunals for ex-politicians; Decree Two, under which persons suspected of acts prejudicial to state security could be detained without charge; Decree Four, under which journalists could be arrested and imprisoned for publishing any information about public officials. My father kept asking, but I told him I never wanted to go back.

I changed my mind one winter morning, while waiting for a double-decker bus to arrive. The wind popped my umbrella inside out, flipped my skirt almost to my waist. It ripped tears from my eyes and knocked my braids backward into my face. A braid scratched my eyeball. I stood there listening to the wind, whizzing in all directions, colliding with my thoughts, which were colliding with each other. I was thinking of men who were given to acts of cowardice, lying when they should be braver. I was thinking of a certain partner in my firm who stared at my braided hair as if it were a head full of serpents. I thought of partners who walked like they'd never passed wind. I remembered my phone bills. I was thinking that if I returned home, at least, at least I would be warm.

Summer of 1984, I returned home for law school. My father bought me a new car, a white Volkswagen Jetta, which I drove straight to my mother's house. "He spoils you," she said, dusting her hands in disapproval. The Jetta was less attractive to armed robbers than other imported models. When my father bought it, it was selling for six times my salary working for him as a newly qualified lawyer. A year later, a second-hand model would sell for twice that amount. He paid for it in cash. There was no such thing as a car loan, and I couldn't drive it on Tuesdays and Thursdays because during weekdays in Lagos, odd and even number vehicle plates were assigned separate days to ease the traffic flow. And, I would have to continue living with my father because rents in Lagos were paid two, three years in advance.

I was almost tempted to board a British Airways back. Then, one day, a lecturer stopped me along the corridors at law school.

"Yes sir?" I said, startled that he knew my last name.

"Is your father Sunny Taiwo?" he asked.

"Yes," I said.

"He is in the papers a lot these days."

He was.

"How is he?"

"Fine, sir."

"You were studying in England?"

Yes, I said.

"Welcome back," he said. "And give my regards to your father. We were at Baptist High together."

I realized I was glad to be back. There were partners in my old firm who may have been to Cambridge with my father. Heaven forbid they admitted that to me, or to themselves. Some of my law school peers from overseas would continue to complain about Lagos: the surly clerks, lazy air-conditioners, power cuts, traffic we called go-slow, water shortages, armed robbers, bribery. But I would embrace the nuisances of Lagos from then on; all of them, to be acknowledged at last.

My father had recently gained publicity for a case he won. His client, a newspaper columnist, Peter Mukoro, was arrested at a police check point earlier in the year. Peter Mukoro wrote articles criticizing the police. He claimed that they targeted him because of this, but they claimed he was indisciplined at the time of his arrest. My father argued that his arrest was unlawful anyhow and won the case.

Peter Mukoro had initially approached my father over a land dispute. He was nothing like my father's usual clients, wealthy property owners who wished to maintain a low profile. He was a man in his early forties, an unabashed dissident who courted publicity. I met him once and thought he drank too much and talked too loud. I suspected he was driven more by vanity than anything else, but my father was enjoying the publicity, holding press conferences with him, making statements about police harassment. I called him an old rebel, but secretly I was proud. As a child, this was how I'd envisioned a lawyer's work to be. Now all I could foresee was paper-work.

Law school ended the summer of 1985. Within a week of my graduation, there was another military coup and our constitution was further suspended. Days later, I registered for national service. My first month would be spent in military training; the remainder of the year, I would work for my father who had no obligation to pay me since, technically, I was employed by the government. Initially posted to a rural district, I begged the registration clerk to send me to another camp, when I saw signs warning campers not to walk around at night, because they might be abducted and used for human sacrifice. The alternative camp was based in a busier district, on the campus of a technical college that was closed for the summer vacation. I drove there hoping that the new camp would be better than I was predicting, hoping even, that I might finally meet someone nice and honest.

An early morning mist hung over the race tracks of the College of Technology. Fifty odd platoons were lined up on the grass patch within it, awaiting roll call. The grass was heavily beaded with dew. I slid my combat boots along and pulled my cap down. It was too early for roll call, and too chilly for warm blood.

"Enitan Taiwo," our platoon leader called out.

"Yeah," I answered.

My platoon mates laughed as he checked my name on the rota.

"Mike Obi?"

"Yes," said the man in front of me. His voice was deep. I'd noticed him as I joined the platoon for roll call. He was standing with his hands in his pockets: wide back, uniform looking like it had been pressed over him. I would be taller than him if I wore heels. He dug his combat boots into the grass and lifted his cap and I saw that his head was shaved.

Our platoon leader blew his whistle. "Round the tracks!"

There were complaints all around. "See me, see trouble," the woman behind me said. "All this *wahala*," my neighbor said.

Mike Obi turned to me. "That's why they're calling us the pregnant platoon."

"Why?" I asked.

"Because we're the laziest, fattest platoon around."

"None of the above," I said.

He dimpled like side pockets. We began to jog along the race tracks.

"Are you one of the lawyers?" he asked, as we rounded the bend. I nodded in response. I was beginning to feel the stretch in my legs.

"How come you start camp later than everyone else?" he asked.

"Because we are better than everyone else."

He laughed. "I'm not so sure about that."

"Law school graduation ceremony," I said.

A group of joggers passed us, chanting an army song.

"You must have been here during the coup a week ago," I said.

"Yes."

"What was that like?"

"No one really cared. Soldiers go. Soldiers come. We had morning drill, went out during the curfew."

"That's a pity."

He stretched out his hand. "I'm Mike."

"Enitan," I said.

His hand felt coarse. I slowed and he slowed, too.

"What do you do, Mike?" I asked.

"Me? I'm an artist."

"I've never met an artist before."

He pulled his cap down. "Actually, I'm an architect, but I studied fine art for a year."

"Liar... "

"At Nsukka university."

"Liar," I said.

"I *am* an artist," he said. "You should see my mosaics."

"Mosaics? Talk true. What kind?"

"With beads. Very beautiful."

"I'm sure."

"And you?" he asked.

"I've just finished law school."

"You don't look that young to me."

I swiped his shoulder. It felt like wood.

"I'm sorry," he said. "But some of the graduates here look twenty-one. You and I don't."

"Speak for yourself."

"You should be proud of your age."

I smiled. "I am. I'm not a new graduate. I worked for three years after my degree."

"Where?"

"England."

"What made you come home?"

"It was cold. It was time. What made you give up on your art?"

"You know our people. Everyone told me I would starve and I believed them."

"Hm. Maybe you didn't believe in yourself."

"Maybe."

"You don't regret giving up?"

"I don't regret anything."

"And yet you still call yourself an artist."

"If necessary," he said.

"To do what?" I asked.

Impress, he said. We strolled back like old friends. Mike was wrong. Most women I knew would sprint from an artist. It meant that they might have to dabble with poverty and poverty always cleared people's eyes in Lagos. After morning drill, where I learned how to march and about-turn, we parted ways. He didn't know it, but I was ready to reach into his dimples and pluck out a gold coin.

⌁

I walked back to the women's halls located five minutes away from the race tracks. A poorly-lit building normally inhabited by the college's students during the academic year, the halls housed national service participants during military training. At the entrance, a group of women were arguing with the caretaker. "Why can't we have men inside?" one woman asked. "After all, we're not students, and some of us are married."

"Is not allowed," the caretaker said.

"Who said?" she asked.

"Jesus," he said.

The old man wasn't letting any men in. He sat by the entrance, flicking his horsewhip and waiting for those who dared. The day before he had lashed out at one graduate who had studied in the US, and still held his rights dear. "You have no rat!" this graduate screamed at him in a Nigerian-American accent. "You have no rat to whip me like that! Nobady has the rat to whip me like that!" The old man looked him up and down. "You want your rights, you go back to the country where you learned how to shout at an elder," he said. "Now, clear out of here, Johnny jus' come."

Baba, they called him. Every old man in my country was Baba, or Papa. This one was keeper of graduate vaginas.

Walking up the stairs, I smelled urine from the toilets and remembered my old school in Lagos. I was almost tempted to laugh: ten years later and still living in similar lodgings. My fear of inhaling the foul odor prevented me. I placed my palm over my nose and hurried past.

Inside the dormitory, I removed my T-shirt and lay on the bed. The shutters were open, but the air was flat and dry. The dormitory was like a prison cell: two iron spring beds and four walls sullied by the hand prints and head smears of previous inmates. My roommate, a graduate from the university of Lagos, refused to sleep in it. She shuttled from home, but home was far away for me and I wasn't sure I could wake up early enough to make roll call.

I rested a little, decided to buy mosquito coils from the hawker who sat under an almond tree by the parking lot. A few campers were there, chatting in groups. Visitors drove in all day to see friends and family, and sometimes camp felt like an everlasting party. At the hawkers stall, I selected a box of mosquito coils, a packet of Trebor mints and paid for them. Contemplating another packet, I felt a tap on my shoulder. It was Mike. He bent to pick a box of mosquito coils.

"You, too?" he said.

"They're eating me alive," I said.

He paid the hawker and we began to walk toward the halls.

"What are you doing now?" he asked.

"Nothing," I said.

"Come and talk to me."

He pointed to the spectator stand by the race tracks. We walked there and sat on the bottom row. Mike removed one of the coils from the box and lit it. I was lulled by the sounds: crickets chattering and laughter from the parking lot. The mosquito coil turned a fluorescent amber and gray smoke rose from it. Mike caught me watching him.

"I'm afraid," he said. "The way you look at me, like I've stolen your money. Are you one of those women who can't trust somebody?"

"I'm one of those women who wants to trust somebody."

He lifted the mosquito coil and placed it between us.

"That's good," he said.

He spoke softly between pauses. I talked till I almost bit my tongue and delayed swallowing to slip in punch lines.

"You this girl," he kept saying. He rarely laughed.

Mike grew up near Enugu, a city in eastern Nigeria that was the heart of Biafra. His parents were lecturers at the state university. His mother taught drama, and his father, history. During the Civil War, he was sent to a foster home in England and I teased him because years later, he still had traces of an English accent in addition to his Igbo one.

"Eni-ton," I corrected him, when I'd had enough of him mispronouncing my name.

"Eni-tan," he said.

"On! on! Do your mouth like this... on... on."

"An."

"For heaven's sake."

It was terrible that we'd had different experiences of the Civil War. In university, I finally acknowledged the holocaust that was Biafra, through memoirs and history books, and pictures of limbless people; children with their stomachs bloated from kwashiorkor and their rib cages as thin as leaf veins. Their parents were mostly dead. Executed. Macheted. Blown up. Beheaded. There were accounts of blood-drinking, flesh-eating, atrocities of the human spirit that only a civil war could generate, while in Lagos we had carried on as though it were happening in a different country. Our Head of State got married even. The timing of the truce, Mike said, came about because the warring troops wanted to watch Péle play football. Péle. Civil war. I hoped that he was joking.

A trip to Oshogbo in Western Nigeria gave him his love for art. He visited the art institutes and the groves of Yoruba gods. He loved football, played it, dreamed about it. Sometimes when he talked about it, I feared he might gag on joy. He told me about Brazil's Péle, Argentina's Maradona. Nigeria's striker, Thunder Balogun and goal keeper, Okala, his first hero. "Okala had mystical powers," he said. "I saw it with my two eyes."

"Bury your head in shame," I said.

Friday, we left camp for a meal at Mama Maria's, a food spot on Victoria Island. It was owned by a local madam and run by her prostitutes. I'd heard about it from friends at law school and thought it was the sort of place Mike might want to visit. We drove there in his car, an old white Citroen that he occasionally patted like a dog. I noticed a rusty hole in the floor, through which I could see the road below.

"What do you do when the rain comes?" I asked.

"I avoid puddles," he said.

"Doesn't it bother you? This big hole?"

He laughed. "No, neither do my headlights."

"What's wrong with them?"

"They're attached with masking tape."

"One day you'll be driving the steering wheel alone."

We were stopped at every police checkpoint. Some policemen even laughed as we pulled away. As we drove through the gates at Mama Maria's, a group of prostitutes mauled his car. They wiggled their tongues and pressed their breasts to the windscreen. They made shrill noises like huntsmen. Once they realized we were not a couple of white men, they abandoned us.

Walking in, we found the place full of pot-bellied expatriates. We never called them immigrants. I'd seen their faces before, working on construction sites overseas. One or two had prostitutes on their laps. The prostitutes eyed us as we headed for the view overlooking the lagoon. They were majestic, and they were ugly. A man was useless-ing me, they would say, for all my propriety and education, so what was I looking at? I noticed the airline stickers on the wall behind the drinks bar.

"Is that some sort of honor roll?"

Mike glanced at it. "More like a tombstone."

At first, I didn't know what he was talking about, then I remembered AIDS. I didn't know much about the disease, but I was sure that people would hide and ignore it, like the drug problem of the seventies, until it was out of control. So far, in Lagos, we blamed expatriates and prostitutes for AIDS.

One of the women approached us and we ordered two plates of food. She handed us beers and we began to drink. The street lights of Ikoyi shimmered down the lagoon. It was possible to believe that I could swim across with ease. My gaze dropped to the shoreline a few meters from Mama Maria's. There was a broken beer bottle to my right, a car tire to my left. A line of rotten seaweed joined them together.

"Filthy," Mike said.

I fingered the bottle of Gulder beer and wondered if it was the cold malt or his voice making me relax.

"You never talk about your mother," he said.

"I do," I said.

"No, you talk about your father, but never about your mother."

I took another swig of the beer and wiped my mouth clean. A daughter was not meant to be at odds with her mother. Especially an only child. Thinking of my mother made me feel like I'd left the door of a vault wide open for thieves.

"We hardly see each other. She belongs to a church, a cult, actually. One of those, take your money and give you fear. She's been a member for as long as I can remember. I think she was drawn in because of my brother. She thinks I idolize my father. But I've never had illusions about my father. You have to be friends with at least one of your parents. Don't you think?"

"Yes."

"Well, there it is, my mother."

There was a time that I would be more open about our relationship, but the responses I got were the same: "Well, my dear, she is your mother." "Only have one mother." "Shiece your mother! She suffered for you!"

"When was the last time you saw her?" Mike asked.

"I see her all the time."

"The last time was?"

"My graduation."

"You should try to see her soon."

"Should I? Why should I?"

"Because you should."

Our mothers were wonderful, mostly. They shielded us from the truths about our fathers, remained in bad marriages to give us a chance. But I'd seen, met, heard of daughters who admitted their mothers were vain, weak, bullying, sluttish, drunken. The difference between these daughters and I was that I did not know my own mother, and I had kept our lack of relationship hidden, often lied about it. How could I tell Mike about my graduation photograph, the one my mother had refused to pose in if my father were by my side? I asked her to let the day end without fighting, and she accused me of taking his side. My graduation day ended in silence. I posed separately with either parent, and then vowed that they would never involve me in their arguments again.

"Because you should," I repeated.

"Yes," Mike said.

"Everything is that simple?"

"Why stop at B, when you can go from A to Z?"

"Isn't that what life's about? The stops along the way, the unraveling?"

He shrugged. "When death knocks, who remembers the unraveling? Only the outcome is important, I believe."

"Then you might as well be born and die immediately."

"I'm sorry," he said.

"Don't be. I'm just saying, I don't think family ties are as simple as people like to say they are, over here. That's all I'm saying."

He reached for my hand. "Why are we fighting? You're too serious tonight. And this place is depressing anyway, for tourists. Next time I will take you somewhere better."

"Only you knows," I said, childishly.

He bothered me like a white sheet. I wanted to search for stains, hidden dirt.

It was Makossa night. The evening ended with us watching other people make fools of themselves, until Manu Dibango's "Soul Makossa" came on, then we made fools of ourselves.

On our way to camp we slowed through a night market. Fluorescent lights from the stalls lit up the street. The street was narrow and juju music blared from a battered cassette player perched on a wooden stool. Street hawkers sat around selling boxes of sugar, bathing sponges, tinned sardines, chewing sticks, cigarettes, and Bazooka Joe gum. A group of old men huddled together playing a board game. A kerosene lantern lit up their faces, casting huge shadows on a wall behind them. We came to a stop and I edged closer to the window to watch them moving their chips. The air was warm and the sky pitch-black. I heard a loud crack above the music. At first I thought it was fireworks, but it was the wrong time of the year, and since one military regime had banned them, they were scarce.

A man was running down my side of the street. His hands were up and he was shouting. The music drowned out what he was saying. I noticed people in the market stand up, heard another crack. The man was thrown forward. He crashed over the trunk of the car behind us. People in the market began to run. The old men disappeared from their table. Mike was looking in his rearview mirror. His hand went to the back of my neck. My head dropped to my knees. I found myself staring through the hole in his car. One moment I could see the road, the next, dirt. We were moving. I wondered how; there had been other cars in front of us. I heard car engines. Mike pressed on his horn and I covered my ears. We drove over a bump and my knee punched my chin. I no longer saw the hole. His hand touched my back.

"Armed robbers," he said.

I sat up. "They were coming from behind?"

We were now on an expressway with street lights.

"The car behind us drove through the market," he explained. "I followed him and everyone else followed us."

"The people in the market?"

"They scattered."

I was meant to feel something. I did not know what.

"I hear it is university students. Is it?"

"I don't know."

We didn't speak until we reached a police check point. Mike reported the raid, and the policeman asked for his driver's license. For the rest of the journey we were silent.

"How are you?" He asked as we drove into camp.

I'd been rubbing my chin.

"Fine," I said. "You?"

He patted my shoulder. We stopped by the women's halls in the college and I crept past Baba, the caretaker, who was asleep with his horsewhip in his lap. I knew I was meant to feel something; I still didn't know what. In my room I shut my door and leaned against it. It was what people in films did.

～

"It's you?" my mother said.

There was a crease across the bridge of her nose where her frown had set. Gray hair peeped from her hairline and time had cast shadows under her eyes. I knew that would be my fate.

"It's me," I said, forcing cheer into my voice.

"You're still plaiting your hair?" she said.

"Yes."

"You don't want to try something new?"

"No."

She walked to her chair. "You young girls and all these hair extensions."

My mother's house smelled of unused linen, shut cupboards, rusty valves, mothballs, candlewick, and incense for prayer. Her window panes were thick with dust and I was sure that if she'd employed someone, they would be clean; but every house help she had ran away. "How is camp?" she asked.

"Fine," I said.

"Only fine? You can't take that attitude. You must try to enjoy life more."

I almost laughed out loud. She who was always accounting or predicting a bad event. If the sun were shining, rain might fall. If rain fell, piss might follow.

"How are you?" I asked.

"I'm all right, but my medicine, the price has gone up. And my tenants, they are late with their rent again."

"What is it this time?"

"They cannot pay. I will give them till the end of next week. If they don't pay by then, I will have them evicted."

Her tenants just didn't believe in paying on time. My father would send a letter to them, I promised her.

"This is Lagos," she said. "People don't move until they're forced. And your father anyway, what does he care? He keeps talking about human rights. The man still hasn't put my houses in my name. What about my rights?"

"He hasn't?"

"Maybe if you ask him, he will. You know you and your father. He thinks you're his lawyer." She patted her chest. "You didn't even ask after me during the coup. You could have at least come to check I was all right."

"We were not allowed out."

My mother calculated dates, situations, betrayals, and she looked at me long enough to summarize my life. She was still angry about my graduation, I knew. But I was angry too, and that didn't start on the day of my graduation. Grievances had set in her bones like cement and it was difficult to be around her.

"You want me to leave?" I finally asked.

"You met me here on my own," she said. "If you wish, you can leave."

Now, I said what I wanted: "All this over one photograph. Is this what you want? To ruin every good day in your life because of one man?"

"You can leave right now, if this is how you want to speak to me."

"He doesn't care. Can't you see?"

"Go back to that house where you learned to abuse your mother."

"You get angry and he forgets. It's all in the past to him."

"It is not past you're living in his house."

"I don't care who is right or wrong."

"It's not past he struts around like a man of conscience."

"I do not care."

"It's not past I'm living in a house that still doesn't belong to me."

I waved her words away.

"Always," she said. "You were too busy trailing in his footsteps."

"How?"

"You always were," she said. "He never gave you a chance."

"You remember things as you want."

"From the day you were born, feeding you ideas. Don't cook, this and that. Maybe you should have been born a son to satisfy him."

"What is it you won't forgive me for?" I asked. "That I like my own father?"

"He was no good."

"To me, he is."

"If he's no good to me, he's no good to you. The day you realize it, I'll be here waiting for you. The damage has been done already. You're still too blind to know."

I stood up. "You want to make me doubt myself? That is it?"

"Yes," she said. "Yes, you never want to hear it. Never about your father. Go on. Continue to deceive yourself."

I no longer believed her; hurt one moment, hurtful the next. She could recall what my father said ten years ago, and yet she misconstrued my entire childhood. She who took a child to church to heal him. She who swallowed pills regularly. She was like one of those mothers who put their children's feet in fire to stop them convulsing. Why didn't they put their own feet in, if they so believed in its healing powers?

"Go on," she said. "Who asked you to come with your trouble? Not one minute's peace did you give me as a child, now you want to criticize me. Asking me why I won't stand next to him in a photograph. Why should I stand next to him? For any reason? The man gave me nothing. Nothing, for all his education, he's as typical as they come. And I may not have paid your school fees, but remember I gave birth to you. Just remember that, while you're out there walking around with certificate, calling yourself a lawyer. Someone gave birth to you."

It took all my strength to shut her door gently. At her gate, I swore that I would never visit my mother's house again. Some people were happy by habit; others were not. It had nothing to do with me.

⁓

We were thirty minutes into our endurance test, a ten-mile run. I was hoping to make it to my old school, to see what had become of the place. Mike and other healthy people were in front. I had fallen behind. I took shorter breaths as my heart raced. I was trying to run with some dignity, unlike some of my platoon members who were using their hands to support their backs.

This part of Lagos was a shanty town. We passed a house with flaky yellow paint and a group of pot-bellied infants scurried out. One almost toppled into the gutter alongside the road and his mother yanked him out and boxed his ear. He began to howl. We passed a group of palm trees huddled together and a pink and white building with a sign post saying: "Hollywood Hair. Mannycure, Pennycure, Wash and Set. Fresh Eggs and Coca-Cola." A woman, the proprietor perhaps, sat on a stool with a cloth wrapped around her body. She was polishing her teeth with a chewing stick and paused to spit into the gutter. The entire area smelled of goat droppings and morning mist. I decided to head back to camp.

The soldiers on duty eyed me as I walked through the gates of the college. I remembered how I tried to bribe them to sneak out during the day as my roommate did. They waited while I fumbled with the money in my pocket. Mike later said, "You greet them every day, then you give them something to buy beer. That's how you do it. Not bringing out wads of *naira* notes. Where have you been?"

I could have swiped his head.

A car horn tooted. I turned to see a new Peugeot. Stepping on the side of the road, I waited for it to pass, but it came to a halt. The windscreen was tinted so I couldn't see the driver, but as soon as the windows came down, I knew.

"Sheri Bakare," I said.

It was like finding a pressed flower I'd long forgotten about. Her smile was less broad; her pink gums seemed to have disappeared.

"*Aburo*," she said. "Is this your face?"

"What are you doing here?"

She laughed. "I came to see my brother."

"Which one?"

"Gani."

"Gani's here? I'm too old. Far too old."

We were holding hands. She was wearing a yellow *agbada* with gold embroidery around the neckline, and her fingers were laden with gold rings.

"Can I give you a lift?" she asked.

Inside her car I smelled perfume and new leather seats. I sat up because I was wet with sweat. Sheri slowed over a speed bump.

"How come you're in national service?" she asked.

"I'm just out of law school."

"You're a lawyer?"

"Yes, and you?"

"I studied education."

"You're a teacher?"

"Me? No."

We drove past the race tracks and stopped by the women's halls. As we got out, Sheri wrapped her scarf around her head and leaned against the car. She moved with the rhythm of big women I admired; like a steady boat on choppy water. I noticed she was wearing black high heeled sandals with rhinestone buckles. It was ten thirty in the morning.

"You look well," I said.

"You too," she said. "You're still slim and don't even try to tell me I am."

I laughed. "I wasn't going to, Miss Nigeria."

"Ah, don't remind me," she said. "Those skinny girls. I still have a pretty face, *sha*."

"Beautiful," I said.

Even with her big ears. Her cheeks hollowed as she spoke.

"I hear you went to England that summer," she said. "I wish I could have gone, for university at least."

"Why didn't you?"

"My father died."

"I'm sorry to hear that. I only heard that you moved."

"He died," she said, scraping the ground with her shoe. "And we lost Alhaja, too. Not long afterward."

I watched her sandals cloud up with dust.

"You remember Kudi?" she asked.

"How can I forget her?"

"She's in her first year at Lagos University. I've just been to visit her. You should have seen her, all of them, nineteen-year-olds wearing the latest fashions. No wonder she keeps asking for money."

"Aren't they supposed to be studying?"

She sucked her teeth. "Their heads aren't in studying. They are looking for boys with cars. I told Kudi, 'If you want clothes, take some of mine.' But she said she didn't want any of mine."

"Why not?"

"She said I dress like an old mama. Can you believe it? She said that to me? Children of nowadays. No respect. We were never like this, I'm sure."

I laughed. "How is Kudi?"

It was as though I saw her a day ago. She continued to talk about her sister and I encouraged her, only because it was easy conversation to make. Before I left, I took her address and promised to visit her over the weekend. It was an apartment block not far from my father's house, and I knew she couldn't afford to live there without a sponsor. But Sheri was sugary, as we said in Lagos; she had a man, an older man, a man as old as my father even, and he would pay her rent.

"Make sure you come," she said. "I'm lonely there."

Saturday morning I drove into Lagos Island via the mainland bridge to see her. A few freighters were docked along the harbor of the marina. Descending the bridge, I caught a partial view of the commercial center I had come to know by driving. A mishmash of skyscrapers crowded the skylines, scattered between them were dull concrete one-story buildings with corrugated-iron roofs. They were mostly trading stores. Each bore a sign in need of painting. A web of electricity and telephone lines criss-crossed above them.

The Atlantic weaved its way around Lagos. Sometimes dull and muddy, other times strident and salty, bearing different names: Kuramo waters, Five Cowry Creek, Lagos Marina, Lagos Lagoon. It was the same water. Asphalt bridges connected the islands to the mainland and the sky always looked as sad as a person whose lover had lost interest. People rarely noticed it, even its amber sunsets. If the sun were going down, it meant there would be no light soon and Lagosians needed to see their way. Street lights here did not always function.

Millions lived in Lagos. Some were natives, but most had roots in the provinces. They fell in and out with the elements as though the weather were created to punish and reward: "Sun beat my head," "Breeze cooled me." Most days it felt like a billion people walking down the labyrinth of petty and main streets: beggar men, secretaries, government contractors (thieves, some would say), Area Boys, street children. You could tell how well they ate by the state of their shoes. Beggars, of course, went bare foot. If no one noticed the sky, it was because they were busy watching vehicles. There was a constant din of cars, popping exhaust pipes, and engines, commuters scrambling for canary-yellow buses and private transport vans we called *kabukabu* and *danfo*. They bore Bible epitaphs: Lion of Judah, God Saves. Their drivers drove devilishly, and added to the incongruity around: cattle grazing in a rubbish dump, a man crossing the highway in a wheel-chair, a street hawker with a Webster's dictionary in one hand and a toilet brush in the other.

There were countless billboards: Pepsi, Benson and Hedges, Daewoo, Indomie Instant Noodles, Drive Carefully, Fight Child Abuse. All smells joined hands in one: sweaty skin and fumes, and the heat was the kind that made your forehead crease, and crease, until you witnessed something that made you smile: a taxi driver making lurid remarks; people cursing themselves well and good; All right-Sirs, our urban praise singers or borderline beggars, who hailed any person for money. Chief! Professor! Excellency!

It was a hard city to love; a bedlam of trade. Trade thrived in the smallest of street corners; in stores; on the heads of hawkers; even in the suburbs where family homes were converted into finance houses and hair salons, according to the need. The outcome of this was dirt, piles of it, on the streets, in open gutters, and in the marketplaces, which were tributes to both dirt and trade. My favorite time was early morning, before people encroached, when the air was cool and all I could hear was the call from Central Mosque: *Allahu Akhbar, Allahu Akhbar.* All that crooning when the city was most quiet, it made sense.

By the Cathedral Church of Christ, I met a bottleneck and was cornered by a group of lepers. One rapped on my window and I rolled it down to put money into his tin cup. A group of refugee children from North Africa, noticing my gesture, scurried to my car. They rubbed my windows and pleaded with feigned expressions. I felt ashamed for wishing them off the streets. Passers-by trespassed the stairs of the Cathedral without regard. Once a monument along the marina, people could now buy fried yams, brassieres, and mosquito coils inches away from her ebony doors. The traffic gave way and I drove on.

I remembered my mother's medicine and made a detour into a market district to check their prices. The roads there were as tight as corridors and gutters dipped inches from my car tires. Crowded stalls blasted out bluish-light fluorescent lights. Their iron roofs collapsed into each other. I called out to a young man behind the counter at a pharmacy stall. "You have Propanolol?"

He nodded.

"Let me see it," I said.

He hurried over and held the bottle up. I noticed the expiration date.

"This has expired," I said.

He snatched it and walked away.

I drove fast until I approached a large round-about. A group of police wives sat within it, waiting for customers who came to braid their hair. Some had infants strapped to their backs, but they pursued my car. I recognized one who regularly braided my hair and waved to her. Lagos festered with people: drivers, sellers, shoppers, loiterers, beggars. Madmen. The latter sometimes walked the streets with nothing but dust covering their private parts. I once saw a woman like that. She was pregnant.

When I reached Sheri's house my shoulders were as tight as springs. She opened her door wearing another colorful *agbada* and matching head tie. I sniffed.

"What are you cooking?"

"A little food," she said.

"For me?"

She prodded my shoulder as I walked in. Sheri's apartment was like an array of plastic flowers. Each piece of furniture had a flower motif on it; some in powdery pastels, others in strident reds and yellows. I almost expected to smell pungent potpourri instead of the onions and peppers simmering in her kitchen.

"Sit here while I finish," she said.

I sunk into a sofa of daffodils and noticed the miniature porcelain ornaments on her center table. There were kittens, a woman with an umbrella, and a house with the inscription "Home is where the heart is." The kittens were lined up. I was sure that if I moved one, she would notice. Her cushions were lined up the same way on the sofas, equally spaced.

Pepper smoke scratched the back of my throat. I heard a pot rocking over a hot plate. "I hope I'm going to eat some of that," I said.

"Eat what you want," she said. "Ibrahim doesn't eat much."

"Ibrahim ?"

Her head appeared around the corner. "Hassan," she said. "The Brigadier. Have you heard of him?"

A tall, skinny man who played polo. He collected polo ponies and women as young as his daughters and was always in the papers during the Lagos tournament.

"He has a stomach ulcer," she said, and disappeared into her kitchen.

I stared at the spot where her face had been.

"Does he treat you well?"

She came out again, cleaning her hands with a dish towel. "I live here. I don't have to worry about money."

"Yes, but does he treat you well?"

She sat down. "Which one of our men really treats women well?"

"I don't know many."

"So," she said.

I inspected my nails. "Isn't he married, Sheri."

Polygamy was considered risqué. Women in our generation who opted for it ended up looking quite the opposite of traditional.

She nodded. "To two women, and he can marry two more if he wants. He's a Moslem."

"Is that what you want?"

She laughed. "Want? I beg you, don't talk to me about want. When my father died who remembered me? Chief Bakare done die, God Bless his family. We didn't even know where our next meal was coming from, and no one cared. Not even my uncle, who took all his money."

"But your father and uncle were close."

She shook her head. "Don't let anyone deceive you. Pray you're never in a situation to need them. It is then you will know what two plus two really makes. Listen, I take care of my family, I even take care of Ibrahim. Since morning I'm cooking. He may not show up, and this won't be the first time. So if I have to tie my head up when I go out... "

"You have to tie your head?"

"He's a strict Moslem."

I rolled my eyes. I knew strict Moslems. Uncle Fatai was one. He was gentle and monogamous. His only vice was gluttony. His wife was a Lagos state judge and her head was covered because she wanted it to be.

"And if I can't go out once in a while," Sheri was saying.

"He stops you from going out? What's next? Purdah?"

She laughed.

"You think it's funny?" I said. "You're better than this, Sheri. Anyone you want, you can have."

"Who said? You remember what happened to me?"

I remembered only that she was the most powerful girl I knew, and then she wasn't anymore, and I became disappointed with her.

"Not that," she said. "You can say it. I did not rape them; they raped me, and if they see me they'd better cross the road."

"The border and hemisphere even," I mumbled.

"Yes," she said. "They can cross that too, because if I get my hands on them, there will be nothing left to cross with."

The boys were absurd in my mind, with their red eyes and hemp, and skinny bodies. I would have to exaggerate them to explain why they jinxed her life and why I still couldn't open my mouth to talk about them.

"I didn't know," I said apologetically. "I shouldn't have talked to you as if it was your fault."

"And me, myself," she said. "What did I know? Taking a hanger to myself, with all the biology I studied. I still thought I had a black hole inside me. So, which single man from a normal family would have a person like me?"

Better to be ugly, to be crippled, to be a thief even, than to be barren. We had both been raised to believe that our greatest days would be: the birth of our first child, our wedding and graduation days in that order. A woman may be forgiven for having a child out of wedlock if she had no hope of getting married, and she would be dissuaded from getting married if she didn't have a degree. Marriage could immediately wipe out a sluttish past, but angel or not, a woman had to have a child. For me, coming home to Nigeria was like moving back to the fifties in England.

"You are strong," I said.

"Have no choice," she said.

I'd been looking at my hands. I had feeble nails and they wouldn't grow past the tip of my fingers. I never bothered to paint them. Sheri's nails were varnished and sometimes she clicked them as she spoke. If she sounded cynical, I'd always found the cynical to be honest, like the mad: they could not be manipulated into pretending that it was good to ignore the bad things in life.

"Let's eat," she said.

Her stepmothers had kept their family together by buying and selling gold jewelry. Gold from Italy was the best, Sheri said. It was eighteen-carat, and the Italian traders were no different from Nigerians: they loved to shout and bargain. Saudi gold was also good. They had those twenty-four-carat pieces Lagos people wore for traditional functions. Sheri didn't care much for the gold from Hong Kong. It was too yellow, and didn't suit our skin color. Neither did the gold from India. She would never buy fourteen-carat gold, like the Americans, or nine, like the British. Never.

My mouth watered as she brought out one steaming Pyrex dish after another. Sheri had prepared food I hardly saw in my father's house: *jollof* rice; *egusi* stew with crushed melon seeds, and *eba*, a meal made from ground cassava. She cooked with enough pepper to tear the roof of my mouth off. I was crying and eating. Sheri meanwhile sprinkled dried pepper over her stew, because none of it was hot enough for her.

"I cook for a week," she explained. "Ibrahim sometimes shows up with friends, and there has to be food. I make his separately. He can't eat pepper because of his ulcer."

"That's nonsense."

"Why?"

"You are not his cook."

"You have that attitude?"

"Who has time to sit in a kitchen from morning to night?"

She shook her head. "You've been away too long. You've become a butter-eater."

"It's rude for him to behave that way, that's all."

She laughed until she spilled her water.

"Is this what you learned abroad, *aburo?*"

I waited for her to stop.

"You want to marry someday?"

"I might," I said.

She leaned forward. "Maybe you don't know this because you were raised by your father, but let me tell you now, to save you from unnecessary headache in the future. Forget that nonsense. Education cannot change what's inside a person's veins. Scream and shout, if you like, bang your head against this wall, you will end up in the kitchen. Period. Now, where I differ from most women is, if you lift your hand to beat me, I will kill you. God no go vex. Secondly, while I am there cooking for you, I won't be thinking of dropping some poison in because you've gone to eat another woman's stew."

"Because?"

"I'm getting what I want in return," she said.

"Love?"

"Please, my sister."

"Sex?"

She sucked on a bone. "I beg, which one of them can do."

"Money?"

She threw the bone on her plate.

"One day your eyes will open."

By the time I was ready to leave, I was bloated, but Sheri wouldn't hear of it. She served more *jollof* into a Tupperware container and handed it to me.

"You should start a catering business," I told her.

"I wish I could," she said.

"What's stopping you? You have property in a good location; your stepmothers can cook, and you trust them."

"I can't come and go as I like."

"I don't want to hear that, Sheri."

"I can't," she said.

I realized she was serious.

"Okay," I said. "My father sometimes entertains and his

cook is terrible. I will mention you to him."

She patted me toward the door. "Thank you, *aburo*."

As I left her home, it occurred to me that I was glad I was not pretty. Prettiness could encourage people to treat a woman like a doll, to be played with, tossed around, fingered, dismembered, and discarded. Prettiness could also make a woman lazy, if she were congratulated for it too often and remunerated too long. Sheri was the Nigerian man's ideal: pretty, shapely, yellow to boot, with some regard for a woman's station. Now she was a kitchen martyr, and may well have forgotten how to flaunt her mind.

I took her *jollof* to my father; the Tupperware was still flexible and warm when I arrived. Over the years, our neighborhood had changed. New houses and condominiums stood where the park once rambled and most of them were now sinking in marshy land, and yet Ikoyi Park was still considered prime property. I found my father sitting on the veranda, reading a brief.

"My dear," he said.

"You're on your own?" I asked.

"Yes."

I sat in the cane chair next to his. "Hm. Working on a weekend. Don't tell me Peter Mukoro is in government trouble again."

My father didn't confirm, but Peter Mukoro had enough law suits to keep fifty lawyers fully occupied, I was sure.

"Where is Titus?" I asked.

"Day off," he said.

"You're lucky. I brought you *jollof*."

He made a show of being shocked. "I know it is not you who cooked that. Is this part of military training?"

I smiled. "It's my friend. She has a catering business."

"Which friend of yours does that?"

"Sheri."

"I don't remember her."

"She lived next door."

He followed my finger. "Chief Bakare's daughter?"

I nodded.

"The one who?"

"Yes, the one who, and now she's catering, so if you ever need help... "

My father resumed his reading. "Let us see if her cooking is any good."

I went to the kitchen and placed the Tupperware container into the refrigerator. Except for two bottles of water, a shriveled orange and three pots, my father's refrigerator was bare. Titus, his cook, was a myopic old man from Calabar. He could barely discern peppers from tomatoes, and yet he would come into the living room and announce, "Dinner is served." The first time I witnessed this, I asked my father what was happening in his house. Dinner was beans and fried plantain. Dinner was always beans and fried plantain, except when it was boiled yams and corned beef stew. My father replied, "Titus used to work for an English family. Let him say what he wants, so long as he doesn't cook potatoes."

My father trusted Titus, enough to leave him in the house alone. Titus sometimes corrected my English.

I returned to the veranda.

"How are you?" my father asked.

"Fine," I said.

He patted my arm. "That will end when you start work with me."

"Pay me well, that's all I ask."

"I will pay you according to your experience."

"You better not be miserly."

He pretended to be deaf. "What?"

"I said, you better not be miserly with me because there are plenty of people who would like to employ me."

"Like who?" he asked.

"Uncle Fatai," I said.

"Fatai is cheaper than me."

"Well, be careful how you treat me. One day you'll be begging me to run that place."

We watched the Lagoon. There wasn't a movement, not even a ripple around the sticks the fishermen had left to mark their fishing traps.

"We had trouble during the week," my father said.

"Eh, what happened?"

"Fishermen. They scaled over the fence and stole three chairs."

"I thought they were in the garage or something."

"They were stolen."

"What will fishermen do with cane chairs?"

"Sell them."

"We've had those chairs for years."

"I don't care about them," he said. "It's about what is happening to our country. Men who fish for a living becoming robbers. We're in trouble."

I shook my head. "What will save us in this place, Daddy?"

"When the army leaves. When we can vote in a good leader."

"But, look at the last civilian government; throwing champagne parties, embezzling, and all that."

"That was 1979."

"It is the same kind of politicians who will surface next time around."

My father nodded. "Let them come. We will drive them out with votes. Anything but this. These military boys don't care. They step in with one policy or the other, suspend the constitution, mess up our law with their decrees... detain people without charge. I'm sure they're deliberately trying to ruin the country."

"How can they benefit from that?"

"Who knows? Most of them are millionaires now. Maybe it's a sport. I don't understand it either."

My father was still passionate about politics, but one single event had catapulted me into another realm. I viewed the world with a bad squint, a traveling eye, after that, seeing struggles I could do little about. Sheri's brigadier, for instance, was he one of the military men who deprived me of my right to vote, or one of those house dictators who seriously made me wish I could beat up somebody.

"Twenty-five years after independence," my father continued. "And still this nonsense. No light, no water, people dying all over the place, before their time, from one sickness or the other."

I remembered my mother.

"I saw her last week," I said.

"You did? How is she?"

"She says the price of her medicine has gone up."

My father said nothing.

"And her tenants are late in paying their rent. Can you send them a letter?"

"It's a waste of time. I'll send one of my boys over."

"She also says the houses are still in your name."

My father rubbed his brow. "I haven't had time to transfer it to her."

"In ten years?"

"Your mother doesn't speak to me, how will she remind me?"

"Well, I'm reminding you. Please, put the houses in her name."

"She can wait," he said. "After what she's done, bad-mouthing me all over the place, trying to get me disbarred. If I put the property in her name, she will probably give it to that church of hers."

"Please," I said. "Let her have the house in her name."

"She collects rent. What difference will a name make?"

"It's hers," I said.

I didn't say any more, but wondered about him, acting like he didn't know better. I heard my mother's voice again, accusing me of always taking his side and decided to pursue the matter from then on.

I stayed with him until the sun began to fall. My father urged me to return to camp, because of armed robbers who prowled the streets at night. It was dusk as I drove up Third Mainland bridge, and the Lagos lagoon looked like a sheet of iron beneath it. The bridge was smoother than most Lagos routes, which had crevices, but there were no street-lights, and some of the steel barriers had been broken by thieves who melted them down to make forks and knives. I could smell burning wood from a village nearby. Logging was their industry. I thought of Mike. I'd missed him. He was working on a piece and wouldn't be back until tomorrow. I decided to surprise him. It wasn't that late.

There was a power cut in the area when I arrived. In this part of Lagos, houses huddled together separated by high brick walls, topped with broken glass pieces to deter thieves. A few teenagers loitered on the other side of the street. I parked my car outside the house and rattled the gates. A man emerged from the front door wearing his pajama bottoms and a white undershirt.

"Good evening," I said.

"Evuh-ning," he said, rubbing his belly.

"I'm here to see Mr. Obi."

"Obi? He lives behind."

He pointed to the back of the house. I saw someone

stepping out with a lantern. It was Mike. The man returned to the house.

"Who was that?" I asked as Mike unlocked the gate.

"My landlord," he said.

He slid the fat chain through the gate's rails and pushed the gates open as though he'd been expecting me.

"Aren't you a little surprised that I came?" I asked.

"I'm happy," he said, holding my hand. "Come, I was about to start something."

He led the way, keeping his lantern up. We walked down the side of the building.

Mike's apartment was an art studio, or so it appeared. It was normally occupied by his landlord's son, a former classmate who was out of Lagos on national service. Mike was renting it from him for the year: one large room with two doors leading to a small kitchen and bathroom. In the corner, on the floor, was a mattress with a patchwork spread made from various tie-dyed pieces, and next to it was a wooden rack over which he hung his trousers and shirts. The only seating space was an old sofa, on which he had a large Fulani rug with black and red embroidery. Everything else was related to his work: an easel, a drawing board, tracing paper, brown paper, pencils, chalk, a black leather portfolio, tape. Leaning along the walls were several mosaics he'd completed, and on a table was a plywood board surrounded by colorful bottles.

"What are these?" I asked, picking one up.

"Beads," he said.

I headed for the nearest mosaic and knelt by it. "Bring the lantern closer."

He did and it cast my shadow over the mosaic. I stepped aside and looked again. It was a woman's profile. She was brown with green flecks in her eye.

"What's this one?"

"Ala."

"Who?"

"Earth mother."

"Of whose earth?"

He smiled. "She is an Igbo goddess."

I moved to the next. "Em, what is this one?"

On a wooden board almost the length of my arms outstretched, was the form of a naked woman with muscular shoulders, in black and white beading. I reached for it.

"Can I touch?" I asked.

"Gently," he said.

I rolled my fingers over her brow and it tingled. "Beads," I murmured. "You stick them on?"

"One by one," he said.

"How long does it take?"

"Eight months for that one," he said.

I breathed in. "Is she a woman or a man?"

"Neither."

"A hermaphrodite? I once thought I was a hermaphrodite. Before my periods started."

He laughed, shaking the light all over the room.

"He's Obatala."

I screwed up my nose. "Who?"

"You're Yoruba?" he said.

"Born and bred."

"And you don't know your gods?"

"Should I?"

"We don't respect our heritage enough."

"I respect my heritage; its right to evolve and change."

He walked over to the table and placed his lantern on it. "The Yoruba religion is the most exported African religion. Cuba, Brazil, Haiti."

Yeah, yeah, yeah, I said for each country. He ignored me.

"Everyone knows about Aphrodite, but ask them about Oshun... "

"Who dat?" I interrupted.

I smiled. I'd been teasing him from the start. What was

he saying? He was Catholic, and he wasn't even Yoruba. How much did he really understand about our gods? And my Yorubaness was like my womanness. If I shaved my head and stood upside down for the rest of my life, I would still be a woman, and Yoruba. There was no paradigm. Every civilization began and ended with an imperfect human being.

"Oshun is your Aphrodite," he said.

"And this Obatala?"

"The creator of the human form."

"Yet you've made him a woman."

"Some cultures, I think the Brazilian descendants of Yorubas, worship him as a female."

"Why is she in black and white?"

"They say all things white belong to him: milk, bones."

I tapped the edge of the mosaic. "I like her," I said. "Although, I'm a little scared."

"Of what?" he asked.

"Evoking gods."

"It's art, not idolatry."

I shook my head. "It's not right."

He walked to the wooden board on his table.

"Who's to say what is right? The Yorubas believed that the world was water. The gods came down on a chain carrying a calabash filled with soil, a cockerel, and a chameleon. They poured the soil over the water. The cockerel spread it around, the chameleon walked around to make sure it was safe, other gods came and the world was born. A beautiful story. Less believable than a story of two naked people in a garden? I don't know."

I dodged an imaginary lightning bolt. Between my mother's worship of religion and my father's disinterest, I, too, had found my own belief, in a soul that looked like a tree covered in vines: vanity, anger, greed, I stripped them off before I prayed. Sometimes I wouldn't make it before I fell asleep. God was the light toward which my tree grew. But the

God of my childhood, the one who looked like a white man, eight foot tall with liver spots and wearing a toga, kind as he was, he was still a God I feared, beyond reason. I was not ashamed to say it. Those who wanted to challenge Him were free to. I'd been burned before, on one finger or the other, and I did not want to feel that all over my body, for eternity.

"Come here," Mike said.

I walked toward the table.

"Pick a bottle," he said.

I chose the red beads.

"Open it," he said.

I unscrewed the top.

"Now, take a few in your palm and cast it over the board."

"Over it?"

"Yes. They will stick wherever you throw them. There's glue on the board."

I poured some beads into my palms and cast them over the wooden board like an Ifa priestess. "I'm an oracle," I said, looking at the spray of beads on the board.

Mike took my hand. "Now, stand here and tell me. What do you see?"

I looked at the beads. "Beads."

"Look again."

I squinted for a moment. "Nothing," I said.

He drew me closer and wrapped his arms around my waist. "Think."

I felt his breath on my neck. He was like a blackboard behind me.

"A sky," I said.

"Are you sure?"

"It's a sky," I said.

"That is what I will do next."

"My sky?"

"Your sky."

I clapped. "Mike, you're the true son of your father."

Mike worked like a seamstress. His fingers moved fast as he dived in and out of the board. He had had one exhibition in Enugu already. There was talk about an exhibition in Lagos, from a French woman he met at the consulate. "I think she just wanted to sleep with me," he admitted. The woman commissioned work from him, so did some of her friends. He wanted to experiment with murals. It was what he'd been searching for, the opportunity to go beyond designing homes.

Soon he began to stalk the board, murmuring to himself. I felt like I was intruding on a confession, so I went to his sofa to lie down. There was a cigarette wrapper tucked in a corner.

"I didn't know you smoked," I said.

"I don't," he said.

I pushed it further in. If it belonged to him or to someone else, I did not want to know.

"You're getting tired," he said.

"I can't believe I have to drive back to camp tonight."

"At this time of the night? You're not going anywhere."

"It's only past eight."

"Still, you're not going. You've forgotten already? Armed robbers?"

"I have nothing with me. No spare clothes."

"You can wear one of my shirts."

I propped myself up." I don't want to go. But your landlord..."

"He minds his business. Your worst fear is your new car outside. We should bring it in."

Mike went to his bathroom to wash his hands and afterward, we went outside to park my car behind his. Returning to his apartment, the air seemed heavier.

"It's hot," he said, as if reading my thoughts.

"Hope they bring back light tonight," I said.

We settled on the sofa. He placed the lantern on the table and drew me to his side.

"Rest your head."

I place my head on his belly. It was as tight as a drum.

"What did you do all day to make you tired?" His voice resounded within him.

"I went to see my father," I said.

"You had fun?"

"I always have fun with my father."

"What else?"

"I went to see an old friend."

"An old friend. Which old friend?"

"Sheri Bakare. My best friend when I was small."

I listened to his heartbeat for a moment.

"And you?" I asked.

"I went to see my uncle."

"Your uncle. Which uncle?" I mimicked him.

"My uncle, the architect I was going to work for."

"Until?"

"He gave me a job that changed my mind."

"What job was this?"

"Some man who wanted his house extended."

"What's wrong with that?"

"I saw the house. It's a series of extensions. Like an anthill inside."

"Why does he keep extending it?"

"New wives. More children."

I smiled. "So you feel artistically compromised?"

Mike sighed. "Here is a man, who has in his living room a portrait of himself inside his aquarium."

"No."

"I swear to God."

"He gave you the job, I'm sure."

"Bent over, eyes closed."

I slapped his arm. "Mike! Everyone needs a job in Lagos. Everyone needs a car that works."

He wrapped it tighter round me. "I'm not doing it

anymore, not after this. The pay is not good, and the work is lousy. My parents never had much money, but they were satisfied with their jobs."

I could easily have told him that was years ago, that they lived on campus, in a house provided by the university.

"So you'll concentrate on your art work?"

He nodded. "Teach for national service, find small work to pay my way. My rent is not much, and I pay monthly."

"That's brave. I'm not sure I want to practice law full-time, but I'm too frightened to think of it."

"Why study law at all?"

"Who knows? Father's business, only child. But it's not bad work. Though he doesn't pay me enough and it pains me that I can't have a place of my own."

"Find another job. Move out."

"A daughter? It's not done."

"What is this 'it' that's not done?"

I sat up. "Don't be difficult. You know where I'm coming from."

"Thousands of single women are living on their own, all over town."

"Well, I am not them and they are not me. I will go back to England penniless before I live in a Lagos slum. What kind of country is this anyway? You graduate and you're privileged to live off your parents, or some old sugar daddy or some government contract. He should at least pay me enough. It's only fair. It's only fair, Mike."

He smiled, satisfied that he'd made me look beyond my small world. Yes, I was acting like a brat, but he hardly ever had to consider his parents and they were not sanctioning his every move. I was curious.

"Tell me about when you were small," I said.

"What age?"

"Eleven," I said, placing my ear to his belly.

As he spoke, I fell asleep dreaming of him, an eleven-year-old boy with khaki shorts holding a rifle made of sticks, dancing to high-life music with his mother and learning how to drink palm-wine from his father's calabash. His parents played card games lying on the floor. It was like a bed-time story.

When I woke up there was light in the room. I was startled by how bright everything seemed. Stretching, I asked. "When did they bring it back?"

"An hour ago," he said.

"And you sat here?"

"Your head," he explained.

"I'm sorry," I said, getting up. "Which door leads to your bathroom?"

He pointed.

Inside, I looked at his shaving cream and toothbrush on the sink. The blue tiles on the shower wall were powdery white from scouring powder. Black mold lurked between them. In the corner was an aluminum bucket for bathing because water pressure in Lagos was too weak to drive showers. I washed my face, came out and found Mike lying on the couch with his shirt off.

"You can pick any of my shirts," he said, pointing to his rack of clothes.

"I don't want a shirt," I said, unbuttoning mine.

He watched me undress and I pulled a face. I walked up to him, willing myself to be confident.

He kissed holes down my back. I cried, only from his tenderness. Later, as he slept, I crept to the bathroom and filled the aluminum bucket with cold water, and washed myself clean. I slept with my nose in his armpit.

～

Military camp ended in a parade attended by government and military officials. Some members of our platoon were chosen to participate in the event, but Mike and I were not among them. We stood in the stands and cheered instead.

Monday, after the parade, I started work at my father's firm. I was a sleeping partner, he said, no matter how hard I worked. "Five years' time and I will be dead according to the latest statistics! Still nobody serious to hand my business over to! This is my lot in life!"

In time my father had become bona fide miserable, not surprisingly. His business was to appease acrimonious freeholders, after the fist fights and juju. Another rental agreement, an old one breached, a reminder letter to an expatriate who had not paid his rent, or a Nigerian tenant who was certain to throw the letter away and still not pay. Court case after court case over property disputes, land disputes, split families, brothers who had not spoken for years, since the old man died.

My father had two senior associates working for him. Dagogo John-White, a quiet man whose name we loved to tease (Da go go, Da come come, Da going gone, and for the brief period he found religion, Da kingdom come, Da will be done.) I made no mention of his white john, left that to Alabi Fashina, a quick tempered man we dared not tease. Whenever my father was away, Dagogo and Alabi sometimes argued about their home cities. Alabi was from Lagos, Dagogo from Bonny Island in the Niger Delta. "Bushman from Lagos," he would say.

"Bushman from Bonny," Alabi would reply. "Hm. Bonny women. They are the most forward women on earth. I visited once. Women were crawling all over me like ants on a sugar, crawling all over me. I did what a man had to do."

"Our man Flint!" Dagogo would say.

"It was a precarious operation."

"007!"

"But I had license to kill."

Our very own double act. They would end with a handshake, snap their fingers and call each other *"man mi,"* my man. Dagogo was tall with a neck at least six inches long;

he naturally looked downward. Alabi was stocky with a one inch neck; he looked upward. Different temperaments, but if they faced each other, they always saw eye to eye.

Thankfully, they were rarely in the office. The others, I saw more of: Peace, the receptionist and secretary whose gymnastics with bubble gum broke new boundaries every day. She would not speak clearly on the phone, because she did not want to smudge her lipstick, and was occasionally off with General Body Weakness—her bones were paining, if you asked her to describe the symptoms of this officially recognized illness. Mrs. Kazeem, a woman who handled the company secretarial work. Her expression was naturally vexed, and we called her mother of twins, because she was expecting some. And finally, Mr. Israel, the lugubrious driver. We called him Papa sometimes, because he was as old as Moses. He spoke Yoruba to everyone, even to Dagogo who couldn't understand a word.

"Who wants groundnuts?" I asked, looking around the office.

Dagogo raised his head momentarily, Alabi said no, and Peace popped her bubble gum. Mr. Israel and Mrs. Kazeem were out. I pulled some dirty naira notes from my bag and went outside to the woman who sat by our gate, selling roasted groundnuts by the bottle.

My father's office was designed like a classroom, without a blackboard. We sat behind desks, facing his room and whenever he came out, it was hard not to react as one might to a school master. He was a different person in the office and kept his face as closed as one of the hardback books he'd stashed along his shelves. I'd also discovered just how stingy he was. He had not increased lunch allowances in over five years and I really wasn't surprised. I couldn't ever remember having much pocket money to spend as a child. My father always told me he had no money. The oil boys were the rich ones, he would say, referring to the handful of lawyers who were counsels for international oil companies. Lawyers like himself, they had to scrape a living.

My father had scraped enough to acquire a large estate. If he worked these days, it was only because he wanted to. He had shed most of his staff now, except for his senior associates, but still, he didn't pay well. I placed the bottle of groundnuts on my table when I returned and invited everyone to eat. Then I headed for his door.

"Come in," he said.

He was scribbling on a sheet of paper.

"What can I do for you?"

"Are you busy?"

"I'm always busy," he said, without looking up.

"Shall I come back?"

He placed his pen down. "No."

I sat in the client chair. "Three things, please."

"Yes?"

"Our lunch allowance."

"What about it?"

"It's too little."

My father's knuckles locked like a zip. "How so?"

"One hundred naira a month?" I said. "I've just bought a bottle of groundnuts for ten naira."

"Please, get to the point."

I spoke slower. "Our lunch allowance needs to be increased, in line with inflation at least."

"In line with inflation," he repeated.

"Yes," I said.

My father sat back. "We'd be doubling allowances every year. Did my staff ask you to do this?"

"No."

"My dear, I've been running this place for over thirty years and... "

I raised my hand.

"Let me finish," he said. "I've been running this place for

many years and I think, by now, I know how to run it well. My benefits are fair. Ask my people outside. If any of them are dissatisfied, they will leave."

I thought of the scruffy lawyers who stood outside the courts, begging for affidavit work.

"To go where?" I asked. "You think it's easy to find work these days?"

"I'm busy," he warned.

"Just think about it," I said.

"The next thing was?"

"I've drafted the transfer letter," I said.

"What transfer letter?"

Of his houses, to my mother, I explained. My father listened without commenting.

"The third thing?" he asked.

"Can Sheri do the catering for your dinner party?" I gabbled the words. "She's very professional. Please. Her father died, and her uncle took her inheritance. And she has no job. And Titus cooks so bad. Sheri can do better. Please."

My father looked irritated enough to throw his pen at me.

"You're wasting my time," he said.

"Thank you," I said, getting up. "Thank you. I knew you would say yes."

Back at my desk, I lifted the bottle of groundnuts and found it half empty.

"Who ate my groundnuts?" I asked.

No one raised their head.

⁓

"How are you coping?" I asked Sheri.

Our kitchen was unusually clean. She wiped the water around the sink, and grease from the stove. There wasn't a dent in her gown, not even a stain, while my own dress was creased from shoulder to hem. I was glad I was wearing black because I'd spilled wine on myself.

Cooking was a skill, I thought; an art form. In our country, we appreciated the end result, but not the craft, perhaps because we didn't have fancy names. Paring was "cut it." Julienne was "cut it well." Chopping was "cut it well well," and so on till you had puree, which would probably be "mash it." And, if anyone was measuring any ingredient in a kitchen, it meant that they really didn't know what they were doing.

Sheri was preparing what she called a continental dinner for my father's party: chicken curry with coconut fried rice, grilled fish, shrimp kebabs, and a bowl of Nigerian salad that would put any niçoise to shame. It had tuna, baked beans, potatoes, eggs, and dollops and dollops of mayonnaise. For dessert, she'd made a pineapple crumble and a platter of sliced mangoes and pawpaws over which she sprinkled lemon juice. I checked one of the bowls.

"Shall I take this to the table?"

"Please," she murmured.

She folded a dish cloth to take the crumble out of the oven. In the dining room, I checked the table. Sheri had insisted we used another table for the food. The guests would have to serve themselves buffet-style, she said. I agreed only because I wasn't that interested in the logistics of a dinner party, or entertaining. Growing up with my father, I rarely stepped into a kitchen, and my father was easily satisfied with meals his cooks prepared. Tonight the food would at least be edible, I thought. His guests were out on the veranda and I would call them in soon.

I wondered about Mike. He was meeting my father for the first time and we planned to sit on the veranda during the dinner. The doorbell rang again as I adjusted the napkins on the table. It was him.

"I was just thinking about you."

He was in traditional wear: a white tunic and black

trousers. He bent to pick up something leaning against the wall and dragged it into the doorway. It was a mosaic of different colors, like a jagged rainbow.

"My sky," I said.

"I didn't say I was going to give it to you," he said.

I steered him toward my father, who was talking to Aunt Valerie, a Jamaican woman whose voice skipped like calypso. At first my father looked as if he were under siege, then I presented the mosaic to him. My father perched it on a table.

"What a stunning piece," Aunt Valerie said. "Did you do this, young man?"

"Yes," Mike said.

"He's an artist," I said.

"That's wonderful," she said. "Sam, come and look at this."

Her husband, a baldheaded man, walked over with Uncle Fatai. Uncle Fatai's wife, Aunty Medinot, hovered in the background. In support of my mother, she rarely came to the house. Just seeing her made me feel guilty, but my father had invited my mother, and she refused to come. "For what reason?" she asked.

"This young man did this, Sam," Aunt Valerie said. "Isn't it wonderful?"

"It looks like a sunset," her husband said.

"Or fire," Aunt Valerie said, throwing her head back.

"Both," Uncle Fatai said.

I drew close to my father.

"He's an architect," I said, "but he does this on the side."

"Really," my father said.

Mike approached us with an apologetic smile. "I never thought they would... "

I patted his shoulder as we returned to the living room. He deserved to be embarrassed for bringing a gift for my father.

"That woman says she wants to see my work," he said.

"Show it to her," I said. "But save Obatala for me."

I snatched the mosaic from him and carried it to my father's room. There, I smoothed my dress and dabbed some cologne behind my ears.

I hurried back. Peter Mukoro had arrived in my absence. A huge man with a thick black mustache, he was already holding court.

"Our last regime claimed they wanted to wage war against indiscipline, and yet they couldn't fight it among themselves. Military coups are the worst form of indiscipline. No respect for the constitution. No respect for those in power... "

"Our people are indisciplined," Uncle Fatai said.

"How?" Peter Mukoro asked, stroking his mustache.

"You're driving and someone tries to run you off the road."

"Trying to avoid potholes," Peter Mukoro said.

"Speeding through traffic stops?"

"Running from armed robbers."

"Teachers not showing up for class?"

"Can't afford transportation."

"Hospital staff selling supplies on the black market?"

"Benefits in kind."

"Bribery?"

"Tipping," Peter Mukoro said.

He continued to speak as though he were making a toast and twirled his cigarette. I edged toward Mike. "Come, let me introduce you to Sheri. This man won't stop talking. He loves his voice."

"I've already met her," he said.

"When?"

"She came in here when you were away."

I sat on the arm of the chair. "What did you think?"

"She seems... reserved."

"Sheri?"

"To me, she was."

I stood up. "Excuse me, I have to check on the food."

Inside the kitchen, I found Sheri pouring curry into a big ceramic bowl. Her waiter was standing by to take it into the living room. I could smell the coconut rice and sweet ginger of the pineapple bake in the oven.

"Is everything ready?" I asked.

She nodded. "You can call them in now."

I paused by the door. "You met Mike?"

"Yes," she said.

"What did you think of him?"

"He's nice."

Throughout the evening, they showed nothing but courtesy for each other. I'd expected some interest, some camaraderie even, but soon I realized that they shared nothing in common. Mike would find Sheri too old. She would find Mike far too young.

Peter Mukoro continued to dominate the conversation meanwhile. He was predicting the demise of our country under the new military government. They were making plans to devalue our currency, and to scrap foreign currency regulations. Most of us who needed foreign currency for business or travel welcomed this. We envisioned a time we no longer had to succumb to black market rates. There were places in Lagos you went to buy US dollars and pounds sterling, from hawkers who loitered like drug dealers. You had to be sure you were buying the real thing.

"We're finished," Peter Mukoro was saying. "The naira will be like toilet paper now. And if we take the IMF loan we can kiss our independence goodbye."

My father seemed to be enjoying his tirade, rocking back and forth. I refilled his wine glass. "Fill my friend's as well," he said, pointing to Peter Mukoro's.

Reluctantly I did.

Peter Mukoro tapped my arm. "I was calling that lady, that yellow lady in the kitchen, but she ignored me. Tell her we need more rice. Please."

"Her name is Sheri."

"Yes. Tell her we need more rice. And beer. Wine is like water to me. I'm an African man."

I delivered the message to her word for word.

"He can't be talking to me," she said.

"Who then?" I asked.

"He must be talking to his mother."

I laughed. Titus had already annoyed her, asking her to serve guests from the left and not from the right. Sheri wore her head tie turban style and it dropped over her eye brows. Her profile was hysterical. She was taking her work too seriously, I thought. I could snatch the head tie and make her run after me. I carried a bowl of rice back to the dining room with a cold bottle of beer.

"Ah thanks," Peter Mukoro said. "Brother Sunny, you must ask for a hefty dowry for your daughter. Look at her, good hostess, lawyer, and all that."

"I would be glad," my father said, "if someone would take her off my hands for free."

They laughed hyuh-hyuh-hyuh, as only men with too much money should. I ignored them and returned to the veranda.

"Something wrong?" Mike asked.

"Peter Mukoro," I said. "Every single time he opens his mouth."

Mike smiled. "He's a man's man. Your father seems to like him."

We looked toward the dining room. Sheri had come out of the kitchen and was leaning over my father.

"He seems to like Sheri, too," he said. "Unlike me."

"Close your mouth," I said.

By the end of the evening, my head was full of wine. I saw Mike off and he kissed me so hard he pulled me through his car window. We spoke against each other's teeth.

"Come back with me."

"My father will kill me."

"You're not a child."

"I am, to him."

"Nonsense."

"Hmm. Where are your sisters?"

"Locked up at home, where they belong."

The road was empty, except for a few parked cars. Before he drove off, I did a strip-tease. I flashed a breast, turned to wriggle, only to find Peter Mukoro standing by the gates. "Ah-ah?" he said. "Are we invited? Or is this a private reception?"

He laughed as I hurried past.

I smoothed the creases from my dress before I walked into the house and kept my face as straight as a newscaster's. Sheri and my father were in the living room. My father was writing a check.

"That young man," he said. "What did you say his name was?"

"Mike."

Count one against him: his name wasn't Nigerian. This could mean his family didn't have enough class to uphold our traditions.

"Obi," I said.

I expected his next question to be which Obi.

"An artist, you say?" he asked.

"Yes." Count two.

"And he's given up architecture?"

Count three. I hesitated. "Not really."

My father peered over his glasses. "That's no good."

"Why?" I asked.

He turned to Sheri. "Tell her. Please. If I say anything to her, she thinks I'm old-fashioned."

Sheri laughed. "You have to admit, Enitan. An artist in Lagos?"

My father handed the check to her.

"Thank you," he said. "It's been a pleasure."

I saw her to the door.

"Well done," I whispered. "Now I won't rest in this house. Why did you have to say that?"

"*Aburo*, the artist has jujued you?"

"I think I've outgrown that name by now."

She raised her hand. "I won't use it if you don't like it."

"Thanks."

"Bye yourself," she said, cheerfully.

I shut the door gently and faced my father. He removed his glasses, which usually meant he was about to give a lecture. I braced myself.

"You know," he said. "I may not know much about youngsters today, but I know a few things and I don't think you should be making yourself so available to a man you've just met."

I crossed my arms. "In what way?"

"Your demeanor. A woman should have more... comportment. And you can stop following him outside unchaperoned, for a start."

"Unchaperoned?"

"Yes," he said. "He might think you're easy. Cheap. I'm telling you for your own good."

I walked away. Unchaperoned indeed. Look at him. Just look at him, and that Sheri, calling herself my sister. "This is modern Lagos," I said over my shoulder. "Not Victorian London."

"This is my house," I heard him say. "Don't be rude."

～

During national service, I received a monthly stipend of 200 naira from the government. This, I spent usually within a week. In return for my stipend, every Monday, I took a day off work for community service. For community service, I met with other national service participants who lived in my district to complete half-day chores. Sometimes we picked litter off the streets; other times we cut grass in local parks with machetes. Most days we begged our team leader, a man who reminded me of Baba, to let us go. He stood over us, gloating as we pleaded. The machetes were heavier than I expected and the grass left my legs itchy. The experience gave me respect for the work Baba did in our garden every week.

Now that he had decided not to work for his uncle, Mike was teaching art classes at a free education school near his home. One morning, after community service, I visited him there. The free education schools in Lagos were the legacy of a former governor of Lagos state. Several years later, and still under-funded, they were teeming with children and lacking teachers. Most of the classrooms were unpainted and some were without windows and doors. I passed a classroom and heard children reciting alphabets; passed another, and heard them chanting multiplication tables. Through the door, I saw a teacher standing by a blackboard with a whip in his hand.

The next room was the teachers' mess. Inside, a woman sat on a chair. She was eating an orange. Her skin was bleached and her hair was sectioned into plaits. In the corner, a man placed both his feet on the table. He flexed his whip at a school girl of about fifteen years who knelt facing the corner with her arms raised. The girl's armpits were stained brown and her bare soles were dusty. There were welts across the back of her legs.

"Good afternoon," I said.

"Afa-noon," the man said.

The woman eyed my jeans.

"Is Mr. Obi around?" I asked.

The student turned to look at me. Her face was wet from tears.

"Turn your ugly face to the wall," the man shouted. "Look at you. Tiffing mango from the tree when you have been warned consecu... " He whipped her legs.

"Consecu... " he whipped her legs again.

"Consecutively." He sucked his teeth. "Tiff."

"Is Mr. Obi here?" I asked.

He picked his teeth. "Obi?"

"Yes, Mr. Obi, the art teacher. Please, do you know where he is?"

I spoke with an English accent to offend him. He would immediately think I was trying to be superior.

"In class," he said.

"What class?"

He pointed. "Outside. Fork right, then right again."

"So kind of you," I said.

He reached over and flicked the girl's shoulder with his whip. She straightened up.

Mike's class was the last on the adjacent corridor and smelled like a puppy's pen. There were about twenty-five children in a room, intended for half that number. Their desks were pushed to the walls and they were gathered around five large wash bowls. They squished the contents with their tiny fists. Mike was walking around them.

"Behave yourselves," he said.

"What's going on?" I asked.

"They're making papier-maché," he said.

There was gray mush in the bowls. One of his students, a skinny boy with dusty knees scrambled over.

"Mr. Obi?"

"Yes, Diran," Mike said.

"Pitan fell me down."

"Pitan!" Mike yelled.

Pitan's large head popped up. "Yes, Mr. Obi."

"No more pushing," Mike said. "This is the last time I'm warning you. If one more person gets pushed, you will all run round this school, you hear me?"

"Yes, Mr. Obi," they chanted.

Mike turned to me. "They're getting on my nerves."

I smiled. "I thought you wanted to teach children."

"I've made the biggest mistake of my life."

"I thought you never had regrets. And what kind of teachers are you in this school? I was in your teachers' room and one man there was beating a girl for stealing fruit. You should have seen."

"That's Mr. Salako, our agriculture teacher."

"He's horrible."

"Her mother probably beats her more. Most of them in here, they leave this place and go home to spend the rest of the day selling something. They think I'm a fool because I don't whip them. Everyone else does."

The children's heads bobbed like a sea of life buoys. Their parents beat out of love, it was said, with love, so that they wouldn't grow up misbehaving anyhow-all-over-the-place-willy-nilly-shilly-shally. Teachers beat, neighbors beat. By the time a child turned ten, the adults they knew would have beaten out any cockiness that could develop into wit; any dreaminess that could give birth to creation; any bossiness that could lead to leadership. Only the strong would survive; the rest would spend their lives searching for initiative. This was what it took to raise an African child, a village of beaters, and yet if someone put their hands around a child's neck, and applied the slightest pressure, someone else would accuse them of wickedness, because strangulation had nothing to do with discipline.

Diran sidled up to Mike again. He scratched his head.

"Mr. Obi."

"What is it?" Mike asked. "Why are you scratching your head? Do you have lice?"

The children laughed.

"Pitan banged my head," Diran whined. "Now my head is broked."

Mike clapped. "All right. No more."

There was murmuring around the class. Mike walked to

the center of the room.

"I can see you're all begging for punishment today."

Pitan raised his hand. "Mr. Obi?"

"Shush!" Mike hissed. "I mustn't hear my name on anyone's lips again. No more. Now push your bowls to the side, return to your desks and line up to run around the school."

The children giggled as they dragged their bowls to the corner. We heard the school bell ring.

"God saved all of you," Mike announced. "Come on, let's get out of here," he said to me.

We drove back to his place and ripped our clothes off. Mike had a collection of Bob Marley albums, and we joined in the wailing. We made love on the mattress and then on the floor. He began to talk the way he talked about football. Could I feel it? It was a fusion of time and space. We were the reggae and soul generation. Our parents were the jazz generation. The next would be hip-hop.

"Stop talking," I said.

He wouldn't stop. I wrapped my legs around him.

"Enough," I said. "You like sex too much."

He grabbed my foot and began to tickle it. His landlord, the whole neighborhood, the whole world even, was about to know how much sex he liked.

"They'll think I'm a slut!" I said. "Please! They'll think I'm... shit."

I was hoarse from screaming. I went to his bathroom to wash myself when I heard a knock on the door.

"Would you like a beer?" Mike asked. "I'm going round the corner."

"No," I said.

I knocked the bucket of water over. Mike walked in.

"Are you all right?"

I stood up.

"What is it?" he asked.

I wanted to tell him, but the story was never mine to tell. I was hurt only by association.

"What?" he asked.

I began anyway. The faster I spoke, the easier it became: the picnic, the rain, the lagoon, the van. The boys.

I sounded fake to my own ears. In my mind's eye, I was standing there, that day, thankful to be safe, glad to be untarnished.

"Come here," Mike said when I finished.

He wrapped his arms round me so tight I thought my fear might drip out. He took the bucket from me, filled it with water and brought it to the shower. He lowered me and began to wash me. I shut my eyes expecting some pain, some probing, something.

The last person who washed me was Bisi, our house girl. I was nine. "Spread your lecks," she would say, and I would spread them hating her sawing motions. But Mike washed me with the gentlest motions, like a mother washing her baby. I felt sure my fear was like any other fear; like the fear of a dog bite, or of fire, or of falling from heights, or death. I was certain I would never be ashamed again.

We didn't drink beer. We drank the palm wine from his refrigerator instead and ate the remnants of a peppery stew with yams. The stew had mellowed nicely, and after about two glasses, the wine made my eyes slip.

"Who taught you to cook?" I asked.

"My mother," he said.

"You'll make a good wife," I said.

I reached for my glass. Of course he was right for me. Even Obatala seemed to be winking at us.

The Bakares started their catering business. As I predicted, it wasn't a difficult transition for them. Their house in Victoria Island was spacious and part of their back yard was conveniently cemented. Their hands were many. Sheri's stepmothers took charge of the cooking, while she handled the money. Her brothers and sisters took on smaller tasks. The back yard was used for cooking, and they converted their chalet into a cafeteria with locally carpentered benches and tables. Most of their customers were office workers from surrounding banks who came in for their meal of the day. I visited once, only because I hadn't entirely forgiven Sheri for siding with my father, and also because the drive to Victoria Island was too long for my one-hour lunch-break.

Nearing lunch time in the office one afternoon, Mrs. Kazeem looked out the window. "Our friend is here," she said.

"Who?" Peace asked.

"Miss Nigeria," Mrs. Kazeem said.

We looked out of the window to see Sheri.

Sheri was one of those women. Other women didn't like her, and I'd often wondered if she noticed. She rarely came to our office, but whenever she did, the women behaved as if she'd come in for a fight. The men, meanwhile, found excuses to come to my desk. Today, the men were out and only the women remained. Mrs. Kazeem crossed her arms over her belly, Peace clicked her gum. Sheri opened the door.

"Enitan," she said. "Will you come out for a moment?"

I got up, aware that the others were watching me. Not greeting was considered rude. Outside, the sun warmed my head. We crossed over to Sheri's car, parked by an orange seller who sat with an infant strapped to her back. She was peeling an orange with a rusty pen-knife.

"Why didn't you greet the others?" I asked.

"Those jealous women," Sheri said.

"No one is jealous of you."

"Who cares? I've lived with this too long, and I didn't come here to see them anyway."

"What did you come for?"

"Are we fighting?"

"No," I said.

"Why haven't you contacted me?"

"I've been busy. My father keeps me busy. All morning I've been drafting letters."

"Don't you go to court at all?"

"He tries to keep me here," I said.

"I'm surprised."

"You don't know him. He runs this place like an army."

We heard a cry from the road.

"*Pupa!* Yellow!"

A taxi driver was leaning out of his window. He was holding the window lever he would pass to passengers who needed to "wine down." One of his front teeth seemed longer than the rest.

"Yes, you with the big *yansh*," he shouted.

Sheri spread her fingers at him. "Nothing good will come to you!"

"Whore," he jeered. "Wait till I get down on you."

"Don't let me curse your mother," she said. "You'd better use that long tooth of yours to push down your windows. It might straighten it out, and your passengers might not suffocate from your stinking armpits."

I lowered my head.

"And you, *Dudu*," the taxi driver said.

Startled, I looked up.

"Yes you with the black face. Where is your own *yansh* hiding?"

I glared at him. "Nothing good will come to you."

He laughed with his tongue hanging out. "What, you're turning up your nose at me? You're not that pretty, either of you. Sharrap. Oh, sharrap both of you. You should feel happy that a man noticed you. If you're not careful, I'll sex you both."

Sheri and I turned our backs on him.

"Fool," I said.

"Penis like Bic biro," she said.

We huddled together laughing.

"So what happened?" I asked.

"Ibrahim wants me to stop my business," she said.

"Because?"

"He doesn't want me going out."

"Is he willing to give you the money?"

"No."

"Then, why are we wasting time talking about this?"

"I wanted your opinion," she said.

"Since when?"

"Please," she said.

"Drop him," I said. "You don't need him."

She raised her hand. "What will happen to me when my rent is due? Where will I live? I can't go back to my father's house. Have you seen the place?"

The day I went, it was teeming with customers and friends. I wondered if they ever had private moments.

"Bide time," I said. "Until your next rent is paid. After that, find more clients. There are weddings, burials, christenings, every weekend in this place. Next year you'll be paying your own rent. But this, this, I have to tell you, is rubbish. You're bright, you're young, and this man is treating you like his house girl."

"It's easy for you to say."

"You asked my opinion."

"You've never had to worry."

"If ever I do, please talk sense to me."

She turned away.

"Sheri," I said.

"What?" she snapped.

"It's for your own good," I said.

"How? I'm not even sure we can continue the business. My uncle comes to the house, complaining that we are misusing his property. He wants to take the house from us, I'm sure."

"He can't do that."

"Why not?" she said. "He took everything else under native law as my father's rightful heir. Why would the house be different?"

"Whose name is the property in, now?" I asked.

"My father's."

"Did he leave a will?"

"No."

What place did the law really have in family matters? At law school I'd learned those indigenous set of codes collectively called native law and custom. They existed before we adopted civil law, before we became a nation with a constitution, and they established individual rights under inheritance and marriage. A man could marry only one wife under civil law, but he could bring another woman into his home under native law. It was polygamy, not bigamy. If he pleased, he could beat up his wife, throw her out, with or without her children and leave her with nothing. His relations might plead with him to show her mercy, but she had no claim over his property. If he died, under some native customs, his son would inherit his estate instead of his widow. Sometimes, a widow couldn't inherit land at all. Even with the progressive customs, widows inherited according to how many children they had, and sons could have double the rights of daughters.

The courts determined how to share a man's estate, according to how he lived his life: the traditional or "civil" way. In reality, his relations could come into his house, "drive his wife comot" and sit on her front porch threatening to put a hex on her if she dared to challenge them. Of course there were exceptions; women who fought in and out of the law courts and they nearly always won.

"There are steps you can take," I said. "But the most important thing is to find a good lawyer."

"Your father's a good lawyer," she said. "Can I ask him?"

I wasn't sure I wanted Sheri to ask my father about this. I wasn't sure I wanted her to ask my father about anything, especially as he had not settled the matter with my mother.

"Yes," I said, since I'd opened my mouth.

"Thank you, my sister," she said.

As she drove off, I turned to the street seller who had finished peeling her orange. A complete spiral of green orange skin bounced off the edge of her pen knife. The infant on her back had his mouth wide open.

"Mor'ing," she said.

"Good morning," I said.

～

They began with Peace, the events following Sheri's visit to my father's office. They began and ended with Peace. She brought the magazine to the office one afternoon and announced, "Come see, our client Mr. Mukoro in a love triangle."

We gathered round her desk. It was a copy of *Weekend People*, a gossip magazine. Peace bought it monthly and I borrowed it each time. Sometimes Sheri appeared as a former Miss Nigeria, "Veteran Beauty Queen Steps Out" and such. On the front page of this issue, was a photograph of a woman with a head tie. The camera had caught her sneer. The headline read "Mukoro is a hypocrite."

The woman was Peter Mukoro's wife. They had been married for 22 years and he had recently taken a second wife. Peace improvised her way through the woman's allegations of affairs, adding gasps and squeals. The highlight of the interview was the story of how Peter Mukoro came home with a bald patch in his pubic hair. His lover had helped herself to a sample while he was asleep. The proceeds went to a medicine man to brew a potion to ensnare him. Alabi kept laughing, Dagogo pretended to be above it all, but he was stapling the same sets of papers together. I had to show it to my father.

"I don't want to read it," he said.

Then he read the whole page.

"Can you believe it?" I said.

He looked bored as he pushed the magazine toward me.

"The woman disgraced herself."

"Him," I said.

"Only herself," he said. "She has nothing better to do, going to the papers with this nonsense."

"He goes to the papers," I said, "For everything. He calls himself a social critic."

"It's not the same," my father interrupted. "This is a private matter."

"Oh," I said, taking the magazine.

"What is 'Oh'? You have something to say?"

I shook my head.

"Speak your mind now," he said "Since you've already come in here."

"I don't think it's a private matter," I said. "A social crusader practicing bigamy. I think it is good that people are being told."

"By *Weekend People?*"

"Yes," I said. "It's good they consider the story newsworthy. And really, I don't know why we continue to follow native law anyway, when civil law is in existence. It has no moral grounding, no design except to oppress women... "

My father laughed. "Who's oppressed? Are you oppressed?"

"I didn't say me, but yes, in a way."

"How?"

"I'm part of this... "

"This what?"

"This group, treated as chattel."

"Let's not get hysterical."

"Show me one case," I said. "Just one, of a woman having two husbands, a fifty-year-old woman marrying a twelve-year-old boy. We have women judges, and a woman can't legally post bail. I'm a lawyer. If I were married, I would need my husband's consent to get a new passport. He would be entitled to discipline me with a slap or two, so long as he doesn't cause me grievous bodily harm."

"You've made your point," he said. "Your grandmother was married off at fourteen, into a household with two other wives, and she had to prove she was worthy of her dowry by cooking better. I'm not sure what your gripe is. I made sure you had a good education, encouraged you to fulfill your career goals... "

"Can you change our culture for me?" I asked.

"What?"

I had not meant to be hysterical. I came in to laugh. Now my heart rate was rising, and I wasn't even sure why and my argument was a mess.

"Can you change the culture?"

My father placed his hands together, still looking bored. "We know there are problems with native law and custom, but these things are changing... "

"How do we know? The women don't come to court, and when they come, it's men like you who conspire... "

"Me? Conspire?"

"Yes, all of you, conspiring."

He laughed. "When did I conspire? I can't believe I spent money sending you to school. This would be endearing, if you weren't getting old."

"I'm not old."

"Accusing me of conspiring. You are not oppressed; you

are spoiled. Very. At your age, I'd bought my house already, I'd started my practice. I was supporting my parents. Yes. Not the other way around."

At his age there was less competition for lawyers. At his age there wasn't an economic recession in our country. It was easier to be a kingpin, and most professionals from his generation were. They substituted the colonialists' sir-and-madamism for theirs, stood by while military men led us into a black hole. Now, we their children were dependent on them. I didn't say any of this.

"Why won't you take me seriously," I grumbled. "Even as a professional. For three years I was respected, paid well. I come back home, you treat me like an idiot, pay me nothing... "

My father stopped laughing. "Shouldn't you be working?"

"It's lunch time," I said.

He leaned back in his chair. "Get Dagogo in here before you disappear for lunch. And stop reading trash."

"It's not trash," I said.

"Yes, it is," he said. "And I hope you're not using an article in *Weekend People* as a springboard for discussing the plight of women in this country."

"Why not?"

"You shouldn't even be discussing the plight of women at all, since you've done nothing but discuss it. How many women do you know anyway, in your sheltered life?"

I felt my heart racing, unnecessarily, and told myself I must never argue with him again, not over this. It was a stupid article, anyway.

"Discussion is a start," I said, steadying my voice.

"Get Dagogo in here," he said.

At his door I said, "I think Peter Mukoro is a hypocrite, too," and quickly stepped out.

The others welcomed me with glances. I knew I had to say something. I handed the magazine back to Peace and said, "Men like Mr. Mukoro should be... "

"Should be what?" Mrs. Kazeem asked, looking me up and down.

"Sued," I said.

They all laughed.

"So sue the lawyer who is representing you," Mrs. Kazeem said. "Sue the judge hearing your case. Sue the driver who carries you from court to your house after your case has been dismissed. Then, when you get home, sue your landlord."

"Sue everybody," Dagogo said.

"Sue God," Alabi said.

Peace clicked her gum and sighed.

"Welcome home," Mrs. Kazeem said.

~

"Kukuruku," people say in my country, whenever they imitate a rooster's crow. Kukuruku. Some might say a rooster sounds more like cock-a-doodle-doo, even though roosters all over the world make the same sound.

It wasn't that I no longer belonged, that I'd become a stranger. Being overseas never changed what I instinctively knew before I left. What had changed was other people's tolerance for me. I was old; too old to be deceiving myself.

Sheri took my advice and began to cater for more social functions. As she predicted, her uncle did take her family to court over possession of their home and my father agreed to represent them. The day she called to tell me, I could do no work. I'd been trying to get my father to sign the transfer letter to my mother for weeks. "All I need is five minutes of your time," I kept saying, but he said he had no time.

I tried again.

"Have no time," he said.

I hovered by his desk. "It's just a signature."

"Have to read it first," he said.

"Why?"

"You're asking me this? You're... asking me this?"

I waited for him to calm down. "Can I leave it here, until you're ready?"

"No," he said. "I have enough papers here."

I retrieved the letter from his table.

"Sheri says you're going to take their case."

"Who?" He looked up.

"My friend, Sheri Bakare. She called today to say you're going to take their case."

"Yes, Miss Bakare."

"Are you?" I asked.

"Am I what?"

"Going to take the case?"

"Yes I am."

"Do they have a chance?"

"There's nothing to prove. Their uncle doesn't have a chance. He swindled them out of their inheritance. The children and the wives, they own that house."

"Under native law?" I asked.

"You should know this. They share his estate amongst his children, according to how the man lived his life."

"Not according to how the wives wish to live theirs?"

"Wives are not always in agreement. These women just happen to be. They want to incorporate and transfer the property to the company."

"They do?"

"What do you think? They're Lagos women. They were trading before you were born. Give them the options and they will do what they have to."

I peered at his papers. "Are you really that busy?"

"Why?" he asked.

"If you're busy, why are you taking a case like theirs?"

He put his pen down.

"I take whatever case I want, Enitan, and at least your friend is a respectful girl, unlike some."

~⌒∽

It was like trying to trap a tadpole. I reproached myself, but the next time Sheri came to the office, I watched her as closely as the other women did. She came to my desk before stepping into my father's office. She stayed ten minutes in there and came out.

"He's so nice," she said. "He's not charging us anything. Can you believe it?"

"Let's hope he's doing it out of kindness," I said.

My father never did pro bono work. He too came out of his room smiling. He never smiled in the office. If you do such a thing, I thought, chase my friend, you will never forget what I have to say to you and after that, I will have nothing left to say to you.

It wasn't improbable, he with a younger woman; Sheri with an older man. There were men in Lagos who chased their daughter's friends. You called them Uncle and curtseyed before them. There were women in Lagos who would chase their best friend's father for money.

Sheri smiled. "Why else would he do that for us?"

"He alone knows what he does," I said, "and why."

~⌒∽

As a child, I knew that he strayed. I chose not to think about it. These days, when he brought women home, I treated them like any of his friends. It was hard to discern if he was interested in one or the other. I did not care to know. I discovered that after one of his clients, a married woman, started visiting him regularly. I thought her visits were work-related, until I met him at the airport after a trip abroad and saw her there. My father was a tricky man, I thought. Tricky enough to warrant an ambush. One afternoon, I arrived home early hoping to catch him. I found him in the living room with Peter Mukoro.

"Hello," I said, deliberately fixing my gaze on my father alone.

I couldn't bear my finger nails scratching a blackboard, the tips of my teeth running along cotton cloth. Peter Mukoro's mocking looks, I couldn't bear them either. He was stroking his mustache and watching me.

"You're back?" my father said.

"Yes," I said, heading straight for my room.

"Enitan," my father called after me.

"Yes," I said.

"You can't see Mr. Mukoro sitting here?"

"I can see him."

I knew I was in trouble. I almost welcomed it. My father came to my room after Peter Mukoro left.

"I've been watching you," he said. "Frowning all over the place and I've been very patient with you. Whatever you think is bothering you, never, ever again do that in my presence."

"I don't like him," I said.

"I don't care if you like him."

"Why won't you sign the transfer letter?" I said. "One minute you're helping someone else. Sheri, this... awful man."

"What has he ever done to you?"

"Sign the letter."

"When I am ready."

"Do it. Now."

My father stepped back. "You think we're equals? You think we're equals now? I treat you like an adult and you repay me this way? Your mother always said I was lax with you. But that will change. If you can't respect me in my house, you're 25 now, go wherever you want."

"Sign the letter."

"I won't tell you again. This has nothing to do with you. I've given you a choice. You either do as I say, or you leave this house."

He left me staring at my door. Leave my friend alone! I wanted to shout.

~~~

It was there; an old anxiety. But I was too old to be playing child and he was too old to be playing parent. If we forced the old ways upon ourselves now, we were liable to come to blows.

Sheri was counting old naira notes into separate piles on the desk in her office when I arrived. She licked her thumb and dealt them like cards. "One minute," she said.

"Take your time," I said.

It had taken me most of my lunch break to drive, but the anxiety was out of control. It was keeping me up at night. I wanted it to stop.

There were two stacks of boxes in the corner of the room: Peak milk, Titus sardines, Tate and Lyle sugar. A portrait of her stepmothers and another of her father alone. A pile of old mustard colored curtains were folded under the window. The green mosquito screen had ripped in two places. Dust. Everywhere. Sheri could not bear the mess, I was sure. She finished and flopped back in her chair.

"How come you're here today?"

"I came to see you," I said.

"Did you see the people outside? Did you see them?"

"I saw them."

"We're making money."

"I know."

There was a large lunch time crowd. They would have to wait for seats and their cutlery would not be clean or dry. Some would cut fried meat with spoons. If they complained, the cooks would ignore them. They had the same expression as cooks in the best food spots in Harlem, Bahia, Kingston: *Do not bother me.* The people came regardless. The food was good: black-eye peas, fresh fish, rice, vegetable stews with cow foot, intestines, lungs, and all manners of innards because in this part of the world we wasted no meat.

Sheri's nails galloped over the table.

"I'd better get back to work," I said.

"But you've just come," she said.

"Lunch-break over."

She laughed. "Why did you bother?"

"I was passing. I wanted to see your face."

If we didn't share our childhood, would I like her? Sheri was rude and vain. Sheri had always been rude and vain, except that as a child it was endearing. And whatever she said, it was clear that she did not think much of herself. She liked rich men. Yes, she did. In Lagos we used the word "like" this way. You liked to stare, you liked to criticize, you liked to make appointments and not keep them. There was an assumption, bad English aside, that if you did something often, you liked it.

If you do that, I thought, chase my father, I will have nothing to say to you. It would be sufficient, more than sufficient, to know that you think so little of yourself.

"You've seen my face," she said in Yoruba.

"It's the same face," I said.

We walked together to my car. Outside, the lunch-time traffic blocked the road. Someone leaned on a car horn. The sun was fierce. I shielded my eyes.

"Has my father been here?" I asked.

"No."

"Did he say he was coming?"

We faced each other. Sheri looked beyond me at the road.

"I hope he doesn't come," she murmured. "This place is a mess. Look, this man is going to... "

A Peugeot had moved too quickly on the road and rammed into the back of a Daewoo. The Daewoo driver got out and smacked the Peugeot driver through his open window. Mr. Peugeot jumped out and grabbed Mr. Daewoo's shirt. Mr. Daewoo was bigger. He slammed Mr. Peugeot against his car, held him by the scruff of his neck.

"Are you mad?"

"You're crazy!"

"Bang my car?"

"Slap my face?"

"I'll kill you!"

"Bastard!"

People came from the surrounding buildings to watch: men, women and children, elders so old their backs had given way. On a Lagos street, justice happened straight away. You knocked someone's car and they beat you up. The people would come out to watch. You knocked someone, and the people themselves would beat you up. You stole anything, and the people could beat you until they killed you.

The drivers on the road blasted their horns in frustration. They were as gridlocked as my mind; tight and going nowhere. The horns were never about this, two men beating themselves senseless over a dent in a bumper, and after a while, the horns had nothing to do with the delay, at all.

It was like pressing on a painful bump. I could not stop. The phone in my father's office rang one afternoon. Peace was out for lunch so I answered it. It was the receptionist from his travel agency. I told her he was in court.

She dragged her words. "His tickets are ready for collection."

"I'll tell him when he gets back," I said.

I knew my father was traveling, but I'd dropped the phone before I realized she said he was traveling with someone. I found the number of the travel agency, and waited for a dial tone. My father still had not updated our phone system. We waited up to two minutes for a dial tone and every month when we received telephone bills with phantom charges to Alaska, Qatar, places we were not even aware of, he threatened to have our phones disconnected.

The line was busy. I slammed the phone and tried again.

"Star Travel, good afternoon?"

"You called Mr. Taiwo's office?"

"Yes."

"His tickets. Whose names are they in?"

My heart was hammering. She put me on hold, consulted someone who asked who I was. I said I was his secretary.

"One is for Mr. Taiwo," she said.

"Yes," I said.

"Second one is for em, Mr. Taiwo."

I frowned. "Who?"

"Sorry, Dr. Taiwo," she said.

No such person, I thought.

"Dr. O. A.," she said. "Initials Oscar Alpha?"

"There's no such person," I said.

"Hold on," she said.

A man's voice.

"Hello, Peace? Why these questions?"

I wasn't Peace, I explained.

"Who are you?" he asked, brusquely.

"I work here," I said.

"Oh," he said. "Well the tickets are for Mr. Taiwo. And his son Debayo. Are you new?"

No such person, no such person, I thought.

"Peace will know. Tell her. Mr. Taiwo and his son are traveling. Their tickets are ready. She knows about it."

I dropped the phone. It was like shrapnel, being pulled out, I was sure.

~~~

Guilt never did show in my father's face. I'd seen. It was how he won cases. It was how he'd driven my mother to distraction. I'd seen that also.

My parent's mothers were both in polygamous marriages. My mother's mother was a trader. She saved money for her children's education under her mattress. One day my grandfather took the money she'd been saving and used it to pay the dowry for a second wife. My grandmother died broken-hearted for her money. My mother herself had never gotten over the shock. A pampered child, she disguised her embarrassment with snobbishness from then on. My father's mother was a junior wife. The two senior wives would deny my father food, hoping that if he were skinny enough, he would amount to nothing. That was why he didn't eat much; that was why he never gave in to my mother's food threats; that was why, years later, he still preferred to have an old man in his kitchen.

I waited for him that afternoon. My head felt like a shaken jar. Each time I opened it up, I didn't know which emotion to pull out. It wasn't uncommon for married men, especially of his generation, to have children outside. But this? Lying for years? I recalled how he punished me for lying as a child, how he would not forgive me for sneaking out with Sheri. It wasn't her—it was him I couldn't trust.

The joke was that a man's families discovered each other at his burial. That they fought until they fell into his grave. In reality most men who could still afford to lead this kind of double life confessed or were caught long beforehand. What were the requirements for being successful, after all? Telling one family, Don't call me at home, keep away from my real family?

It was nonsense.

He returned late in the evening. I opened the door.

"Do you know a Debayo Taiwo?" I asked.

My father placed his brief case down. "Yes."

"Is he your son?"

He straightened up. Yes, he said. Debayo was his son, four years younger than me. He lived in Ibadan. So did his mother. No, they were never married. He was in medical school there, finished last year. He was born a year after my brother died.

"I would have told you myself," he said.

"When?" I asked.

"I wanted you two to meet. Not like this."

I began to count my thoughts out on my fingers. If I didn't, I wouldn't have known how to speak. But I spoke calmly. He was not going to take control of this argument.

"That I thought I was your only child, I can live with that. That almost everything I've done comes back to it, was my own choice. That I have a mother who despises me because I stayed with you, is my own lot. So is the fact that I live in a place where all sorts of asinine..."

"Be careful how you speak to me," he said quietly.

"Asinine behavior is passed off as manliness."

"Be very careful."

"But don't tell me it is time I meet your son. That is not my choice. Not my lot, and I don't have to live with it."

"I have not asked anything of you."

"Does my mother know?"

He did not answer.

"Does she know?"

"No," he said. Shame had winded him. His voice was too low.

"You see?" I said, just as quietly. "You're the one who did the wrong thing, not her. Not her."

"You do not speak to me like that. No child of mine speaks to me like that."

I turned away. "I'm not staying here."

"Where are you going?" he asked.

"To my boyfriend's house," I said.

My father pointed. "Walk out of that door, and you won't be welcome back here."

"Liar," I said.

I packed a bag, didn't even look at him as I walked out. For all I cared, he could take my hymen, stretch it out, and hang it on the wall next to Mike's mosaic.

The road to Mike's house was choked. I kept punching my steering wheel. Perhaps it was a sign. Daughters didn't walk away like that. It was sacrilege. Costly, too. Under my breath, I cursed our economy that didn't give me freedom to sustain myself.

I had always believed my mother chose to depend on my father. The evidence was there in her dusty certificates. Other mothers walked out every day, to work, but she didn't. Now I felt no different from her, driving the car he had bought. My father would give a car, but he would not pay me enough to buy myself one. If I were taking the car with me, I deserved it. If my mother took a house, two houses even, she deserved them. The power had always been in my father's hands.

I stopped at a junction. A battered Peugeot crossed the main road before me. The driver was gaping at me. He drove as slow as if he were taking time to masturbate. I could not imagine why. A more bitter face than mine, I had not seen.

I banged on my horn. "What are you looking at?"

He scratched his head and accelerated.

When I arrived at Mike's house I rattled the gates. He came out wearing nothing but shorts.

"You didn't say you were coming," he said.

"I didn't know I was."

He opened the gates and I slid through.

He spotted my bag. "What's this?"

"I need a place to stay," I said. "I beg you. Tonight."

He walked ahead of me and I thought nothing of it because he might have been working or playing football. Climbing up the stairs, he stopped by the door.

"You didn't say you were coming, Enitan."

"You want me to leave?"

"No, no. I'm not driving you away."

"You won't... have to," I said, studying him. His shoulders were hunched. "Do you have someone with you?"

He looked away.

"Mike, I'm talking to you."

Still, he said nothing. I brushed past him and opened the door. Lying on his sofa was a girl wearing nothing but a shirt. His shirt. I recognized it. Her hair was cropped like a boy's and she had bronze lips and eyes so haughty they didn't even blink. She was so dark and so beautiful I could have wet myself from grief. She drew on her cigarette.

Mike's hand closed over my shoulder. I wriggled out of his grip and hurried down the stairs. He ran after me, grabbed my waist and I elbowed him. We locked into a knot, breathing heavily into each others' faces. I was tempted to spit at his.

"Let go of me!"

He gripped me tighter and dived lower. I kicked him. He released me.

"Don't open your mouth," I said, pointing at him.

I remembered how I'd called him a liar when I first met him.

"Pretentious bastard." I said, walking away. "You're shallow and your work is shallow."

He followed me. I fumbled with the lock of the gate, then kicked it. It rattled in protest.

"Open this damn lock," I shouted.

The gates fell apart. I pushed him aside and walked out. I reached my car, jabbed my key into the key hole and yanked the door open.

"Listen," he said.

"Why?" I asked. "Tell me? Why should I listen to a single word that comes out of your mouth."

"I don't know," he said.

"You don't?" I said. "Well, neither do I."

He was one of those people. They were either living as they pleased or they were the greatest pretenders. In a room of ten people, how many would call him a berk? I sort of knew. I'd always sort of known.

The thought seized me. She couldn't go free. If I got in my car and drove away without letting my rage go, it would rupture me.

I got out of the car and began to walk back to the house.

"W-where are you going?" Mike asked.

"I don't know," I said, wagging my finger.

He hurried after me. At the top of the stairs, I saw the girl peeping from the doorway. She took one look at me and dashed back inside. I heard a door shut and realized she was running from me. Stupid girl. She was running from me.

I ran up the stairs.

I headed straight for Obatala, grabbed her, seemingly, by the ear and dragged her out. Mike was standing at the foot of the stairs. He was staring at me as if I held a gun in my hands. I raised Obatala high above my head, smashed Obatala over the banister, heard her beads pitter-patter down the stairs. Mike clamped his hands over his head. I placed the broken board on the ground, and walked down the stairs.

"Tell her," I said. "Tell her she should be running away from you, not me."

"Not my work," he said.

"Not my life," I answered.

I drove away. Through the gate I saw Mike's landlord, standing with his mouth open. I could almost read his thoughts: Good women didn't shout in somebody's house. Good women didn't fight on the streets. Good women didn't come looking for men. Good women were at home.

My fingers trembled over my steering wheel and tears pricked my eyes, but they wouldn't fall. I drove fast till I reached Sheri's house. The traffic favored me.

There I cried.

～⌒

Sheri asked me to reconcile with my father. "These things are nothing," she said. I was not the first and I would not be the last. Half of Lagos had an outside family, and the other half wasn't aware. I refused and arranged a transfer to work with the Federal Ministry of Justice for the rest of the year. While my father was at work, I went home and packed a suitcase.

The day I met my new boss, I waited an hour before she arrived, and waited another thirty minutes while she ate yam and eggs out of a Tupperware container. My boss was one of those people—asking questions was unnecessary fussing. Her favorite complaint was that her duties belonged to someone else. Over the next months, I would go to court with her as an assistant, prosecuting in federal cases. The first time I had to address the bench, I tried to adopt an impressive voice. The judge, a middle-age woman, asked, "Young lady, is this some sort of new style?"

"No," I said.

"Speak in your normal voice, please," she said. "This is very tiring."

It was a hot day in court, especially under our wigs, which were made from horse hair, so we never washed them and they itched. The judge's salary would never compensate for the procession she had to witness: a tattered clerk, an illiterate criminal, my boss who was ill-prepared and asking for an extension, "if my lord pleases."

This particular my lord was not pleased. She had to take notes because there was no stenographer. She was taking the notes in longhand and oh Lord, the different ways of speaking. Then there would be traffic on her way home.

Fraud rackets had recently increased. Overseas they were calling it "Nigerian Crime." Here we called it "419," after the criminal code. Drug trafficking had also increased, and if the latest reports were true, Nigerian drug rings were now one of the largest suppliers to the US and Europe. Foreign embassies were reluctant to grant us visas, and those of us who received them risked being strip-searched for drugs at airports. Many of the accused were single women, mules, who were caught en route to Europe or the US from the Far East. Some had swallowed condoms crammed with heroin and cocaine; others had squeezed them up their vaginas. There was a case of a woman who stuffed a condom of cocaine down her dead baby's throat and cradled him on a plane. She was caught when an air hostess noticed the baby wasn't crying.

I hated coming out of court to find relations pleading to spare their son or daughter, old men and women prostrating. In one trial, the accused, a nineteen-year-old girl, claimed she didn't know what she was carrying. Another woman had handed the package to her, then disappeared. The court found the girl guilty. A month before, the new regime had shot people for the same crime, as part of their war against indiscipline. The executions were carried out retroactively, to punish those who had been tried and convicted before the law came into effect, but following a public outcry, further executions were deferred.

The girl's face haunted me. The way her glasses kept sliding down, I imagined her as a school librarian in her hometown, coming to Lagos to earn a better living. When I actually began to believe her story, I realized I was not detached enough to be successful at litigation. I wasn't even sure I enjoyed being in court. The proceedings took too long, relied on too many people. I viewed them through bleary eyes and my heart throbbed like a toothache.

I had lost weight, even with Sheri's cooking. Whenever I remembered Mike and my father, not being able to say a word, I dropped my head. I cared for someone and I enjoyed showing them courtesy. The worst was to be deprived of giving it. I carried some of their shame. Soon I began to keep the same hours as my boss and learned how to disguise my tracks. I didn't even mind the bad looks I was receiving from other colleagues.

Living with Sheri, I saw how she survived as a sugary girl. She limited her involvement in the family business to please her brigadier. She tidied, after me and after her nephews and nieces who came to spend time with her. She dusted with cleaning rags, sometimes with her fingers. She plumped cushions if she stood up, picked fluff from her carpet, listened to the saddest Barbara Streisand songs. The rest of her time she spent preparing for Brigadier Hassan: her hair, her nails, dabbing perfumes and cooking meals. There wasn't a coy bone in her body to spare for the outrage of others, especially those from homes like mine, with errant fathers and mothers who prayed good and hard about which good families their daughters would end up in.

In a bizarre household arrangement that appeared incestuous to me, Brigadier Hassan's wives were trying to recruit her as a third wife. They knew their husband had a number of girlfriends and thought that if he had to remarry, it would be to someone who wasn't liable to sit around the polo club chukka after chukka, wearing expensive sunshades. Sheri found polo boring. Their daughters liked her. She was less than ten years older than the eldest and would never tell if they visited boyfriends. They had all attended finishing schools in Switzerland, and their marriages were to be arranged. Their father also thought they ought to remain virgins until they left his house. The eldest claimed that horse riding stretched her. Meanwhile, he was taking Sheri to Paris, to Florence, first class. Sheri, who had trouble remembering: "That place in Florence with the gold market," "that street in Paris with the shops," "that watch, starts with P? Exactly, Pathetic Philip." I could remember every single trip in Europe, even the names of each poxy pensione I'd stayed in, and if someone had bothered to buy me an expensive watch, I would at least try to remember.

Where two cultures diverged Sheri had chosen which to follow. Her grandmother, Alhaja, had seen to that. A woman widowed in her thirties, Alhaja headed a market women's union and earned enough to educate her children overseas. She was disappointed when her son ended up with a white woman, but she raised Sheri herself so that no other wife would mistreat her. When the other wives did come, they would worry more about Alhaja's rage than their husband's. She would visit their home, if she heard they were fighting. There, she threatened them. Her son had had a white woman, and he would get rid of two squabbling Africans in no time! She would go to the houses of her daughters if their husbands beat them. The husbands would end up begging her. When she learned about what happened to Sheri at the picnic, she visited each of the boys' houses with a mob in tow. The mob started with the watchmen, or whoever was unfortunate enough to open the gates. They broke down doors and windows. As they went for furniture, Alhaja went straight for the boy's crotches. She wasn't letting go until their mothers, fathers, their grandparents even, lay flat on the floor to beg her granddaughter. After, she visited her medicine man to finish what was left of their lineage.

Sheri was her grandmother's true daughter. I once tried to explain the Tragic Mulatto syndrome to her. She said it was nonsense. All sorts of people tried to find their identity. Why was the mulatto tragic? There was nothing tragic about her. At the Miss World contest, a girl from Zimbabwe told her the word "half-caste" was derogatory; "colored" was what Sheri would be called in her own country. Sheri said she didn't care what anyone called her. In the Yoruba-English dictionary there was a whole sentence to describe her: "the child of a black person and white person," and it suited her fine.

It wasn't always that clear to her. She was eight years old when, fed up with a boy at school who laughed at her features, she ran home one afternoon and cut off her hair, trimmed her lashes to stubs and rubbed brown shoe polish on her face. Her grandmother Alhaja found her standing before the mirror and ordered her back to the boy. He was singing that Yoruba song, "I married a yellow girl" when Sheri grabbed him. "I beat him up," she said. "Then I emptied his school bag on his head and pushed him into the gutter. I will never forget his name. Wasiu Shittu."

Like a proper Lagos Princess, nobility surfaced once you got in her way. A fist fight? A person would have to kill Sheri first before she let it rest. Drop an insult? Yes, she would, as fast as she was provoked. Chop a person down in three glances heads, torso, and legs. In no time, if they turned their noses up at her. And whoever they were, she was about to give them their life history: "From where are you coming? From where?"

Still she wouldn't eat pork. And every morning when she said her prayers with a scarf wrapped around her head, she had a humble expression. The humblest she would have all day. Haughty and bored it would be from then on. The kind of haughtiness that came from being a favored child and the kind of boredom that came from not having enough to do.

I avoided her brigadier altogether, catching only the smell of his cigars and finding it strangely seductive. I imagined him according to the stereotype: dressed in a long white tunic with a Mao-style collar, gold cufflinks, fat diamond watch on his wrist. His hands would slip in a handshake. His trousers would flap around his ankles. His feet would be small in his leather slippers. Absolutely no conversation. He would not be used to talking to women. Not that way.

But I dared not say a word, not even about his drinking and smoking as a strict Moslem. I was living in his apartment, the very place I'd urged Sheri to move out of. Whenever he was visiting, I would go swimming at Ikoyi Club, and she was pleased. "Forget that stupid artist," she said.

I swam regularly. My body pressed on. Then it seemed that my mind, which had been lagging behind, soon began to say, "Wait for me. Wait for me."

I was swimming one evening when a tall man with legs like an Olympic swimmer joined me in the club pool. He dived in and paced himself fast. He made me feel slow and clumsy. Once or twice I crossed him in the middle of the pool, but most times we were at opposite ends. Soon I paused to rest in the shallow end. He came to a stop and rose from the water like something aquatic. "Hello," he said.

His smile was the color of ivory. One side tooth popped out a little.

"You too," I said.

He splashed water over his chest. "Would you mind if I told you something?"

"I would," I said.

He tucked his chin in. "Why are you being rude?"

"Listen, I come here to swim."

"So do I," he said. "All I wanted to say was that you have mucus."

"What?"

"Mucus. Hanging out of your nose."

He pointed.

My hand clamped over my nose as he hoisted himself out of the pool. I shrugged and continued to swim. Fool, I thought.

     ~

I was walking up the stairs, two evenings later, from the changing rooms to the pool shower, wearing my swimsuit. He was walking down the stairs from the pool bar to the same shower.

"Sorry," I said, in embarrassment.

I was usually alone in the pool in the evenings. The children, mostly expatriates, were gone. There were married couples at the pool bar, having soft drinks. Most of the activity was in the main club house, where beer and spirits were served, or in the squash courts full of the regular players. I never expected to see him again. He gestured like a cattle herder, I thought, to move me along.

"At least say thank you," he said, when I didn't.

"Why," I answered.

I stepped under the faucet with my backside to him, didn't even care if he saw my stretch marks. He wasn't perfect either. Good legs maybe, startling height, weakish chin, and his stomach could be tighter.

He made a sound, "hm," as my father would, like a warning. Not as women did, stretching the sound and turning their mouths downward. That was the sound I made in response.

"Any time," he said, as I walked away.

We swam as if we were each alone in the pool that evening.

～

Again I bumped into him. This time, in the main club house, after swimming another evening.

"Miss Rudeness," he announced.

"I'm not rude," I said.

He walked past and I turned on a whim.

"Excuse me?"

"Yes," he said.

"My manners are mine," I said. "You don't have to remind me of them, or my mucus for that matter. It has nothing to do with you. And whenever you see me, try not to say anything, if you really want to avoid an insult."

He smiled. "Let it go. Let it go."

"What go?"

"Bitterness," he said. "It eats you up."

I looked him up and down. "I see your mouth is sharp."

"So they tell me."

"What do you know about me? You know nothing about me. All I'm saying is, stop passing comments whenever you see me."

"Let it go."

We were both smiling now, except he was making fun of me. There was no need to be angry with him, I thought. He was a big fool.

"What's laughing you laugh?" I said.

He continued to smile and I wanted to shock him.

"Would you like to have a drink?" I asked.

He cupped his ear.

"I said would you like to have a drink?"

"I come here to swim," he said.

"After you swim," I said.

I pulled a face behind his back. I'm not afraid, I thought. Of any of you. If I want a drink, I will have one.

~ා

He joined me in the club house. We sat at the bar, while the bartender gave me disapproving looks.

Niyi Franco. He was a lawyer, though he was now a manager in an insurance company. His grandfather was a lawyer. His father and four brothers were lawyers. His mother retired from nursing the year he was born. He swam for Lagos State, and thought he would do so for the rest of his life. Then he cracked his head on a diving board, and his parents banned him from entering a pool for life.

"Africans can't swim," I joked.

"I'm a Brazilian descendant," he said, lifting his chin.

"My friend," I said. "You're African."

I told him about my recent experiences in court, saying little about my family. We walked to our cars together and it was hard to keep up with him because he took such long strides. This time we were talking about lawyer's wigs and gowns. There was much debate in the press about changing the uniform to reflect our heritage.

"We'll never change it," he assured me.

"I hope we will," I said. "Those wigs look terrible."

"Thank God I don't have to wear one."

"When was the last time you did?" I asked.

"A year after I graduated," he said.

"When did you graduate?"

"'77."

I stepped back. "No."

"Yes," he said.

That was the year of the Festival of Arts and Culture we called Festac. Stevie Wonder came to play at our national theater, Mariam Makeba, Osibisa, every African person in the world represented in Lagos. I thought I would die because I was in boarding school in England. We had color television for the first time in our country, and everyone was growing vegetables in their back yards in support of the government's Operation Feed the Nation. My mother grew an okra patch, my father said the whole regime, its Operation Feed the Nation and Festival of Arts, was all nonsense.

"See my eyes," he said. "I never lie. I have a six-year-old son."

My mouth fell open. "You're married?"

"Divorced," he said.

"You're married," I said.

As far as I was concerned.

"Well," I said. "Nice meeting you."

"You too," he said.

"I'd better get home."

"I've enjoyed talking to you."

"You're welcome," I said, without thinking.

I almost curtseyed. How old was I in 1977? Seventeen.

~⁀∘

I was determined to find out about his wife the next time we met. This time, we sat in the drinks lounge.

"You must miss your son," I said, as we waited for our beers to arrive.

"Yes."

"You get to spend time with him, I'm sure."

"No," he said.

"That is a pity," I said.

I thought I should give up prying. It was not my business.

"He's in England with his mother," he said.

"Your wife's in England?"

"She's not my wife."

Our waiter arrived with the beers. Niyi immediately reached for his wallet and paid. The waiter obscured his face for an instant.

"You drove the poor woman to England?" I said.

I reached for my bottle.

"She left," he said. "I was twenty-three. Let me see... she was pregnant, still in medical school. I was working for my father. My parents are strict Catholics, but I didn't get married because of that. My father was not an easy man to get along with. He kept threatening to sack me. One day I said, 'I've had enough' and walked out. That was the beginning of our troubles.

"I found a new job, but it was hard. She was working in the teaching hospital, we were living in Festac Village. My son is an asthmatic. One day her car was stolen, this, that, you can imagine. But she had this group of friends. Like rats those women, shoe-and-bag girls. They were always wearing something, traveling somewhere. She wanted all of that. One day her parents gave her a ticket and she took off. She went to England with my son. She didn't even call until she found a job then she phoned crying and asking me to come and join her."

"What did you say?"

"I had a job here. I wasn't qualified over there. What was I going to do? Who would employ me? She was a doctor, and I would be what? All the time we were in Lagos, she was telling everybody I couldn't provide. Now she wanted me to go to another country and take an odd job?"

"That would have been difficult."

"I could have gone, for my son."

"Would she have done the same for you?" I asked.

As he drank his beer, I watched him. Every movement he made was large.

"No," he said, rubbing his forehead. "She knew exactly what she wanted. She always knew what she wanted. She wanted to get married. She wanted to travel. She wanted to work in England. She just wouldn't admit it. Women do that, you know."

"What?"

"Dribble past you and score. Phoosch! Mental football."

I smiled. "You generalize."

"You're not like that?"

"I'm not perfect."

"Tell me your faults," he said, smiling.

"I trust too fast," I said. "I don't forgive easily. I'm terrible, terrible with that, and I'm scared of death."

"Yours?"

"Mine, and others."

"That's not a fault."

I pictured myself as a drunken woman, ramming my head into a wall, thinking I would eventually walk through. I was always hopeful about men.

"I'm hopeful," I said.

"That's good," he said, taking another drink.

I glanced at his hands.

"Do you play the piano?"

He studied them, looking pleased. "How come you know?"

I brought my glass to my lips.

"How did you know?" he said. "You must be a mammy-water, hanging around pools, looking for men to entice and wagging that ass of yours."

My beer went down the wrong way.

⁓

Sheri was sitting on her bed. I stood before her mirror, wearing work clothes: a black skirt suit that always needed to be coaxed down.

"You can't go out like that," she said.

I checked my lipstick. "Why not?"

"To the Bagatelle? People dress up to go there. Your suit looks un-ironed."

"Who's looking?"

She walked to her wardrobe and began to sift through.

"You'll never find anything in there for me," I said.

"Wait and see," she said.

"I won't like it, Sheri. I know I won't, and I'm not going to change to please you."

Always. She asked if I'd eaten. She fixed my hair as I walked out of her door, made me iron my clothes. I told her she had an old woman's soul. She said that was why she was wiser. She pulled out a black gown with a large gold print. It was narrow and the neckline was a little wide, Senegalese style.

"Tell me you don't like it," she said.

I wore it. Niyi arrived early. I thought he would have made an effort, but he was wearing work clothes. Sheri was looking forward to meeting him, and he ended up not staying. We were running late, he claimed, then he later confessed he was hungry.

"How long has she been living here?" he asked as we drove out of the apartment complex.

"Two years," I said.

"She's come far," he said.

"What do you mean?"

We approached the junction leading to the main road.

"Living here and no job," he murmured.

I watched one car whiz past, then another. I was about to answer when he whistled. His gaze followed a red car which looked like a miniature space ship on the antiquated road. The car slowed by the gates of the large apartment complex across the road. "What?" I asked.

"The new BM," he said.

"BM what?" I asked.

"W," he explained.

He stared at the red brake lights. The gates opened and the car rolled in.

"Em, can we go, now?" I asked.

The main road was clear. He gave it a cursory look before coming out.

I sniffed. "So materialistic."

He looked me up and down. "You don't like good things, Madam Socialist?"

I turned my face to the window.

He patted my knee. "It is good to see that your politics doesn't affect your dressing. You look nice in your black and gold."

I kept my face to the window. I did not want him to see me smile. How the man annoyed me.

But I knew he joked because he thought he was flawed. Not flawed the way most people were, secretly, for their own self-obsession, but flawed publicly, so that everyone could see: a wife who had walked out on him, a son he was not raising. Anywhere else in the world it would be hard to deal with, more so here. A woman was used to humiliation by the time she reached adulthood. She could wear it like a crown, tilt it for effect even, and dare anyone to question her. A man would wear his like an oversized cloak.

"Move your broken down car," he shouted.

He drove terribly, as if we were rushing to the airport for the last flight out of Lagos, and accused other drivers of sleeping.

"Please," I said. "Don't crash us."

The Bagatelle was one of the oldest and best run restaurants in Lagos, owned by a Lebanese family. Throughout dinner I was laughing. Niyi ordered falafel as lafa-lafa. When it arrived, he said it would give him gas. I asked if any food pleased him. He said home cooking.

"I'm sorry, I don't cook," I said.

"Serious?"

He contemplated my confession for a moment then thumped the table.

"I'll marry you, anyway."

"Oh, Lord," I said, holding my head. If I did, I would be in trouble.

"Eat up," he said.

"I'm full," I said.

"You're wasting good food," he said. "I thought you were a socialist."

"You've been calling me names since you met me."

"Eat up, o-girl."

"Please, let me digest."

How the man annoyed me. He had a wicked mouth, even to kiss.

~

I was surprised to find Sheri's door ajar when I returned. I pushed it open and peered into the living room. There was a pot on her sofa, overturned. I slipped and realized there was okra on the floor.

"Sheri," I said, placing my hand to my chest.

I walked around the sofa, found more stew on the floor. In the kitchen, I saw a bag of yam flour lying half empty on the floor.

"Sheri!" I said.

Her voice came from her room. I hurried there and found her lying on her bed.

"What happened?"

She propped herself up slowly.

"Nobody hits me. You hit me and I will hit you back. God no go vex."

There was yam flour in her hair.

"Who hit you?"

She patted her chest. "Telling me I'm a whore for going out. Your mother is the whore. Raise a hand to hit Sheri Bakare, and your hand will never be the same again. Stupid man, he will find it hard to play polo from now on."

"Sheri, you beat up the brigadier?"

With a pot, she said. The Civil War hadn't prepared him for her. She beat him for every person who had crossed her path in life. I told her she didn't have a drop of white blood in her. Anyone who had white blood wouldn't beat up a whole brigadier, like that, with a pot of okra stew.

"I was raised in downtown Lagos," she said. "Bring the Queen of England there. She will learn how to fight."

She swept the yam flour off the kitchen floor.

"You know you will have to leave this place," I said.

"I know," she said.

"And you know he might send people over to harass you."

"Let him send the president," she said. "United Nations troops, even."

"You're prepared to die?"

"I know people who will beat him up for ten naira alone," she said. "And I know things about him that will land him in Kirikiri maximum security prison for the rest of his life, if he tries any nonsense. The man is a coward. That is why he hit me. He won't dare send anyone here. If he does, he will read in *Weekend People* how a woman beat him up."

I shook my head.

"Me and you, I don't know who is crazier."

"After what my eyes have seen? If I'm not crazy, what else will I be? The man is jealous of me. Can you believe it? He's jealous of my success. With all he has. He wants me to have nothing, except what he gives me. He says he will take it all back. I said take it! All of it! I did not come to this place naked."

I looked into the living room.

"What about your furniture?"

"We don't have tables and chairs in my father's house? Let him keep them. All I want is my Barbara Streisands."

I could see she was struggling with the broom.

"Let me do that," I said.

She dragged a chair as I gathered the flour into a pile.

"Enitan," she said after a while. "I'm telling you this, not because of what happened tonight, and I hope you will listen."

I was about to kneel. "Yes?"

"My mother is not dead. My father told me she was, but the truth was he took me away from her."

"What?"

"You know how England was in those days. Black people were like monkeys to the *oyinbos*. He had just graduated. She was working in a hotel. She used to bring him food. They never married, and he wanted me to know our traditions."

I whispered. "Traditions of what?"

The man didn't even bother to raise Sheri. He handed her over to his mother and then to his wives.

"Alhaja told me everything before she died. She apologized. I told her it was in the past. Stop looking at me like that. I'm not the first or last. At least he didn't leave me in England like some did, and anyway, I have two mothers."

"But your real mother... "

"The person who never came to look for me. That isn't a real mother."

I shut my eyes. "What your father did was wrong. Wrong!"

"I can accept it; so can anyone else. Are you trying to tell me you feel my pain more than me?"

She was smiling; I knew not to probe.

"Sorry."

"Just make up with your father. That's all I'm asking. It's enough now. I'm moving out of here tomorrow, and I'm going back to my family. I think you should do the same. These things happen in families. They happen. It's what you do afterward that matters. Your father raised you. He never abandoned you. Don't be stubborn."

"I have a right to be angry."

"So you deny the person who raised you."

"It's more than his lies."

"What more?"

"I can't trust him. Not even with my friends."

"Which friends?"

I pointed.

Her eyes widened. "You think your father is after me?"

I imitated him: "'My dear this, my dear that.'"

"He does the same to you."

"Well, I know him. He thinks I don't, but I do."

I stood up, aware that I was sounding like my mother.

"This is Lagos," she said. "You can't behave like this. You won't be the first, and you won't be the last. Our fathers, we know what they're like. We just have to accept them as they are."

I emptied the dust pan into the large waste bin.

"Enitan!"

⁓

Walking down the graveled path, I felt ashamed. Daughters were meant to listen and I hadn't listened. I paused before I rang the door bell; rang it twice and heard footsteps. The door opened. Her hair was completely gray. Perhaps she'd forgotten to dye it. For the first time, I worried that my mother would die without forgiving me.

"It's you?" she said.

"Yes," I said.

"Come in," she said.

She listened to what I had to say.

"You were rude to him," she said, "You will have to apologize. That is taboo, to call your father a liar."

She kicked her bedroom slippers off. They were originally light blue, but her feet had left brown imprints and the fabric was matted with dust.

"He was no good. After you were born, I told him I didn't want another child. God had blessed us with a healthy child. Why risk having another? But his family wouldn't hear of it. He had to have a son, so they started threatening that he would take another wife, and his mother, that woman who suffered so much herself, threatened me too. Your father never said a word to support me.

"I was very reserved, you know. Aloof. Your father liked that. Sunny, he always felt he had to be above others. Maybe because he was so neglected as a boy. And I did not mind wearing what he bought, clothes, jewelry. I had it all, but when your brother was born, who cared about them? Imagine the pain for a child? He would scream and scream and we couldn't touch him. I couldn't touch my son. For what? For a man who wouldn't be kept. Going out all the time, as if my son didn't exist, as if I didn't exist. He said I stopped looking after myself. I did not have time for myself. He said I was angry all the time. Of course I was angry. It was like swallowing broken glass. You can't expel broken glass from your body. It will tear you apart. It's best that it remains inside you."

"Never make sacrifices for a man. By the time you say, 'Look what I've done for you,' it's too late. They never remember. And the day you begin to retaliate, they never forget. Pray you never know what it means to have a sick child, either. You don't know whether to love them too much, or too little. Then as they become sicker, you love them the only way you can, as though they are a part of you.

"The day your brother died, your father was out. I took your brother to church. We were praying. How we prayed that day. Your father wouldn't forgive me, kept talking about hospital. Why didn't you take him to hospital, why didn't you take him to hospital. What can hospital do? Hospital can't take sickle cell out of a child, hospital cannot make a dying child live. I am not an ignorant woman. There isn't a mother in the world who wouldn't believe that faith can heal her child after medicine has failed, even the young women of today, who are so smart about family planning."

I nodded. In those days, couples took chances. These days, couples who could afford it, traveled overseas for a test in their first trimester. If the result showed a sickle child, the woman would have a quiet abortion. We believed in reborn spirits no more than we believed in the sanctity of early life.

"Yes," my mother said. "A son, you say. I'm not surprised. It was a question of time before he surfaced. I'm glad I know. All those years, I wanted your father to admit he was doing wrong. He never did."

I tried to picture my brother. He was scrawny; always being tossed in the air and tickled, even by me, except when he was sick. Sometimes I wanted to know how it felt to be sick. Once, I tried to pretend that I was having a crisis. He laughed and poked me off my bed, screamed until my mother rushed in.

"You think it's funny?" she said to me.

The day of his funeral, none of us attended. My parents didn't, because parents couldn't bury their children, according to the custom. I stayed with them because my father said I was too young. Years after, I fantasized that my brother was playing another prank, this time, pretending to be dead. I wanted to see him again, getting me into trouble and sneaking peeks to gauge my reaction, but I was afraid of ghosts. My brother was the brave one, I thought. Whenever he was in hospital, I preferred to hide under my bed than to visit him, and after he died, I worried that he would visit me like an ugly masquerader. For a while, death became the logical conclusion to every situation. My head itched, so I would scratch it, so I would bleed and bleed until I died. A spider on the curtain, so it would fall into my mouth, bite my throat, my throat would swell up and I would die. As I grew older, the links between events became less precarious.

There were things I remembered about my mother also, how she brewed lemon grass tea whenever I was ill and checked on me several times a night, like a nurse, without pity: "Open up. Good." In another country, she might have sought help through counseling or therapy. Here, people were either mad or not mad. If they were mad, they were walking the streets naked. If they were not mad, they remained at home. My mother once had thirty-three bottles of perfume on her dressing table, before she started wearing those church gowns smelling of bleach and starch. I counted them. I could still remember the glamour days, the velvet caftan with circular mirrors. I imagined her with broken crystals in her stomach. They were there in her eyes. She was a beautiful woman. I had long forgotten.

1995

People say I was hot-headed in my twenties. I don't ever remember being hot-headed. I only ever remember calling out to my voice. In my country, women are praised the more they surrender their right to protest. In the end they may die with nothing but selflessness to pass on to their daughters; a startling legacy, like tears down a parched throat.

The first time I spoke to Niyi about marriage, I'd discovered my mother was scavenging our trash bags for my used sanitary towels and taking them to church for prayers. Her priest had said I would remain childless otherwise. She was still a member of his church, a senior sister now. She lit candles in the mornings and evenings to pray, mumbled to herself and hummed church songs. Her front door was padlocked by six o'clock and her curtains drawn. I would go out to see Niyi just to escape from her, from her house where I often felt shackled by afterbirth. It was hers now, since my father relinquished it. That happened three weeks after I moved in with her. I received a transfer letter from him with a covering letter accusing me of de-camping. I replied, thanking him for raising me and reminded him that I was never given a chance to decide what camp to be in. I apologized for my rudeness meanwhile. Really, I shouldn't have called my own father a liar.

My mother began to boast to her church friends that I'd seen his hypocrisy first-hand. I watched her disappear every Sunday only to come back and accuse these same people of meanness. I pretended to listen. I knew that she hurt because of the sacrifices she'd made in her marriage. I finally understood why she turned her mind to church with such fervor. Had she turned to wine or beer, people would have called her a drunkard. Had she sought other men, they would have called her a slut. But to turn to God? Who would quarrel with her? "Leave her alone," they would say. "She is religious."

I had watched my mother worship, and seen the way she waved her hands and exaggerated her smile. Whenever she said amen, I thought she might have well have been saying nyah-nyah. She had tricked us all. Her fixation with religion was nothing but a life-long rebellion. Faith had not healed her and I hoped that one day, the birth of a grandchild would.

But when I told her I was going to marry Niyi she said they had madness in his family. Oh yes. One of his aunts was always washing her hands, and another one, pretty thing like this, had a baby and would not touch it for days. "Imagine that for a mother," she said. I told my father about my engagement and he, too, suddenly became religious. "Not allowed," he said, raising his forefinger; not allowed by the Pope, he meant. Niyi was a divorced Catholic, so he would not give his blessings. Not until Uncle Fatai persuaded him would he agree to the wedding, then he lectured Niyi about how our marriage would have to work. That ended any father-son relationship they could have developed, and Niyi, disturbed by my mother's church activities, avoided her as if she were a sorceress.

On the day of my traditional engagement, I knelt before him according to the rites. He presented a dowry to my family, of hand-woven cloth and gold jewelry. I did not want a dowry and I did not want to kneel. Niyi, who was reluctant to participate in rites that would proceed as if he were 21 and without a child of his own, did not want to be there at all. During the ceremony my parents argued. My mother refused to sit by my father. He told her she was quite welcome to stand outside his gates. A week later, at the civil ceremony, I almost suffocated from the ill-feeling in the Ikoyi registry.

I did not shed a tear over leaving home. I, who cried easily. After the final rites, when a bride knelt before her parents and they blessed her, she was supposed to cry. An entire wedding party waited for this moment, so that they could say "Ah, she wept. She wept, that girl. She loves her parents no end." But I'd always been suspicious. What were the tears for, on cue like that? One bride, almost 40, gray hairs all over her head, she was crying as if her parents had sold her. They had all but given up on her. What was she crying for? I was not bitter about my parents. We had healed the way most families did, enough to hold us together from one day to the next, but liable to split under any great stress. I still had not met my father's outside son, my half-brother. At first it was about letting my father know I hadn't forgotten about his deception. Then it was about being loyal to my mother. After a while, it was really about having other matters to worry about, like work.

At the time, I was working for the Ministry of Justice and supplementing my income with the odd business incorporation. After we got married, Niyi introduced me to some of his friends in banking and I found a job in credit control. I was not prepared for my new environment, handling large sums of money within tight deadlines. On the one hand, I had the hustlers from treasury pushing me to pass deals; on the other, management cautioning me to check credit lines. The treasury guys would come ten minutes to cut-off time, tallying exactly how much the bank would lose if I didn't approve their transactions. I would get heartburn from arguing with them. Then, one day, I mistakenly approved a deal with an insufficient credit line and management hauled me in for a reprimand.

After work I drove home crying. Niyi took one look at me. "You have to be tougher than this, o-girl," he said. "You can't let people push you around. Tell them to go to hell if they pressure you."

"You have no idea," I said. Bankers were not like lawyers. We were accustomed to waiting for due process. We expected delays. Niyi pulled my nose. "Stop," I said and slapped his hand away.

He patted my head. "That is what I want to hear."

I was able to face work the next morning. From then on, Niyi led me through similar rites. Months later, when the company secretary left, I stepped into her position.

At work I consciously tried to imitate him. How he said "no" without moving his head; how his eyes, once locked, wouldn't shift. At home, he had me howling with things he would do and say with that look. He played pieces on my piano and dared to call them jazz. I thought they sounded like a petrified rat scurrying back and forth over the keyboards. He walked around with nothing but Y-fronts on. On more than one occasion, he turned his back and pulled them down; to check. He had hemorrhoids, at least two episodes a year. I told him it said something about his personality, that he had a hidden weakness in his gut. He said I should get used to it, the pesseries and the ointments. I would eventually grow accustomed to this and other marital surprises. I didn't know a man could have his own way of squeezing toothpaste. I didn't know I could come close to lunging across the dining table to throttle a man, because of the way he chewed. Then there were more serious times, when Niyi's brows knotted and I knew that silence would follow. This happened whenever he was reminded of his grudges, against his ex-wife, against their friends who had taken sides and his own family. That I would never get used to.

After he left his father's firm, Niyi's brothers avoided him for fear of offending their father. Only his mother sneaked visits to him. Then his wife left him. The day she found a new boyfriend, their son stopped calling. Now, years later, although they were all on speaking terms, Niyi swore he would never forget each person's role. Whenever he wanted to speak to his son, I was the one to call his ex-wife. He was wary of his father and brothers, and he protected his mother like an egg.

Toro Franco. She was one of those women who swallowed her voice from the day she married. She was a nurse, and yet her husband and sons, all lawyers, thought she couldn't grasp the rudiments of Offer and Acceptance, so she acted like she didn't. She called "precedence" "presidents," walked around with her underskirt hanging out. Whenever she tried to join in their legal discussions, they teased her, "Mama, look at you. Your Saturday is sticking out of your Sunday." They laughed as she adjusted her underskirt. If they mentioned the word hungry, she ran into her kitchen and began to boss her house boys around. Soon she would summon me to help. I knew that she watched me botch my kitchen duties, dropping spoons, recoiling from hot handles, slicing my fingers.

"It's hot in here," I would say.

"Don't worry," she would say.

"The boys should help."

"Boys? What can boys do?"

"They know how to tease you."

"Who else can they tease?"

Once, I tried to trick her into a confession. "Don't you ever feel lonely in here, ma? Isn't the kitchen the loneliest room?" She looked at me as if I'd offered to strip.

"Enough," she pleaded. "Enough now."

I continued to stir her stew, imagining her in a mortuary, on a slab, underskirt hanging out, husband and children saying how nice she was.

Everyone said my mother-in-law was nice. I wouldn't believe them until I'd heard a true word pass her lips. Her husband was a man who liked his stews prepared the traditional way, meat fried in thick groundnut oil, and he loved his wife so much he wouldn't eat stews prepared by anyone but her. Forty-five years later, he had bad arteries and her hands were as dry and shriveled as the meat she fried. Francis Abiola Franco, Esquire. The first time we met he asked, "You're Sunny Taiwo's daughter?"

"Yes, sir," I said.

"Good breeding always shows," he said.

"I'm a horse?" I asked Niyi later.

"He's a horse," Niyi said. "An old nag."

He was one of those Senior Advocates of Nigeria, though he was now out of touch with the Law, and with reality. He asked his sons to dial if he needed to make a phone call. He sat in the back seat of his car, always, even when one of his sons was driving. He stopped speaking to me after I challenged him on a point of law. I disagreed with him just for the sake of it. I didn't care much for him, but my brothers-in-law, I loved. They would all troop into my house, all four of them looking like Niyi with the same dark skin and thin nose, and I would kiss each of them feeling a rush of libido and motherliness as they greeted me, "Enitan of Africa!" "*Obirin Meta!* Three times a girl!" "*Alaiye Baba!* Master of the earth!" It was like welcoming my husband four times over. I didn't even mind sitting with them as they scratched their groins and christened women's parts: her foward, her backward, her assets, her giblets. About Sheri: "She's, em, very talented. Hyuh-Hyuh-Hyuh."

I knew. They were petrified of women, though they denied it. "Who? Who's scared of chicks?" they asked.

"Sneaking," I said. "Lying. Lying on your last breath. Then you cannot even face somebody to say a relationship is over? That is petrified."

"If you say so. Hyuh-Hyuh-Hyuh," scratch, scratch, scratch.

Sometimes they brought girlfriends who disappeared by the next visit. Sometimes they played hide-and-seek games with their girlfriends. I once asked, "Are you boys waiting to marry your mother, or what?"

"Of course," they answered, including Niyi.

"Well, em," I said. "Don't you think you should drop your standards a little?"

"No," they said, except Niyi.

Niyi bullied his brothers the same way he bullied me, but

he could easily become vexed in the middle of our playing. Then he would call me aside and warn, "Better watch what you're saying. Next thing they'll be calling me woman wrapper." Wrapper was the cloth women tied around their waists. Woman wrapper was a weak man, controlled by his woman. I thought he was paranoid. I said it was too bad. He was the very person who had encouraged me to be strong at work. He was asking me to fly within specified perimeters. I would have shouting fits about this and he would remain totally silent. He said he wasn't used to arguing that way. "In our family," he said, "we don't raise our voices."

The Francos were one of those Lagos families, descendants of freed slaves from Brazil, who once formed the cream of Lagos society. They considered themselves well-bred because their great-grandfather, Papa Franco, was educated in England. In his time, Papa Franco acquired a huge estate which survived the slum clearance that wiped out most of the Brazilian Quarter in Lagos. Some of the buildings now looked as if a giant fist had come down from heaven and punched them into the ground. Those that remained standing were rickety with tall shutters and wrought iron balconies. Nothing had been done to improve the drainage system: gutters and pit latrines dating back to colonial times. They were occupied mostly by street traders and market people.

Papa Franco's only son, Niyi's grandfather, had twenty-six children by three different women who died before him and there had been several documented court cases over his estate. Each faction of Franco occupied separate pews in the Catholic church they attended. Their church reminded me of my mother's: the incense, white robes, and chants. When the collection tray passed, they gave very little. Oil wealth hadn't touched their palms and civil service wages were paltry. The Franco men tilted their noses heavenward, the women fanned their cleavages laden with gold and coral beads, their clothes reeked of camphor balls. They had the pride and lack of ambition of a generation that wealth would skip, and ignored each other because they thought it was common to quarrel openly. That was how they settled differences: Aunty Doyin, The Pretty One, locked herself in a room until her father allowed her to marry a Protestant; Niyi's father stopped speaking to him for a year after he left Franco and Partners; Niyi, himself, would ignore me for days.

The first time this happened, we'd argued over drinks. Drinks. His brothers were visiting and I had just returned from work. As usual, he asked, "Enitan can you get these animals something?"

Niyi claimed he was totally inept inside kitchens. His favorite trick was to feign panic attacks by the door, clutching his throat and keeling over. Normally I humored him, because we had house help, but this evening, I only wanted to stop trembling from the lack of sugar in my blood. I'd spent the day fending off the treasury guys.

"You have hands," I said.

"My friend," he said. "Show some respect."

"Go to hell," I said.

In my 29 years no man ever told me to show respect. No man ever needed to. I had seen how women respected men and ended up shouldering burdens like one of those people who carried firewood on their heads, with their necks as high as church spires and foreheads crushed. Too many women, I thought, ended up treating domestic frustrations like mild cases of indigestion: shift-shift, prod-prod and then nothing. As far back as my grandmother's generation we'd been getting degrees and holding careers. My mother's generation were the pioneer professionals. We, their daughters, were expected to continue. We had no choice in the present recession. But there was a saying, and I'd only ever heard it said by other women, that books were not edible.

It was an overload of duties, I thought, sometimes self-imposed. And the expectation of subordination bothered me most. How could I defer to a man whose naked buttocks I'd seen? touched? Obey him without choking on my humility, like a fish bone down my throat. Then whoever plucked it out would say, "Look. It's her humility. She choked on it. Now she's dead." This may have been my redemption, since my husband needed a wife he could at least pity. Later that night, he called me aside to say, "Why did you have to say that in front of my brothers?"

"Well, why can't you ever get them drinks for once?" I answered, "Why can't you go to the kitchen? What will happen if you go? Will a snake bite your leg?"

He did not speak to me for two weeks and I contemplated leaving him for that alone—he could at least have remembered his age, even though I deliberately bumped him and poked my tongue behind his back. But no one I knew had left a man because he sulked, and I wanted a family, and I'd seen how Niyi grieved for his. I knew him down to his breath in the mornings. When we were not quarreling, I liked to watch him writhing to one whiskey-voiced woman or the other, like the one he called Sarah Vaughn. I could not tell one scat from another, but she said just about everything I wasn't prepared to, using ten words:

Sometimes I love you
Sometimes I hate you
But when I hate you
It's becau-au-au-ause I love you

I got pregnant and shortly after had a miscarriage. I was at work when I felt the first contraction. By the time I arrived home, it was too late, I'd passed a blood clot. I cried until I soaked my pillow. Nothing is worse than the loss of a child, even if the child is never born. If a child dies in your care, people understand that you feel responsible. If a child dies within you, they immediately try to absolve you: it is God's way, there is to be no mourning. You never understand why.

I got pregnant again. This time, the baby grew out of my womb and could have killed me had it not been for one smart doctor. I had to have an emergency operation. The doctor told us my chances of having a child after that were reduced. "But keep trying," he said. A year later, we still were. Niyi's relations began to press, "Is everything all right?" They looked at my stomach before looking at my face. Some scolded me outright. "What are you waiting for?" My mother invited me to her vigils; my father offered to send me overseas to see other doctors. I asked why they harassed women this way. We were greater than our wombs, greater than the sum of our body parts. "For God's sake," my father said solemnly. "I'm not playing here."

Sheri suggested I tried fertility drugs. Didn't I know? Everyone was taking them. They were? I asked. "Of course," she said. "One year and nothing is happening? Six months, even."

"Six months!"

She began to name a few women. One who didn't have children. Another who had two, but both were girls. One who did it to trap a man. Where did they get the drugs? I asked. "Doctors," she said. Infertility specialists? I asked. Um, she didn't know, but they treated infertility all the same. Where did the doctors find these drugs? Black market, she said.

Multiple births, laparoscopies, drug cycles. She gave me details, asked if I wanted a telephone number. I only wanted to be left alone, I said. At least my husband had a son of his own. No one could accuse me of ending the Franco lineage.

I never once doubted that I would become a mother. Not once. I just didn't know when it would happen, and I didn't want to be a guinea pig until then. Two more years passed and Niyi and I were still trying. I finally agreed to see a gynecologist who specialized in infertility. He made the appointment and I stuffed my head under a pillow as he spoke to the receptionist, but he refused to use a fake name. "It's not a VD clinic," he said. We arrived and saw the number of cars parked on the street, walked in and I saw that some of the women were as old as my mother. I was one of the few with a man by her side. The doctor arrived an hour later, chin up, stomach forward. He grunted in response to our greetings. I ducked a little, like the other women. Didn't even know why.

In no time at all Niyi and I began to quarrel about the fertility regime. It made us feel like mating animals. Every minor event sparked an accusation, and I shrunk to the size of my womb. I stared at other people's children imagining their soft, sticky hands in mine, worked myself into false morning sickness and cursed out loud when my periods started. Sometimes they didn't, then I'd be buying pregnancy kits and peeing on the sticks. Soon I convinced myself that it was a punishment; something I'd done, said. I remembered the story of Obatala who once caused women on earth to be barren. I made apologies to her. I remembered also, how I'd opened my mouth once too often and thought that if I said another bad word, had another bad thought, I would remain childless, so I swallowed my voice for penitence.

That was how my thirties found me, in a silent state. I felt as though I'd been running in midair for years. The realization had me laughing at myself. "Satisfied?" I asked myself aloud one morning. When I could hear no answer, I said, "Good."

I would not delve below that; I preferred to balance my home on a pin than to delve.

The day I got pregnant, I sat on my bathroom floor crying over a stick. "Thank you, God," I said. "God bless you, God." I waddled to Niyi, already imagining my stomach big, fell into his arms and his eyes filled with tears.

"I thought we were finished," he said.

"We are never finished," I said.

We promised not to argue. This time, my doctor suggested bed rest for three months and I resigned from work because my managing director, the one with the bad sinuses—who once told me I was segsy, very segsy indeed and he would have chazed me but for my sginny legs—he had been looking for an opportunity to move his cousin into my position and refused to approve my request for time off. "Mizeez Frango," he said. "Our bank can ill-afford an abzent company segretary." The bank couldn't afford my lawsuit either, I threatened. This wasn't a position to let go without a fight. I considered suing for a while, then I gave up on the idea because really, I wanted to be a mother more than I wanted to be a company secretary. I knew this when I would vomit into a toilet bowl in the mornings, look at myself in the mirror and smile. I accepted my father's offer for partnership instead.

During my first month of bed rest, I read local newspapers I normally didn't have time to read while I was working. Mostly I read stories in less reputable papers: *Woman gives birth to snake. Hundreds flock to vision of Mary on latrine window.* I also read the obituary pages: *Rest in peace, O glorious mother and wife, died after a brief illness. In loving memory of our father.* Here was the real news, I thought. The obituaries were always timely and uncensored, expect when they were hiding deaths from AIDS.

Sometimes I read editorials about the future of democracy. It was over a year since June 12, 1993, the day on which our country's third transition to democratic rule was to begin. That ended two weeks later when the military government annulled our general election and stepped down. A transitional government lasted three months before there was another coup. This new regime partially restored our constitution; placed a ban on political parties, disbanded both houses of senate and representatives, then instituted something called a constitutional conference to bring about democratic reform.

Not since the Civil War had we seen such resentment. Reading the papers, it was clear that some Yorubas blamed their one-time Civil War allies, the Hausas. But those who were less blind-sided looked to the small but powerful clique of Hausas who sanctioned our nation's military rulers. The majority of people simply cared about their vote. Pro-democracy groups immediately called for a boycott of the constitutional conference. There were organized protests, which ended in gunfire, and deaths. The National Democratic Coalition was formed. Then the winner of the general elections was arrested and detained when he declared himself president. Oil workers went on strike and this led to petrol shortages. The Nigerian Bar Association, teachers' unions, university students, joined the protest. Our military government responded by breaking up meetings, detaining students, lawyers, union leaders, ex-politicians, journalists, any individuals they considered enemies of the state. They passed new decrees to strengthen the old ones, seized passports, imposed exit visas on journalists.

Of the pro-democracy activists campaigning, one was my father's long time client, Peter Mukoro, now editor of a magazine called the *Oracle*. Over the years, Mukoro had gained a wide readership because of the kind of reports he pursued: exposes on drug rings, oil spills in the Niger Delta, cults and gangs in universities, religious wars in the north, Nigerian prostitution rings in Italy. When Peter Mukoro wrote people read, so, quite often, Peter Mukoro was in trouble. He'd had several law suits against him. My father continued to represent him. Some they lost, some they won, others were pending. Peter Mukoro's house was burgled twice, although nothing was stolen. Then there was that mysterious fire in his office. After that Mukoro declared himself "the unluckiest man in town" because, even by Lagos standards, his life was "well and truly jinxed." When he ran an editorial calling for the reinstatement of the general election results he himself was detained. His magazine went underground. He was not formally charged, but his detention was made lawful under Decree Two, that decade-old military decree under which persons suspected of acts prejudicial to state security could be detained without charge. Even I felt sorry for him. At least he wasn't one of those journalists who were government critics until they landed a government job. Mukoro would not work for a state-owned paper. He would not work for anyone with military affiliations.

My father immediately published a statement in the *Oracle*, saying he would continue to petition until Peter Mukoro's release. I worried about my father's safety, given that under Decree Two, any arrest could be justified. These days, my father was going as far as to ask the military regime to step down. I, too, wanted them out, especially after they gunned down protesters during the political unrest. But there were thousands of other ways people were being killed in my country: unseen pot-holes in the roads, fake malaria medicine. People died because they couldn't afford an intravenous drip. People died because they drank contaminated water. People died from hardship: no water-no light, we called it in Lagos. People died because they got up one morning and realized they were ghettoized, impoverished. 1995 had me giving thanks for the calamities my family and friends had escaped, not protesting against the government. I was almost two months pregnant and thought, like many Nigerians, that my priorities were best kept at home. What I hoped for, at the beginning of the year, was to have my baby in peace.

⌐°

Niyi handed the latest copy of the *Oracle* to me.

"Read," he said.

"What is it?" I asked.

"Your old man," he said. "He's talking again."

He left our bedroom and I read the article. My father had given an interview about recent detentions under Decree Two. He was advocating a national strike. I tossed the magazine on the bed and put some clothes on. Niyi was surprised to see me coming downstairs. He lowered his paper. "You're going out?"

"Yes. To see my father. Talk some sense into his head."

"What about bed rest?"

"I'm tired of resting."

He pulled his paper up by the shoulders. "Be careful."

I assured him that I would. As I drove to my father's house, I breathed in deeply. It was a while since I'd been out on my own and during the harmattan season the evenings were cooler. I could see no more than half a mile down the road because of the dusty haze. It shrouded leaves and blew into people's eyes. Children were still calling conjunctivitis Apollo.

I should have planned what to say to my father. I found him indoors. He no longer sat outside on the veranda in the evenings, not since thieves visited the house next door by boat.

"What are you doing out of bed?" he asked.

"I'm not ill," I said.

Over the years, his hair had whitened considerably and the pupils of his eyes had faded to a grayish-brown. His shoulders were also hunched, as though he were permanently grumbling.

"You're supposed to be lying down," he said.

I held the magazine up. "I read your interview, Daddy."

"Yes?" he said.

"You're calling for a national strike?"

"Yes."

"Suppose they pick you up?"

"Did you come here to visit or to fight?"

"I came to visit."

"Then you are welcome to stay. If not, find your way."

He picked up a cushion and gave it several blows before sitting. I settled in his sofa. I could smell the wood wax on the floor. Every month my father's floor was polished. He would never give that up. On his walls there were three fake crystal clocks that looked like corporate gifts. They had all stopped working: quarter to five, half past seven, twenty-seven after two. My father could not be bothered to replace a battery and he surrounded himself with clutter: unhung paintings, lava lamps so old they were fashionable again. The spot where my piano had stood was now a storage space for records and gifts. From the mess he would pull out a bottle of port, a biography, a Nat King Cole or Ebenezer Obey record.

"How shall I beg you?" I asked.

"For what?"

I didn't have to explain. "You know."

He waved his arm. "So I mustn't talk? An... an innocent man is locked up and I mustn't say anything?"

"Just be careful is what I'm saying."

"Of what should I be careful? Walking outside? Driving down the road? Sleeping in my house? Eating food? Breathing air."

"Don't make fun."

"But you are funny, all of you, Fatai and the rest. 'Don't do this. Don't do that.' Maybe I'm the one who's ruining this country."

"We're worried."

"Well, worry yourself with your own worries. Let me worry about mine."

He was not ready to listen.

"Do you have any idea," he said, in his normal voice. "Do you have any? One hundred million of us, less than ten thousand of them and they want to run this country... " he searched for words. "Like it's a club that belongs to them?"

"Yes, I do."

"Then they tell us." He patted his chest. "Tell us that we can't talk? We can't say anything, or we'll be locked up? Fatai, too, comes here this morning telling me that I should be careful. I'm disappointed in him. He is afraid like a woman."

He noticed my expression and pulled a face to imitate mine.

"What? How come your husband let you out of the house anyway?"

I laughed. "I'm not a pet."

"You modern wives."

"I see everything is a joke to you."

He folded his arms. "Humor is all I have left."

His anger was not controlled. He was like a child with a bloodied nose, waiting for the opportunity to strike back.

"So," I said. "Nothing I say will change your mind."

"Nothing," he said.

"Activists end up in prison."

"I'm not a criminal. Why should I fear going to prison? Anyway who's calling me an activist? Have you seen me join any pro-democracy group?"

"No."

"Do you see me running off to Amnesty International?"

"No," I said.

"Well then. I'm only doing my job, as I've always done. My business is to look after other people's legal business and I can't let this go, not as easily as they want. They must free Peter Mukoro. He has done nothing wrong."

There were lawyers who made their names in the struggle for human rights. My father was not one of them. He never cared for groups and had lost favor with some in the bar association, because of his association with Peter Mukoro, who had called senior advocates "senile advocates."

"Now, look at the situation we're in," he was saying.

"Older people afraid to talk, the young ones too busy chasing money. Doesn't the situation bother the youth at all?"

"It does."

"Yet none of you are saying anything?"

"We worry about no money, no light. You form your groups and they beat you up and throw tear gas in your face. What can we do?"

"Women," he grumbled. "We never hear from them."

"Women? What do you want to hear from women for?"

"Where are they? More than half our population."

"We have our own problems."

"Like what? More important than this? People ridiculing our constitution?"

I began to count on my fingers. "No husband, bad husband, husband's girlfriend, husband's mother. Human rights were never an issue till the rights of men were threatened. There's nothing in our constitution for kindness at home. And even if the army goes, we still have our men to answer to. So, what is it you want women to say?"

"Two separate issues," he said.

"Oh yes," I said. "Bring on the women when the enemy is the state. Never when the enemy is at home."

My father eyed me. Whenever I stood on my soap box, he wanted me to step down. When he stood on his, it wasn't a soap box; it was a foundation of truth. I smiled to annoy him more.

"Is everything all right at home?" he asked.

"Shouldn't it be?"

He glanced down at the sofa. I knew he was looking for his reading glasses. He simulated fist fighting movements. "You're too... "

"Me?" I said. "I'm not like that anymore."

"Since when?"

"I'm a peaceful woman now."

"You gave me *wahala*."

So did you, I was tempted to say.

"Just don't end up in prison," I said. "I won't come to visit you there."

He found his glasses between cushions. "I don't need your warnings."

"You're not getting any younger."

He slipped his glasses on. "If you came here to remind me of my age, then you've wasted your time and mine, because I know how old I am."

"I've told you, Daddy."

"I heard."

"You'll be sorry."

"I can't be sorrier than I am now."

We spent the rest of the evening discussing our plans to work together after my baby was born. "Practice some real law," he said. "Instead of taking minutes or whatever you do in a bank."

My father was suspicious of my generation of bankers, with their MBAs and other qualifications. Slick and rude, he said about them. They wanted to run before they could walk. Time had proven him right. Some managing directors I knew had been locked up under a failed bank decree.

On my way home, I passed Lagos Lagoon. I could smell animal cadaver, sweet fruit, and burnt tires. Smells were still strong though I'd managed to overcome nausea. A motorcycle growled past. The rider hunched over his handle bars. The woman behind him held on to his waist. Her white scarf blew like a shrunken peace mast. I touched the hard mound below my navel and imagined my child curled up. Nervous bubbles popped inside me. It had to be good this time. I could not bear another mishap.

I drove past a row of houses with balconies and green pyramid-shaped roofs. They were concealed behind high walls, above which coconut and oil palms grew. In this part of the suburbs, there were a few free-ed schools. Uniformed children walked around in shin-high socks. They came from nearby slums. From here, only their El-Shaddai and Celestial church spirals were visible. I stopped by the vigilante gates of our housing estate. Street hawkers sat behind wooden stalls in a small market along the front wall. They were Fulani people from the North. The men wore white skull caps and the women wrapped chiffon scarves around their heads. Their stalls were illuminated by kerosene lanterns. They talked loud in their language, and together they sounded like mourners ululating. Recognizing my car, the guards pushed the gates open. "Evening, madam," one of them said.

"Evening," I said.

Our estate, Sunrise, was on the outskirts of Ikoyi, though people here claimed to live in Old Ikoyi. They were mostly young couples in well paid vocations. Plot one was a banker and his wife was a lawyer. Plot two was also in banking and his wife sold Tupperware and baby clothes. No one knew what Plot three did, but he wore good suits and his wife Busola ran a Montessori school from a prettily painted shed in their yard. We lived in Plot four and so on. Our roads had no names.

There was a lot of gossip in Sunrise: who was earning less than they claimed, whose husband was shooting blanks, who owed money to the bank. Whenever we came together, the women sat on one side, and the men sat on another. The men chatted mostly about cars and money; the women about food prices, pediatric medications, work politics, and Disney toys. The advertising world may not have been aware of us, but we bought the merchandise they targeted at others nevertheless, whenever they arrived in our country and when we traveled overseas. We bought to hoard, to show off, to compensate for affairs, for ourselves. We bought what someone else had bought, what everyone else was buying. Consumerism was someone else's embarrassment; we felt privileged to be able to be part of a circle that didn't change much, except with fashion.

Some would say we were New Money. But I thought all

money in our country was new, because our money itself, the naira and kobo, was new, devaluing fast and never able to make our country work anyway. So what car was anyone driving? To where, with craters in our streets? What watch was anyone wearing, when a thief could grab it from their wrist? What stereo system; what shoe; what dress. And no matter how much money a person had, they would find their bowel movements floating around in their toilet bowl, not going anywhere, because there was no water to flush our toilets.

We were living in enviable conditions, pre-fabricated homes worth millions of naira, because the naira was worth so little. We were in the middle of another water shortage. On Tuesdays a tanker brought water which we stored in large drums, for flushing toilets and bathing; for cooking and cleaning teeth. Drinking water we bought by the carton. Sometimes we found sediment in it. We drank it anyway. There were no phone lines on the estate, so we carried mobile phones. Power cuts turned our meat rotten and our pots black with kerosene soot, unless we owned electricity generators. At night, mosquitoes bored holes into our legs and every year there was another death to mourn: someone shot in the head by armed robbers; someone crushed by a wayward lorry; someone suddenly taken ill with malaria, typhoid, they-don't-know.

Afterward we congregated in the deceased's house to mourn. Mostly we came together to celebrate: birthdays, holidays, and christenings. My one rule, whenever I was hosting, was that the women should not serve their husbands food. That always brought a reaction, from them: "Well, you always speak your mind." From their husbands: "Niyi, your wife is a bad influence!" From Niyi himself: "I can't stop her. She's the boss in this house."

I contributed to that illusion, claiming to be free from domesticity, and encouraged our friends to argue about division of home duties. The men would profess how they took charge of manly tasks like programming videos, opening jars, and changing light bulbs. The women would respond with such halfhearted attempts to appear indignant, that I would be tempted to take the men's side, just to stimulate a real discussion. But I wouldn't. Then from the opposing side would come an accusation so venomous, I'd almost fall backward from the force of it: feminist.

Was I? If a woman sneezed in my country, someone would call her a feminist. I'd never looked up the word before, but was there one word to describe how I felt from one day to the next? And should there be? I'd seen the metamorphosis of women, how age slowed their walks, stilled their expressions, softened their voices, distorted what came out of their mouths. They hid their discontent so that other women wouldn't deprive them of it. By the time they came of age, millions of personalities were channeled into about three prototypes: strong and silent, chatterbox but cheerful, weak and kindhearted. All the rest were known as horrible women. I wanted to tell everyone, "I! Am! Not! Satisfied with these options!" I was ready to tear every notion they had about women, like one of those little dogs with trousers in their teeth. They would not let go until there was nothing but shreds, and I would not let go until I was heard. Sometimes it felt like I was fighting annihilation. But surely it was in the interest of self-preservation to fight what felt like annihilation? If a person swiped a fly and the fly flew higher, would the fly become a flyist?

I thought not, but that was before, in my twenties. These days, if ever I carried on that way, on my soapbox, it felt like an exercise in vanity, childish, in the scheme of dangerous living.

The houses in our estate lined up along the road trying to assume separate identities within cramped· spaces. One had a palm tree in its front yard, another a thatched gazebo. Several had wide satellite dishes perched on their roofs to capture CNN and other television programs from overseas. All had barred windows and doors. My headlights beamed on our iron gates. Beyond them was our house with a bush of violet bougainvillea. Our gate man unlocked the gates. His prayer beads hung from his wrist. I realized I must have disturbed his prayer. Soon it would be the Moslem fasting period, Ramadan.

"*Sanu*, madam," he said.

"*Sanu, mallam*," I replied in the only Hausa I knew.

~

"How now," Niyi said.

He aimed his remote at the stereo system. The sound of trumpets jarred my ears like Lagos traffic. He was trigger happy, my husband, and listening to jazz again.

I dropped my car keys in my bag. "How now," I answered.

"What did he say?"

"You know him. He won't listen."

He pressed a button to lower the volume. "He has to this time."

"I'm nervous about working with him again. The man doesn't compromise."

Niyi was busy nodding. He liked the women who sang or the men who played. Never the other way around. What if a woman could blow a horn? I would ask. "Can't," he would say. What if a man could sing? "Can't," he would answer. He dreamed of buying a Bang and Olufsen by the year 2000 so he could hear each instrument clearly. I only hoped he would be satisfied with our Hitachi in the year 2000. Our savings were geared toward replacing our electricity generator since it had broken down.

I slipped my shoes off, and turned down an offending light. Our living room was furnished with black leather seats and glass tables that matched the keyboards of my old piano, on top of which were financial magazines. The room reminded me of a chess game. We had plants, but no flowers, because flowers flopped within a day. I owned nothing except a framed print of gazelles from the Ivory Coast and an ebony stool on which Niyi rested his feet.

I turned the music down and walked toward him. Niyi placed both feet on the floor and his knees jumped up. There was never enough space for him wherever he was.

"You have giant in your genes," I said, placing my hand on his head.

"Good. I will pass it on."

"What if she's a girl?"

"She will be a giant, too."

"Who will go out with a giant?"

"She won't go out with anyone. But she will be beautiful and she will look like me."

"Big feet and a skinny nose?"

He turned his profile. "It's my foreign roots."

My laugh rushed through my nostrils. "Foreign my ass."

Niyi liked to remind me of his Brazilian ancestry the way an English person might say he were part French or part something else. He grouped himself with black people who had a direct claim to foreignness: West Indians and African-Americans. I kept reminding him that there wasn't a single black soul who hadn't descended from Africa. His ancestors would be rejoicing. They were back where they belonged.

I watched him in amusement. With his bald head he could pass for one of those American basketball players, but a girl who looked like him would be finished in a place where men loved small shapely women.

"Did you get through to London?" I asked.

He nodded. "That crazy woman answered the phone."

"What did she say?"

"He's doing it for attention."

I shrugged. "Well, teenagers. Maybe he is. It's tempting to play your parents against each other."

He'd been trying to reach his ex-wife all day. Their son was refusing to call his stepfather "Daddy." His mother was insisting that he did, and Niyi was saying the boy never should have in the first place.

"Stupid woman," he said. "I stayed with him while she was working. She practically kidnapped him. Now she's complaining he's difficult. I told her if she can't live with him, she should send him back here. He can go to school here. I didn't go to school abroad and there is nothing wrong with me. She didn't go to school abroad and there is nothing wrong with... "

He realized he was about to pay her a compliment. He straightened his leg so fast he kicked my wooden stool over.

"Foolish woman. If she were here, she'd be begging me to see him."

"Don't break my one piece of furniture in the world," I said, smiling.

Two disgruntled men, one evening. The truth was that neither was used to feeling powerless. Niyi would not rise above anger for his son's sake. He preferred to disrupt the boy's life and bring him home twelve years later.

"She doesn't know how lucky she is," he muttered.

"For the sake of this child," I said. "Forget how much you hate her. It doesn't matter who is right or wrong."

"Why do people say that rubbish?"

"Okay, it does matter. But try to make your own phone calls from now on. I didn't escape my parent's home to become a mediator in mine."

He did not answer and I thought I'd been insensitive.

"At least," I said. "Give me a chance to despise her, or to be jealous of her or whatever it is I'm meant to feel for her, instead of acting as your counselor. Look at you, you worry, you phone, you write, you listen. There is no better father than you. It is her loss. No one can come between father and son. Have you eaten?"

I asked only to appease him.

"Nothing to eat."

"Did you bother to look?"

"It's stale. I don't want any of it."

I waved my free hand regally. "Hm. Maybe someday I can sit with my feet up and grumble about food. I will have to go shopping this weekend, since my lord and master is not pleased with the food I have at home."

"Woman, what d'you think I paid your dowry for?"

"Good sex," I said, strutting away. Since I was out of bed and running all over the place, he said, I would have to perform my wifely duties and give him some.

"You speak like that to the mother of your child?"

"Your breasts have grown."

"So have yours, and you'll be lucky if I ever have sex with you, after all the sex I've had to make this baby."

"What about my needs?"

"Handle your needs yourself," I said.

I had married a man I could fall asleep with, not a man who would keep me up at night. I told him, the only way he could make me scream in bed was if he farted under the covers. I would repay him my dowry one day, have a ceremony and return his gifts. I went to bed dreaming of market shopping instead. Sex my ass.

⁓

"Give me another tray," Sheri said.

The market woman passed her a tray without looking. She neatened the tray of tomatoes Sheri had rejected.

"How much?" Sheri asked, surveying the new tray.

"Twenty," the woman said. Her hair was bound in thread and her cheeks were lined with facial marks.

"You must be joking," Sheri said. "Twenty naira for this?

Fifteen only."

"Fifteen is not possible," the woman said.

She swatted flies from her ware. The sun bore holes in my back. I dipped under the corrugated-roofed shack and swiped flies from my braids. The flies swarmed the marketplace, perching on mangoes, between spinach leaves and lumps of cow flesh. Later they would settle in the gutters and clotted drains and fly back to the food. I had left Sheri to bargain. She was better at it. Sometimes the women misjudged her and she immediately told them, "Do you know where I'm coming from?" One woman answered, "It's not my fault. I've never seen a white person who acts like you."

In the same shack, another woman sat behind a wooden table laden with okras, cherry peppers, and purple onions. She had tattoos on her arms. A naked infant sat on a mat by her feet. Spit drooled from his lips and yellow mucus dangled from his nostrils. His eyes were lined with kohl.

"How much is this?" Sheri asked.

"Ten naira," the first woman said.

"Ten naira!" Sheri exclaimed.

It was a game. I watched the second woman. She lifted the infant and sucked on his nose. The infant gasped as the woman spat his mucus into the gutter. The first woman wrapped our tomatoes in the obituary pages of a newspaper.

The marketplace was a series of meddlesome shacks like this, built row by row for a square mile. They were topped with rusty iron sheets and had no light except for sunlight. A small tarred road, wide enough to contain a car, separated the east side from the west. Cars and bicycles were not allowed in. They were parked by the entrance, near a high rubbish dump that smelled of rotten vegetables. Shoppers filled the road, walking in one direction like pilgrims. Above their voices I heard car horns from nearby streets.

At the butchers, I preferred to stand in the hot sun, rather than stand near the stall. I couldn't bear the smell of cow's intestines. From a distance I watched Sheri giving the butcher instructions. He laughed and hacked through a cow's flank with a machete. Soon he paused to wipe sweat from his forehead using the neckline of his bloody undershirt.

Sheri returned to me. She had lost some weight and it showed in her face.

"You're skinny," I said.

"You think?" she said.

"Are you fasting?"

"It's my gym. I never fast."

I fanned my face with my hands. The sun seemed to be melting me.

"Everyone is going to the gym these days," I murmured.

I'd heard men say that women like Sheri didn't age well: they wrinkled early like white women. It was the end of a narration that began when they first called her yellow banana, and not more sensible, I thought. Thankfully, Sheri never relied on their praises, so she didn't pay attention to the insults. She was not one of those retired beauties who walked into a room and immediately began to assess who was better looking than her before she could relax.

We stopped by a fabric stall across the road, then loaded our bags into the trunk of my car and drove out of the market. By the exit, a hawker sat before a gutter selling roasted corn.

"Want some?" Sheri asked.

"No," I said.

I couldn't risk getting typhoid. She stuck her head out of her window and beckoned to the hawker. I drove into the usual Saturday traffic. Cars formed two lanes on the narrow one way street. Some stopped by hawkers on the side walk, causing temporary bottlenecks. Shoppers scurried between them. Before us, a yellow bus staggered along. A conductor hung from its door, shouting the destination of the bus: "C.M.S! C.M.S!"

C.M.S. was the Christian Missionary Society school near

the Marina. Only two people came out of the bus and about ten hurried in. There would be no space for them inside. Lagos was getting more crowded. Most of it resembled a shantytown. Buildings were never repainted, roads never repaired. My car began to make grinding noises. Ten years old, it gave me a reason to visit my mechanics almost every month, though in its present state, it could fetch three times the amount it had cost. I still used it for what I called my rugged trips. These days, people budgeted for cars the way other people in the world budgeted for houses.

"Niyi is talking about a party for my birthday," I said.

"He is?" Sheri said.

"Yes. I've told him it has to be small and only people I want. Will you cater for us?"

"Yes."

"Discount?" I asked.

She finished her corn and threw it out of the window. I would get my discount, she would help cook, but Sheri would not come to my party. She was not interested in people who would gossip about her or boast about their possessions. And the people I knew, Sunrise people in particular, scrutinized her whenever they saw her, for unhappiness, sexual frustration, and other deprivations, so that they could say her life was well and truly ruined. Sheri, who had always divided people into those who would die for her and those who were jealous and wished for her downfall, ignored them in a way that made me want to jump up and cheer, so desperate was I to rise above our social circle.

Niyi wasn't home when we arrived. "He's at work," I explained as we separated our bags in the trunk of my car.

"Your husband works too hard," she said.

"Everyone works too hard," I said. "I'm about to work too hard."

"You must take care of your husband's home," she teased like an old woman.

"Ah, I hate it," I said, peering into a package. "And for a man who won't even take a glass to the kitchen."

"He won't?"

"I've never seen anything like it before. The man behaves as if I'm his personal servant."

I told her about our living room, how I found beer glasses left overnight, stuck to our glass side tables, stuck so hard I could lift the tables. In our bedroom, I picked up his clothes as he dropped them. In our bathroom, I found stains around our toilet rim, which looked like beer stains, except they were misdirected urine.

"You must have known before," she said.

"I haven't been at home this long before."

"It's his mother, I'm sure."

"The statute of limitations has run out."

"Show him sense, *jo*."

I handed her a bag and sighed. "These are peaceful times."

Our conversation was as idle as conversation was in Sunrise. We separated parcels of vegetables wrapped up in censured news. Sheri recounted how she'd seen a man knocked down by a car the week before. The driver who hit the man drove off for fear of being mobbed. Four passersby carried the man off the street, one for each limb. They were shouting and the man himself was shouting, from pain.

"Please," I said. "Why are you telling me this?"

She sighed. "How-for-do?"

I ruffled through more bags.

"You must break fast with us this year," she said.

"You don't fast, Sheri."

Allah had to forgive her. She couldn't go an hour without eating.

"Still come. We're going to cook."

"I'll be there."

She sighed. "Hopefully we will have light that day. All this talk about democracy. I will take any kind of government that can guarantee me electricity."

"Any government?"

"A communist regime even."

I knew she wasn't serious.

"Only electricity?"

"That's all I need," she said.

"Some people don't have power lines."

"Who? People in the villages? What do they care? They light their fire at night, the smoke drives mosquitoes away. At night they quench the fire and sleep. Clean water to drink is their problem, not electricity. Guinea worm? Can wipe out a whole village."

Two children rode past my gates on bicycles. They pedaled fast and screamed.

"We're still better off," I said.

Sheri handed a package to me. "I wonder."

I arched my back. "Have to be grateful, Sheri, for everything. Good health, food, roof over your head and bed to lie in."

"With a grumpy husband," she said.

"At least he's not one of those running around."

"No other woman will have him."

"You see? What more do I want? And at least I have a car of my own. Even if it hardly works, I can still get up and go. Someone can't knock me dead on the streets. Hm-hm. What are we going to do? 1995 and we still have no decent ambulance service in this city. No decent hospitals. No nothing."

"I'd rather die on the streets than go to any hospital here."

"I'm telling you. If you get a headache, start packing your bags."

"If you can afford to get out," she said.

"If not," I said. "Start digging your grave."

"Gather your family for last rites. And oh, don't forget, on your tombstone: 'The wicked have done their worst'."

We laughed. Sheri handed me a tight obituary parcel.

"But people suffer," I said.

"Country hard," she said.

Our bags were finally separated.

"My sister," I said, tapping her back.

"Greet Papa Franco," she said.

~~⌒

Sheri called Niyi "Papa Franco" behind his back, because he was always scowling, she said. I couldn't tell her he scowled because he thought she was bad company. "Used-up like dry wood. That's why no one will have her." I would get hoarse arguing with him. Sheri didn't need any man. I was there when she walked out on her lousy brigadier. "Yeah, yeah, she has a past," he would say.

"Has a future," I would say.

When she took money from her brigadier, she wore evening shoes in the day, bought any ornament with flower motifs and didn't even stay abroad too long because it was too cold. Now that she earned her own, she watched it like an accountant. I envied her freedom to spend as she wanted; her business knowledge, which came from bargaining. Sheri said she didn't have a head for books, but she saw a clear margin before a deal started. It was true that she rarely read anything, not even the gossip magazines I sometimes read. She said they were written by idiots, for idiots, especially on the rare occasions she was captured by the handful of tiresome Lagos paparazzi at the society events she catered for. "A half caste and a half" one recently called her. Sheri only ever read the romantic novels she'd been reading since she was a child. She used leather bookmarks to save a page. It took her several weeks to get through one, and yet trading came naturally to her. A wake, a wedding, a christening, she was there, haggling and keeping her client's dirty secrets as a doctor would. Within a year of starting her business, she was able to buy herself one of those second-hand cars people called "fairly used" and after two years, she was able to rent a place of her own.

No, Sheri didn't love men or money. What she loved was food. She was always munching on fried meat, corn, biscuits. She could suck down a dozen banana ice pops and her eyes grew wide as food entered her mouth. I was there when her worship of food began and it didn't make sense because I was learning to starve myself through my tribulations. Now I knew some women did exactly the opposite. Sheri had gained weight from it over the years: English size 16, American 14, Bakare household size 2, she would say. But she had shed most of her childhood spirit, and I often remembered the time she laughed till hibiscus toppled out of her afro. It still brought tears of laughter to my eyes.

She was my oldest friend, my closest friend. We had been absent friends, sometimes uncertain friends, but so were most sisters and she was the nearest I'd come to having one in this place where families were over-extended.

In my kitchen I removed the food and stored the plastic bags away for future use. My kitchen was equipped for preparing local meals, nothing else. There was a wooden table, two collapsible iron chairs, an electric cooker, a kerosene stove, in case of power cuts, a deep freeze large enough to store a human body, and a refrigerator with an ice maker I'd never used. In my store room, I kept plastic bags, which were hard to find in Lagos, kegs of palm oil, groundnut oil, sacks of rice, yam flour, dried ground cassava, a bundle of dusty yams and sticky plantains. On the shelves there were piles of dishes, Tupperware, enormous steel pots, plastic bowls and calabash quarters for scooping. The door leading to our back yard was barred. The windows were also barred and covered in green mosquito netting. The netting garroted mosquitoes, trapped dust and raindrops. Sometimes, if the wind blew, I smelled all three and sneezed.

Pierre, my present house boy, began to wash the vegetables in a bowl of water. He was a burly boy about nineteen years old from the neighboring Republic of Benin. French was the only language we had in common. He spoke it fluently with an African accent, and I vaguely remembered it from secondary school. Pierre couldn't cook. He cleaned, fetched water, and thought himself a lady's man in between. Unable to get the French accent quite right, we pronounced his name, "P'yeh" and Niyi said it served him right anyway, because Pierre was lazy and never around when you needed him.

I needed Pierre to place the okras on the chopping board. "*Ici*," I said pointing. "Over there, please."

Pierre raised a brow. "*La bas*, madame?"

"My friend," I said. "You know exactly what I mean."

It was my fault for attempting to speak French to him. Now he raised his eyebrows twenty times a day.

"I beg, put am for there," I said.

Our continent was a tower of Babel, Africans speaking colonial languages: French, English, Portuguese, and their own indigenous languages. Most house help in Lagos came from outside Lagos; from the provinces and from neighboring African countries. If we didn't share a language, we communicated in Pidgin English. Night watchmen, washmen, cooks and gardeners. The general help we called house boys and house girls. It was not our way to feel guilty and adopt polite terms. If they had friends over, we worried that they might steal. If they looked too hard at our possessions, we called them greedy, and whenever they fought we were amused. We used separate cups from them, sent them to wash their hands and allowed our children to boss them around. They helped with daily chores in exchange for food, lodgings, and a stipend. Most were of working age, barely educated, but some were of pensionable age, and many were children. In good homes, they could be treated like distant cousins; in bad homes, they could be deprived of food, or beaten. I had more than once suggested that they were a few degrees separated from blacks in old Mississippi and in apartheid South Africa. "But that's racism," someone would say.

Pierre began to chop the okras. I ground the peppers and onions. Later he washed and cut the meat and I braised it. We worked together, cutting and frying, stirring and pouring. My eyes streamed from pepper and palm oil fumes settled in my braids. Steam scalded my wrists. Three hours later, we'd finished four separate stews. Pierre scooped them into Tupperware containers and placed them in the freezer. I handed him a plate of lunch and decided to have a wash.

Behind our bathroom door, we kept a drum of water. I filled my bathing bucket and topped it up with boiling water from a kettle. But for the bump under my belly button, my body was the same as it was before I became pregnant. I'd finished soaping myself when the electricity generator next door began to roar. "Shit," I said, remembering the food in my freezer. Quickly, I scooped bowls of water from the bucket over my body and came out. Niyi was coming upstairs.

"No light?"

I stamped my foot. "It's just gone."

"Why are you getting angry?"

He looked just as irritated.

"I've been cooking all day."

"You cooked?" he said. "Good."

He headed downstairs as I grumbled on: "Someone ought to call a national conference for diet reform. The day an African woman can prepare a sandwich for a meal, that will be the day. I've spent the whole day in that bloody kitchen... "

"Where is this food?" Niyi interrupted.

I leaned over the banister. "When you are truly hungry, those bearings of yours, you'll find them very quickly."

He knew how serious I was. If he liked, he could try me, then he would see the African version of the girl from *The Exorcist*.

~⌒

Electricity returned before midnight and my food was saved. Niyi said it would taste so much better if only I learned to cook with a sweeter disposition. "The trouble is," he said, before we went to sleep. "You are not a domesticated woman. You just don't have that... that loving quality."

He pinched his fingers together as if I couldn't grasp the essence of what he was saying. He was lying on my side of the bed. I pushed him over.

"I'm very loving," I said. "What do you know? Move, I beg."

I was a scrotum shrinker, he said. And I would not stop until he was as small as raisins.

"What are you doing for my womanhood?" I said, spreading my arms. "Am I not a temple of the miracle of creation?"

Every picture, advert, film, I'd seen of pregnant women, showed their partners rubbing their feet and such. I didn't ask that of him; never once expected him to tell me I was beautiful. It was a miracle, I had to admit, that he never complained when I came to him in the mornings with a puffy face after vomiting. That was his best loving ever; his best romance from the time I met him.

We held hands to sleep. The next morning, we shared the Sunday papers, though Niyi remained downstairs while I stayed upstairs reading what he handed to me from time to time. I was flicking through a government-owned newspaper. A group of army wives had founded a program for women in a village. They promised to train the village women to eradicate infant dehydration. On the front page, an army wife was put on display with a gold choker around her neck. I turned the page and a man had thrown acid into his lover's face. On the next page was a charity drive for a boy's eye. He had a rare type of cancer and would have to be flown overseas for treatment. Underneath, a bank director in tortoiseshell glasses was discussing capital investments. A page later there was an update on our peace-keeping troops in Liberia, directly over the story of a child hawker who had been molested. She had had difficulty expressing herself during the court case, and untied her wrapper to show where the man had touched her. The magistrate ordered her to cover up. The caption read, "No Need for Nakedness."

Niyi walked in. I held the paper up.

"Have you read this?" I asked.

His mouth was open. My heartbeat quickened.

"What?" I asked.

"They've arrested him," he said.

"Who?"

"Your father."

I grabbed my head. "No."

"This morning. Baba came to tell us. He's downstairs."

I scrambled out of bed. "I told him. I told him."

I ran down the stairs. Baba was in the dining room. His eyes were yellow and watery. A fly settled on his white lash and he brushed it away with a trembling hand. "I was doing my work," he said. "Doing my work, as usual. A car came. Two men. I let them in. I went back to work and time passed. Then your father called me to the veranda. 'Tell Enitan,' he said. 'Tell her they've taken me. And let Fatai know, too.' Then he got in the car and they drove off."

"Policemen?" I asked.

"Like policemen."

"What were they wearing?" Niyi asked.

Baba ran his heavily veined hands down his chest. "Em, something. Something... "

I was trying to recall the last detainees I'd read about.

Ten-millimeter names, blurred photographs, newspaper phantoms. People invited for questioning by state security. They disappeared for months.

The rest of the morning, we tried to telephone our friends and family. I couldn't recall any telephone numbers and Niyi had to find my address book. My mother still didn't have a phone. We called Uncle Fatai, then Niyi's parents. Later, Sheri. By lunch time, they were in my home.

They eased into my father's disappearance the way people in Lagos eased into death. At first there were the usual questions. How? What? When? Then resignation set in. My father-in-law began to talk about other people who had been detained: journalists, lawyers, a trade union leader. "I know him well," he said.

He talked slow and savored his pronouncements. Whenever my father-in-law spoke, he lifted his chin as though he was making a great contribution to humanity, and kept his eyes shut, confident that when he reopened them, someone would still be listening. My mother-in-law always was.

Niyi walked over to me. "We should get them lunch at this rate."

"Lunch?" I said, as if he'd suggested horse manure.

"Yes. They've been here all morning."

I began to gabble. "Pierre has his day off and I don't know if... "

"I'll help," Sheri said.

Niyi tapped my shoulder. "Thanks."

I was getting lunch, Niyi told everyone. I stood up and my mother-in-law stood up, too, but I waved her down. "No ma, Sheri will help."

My voice was unnaturally high. It was nothing but a minstrel show, I thought, except no one bothered to watch as Sheri and I headed for the kitchen.

Inside, I slammed an empty pot on a stove. "What am I doing here?"

"Where do I start?" Sheri asked.

"My father is detained and I'm cooking?"

"People have to eat."

She looked around as though searching for a weapon. I imagined us finding plates and breaking them; both of us banging pots.

Sheri beckoned. "Be quick. Where do you keep your cutlery?"

I did not eat. My father-in-law and Uncle Fatai sat on opposite ends of the table. Their chewing inspired me to imagine new ways of throttling.

"I want to talk to you," Uncle Fatai said, as I collected his plate. Niyi and his father inclined their heads like world leaders at a conference. On a whim I asked, "Can you help?" Niyi looked up like a world leader confronted by his mistress at a conference.

My father-in-law cut in, "The young lady can do that."

Sheri stood up hurriedly and nudged me through the kitchen door.

"I want them out of my house," I whispered. "Out."

Sheri touched my shoulder. "They won't stay here forever. Go and speak to your uncle. Go on."

She pushed me through the door. I joined Uncle Fatai at the dining table. He pressed his hands together and his knuckles dimpled. "Who will mind your father's business now?"

"I will," I said.

"Good," he said, covering his mouth.

"Is there anything we can do meanwhile?" I asked.

He rubbed his mouth with a napkin. "Nothing."

"Shouldn't we try to look for him?"

"Where?" he asked.

"I mean, can't we contact someone?"

He noticed my expression and leaned forward. "Enitan, your father knew what he was doing. You understand? I'm sorry but this is the result of a decision he made on his own. When he started saying things, I told him, be careful. All we can do now is to make sure his practice continues. You understand?"

The aftermath of his belch hung between us.

I nodded. "Yes, Uncle."

"By the grace of God he will be out soon," he said. "Now, I will need a bowl of water."

His knuckles dimpled as he held his hands up.

"To wash my hands," he explained.

I couldn't sleep. All that my father had told me about prisons came to haunt me: the darkness, damp, smell of stale urine, cockroaches, rats. There were no beds, no ventilation, too many inmates. Some were arrested for being out on designated sanitation days; others belonged in mental institutions, cemeteries.

At dawn I forced myself to imagine my father. I could see only his hands and they were covered in sores. "Look where I've landed myself," he said. "We sleep in each other's urine in this place. The food is like the bottom of a pit latrine. I have not touched it."

"Your hands," I said.

He lifted them. "It's going around. Itches like mad, but they won't get a doctor. They keep sending the prison matron in. That woman doesn't know what she's doing, but the men love to see her."

"Men?"

"I'm not alone. I have friends. An armed robber, Tunji Rambo, he calls himself. Too much heroin in his blood and too many American movies in his head. He says that he's no more a murderer than a general here who fought in the Civil War and killed Biafrans, than a government minister who embezzled money set aside for healthcare. He says that God will judge them the same."

"Death is death."

"The general used to be a fat man, now he's thinner than you. They put him here for plotting a coup. He could have been our president. Today, he's just another criminal. He prays with the librarian. That one we call Professor. The man has more knowledge than an encyclopedia. He was picked up for wandering on a sanitation day. Now, he prostrates to rats and calls them gods."

"Please don't end up like him."

⌒

Monday morning I went to my father's office. Peace began to cry as soon as I mentioned the word detention. I felt dishonest standing there and promising them that their jobs were secure. What did I know about running my father's business? I'd worked in a bank since national service. My experience in estate transactions was limited and outdated.

"We will just have to continue until he returns," I concluded.

As they dispersed, I gritted my teeth. My father's table was littered with papers. He never shared what he called sensitive information and his filing system was held in his head. Mr. Israel, the driver, walked in. "Someone to see you," he said.

"Who?"

"Journalist."

"Tell him to come in."

The journalist was a woman. Her smile was so benign, she could pass for a Bible seller.

"Grace Ameh is my name," she said, extending her hand. "*Oracle* magazine. We interviewed your father last week. We had another appointment this morning and I hope you won't mind speaking to us."

She had a gap between her front teeth and her gums were the color of dark chocolate.

"What about?" I asked.

"His detention. The driver, Mr. Israel, told me. I'm sorry to hear about it."

"It happened only yesterday."

I wasn't ready to confer with a stranger. She was thick-set from her waist up. Her dress had a butterfly collar and she carried a wrinkled brown leather portfolio. She removed a notepad from the portfolio.

"All I need is a few words from you, about what transpired."

There was a drum roll in my chest. "Is it safe?"

"To talk? It's never safe to talk."

"I haven't done this before."

"You're afraid?" she asked, glancing up.

"I'm not sure you should be here."

She waited for me to recant my statement. I was first to look away. Grace Ameh was older, self-assured, and her disapproval was beginning to cloud up my father's office. She had an intense stare.

"That's a pity," she said. "I would have thought you would be willing."

"Last week," I said, "my father spoke to your magazine. Today he's in detention."

"Perhaps we started off on the wrong foot... "

"I don't know who 'we' are."

"Please, let me tell you what we're facing." Her voice remained calm, but her lips moved with a hint of impatience. "Our reporters are being dragged in every week, no explanation given. They're kept in detention for weeks, questioned, or they are left alone, which I'm told is worse. Nobody speaks to you in detention, you see. If you don't cooperate, they transfer you to a prison somewhere else, packed with inmates. Sick inmates. You may end up with pneumonia, tuberculosis, and you won't get proper medical attention. Jaundice, diarrhea— food in Nigerian prisons isn't very good. I'm sorry. I'm sorry. Am I upsetting you?"

"No." But she was.

"I want you to understand why people must hear from you. This can happen to anyone these days. Your father had no reason to be involved. He could easily have been silent, too. So, are you willing to talk to us?"

I nodded reluctantly. "Yes."

"Thank you."

Her hand whisked shorthand notes over her notepad.

"My father is not a criminal," I began.

⤳

I visited my mother in the afternoon. Uncle Fatai had promised to tell her about my father, but I could not be sure. When I arrived, her neighbor's daughter was sitting on top of their gate. A girl of about seven with dusty knees, she was wearing a white T-shirt with the words "Kiss me I'm sexy" across her chest. She had top teeth missing. Behind her, two of her brothers played a loud game of table tennis; a third brother twisted his mouth in time to the ball. The girl looked liable to fall.

"Kiss me I'm sexy," I called out. "Be careful sitting up there."

Her brothers collapsed over the tennis table laughing.

"My name is not Kith me I'm Thexy," she said.

"Sorry," I said. "What is your name?"

"Shalewa."

"Shalewa, you have to get off."

She scowled. Her brothers were dancing around the tennis table singing: "Kith me I'm Thexy!" One of them tugged the corners of his mouth. I felt bad for causing them to laugh at her.

Shalewa hopped down from the gate. Her spindly legs trembled. "Bombastic elemenths!" she said.

My mother opened her door. "Those children are so rowdy."

"They're your tenant's children?"

"I've had enough of them. But at least their mother is pleasant."

Over the years my mother's expressions had become one: sad that a good thing had happened, happy that a bad thing had. I could smell menthol. As usual we spoke in Yoruba.

"Fatai told me about your father," she said.

"Yes," I said.

"It happened yesterday, he said."

"That's all we know."

"So," she said. "What is being done now?"

"We can't do anything. We don't know where he is. A journalist I spoke to this morning thinks he might be in one of the state security offices."

I pressed my temples. My mother watched my hand movements.

"What journalist is this?"

"From *Oracle* magazine."

"You spoke to him?"

"Her. I gave a statement."

"You're giving statements now? You're giving statements to the press?"

"It was nothing."

"Not in your condition," she said, clapping her hand. "Not for your father, either. God forgive me, but that man caused his own problems. Fatai told me. He said he warned him. He said you too warned him. Now what are you going to do? Get yourself locked up, too?"

"I'm not going to get locked up."

"How would you know? The government has been doing what they want for years. What do you do? You leave them to it, that's what you do. Does your husband know about this?"

I didn't answer. My mother coughed and rubbed her chest.

"Be careful," she said. "This kind of thing is not a woman's place. Not in this country. You don't need me to tell you."

"I want my father out of there."

"What if they take you, too? You're pregnant, are you not? Do you or do you not want this child?"

"Yes."

"So," she said. "You've waited this long. None of this. You hear me? Not for a man who... who showed me nothing but wickedness."

I was about to answer when a girl about twelve years old came out of her kitchen. She had robust cheeks and a pointed chin. The hem line of her dress was askew.

"Ah, Sumbo," my mother said. "You've finished in there?"

"Yes, ma," she said.

"Good. You can go now."

The girl disappeared. Her bare feet scraped the floor like sandpaper. There were cracks in her soles.

"You've got a new girl?" I asked.

"Yes," my mother said. "But I need to train her. She never washes her hands."

"How old is she?" I asked.

"Her parents say she's fourteen."

"She's young," I said.

My mother shrugged. "The parents brought her here themselves. Look at her fat cheeks. She's better off. She eats well and sends money home. She's not too young. She's probably seen more than you have. Turn your back on that one and she'll be dipping her hand in your bag or following men."

"Mummy."

"It's true."

I saw her regularly, out of choice. I was capable of deciding my answers and silences. If I remembered the bad times, I stopped myself from thinking about them. Whenever I felt overly criticized, I knew the feeling would pass. I did not retaliate in any way, and I wasn't analyzing how or why I had this reserve. To me, it was like picking fresh fruit from a basket of mostly rotten ones.

"Your new tenant," I said. "Is she paying her rent on time?"

"No problem with that."

"That's good," I said.

My mother looked me up and down. "You look tired, Enitan. If I were you I would go home and rest."

"I'm not that tired."

"Still go. You need your rest. Let Uncle Fatai run around for your father, if he pleases. After all, they are friends."

"Uncle Fatai is busy."

"Then it is too bad. Too bad for your father. He can't keep a family together, now he wants to save his country?"

My father couldn't even save himself, she said. She began to recount their past battles. I did not say a word. When I left her house, Shalewa next door was drawing circles in the ground with a stone. Her tongue jutted out from the side of her mouth. Her brothers were nowhere to be found. They must have abandoned her, I thought.

～⌒つ

"What time did she come?" Niyi asked.

I was sitting at the top of the stairs, watching him through the banister. He placed his briefcase down.

"About ten," I said.

"Ameh," he said.

"Grace," I said.

"She must be from Benue with a name like that."

I wrapped my dressing gown tighter. What did I care where in Nigeria Grace Ameh was from? Our air-conditioner was too cold. I was shivering.

"Where are they publishing from now?" he asked. "Didn't they close down?"

"They're underground."

"What does that mean?"

"I don't know."

"How do you know she was one of their reporters?"

"She said she was."

"Did you ask her for an ID?"

"No."

"Suppose she was state security?"

"She wasn't."

"How do you know?"

"She wasn't."

He would know if he'd seen Grace Ameh himself, and why was he questioning me? He threw his keys on the dining table.

"You should have called me first."

"I didn't have time."

"What if they pick you up, after the article is published?"

"They won't pick me up. Not for this."

"She took advantage of you. I'm sorry. The woman knew exactly what she was doing. They will do anything to get publicity, these journalists."

"What publicity?"

"Asking you to give a statement, jeopardizing your safety at a time like this. You shouldn't even be going to work."

"I shouldn't be entertaining people, either, but I did."

"What?"

"Yesterday," I said.

"I'm serious," he said.

"So am I," I said.

There was no precedent for this, nothing to draw on. We went to the authorities to report crimes. Where could we go when the authorities committed one? It was as if I'd opened a Bible and found the pages blank.

"Call me next time," he said.

～૭

Wednesday morning I paid my father's staff their salaries: Dagogo and Alabi first, and then the others. I was surprised— Dagogo and Alabi's paychecks were a fraction of what I had earned at the bank. I'd heard them joke before about eating two meals a day, about substituting beans for meat. It was the principle of "at least" on which people persevered in Lagos: at least they had food in their stomachs, at least they had a roof over their heads, at least they were alive. People said there was no middle class in a country like ours, only an elite and the masses. But there was a middle class, and all that separated us was a birthright—a ridiculous name for a right, because there wasn't a person dead or alive who hadn't been born at some point. We were a step-down society compared to those by which we would be defined. The Nigerian elite were middle class people. Few had the sort of wealth that would rank them amongst the world's elite, and they were usually government or ex-government officials. The middle class, in turn, were working-class people, and the masses were poor. They begged for work and money, served, envied and despised the elite, which actually made the elite feel more special and important. But for Lagos, always reminding me where exactly in the world I was living, I grew up feeling like I was part of landed gentry in England. That uppity.

I left the office that afternoon with my head down. How could my father be paying his senior associates so little? I asked Niyi at home.

"It is the cost of living that's high," he said.

"Don't employers have a responsibility to compensate?"

He rubbed his eyes. "It's the northerners. They are responsible for the problems in this country. They've completely ruined the economy."

"Beggars on the streets, our night watchman, he's from the north. The hawkers by our gates, they are from the north. I don't see them ruining any economy."

Niyi wasn't convinced. "Who heads our government?

Northerners. Who heads the army? Northerners. One southerner wants to be president and they lock him up. Come to my office. The whole place is full of them. Barely educated and yet they want to bring in more of their people. They've completely ruined the economy. How can men like Dagogo and Alabi survive?"

Increasingly, I was hearing this type of sentiment; north versus south. We had the oil fields, the northerners had enjoyed the revenues for so long. Some southerners were calling for a secession. I thought it could end in the kind of bloodshed we'd seen in the Civil War. From his little experience with office politics, Niyi had come to distrust northerners, and Moslems, if he cared to admit. He called them Allahu-Akhbars. His chairman, a northerner and Moslem man, had little education. He bypassed senior staff for another northerner. Round them up and shoot them, Niyi would say. "Then what?" I once asked. "No one will ever bother you at work again? No official will ever dip their hands in our treasury and deposit half the proceeds with the Swiss? Please."

I imagined my father in a prison cell again. Under a detention order he would have no right to know the reason for detention, no access to his family, or legal counsel. The detention orders were renewable and the law courts could not review them. Some detainees were released after a few weeks; others were held for longer periods and no one could decipher why. It didn't matter to me if a northerner or southerner was responsible for this.

"Do you think they will let him out soon?"

"Yes," Niyi said.

"What if they try to kill him?"

"They won't," he said.

I moved closer toward him and rested my head on his shoulder.

"If anything happens to him," I said, "someone will pay."

He stretched and the leather sofa grunted.

"You're tired?" I asked.

"Exhausted," he said.

He put his arm around me. Family rifts, losses, absences. The stress brought us closer. Niyi's heartbeat was almost in time with mine when our air-conditioner shuddered to a halt. We were sitting in the dark.

"Jesus," he said.

We heard the electricity generator start next door. He went to the kitchen and brought back a huge battery-operated lamp. I watched the stark light, like the moon. Outside crickets chattered. I began to feel hot.

"It really is more than north and south," I said. "We have all played a part in this mess, not caring enough about other people, how they live. It comes back to you. Right back. Look at us in this house, paying Pierre pittance... "

"Pierre's lazy," he said. "I work harder than him."

"Living in quarters... "

"He's lucky to have a roof over his head."

"Bad ventilation and a pit latrine? Would you like to live there?"

A mosquito buzzed around my ear. I swiped it away. If I wouldn't like to live in our quarters, why would anyone else?

Niyi turned to me. "Why are we talking about Pierre? Don't we have enough problems of our own?"

The skin on my belly was beginning to feel moist. Niyi once said I was guilty of thinking too hard. I told him that it wasn't possible, even with a million thoughts, colliding with each other, my thoughts wouldn't be enough. I envied his ability to be certain.

He placed his hands behind his head. "You live in this country, you suffer in some way. Some more than others, but that's life." He noticed my expression. "That's life, o-girl, unless you want Pierre to come and sleep in our bed tonight?"

I resented him, enough to shift inches away from him, then I shifted back again because none of it was his fault anyway. If people didn't care, it was because there was so much to care about. After a while the suffering could seem like sabotage; salt in your sweet pap. A beggar's face at a car window could appear spiteful, a house boy's clumsiness deliberate. Sheer wickedness could begin with the need for self-protection.

We slept without electricity that night. The next day, Niyi returned from work with two potted plants. "Anything?" he asked.

"Nothing," I said.

He shook his head. "Man... "

I walked toward where he stood in the veranda. We'd had the same conversation several times during the day: Anything? Nothing.

"All day," I said. "People were calling the office. I had nothing to tell them. I mean, if you detain someone, shouldn't you at least tell their relations?"

I held his hand as it came over my shoulder. What little garden we had, Niyi was responsible for: the golden torches I liked, the spider lilies he liked. He bought them from a nearby nursery and performed tricks with them: cutting up the leaves and replanting them, halving a plant to make two. I'd even found him polishing the leaves of a rubber plant. These new plants were pinkish-white and waxy. I couldn't remember what they were called.

"You love this house so much you bring her flowers every week," I said.

He rolled his shoulder. "Hm."

"You strained something?" I asked.

"It will go," he said.

"You should have asked Pierre to help."

"What, I'm not a slave driver today?"

I'd been looking forward to seeing him. What I wanted was to share every thought I had during the day.

"No one is calling you a slave driver. I'm just saying,

maybe we can't see things the same way. Not anymore."

I expected an answer, instead he began to punch the air with his free hand.

"How was work?" I asked.

"Same. Akin called, just before I left."

My mind was drifting. Between phone calls at work, I was thinking that the one person I could ask for advice was the one who needed help. My father. There was no one else.

"He and a group of other guys," Niyi was saying. "They are starting a firm. Stock-brokers. They are looking for people who want to join. It seems like a good idea, I mean, privatization is bound to happen soon. Can you imagine? If it means we can have an electricity system that works in this country, a telephone system that works... you're not listening." He tugged my chin.

"Sorry," I said. "I was thinking."

"Yes?"

"All day I've been thinking. So many things. Decree Two. You remember when they first passed it? You remember? I didn't care then, and I called myself a lawyer. Now... " I waved my arm around. "Now, we don't have a safe country. Not even to have a thought."

"So?"

"So, this is the result, can't you see? Nothing, nothing will get better if we don't do something. That is what I was thinking."

His hand dropped. "Something like... "

I stepped back. "It is blood money if they privatize. I wouldn't join a firm like that. What is it? These military bastards are always on to something: Indigenization decree, Structural Adjustment Program, Operation Feed the Nation, War Against Indiscipline, National Conference for Democratic Reform. Now, privatization. I'm sick of it. Their damn initiatives. Someone gets rich and people continue to drop dead. What, are we to rejoice because a group of generals and their friends are about to buy up what the public owns in the first place? Let them privatize if they want. They can't deceive the people anymore."

I could have been bragging about an old boyfriend the way Niyi was looking at me. He worried more about the loss of financial power than any other. But I was not interested in the profit ventures of my father's captors; not even if it meant a career change for him.

"I take responsibility for what I have done," he said. "Only for what I have done."

"And what we have not done?" I asked.

I was hoping he would tell me I was right.

"At some point," he said, "We have to let it go."

Letting it go. My father, backdoor house boys and house girls, child hawkers, beggars. We saw their faces every day and we were not stirred. There was a feeling that if people were at a disadvantage, it was because they somehow deserved it. They were poor, illiterate, they were radical, subversive, and they were not us.

How did we live comfortably under a dictatorship? The truth was that, we in places like Sunrise, if we never spoke out, were free as we could possibly be, complaining about our rubbish rotten country, and crazy armed robbers, and inflation. The authorities said hush and we hushed; they came with their sirens and we cleared off the streets; they beat someone and we looked the other way; they detained a relation and we hoped for the best. If our prayers were answered, the only place we suffered a dictatorship was in our pockets.

I should have reached the end of my self-examination, but I didn't until Friday morning. I arrived late to work. It was a few minutes past eleven. Everyone was present in the office, except for Mrs. Kazeem who was normally late. I was in my father's office when his phone rang. I thought she was a client. "This is Grace Ameh," she said.

"Yes?"

"I have news. About your father. Please, don't say anymore."

She would not give details. I scribbled her address down.

"Is he... how is he?" I asked.

"Come to my house," she said.

I telephoned Niyi's office as soon as I had a dial tone.

"It's me," I said. "That journalist, Grace Ameh, has heard from my father. I'm going to her house."

"When?"

"Now."

There was silence.

"Hello?" I said, impatiently.

"You think you should?"

"Yes," I said.

Again, silence.

"Okay, but be careful."

"I will."

As though I had any control.

"And call me afterward."

"Don't worry."

They made me nervous, the way close families made me nervous. They talked loud to each other and walked around in disarray. Behind us was a shelf stashed with books. Grace Ameh was by my side on a sofa. She was a wife and mother now. Her hair was in four chunky plaits, and she had the habit of scratching her bra strap as she spoke. Her husband dragged his flip-flops across the room. He was wearing faded blue shorts and his white undershirt clung to his belly. Their daughter, a girl of about fourteen or fifteen, watched her brother who sat before a computer. He looked a couple of years older.

This was Grace Ameh's study, she explained as she escorted me upstairs, but it was where her family had been coming to escape from the people who were dropping by since her release from detention. The room, with one fluorescent light, gave the appearance of a store room. The rest of their house was too spacious for a family of four, and under-furnished. They'd either rented or inherited the property. This part of Lagos had residential buildings abandoned in various phases of completion and during the day armed robbers ambushed residents as they drove through their gates. At the top of their street there was a Viligante barrier.

"Joe," Grace Ameh said to her husband.

"Grace," he answered without looking at her.

"If any more reporters show up, tell them no more interviews."

He picked up a newspaper from her desk and walked out.

"I suppose I was talking to myself," she whispered.

His head popped back in. "My wife writes. She doesn't get royalties, instead she gets locked up. You see my trouble?"

"Joe," she warned.

"I too suppose, that it could be worse for me. I could be cuckolded."

"Joe!"

"I'm going," he said.

She turned to me. "Don't mind him. He thinks he's married to a renegade. Now."

"Mummy," her daughter interrupted. "Isn't '*Nkosi sikelel' iAfrika*' God bless Africa in Swahili?"

"Swa?"

"Hili," her daughter said.

"No, it isn't."

"I told you," her son said.

Her daughter looked angry. "What is it, if it's not Swahili?"

Grace Ameh sighed. "Xhosa, Zulu. Why are you asking me? *Na wa*, can't you children take pity on me? Why are you here anyway? You know this is my quiet room."

"Sorry," her daughter said.

"Both of you," Grace Ameh said. "Go downstairs, in the name of God, before I lose my head."

As if by cue, they disappeared. Their legs were too long for their bodies and they had the same teenage slouch.

"I can't wait until they graduate," Grace Ameh said. "Now. I was at Shangisha last night, State Security Service headquarters. I was coming back from a conference in South Africa. They read one of my manuscripts and said I was in possession of seditious material. I asked how my work of fiction can be seditious. They took me to Shangisha to explain why I made mention of a military coup in a work of fiction. I begged them. What else was I to do with philistines? I was not going to stay in that place. I asked them to take pity on me, left with the names of some of the people they had in there. They said your father was there, but he has been transferred. No one knows where."

"You didn't see him?"

"No."

"Should I go there?"

"To Shangisha?" She shook her head. "Don't do any such thing, my dear. These days if they can't find you, they take your family. What will they do with you if you present yourself? They don't interrogate prisoners in detention; they torture them. Nail pulling, ice baths. If you're one of the lucky ones, they will throw you in a cell and leave you on your own. Mosquitoes? Plenty. Food? Unbearable. Grown men cry inside there. They cry like babies and run away from the country to avoid it. I told you, I begged them on my knees."

I pinched my mouth. She had become a blur.

"At least you know he is alive," she said. "This is better than nothing, isn't it?"

I couldn't tell.

"Dry your tears. You have to be strong."

"Yes," I managed to say as she rubbed my shoulder.

⁓

"She sounds strange to me," Niyi said.

He had listened to my experience at Grace Amehs' house as though it were a party he missed. I thought he sounded resentful.

"She wasn't," I said.

"What does she write anyway?"

"She writes for the *Oracle*."

"I've never heard of her before."

"Well," I said. "She writes."

We were sitting on the floor in the living room. He winced as he struggled to his feet. Sometimes his knee joints gave him trouble.

"She's brave though," he said.

"Yes. She was begging them and thinking of a way to outsmart them."

His stomach groaned loud enough for me to hear.

"Man," he said. "I'm hungry... "

He had that dazed expression, as if he expected food to appear magically. I ignored him and dragged my forefinger around the carpet.

"I have to tell the people at my father's office about this."

"I wouldn't do that."

"Why not?"

"The last thing you want is to tell anyone about this."

"Why?"

"It is not safe."

I stood, supporting myself with the chair and walked toward him.

"Whose safety are you worried about?"

He raised his hand. "We'll talk about this later."

"When?"

"Later."

He was near the kitchen door. I hurried there and blocked his way. "You know I hate for you to walk away."

He reached for the handle and I placed my own hand over his.

"Talk to me now," I said.

He laughed. "Out of my way."

"No," I said. "What do you want in there anyway? When have you ever entered a kitchen before?"

"I'm a hungry man."

"You're always hungry. Answer me."

"Okay!" he said. "Who the hell are these people?! They come to your office and you speak to them. They call you and you go. How do you know they won't get you into trouble?"

"Do you see me in any trouble here?"

"That is exactly what your father said. Now look where he is, and I'm surprised... "

"Surprised that what?"

"You are pregnant."

"I know."

"You've already had one miscarriage."

"I. Know."

"You don't seem to care."

I wagged my finger. "Not from you will I hear a thing like that."

"This has nothing to do with us!"

"Why didn't you say that before? That you didn't want to be involved."

"You. I don't want you involved."

"I am involved."

"Not yet," he said. "But the way you're going, you will be, and yes, I am scared, but I don't have to announce it before you're satisfied. Now please."

He made shooing movements with his hands.

"No," I said, jabbing him several times.

Niyi checked his torso as if it had sprung leaks. "Is something wrong with you?"

"Don't you dare speak to me like that."

His voice dropped. "Listen, I'm not used to this... this melodrama."

"Ah," I said. "Just because one person chose to live like a zombie in your family doesn't mean you didn't have problems of your own."

He put his fist against his mouth. "Step away from the door."

"No," I said.

"I won't tell you again," he said.

Niyi was as tall as the door. He moved closer and I stepped aside.

"Go," I said, as he walked through. "See if that solves anything. And when you've finished in there, why don't we buy our way through our problems as we always have?"

I heard him slam the refrigerator door. He marched back with a bag of frozen bread. "If you had any concept," he said, "any, of what it means to pray for money, like most people do in this country, you wouldn't be standing there making such a stupid statement."

I pointed at the kitchen door. "Isn't that why we spend half our lives inside there? Cooking this, cooking that, so that you can take charge, at a time like this?"

He was struggling with the knot in the bag. "Say what you like. You're heading straight for trouble and I'm not going to let you."

"Let?" I yelled.

"Yes," he said. "If you have no sense in your head, at least I do. What, I should walk to the presidential palace and ask them to release my wife's father? Should I? 'Please, sir. My wife's father is locked up. Please release him, sir.'"

"Have no electricity," I continued. "Buy a generator. No water, pay for a bore hole. Scared? Hire your safety. Need a real country to live in? Buy a flag. Stick it on your roof. Call it the republic of Franco."

"And while you're living here," he said, "don't even think of trying to ruin it for everybody by playing... "

"Playing what?" I shouted.

He ripped the bag apart.

"Fucking political activist," he said. "Or any of that shit."

He said nothing to me for the rest of that evening, and I moved into the spare room, vowing to stay there until he apologized. People like my father, did they come from a different place? Were they born that way? Ready to fight, tough enough to be imprisoned? I checked the doors and windows twice before going to bed. I fell asleep after midnight. When I woke up three hours later, my gums throbbed and my mouth tasted as if I'd been chewing on iron beads. Going downstairs to get a drink of water, I saw a strip of light under Niyi's door. No, I thought, this wasn't one of our house fights. I would give him time. He just hadn't accepted it yet. We were all under attack.

My memory liked to tell lies. Huge lies. Sometimes, I remembered my father standing tall, my mother cracking jokes. My memory could blank out all but one sensation: a sick feeling in my stomach, a smell, a taste, like the creamy sweetness of banana ice-pop in my mouth. Then there were times my memory became a third eye, watching from a distance. This was always how I remembered the conquering moments; the moments I transcended myself: my first free rotation on a bicycle, my first paddle without arm bands, first plunge into a pool.

My father was standing in the shallow end. I was on the very edge, swimsuit in my butt crack and nose streaming. I crouched like I was about to pee, then flopped in.

He grabbed me. "You see? It's not so bad."

I buried my face in his chest. The water had smacked me good and hard. My father had given me my first swimming lessons, though he wasn't a good swimmer himself. Half of it was a lesson in courage, he said.

I couldn't shift the feeling that I had failed him. I told my friends and family about Grace Ameh, and no one else. Uncle Fatai said we could do nothing but wait for his release.

I waited. In the silence of my home I waited, as harmattan season passed and the Moslem fasting period, Ramadan, approached. Those who could afford time and money began to look forward to the day of the new moon on which Moslems feasted. Niyi's silence continued as the mound in my belly grew. My thirty-fifth birthday came and went like any other day. I was relieved.

As soon as the February issue of the *Oracle* came out, I drove to nearby Falomo to buy a copy. As usual there was a traffic jam there. Traffic to and from Victoria Island converged in the same place, under the bridge at Falomo. On one side there was the Church of Assumption; on the other, the local council had built a line of concrete stalls by the police barracks. Mammy Market, it was called. The road was filled with potholes. The barracks looked like slum dwellings over the marketplace: dusty and gray from cauldron smoke, wooden slabs for windows, barefooted children. Hens.

This was suburbia. A vagrant woman scraped ash from a burnt pile, using a piece of cardboard. A man hawked small plastic bags filled with drinking water. Someone had hung four fake Persian rugs over a public wall, for sale; another displayed a set of children's tricycles on the sidewalk. A man walked by with a sewing machine on his shoulder, ready to fix a zip or tear. There wasn't a corner free from baskets and wooden stalls. A watchman performed ablution into a gutter, another peed by a wall that said *Post no Bill.*

While people moved slowly, they were not idle. They were skewering meat, pumping tires, hawking suitcases of fake gold watches. If no one would employ them, they would employ themselves. The State gave them nothing, not even what they paid for. Sometimes they were begging, and sometimes the beggars were children. A girl stood with a tray of coconut slices on one side of the street. Next to her, a boy carried a board: *Please help me. I am hungry.* Billboards told the story of trade: Kodak was keeping Africa smiling; Canon was setting new standards in office copying; Duracell lasted up to six times longer. Redeemed Church, rug cleaners, Alliance Français. A bank, vet services, a nursery of potted plants, *fresh salad sold here.* No pesticides or dyes so cucumbers were small and oranges were yellowish-green.

Initially, finding myself unexpectedly nervous, I couldn't read the article, but driving back home, I pulled into a private driveway to search for it. It was a three-inch column: "Sunny Taiwo's daughter speaks out." Grace Ameh recounted the events as I'd told her, and then finished with: "When asked to comment on her father's detention, she stated, 'My father is not a criminal.'"

I placed the magazine on the passenger seat and drove off. A few meters down the road there was a police checkpoint. Two policemen stood by rusty oil drums placed on either side of the road. Their rifles were hanging over their shoulders. One of them flagged me down and I came to a stop. He searched the interior of my car.

"Your lishense," he said.

I reached into my glove compartment. He flicked through

breathing heavily and handed it back.

"Insh-wurance?"

I passed my insurance certificate and he held it upside down.

"Sistah, why you stop like dat?" he asked, giving it back.

"Where?" I asked.

"Yonder."

He pointed down the road where I'd stopped.

"I was looking for something."

"What?"

"My glasses," I said.

He scratched his chin. "Is not allowed to stop like dat, Sistah. Is not allowed. You almost caused accident for dis side."

His eyes landed on my handbag under my legs. There wasn't a traffic sign on the road. I knew not to argue with the police. Give them money, or apologize. Move on.

"That is not true," I said, quietly. "There are no traffic signs, nothing to say I can't stop there."

"Eh," he shouted. "Who tol' you dat? Comot. Comot."

He banged on my car door. I got out of my car and stood before him. Across the road, his partner glanced at us and carried on watching traffic. The policeman screwed up his face attempting to look angry. "Sistah, you no fear? I can arrest you right now."

"What for?"

He snatched my arm and I snatched it back.

"I'm a pregnant woman. Be careful how you handle me."

His gaze dropped.

"Yes," I said. "I am."

His face creased into a wide grin. "Why you no talk before? You for enter labor small time."

I didn't answer.

"Begin go," he said waving me into my car. "Go on. You're very lucky today. Very, very lucky. It could have been another story."

His mouth hung like a hammock from his ears. The dead and the pregnant, I thought.

⁓

Niyi was sitting on the couch with his legs propped up on my ebony stool. As usual, he was listening to his noise. I heard a clarinet.

"How now," I said.

Drums.

"The article came out today. We have nothing to... "

Trumpets.

"Worry about."

The instruments clashed like a marketplace brawl. Niyi nodded in time to the bass. I placed the magazine on the dining room table and went upstairs.

The spare room seemed smaller. I imagined it was the same size as my father's cell. I drew the curtains and lay down. Slowly, I rubbed my belly, trying to picture my child inside, skin stretching, bones forming. My palms ached from being snubbed, but I was no longer alone.

My father appeared leaner in my imagination, with yellow eyes. I strained to see him. The rest of him was a shadow.

"I spoke to the *Oracle* about you," I said.

"You did?" he said.

"They are calling you a prisoner of conscience."

"They are."

"Do you think I was right to speak to them?"

"Do you think you were?"

"Yes."

"Nothing left to say then," he said. "Let your mind be at rest."

Downstairs I heard the thud of a bass. Outside I could hear children playing. There was a hush over my country. I heard that too, and in my frustration, it sounded like men learning how to be women.

In my first year of marriage, there was a hawker who sat by the vigilante gates of our estate. She was one of those Fulani people from the north. We never said a word to each other: I could understand her language no more than she could mine. But I would smile at her, she would smile at me, and that would suffice.

Fulani people, traditionally, were cattle herders, but those who lived in Lagos worked as stable hands, night watchmen, craftsmen, or as street hawkers. Lagos people would say they spread tuberculosis because they were always spitting. Their elite were the sort of people Niyi held responsible for the demise of our country, the power hawkers. They were Moslems, influenced by Arab culture, and wealthy. Sheri's brigadier was one of them.

This hawker sold confectionery out of a portable display box: Trebor mints, Bazooka Joe gum, Silk Cut cigarettes, local analgesics, and I would often find her crouched over her box, arranging the contents of her display, as if she were playing a solo chess game. Occasionally I stopped to buy something from her and I soon began to call her "my woman." She pressed her palms together whenever she smiled, and I thought she was truly graceful and enjoyed seeing her, the way a person might a beautiful tree, or a view.

Niyi asked if I was a lesbian, calling her that. I told him that I'd always wanted men, but women interested me. Still, one day, I came back from work and my woman was not there. I thought she might be preparing for prayers, or resting in the dilapidated building where she and others in her community squatted at night. I asked a gate man and he confirmed that she'd gone. I wondered where. I watched the other Fulani women. They were lighting kerosene lanterns for night time and perching them on their display boxes. I imagined a story about my woman. Her name would be Halima. She would be the wife of a stable hand. His name would be Azeez. One day Halima got tired of being stationary in Lagos. She left on foot, walked to Zaria up north, crossed the Sahara desert in her robes and chiffon wrap. During the day, the sun beat her head, but she never, ever died, and at night, her gold hoops made music with the wind.

～⌒

February began with the season of Ramadan and a petrol shortage. Sunrise Estate was full of angry residents, none of whom could leave their homes to go to work. The first day, we telephoned each other: What kind of country were we living in? How would we ever get out of our homes? By the second day, children were ecstatic. Two whole days and no school! The third day, and they were driving their parents crazy. Solutions began to emerge fast. A bank was sending a bus around. Someone knew an employee of an oil company with petrol to spare; another somebody knew somebody who knew somebody else who was selling petrol at black market rates.

The queues were three days long. A few petrol stations had opened. They were selling petrol from oil drums using nothing but funnels to get the petrol into car tanks. I stayed at home until the shortage was over. I doubted any of my father's staff would show up. Public transportation had not fully resumed and fares had quadrupled. I saved what little petrol I had for an emergency which never occurred.

Niyi went to work every day. His company driver came for him. Our home was ridiculous. He was carrying on his standoff and I'd retreated fully to the spare room. Silence had become noisy: doors clicking, curtains rolling, and at night, jazz and crickets. Sometimes I heard Niyi laughing on the phone. I wanted to tell him that a heavy plug had settled at the base of my womb. I wanted to tell him that I was finding it difficult to sleep on my belly at night. I wanted to talk to anyone about my father.

On the day of the Moslem festival, *Id-el-fitr*, I left home for the first time that month to break fast with the Bakares. The streets were crowded with vehicles and the heat was heavier than I was prepared for. Harmattan ended in Lagos and we expected something new, the way the rainy season left colors deeper and cleaner and shinier. It was always easy to see that a well-meaning season has passed after the rains. But after harmattan, all that remained was humid heat. Gutters dried up as if they couldn't remember why they started flowing. The dry season was nothing to look forward to in Lagos, and it lasted most of the year.

As I drove through their gates, I heard a ram bleating in the back yard of the Bakare's house. It had been tied to a mango tree for two weeks and would be slain for the *Sallah* feast. I parked, walked past the lunch time cafeteria and emerged in a cement square. Sheri and some of her family members stood around the square. They were watching a butcher untie the ram. Nearby, a bandy-legged butcher's aide waited with his hands on his hips. I headed straight for Sheri's stepmothers and curtseyed.

"My child, how are you?" Mama Gani said.

"Long time we haven't seen your face," Mama Kudi said.

I apologized. It was the petrol shortage. February had been a quiet month because of it.

"How's your husband?" Mama Gani asked. Her gold tooth flashed.

"He's fine," I said.

"And your mother?"

"She's well, thank you."

"Still nothing about your father?"

"Still nothing," I said.

She clapped her hands. "*Insha Allah*, nothing will happen to him, after the kindness he's shown us."

There wasn't a line on either of their faces, as though

they hadn't aged from the day I met them, but they were fatter, with the same lazy walks, high cheek bones, watery eyes, and chiffon scarves wrapped over their heads. Perceptions of beauty had changed over the years, between satellite and cable television and overseas travel, but not for women like these. They wanted to be fat, they enjoyed being fat and worried about foreign women who cried on television because they were fat.

Their husband had married the same woman twice, I thought, regardless of their characters. Mama Gani was the one who had ordered me to kneel before her when I was a girl: the wicked one, but nice. Her wickedness saved their family in the end. She was always disagreeable and confronted her dead husband's relations. She was the one who would fight on cue, Sheri said, remove her head tie to land a slap. Mama Kudi was younger and she spoke three languages: Yoruba, Hausa, English, and a little Italian for bargaining, but she hardly said a word. She was also the one with a boyfriend.

I wondered how they could live according to their traditional roles. I had wondered, also, how they could stay together without the man who had brought them together in the first place. Sheri once said that they rarely quarreled; that they took turns to sleep with her father without once coming to blows. In her uncle's house, the wives fought and tried to poison each other's children, but that was because the man himself was no good. "This one-man-one-wife business," she said. "If it's so wonderful, why are women so heartbroken?" "We don't break our own hearts," I reminded her.

Children of polygamous homes, this was their refrain, that civil marriages didn't work anyway. They boasted about their numerous relations, elevated their mothers to sainthood. "Pity your own self," they would tell me, "we are not unhappy with our family arrangement." They rarely confessed about domestic battles: who got more money from Daddy, which mummy had more sons, whose children performed better in school. I suspected they were embarrassed by their fathers, who had bigger sex than brains. But how successful were civil marriages meanwhile? Couples bound by legal certificates, confused by romantic love. So and so whose husband had an outside child; so and so who slept with her boss, because her husband was sleeping with his subordinate. If this was a country struggling with religious and government structures imposed on us, it was also a country struggling with foreign family structures. On our estate alone, there were affairs from day to day, and above it all, Niyi judging other people as only a jilted man could. It was sad to see women acting out like their fathers, because they were so determined not to be like their mothers; worse, to see women joining born-again churches, seeking refuge from their marriages as some mothers had.

Sheri's younger siblings greeted me as I walked across the cement square.

"Hello, Sister Enitan."

"Long time no see."

"*Barka de Sallah*, Sister Enitan."

I felt awkward smiling. I was about to respond when the ram slipped from the butcher's grip and charged forward. Sheri and I collided. The others fled. Within a moment, the butcher had grabbed the ram. His aide tackled the hind legs. The ram bleated louder and I shut my ears to drown out the noise.

"Are they about to kill it?" I asked.

"Yes," Sheri said.

"I can't watch," I said.

The aide wrestled the ram off the cement square and the butcher brought out a knife. He pulled the ram's head back and dragged his knife across its throat. Blood poured into the dark soil. The younger children shrieked and huddled closer. Sheri's stepmothers laughed.

"I hate this," I whispered.

It reminded me of the fowls Baba killed for my mother.

He beheaded them and allowed their bodies to run around headless until they dropped. It reminded me of Sheri being strapped down by two boys.

The ram lay dead on the floor and the butcher began to slit its belly.

"Let's go," I said, tugging Sheri's elbow.

We sat on the balcony overlooking the cement square. The butcher castrated the dead ram and placed its testicles next to it. They looked like hairy mangos.

"Not once have you fasted," I said. "Yet you celebrate *Sallah*. What kind of Moslem are you?"

"If I don't fast until I die, I will get to Heaven," she said, cheerfully.

"Are you sure? I hear none of you in this house will inherit the kingdom of God."

"Why not?" she scoffed.

I smiled. "It's what the Christians say."

A woman poked her head through the sliding door. She was bouncing a baby boy.

"Sister Sheri, sorry I'm late. It's the baby again."

There was a coin taped to the baby's belly button to tame his hernia.

"What happened?" Sheri asked.

"He hasn't gone for days," the woman said.

"You've given him orange juice?" Sheri asked.

"Yes," she said.

"Bring him here," Sheri said.

Sheri prodded the baby's belly. "You, you're not supposed to give your mother this much trouble."

"He's been so fussy," the woman said. "I haven't been able to leave his side."

Sheri handed the baby back to her. "He's all right."

The woman left, cuddling her baby.

"You're a pied piper," I said.

"Don't mind her, *jo*," Sheri said. "She's just pretending.

Every time it's the same with her, one excuse after the other. We can't get her to help with cooking."

"Who is she?"

"Gani's wife."

"Don't you have enough help downstairs?"

"Ehen? She knows how to eat, doesn't she?"

"Leave the woman alone," I said.

Our country was full of passive-aggressive wives like her, finding ways to challenge their in-laws.

Like her grandmother Alhaja, Sheri expected her brother's wives to run around for their family functions. Sheri's stepmothers expected the same. Through them, the spirit of Alhaja was alive, keeping the next generation of wives in check.

As Sheri read the article, I watched the proceedings on the cement square through the balcony railings. The ram's guts were displayed and the butcher and his aide were contemplating how to carve the body. Nearby, Sheri's stepmothers were supervising the women who had come to cook.

Sheri once said she was not interested in who held the power in our country, the military or the politicians. She had witnessed their corruption first hand, mixed with the underworld of people who got rich on their backs. She who slept with an important man to get her directorship. He who slept with the same important man and received a multi-million naira contract. It was enough to make me doubt we had any legitimate businesses in our country that were not somehow linked to corrupt or lustful government officials. But her stepmothers loathed the military, because they supported the wife of the man who would be president, Kudirat Abiola. Abiola was campaigning for her husband's release, and for a reinstatement of our general election results. She was a southerner, a Moslem, and a Yoruba woman, like them. They loved her, and my mother said of her, "Oh, she just wants to be First Lady," which was ironical to me, because Kudirat Abiola was in an openly polygamous marriage. 1994 had given us our greatest symbol of hope in post-colonial Africa with the inauguration of Nelson Mandela. Rwanda was our despair. Kudirat Abiola had become the symbol of the Africa I'd been at odds with since my return, a senior wife, fighting for her husband's political freedom.

"Well done," Sheri said, after she read the article.

If Sheri sympathized, she never showed it.

"How's work?" she asked.

"A mess," I said. "You should see. Papers all over the place. I will have to start sorting them soon."

"One day at a time," she said.

For a while, we watched the carving of the ram. The butcher skinned the ram and then cut the meat. His aide washed the blood away with boiling water.

"How was your birthday in the end?" Sheri asked.

"Quiet," I said.

"Papa Franco didn't do anything?"

"Doesn't even speak to me."

"Eh, why not?"

I tapped the magazine. "Over this. He didn't want me to talk to them. The man hasn't spoken to me for weeks because of it."

"Hey-hey, I think I would prefer a beating."

"I hate the silence."

"It is my friend," she said.

Most times, I could only guess what was going on in her mind. Sheri had become guarded about her personal life, as unmarried women our age were; as the long-term unemployed were about their job prospects.

I turned to her. "I mean, how can I decide what to do about my father from a kitchen? Come to think of it, how can I decide anything with a mini Idi Amin sitting right there in my home?"

She smiled. "Papa Franco? He's not that bad."

"Yes, he is. Sulking, sulking."

"If he frowns, just don't look at his face."

"I wouldn't be bothered with it, any of it, if I were on my own."

She shook her head. "It is not easy on your own. Men thinking you want them; women pitying you and not wanting you around their homes. Your own mother talking about you as if you have terminal cancer: Ah, Enitan, she's still with us. Ah, Enitan, we pray."

"Nothing can be worse than this, Sheri. We see each other in the morning and no hello even."

"Ignore the man."

"He is so childish."

"Don't let him affect you, or anyone else. The people in your house that day, do you think they knew, or cared, that you were angry?"

I patted my chest. "Asking me to make lunch."

"The day my father died, the people who came to give their condolences wanted to eat."

"What did you do?"

"My stepmothers cooked. Some people even asked for more." She laughed.

"I don't think it's funny, Sheri. We laugh and one day we will be laughing in our graves."

"Ignore the man. He can't do anything. And stop letting people upset you. It's not good for you or your baby."

I could have predicted her advice. Sheri once taught me a lesson when she knelt to greet her uncle who had tried to disinherit her family. "How could you?" I asked, sure that I couldn't muster a nod for him. "It's easier to walk around a rock," she said, "than to break it down, and you still get where you're going." I saw that in the past I'd been inclined to want to break rocks, stamping my feet and throwing tantrums when I couldn't. Acting without grace. So cynical was I about the core of strength an African woman was meant to possess, untouchable, impenetrable, because I didn't possess one myself.

The Bakares had not forgotten how to enjoy themselves. After lunch, I watched them do a line dance called the electric boogie. During the dance there was a power cut, which brought on more laughter: no electricity for the electric boogie.

Close families had affectations, I thought. In Niyi's family, they spoke hush-hush; in Sheri's family, they worried about food: Have you eaten? Why aren't you eating? Are you sure you don't want to eat? I thought it was best to say yes to whatever they handed me. They quarreled with people over food-related misdemeanors, like refusing to eat what they offered, or not eating enough. As they danced, I imagined them in the aftermath of a nuclear attack, no home or hair to speak of, still worrying about food.

Niyi was out when I arrived home, and a sneer met me at the front door. It poked my shoulder and prodded me upstairs, spread its ugly mouth across my bedroom wall. In the distance, I heard sounds of Lagos: car horns, motorcycles, street hawkers. From here, the noise sounded like tin cans colliding on hot asphalt. I sat on my bed. There was a fly perched on my mosquito netting. I couldn't tell if it was resting or trying to pass through. I faced the walls again. At one end, silence could defeat a person, a whole country even. At the other end, silence could be a shield, used as Sheri did. An attack and a defense, and yet people always said silence was peaceful.

My phone rang. It was Busola from next door, inviting me to dinner.

"We're having Bomb Alaska," she said.

I really couldn't, I said.

"I saw your husband at the club today. I couldn't believe it. I said, 'You? Here? Where's your best half?' He looked at me, as if to say, 'This girl, you're certifiable.' I know he hates me."

"He doesn't hate you."

"Oh, I know he doesn't like me."

"He doesn't... "

"Anyway he's one of the decent ones and he works hard, unlike some lazy buggers in this house. Come on, to cheer yup."

"I can't," I said.

Busola was someone I'd known from my student days in London. She socialized with a few Nigerians who drove Porsches to lectures and snorted cocaine for extra-curricular activities. They were called the High Socs, and Oppressors, and they were the envy of those who had time for such emotions after studying and socializing. I'd always thought her crowd was a little tragic: their cocaine habits, the inevitable drying out, which could mean they were in a clinic in Switzerland, or being exorcised by the whip of a juju man in their hometowns. Wasted brains, and the boys nearly always ended up beating their girlfriends.

"Any Rhoda," she said.

The gossip about Busola was that her husband had married her because of her good English and secretly he chased women who could barely string two words together without breaking them. Her father was a retired government minister and my father handled part of his large estate. While the rest of us were filling out university applications, Busola was planning a year in Paris. A year stretched to two years and she returned to London wearing short skirts and saying she was in public relations. No one could understand it. We had to go to university. But Busola didn't, and her parents brought her back home when they discovered she was dating an English boy. Now she was married to a Nigerian whose sole purpose in life was to wear good suits and attach himself to the polo-playing clique in Lagos.

I liked Busola, down to her Chinese hair wigs and bags from Milan. I thought she was stylish, smart even. She had conned a whole bunch of people into submitting their children for her Montessori classes, hosted art exhibitions for artists she knew nothing about, dabbled in interior design. All these things required skills, I told Niyi who started calling her "the blockhead next door." From the day she described the houses on our estate as glorified storage space, he'd lost patience with her. Her father had robbed the treasury and she was not afraid to open her mouth, he said. "Why do you always befriend women that no one else can stand, like that Sheri?" he asked. Sheri, who having spent a mere ten minutes with Busola, asked, "Come, what was she talking about? Is she a joker?"

Being generally offensive was what I had in common with both women, and there were a handful of jokers in Lagos, enough to keep the dinner parties going. They cherished their foreign ways, not like the bumbling colonial copycats of our parents' generation. They were much too savvy for that. They gave their children Nigerian names, wore traditional dress, spoke our languages, and pidgin. They were not that different from me, to be fair. But I lacked their affectations, to be fairer still. I imagined them being accosted by state security men at Busola's party. She would drop her Bomb Alaska and run screaming through the gates of Sunrise.

She was nice. The kind of nice that she would say of her husband: "He took my car, went out and didn't come back till morning, and I was furious. So, so furious. You know what I did? I looked at him. Like this. So he knew how furious I was."

Each time I heard a car that night, I went to the window. How free was I, really, in my marriage? Niyi got in a bad mood and in no time, so did I. When I met him, I followed his eye movements, to see if he would stray. Now that I was sure he didn't, I still worried if he was out late, and not just because of his safety. Infidelity was always my limit. For Sheri it was any form of physical force. But there were other things a man could do. My father-in-law had tamed his wife, almost as if he'd scooped out her brains and left just enough for her to keep on obeying him. His son acted like I was invisible until he liked what he saw.

I went downstairs and padlocked the front door, tossed the key with a flourish. Beaters, cheaters, lazy buggers. The worst were the so-called decent. No one would ever encourage a woman to run like hell from them. Fortunately, my mother had shown me the power of a padlock. Whenever Niyi returned, he would have to wait a while before he entered his own home. Mosquitoes could keep him company outside meanwhile.

~⌒

It was past midnight when I heard the door bell. I opened the door in my crumpled night shirt. My face was swollen. I had not slept. Niyi dropped his keys on the dining table as he normally would. I sat on the bottom stair. I was determined to make peace with him this time. The floor felt cold under my feet.

"Busola says she saw you," I said.

He raised his brows as if to say, "And so?"

Niyi's face was easy to read when he was angry. This was not the case. He was not sulking; what he wanted was a surrender. I'd almost forgotten that he was a man who believed in absolutes: he wouldn't chase other women but he would break my heart for my own good.

"I'm not asking you to talk," I said. "Just listen. I know you're scared for my safety. I too wish my father were not involved. He and I, there are questions I could ask him, but none of it matters now. What if I never have a chance to speak to him again? God knows what is going to happen, but my life has to change, and you have to help me. Please. This is too much for me. Look at me."

Niyi looked as if he wished I were still upstairs sleeping.

"You hear me?" I asked.

His expression didn't change. I gave him time.

"So," I said. "This is how it is. I can't tell a lie—you're hurting me. I've tried my best. Don't forget to lock your door."

⌇

Anger was heavy in my hands that week, weighing them down, and I didn't know where to place it. I would stab a table with a pencil, drag a curtain by the nose, kick a door in its shin. Sometimes I passed Niyi along a corridor when he returned from work. I felt like reaching out to push him, with both hands: "Bombastic element!" But I wasn't going to give in.

I visited Grace Ameh again, hoping for some impartial advice on what to do about my father. She was dressed as I last saw her, in a colorful up-and-down.

"My dear, any news?"

"No," I said.

"*Na wa*, what a pity. Well, come in."

She placed her hand on my shoulder. We found our way to her study. This time I looked around. There were piles of paper in bundles, an ancient computer, a typewriter, two ebony busts used as book ends. I recognized some of the authors on her shelf: Ama Ata Aidoo, Alice Walker, Buchi Emecheta, Jamaica Kincaid, Bessie Head, Nadine Gordimer, Toni Morrison.

"You write here?" I asked.

She looked confused. "What?"

"Write in here," I said.

"You'll have to speak up," she explained. "I'm deaf in one

ear. That's why everybody shouts in this house."

Now, it was obvious she was lip-reading, not scrutinizing, me. I repeated my question.

"Not recently," she said. "I feel their presence too strongly, on the tip of my pen. I want to write a word and I think of treason. I'm too upset to write since I came back. Have you ever been to South Africa?"

"No."

She screwed up her nose. "I didn't feel comfortable there. Racial tensions and all that. I don't understand, wherever I travel, beautiful countries, better countries than ours, countries that function, I am always eager to come home for a reason. What do I get on my arrival?"

I smiled. "Arrested."

She folded her arms. "What is it you do? I never asked. I assumed you were a lawyer like your father."

"I am a lawyer."

"I hear that's curable."

I touched my stomach. "I've been out of practice for a while. I was in banking, and then maternity called."

"How many months?"

"Four."

"*Na wa*, congratulations. My mother was a midwife. She worked in Lagos Maternity. She gave up the day she learned that rats were eating the women's afterbirth."

She caught my expression.

"Afterbirth is nutritious," she said. "But it makes the rats fatter, and she couldn't bear that."

"My husband wants to know what you write about," I said.

I could not forget him for a moment, I thought.

She glanced at me sideways. "You've heard of my play 'The Fattening House?'"

"No."

"You've never heard of my play 'The Fattening House?'

Two sisters locked up in their home and force-fed by their grandmother?"

I smiled. "No."

"Look at you," she said. "That was my first play. I made such a loss. Yes, those were the days. At least we were able to express ourselves freely. I write plays for the stage and television. I'm also the arts editor for the *Oracle*. Now that they've driven us into hiding, I do what I can to make sure they don't completely silence us."

I seized the opportunity. "My father says women are not vocal enough."

"He does?"

"About what is happening."

"Not many people are, men or women."

"I can see why women are silent."

"Why?"

"The usual pressure. Shut up and face your family."

"I don't subscribe to that."

"Neither did my father, but it's reality."

"Not mine."

"Your family must support you."

"I wouldn't have it any other way."

Was she being smug or trying to get information out of me? After all, she was a journalist.

"Not everyone has the will to defy people they care about," I said.

"You?"

"Yes. I hear the warnings all the time. 'Don't get involved,' 'Don't say anything.' Sometimes it's easy to forget who is at fault."

She nodded. "Yes, yes, but you have a voice, which is what I always try to tell people. Use your voice to bring about change. Some people in this country, what chance do they have? Born into poverty, hungry from childhood, no formal education. It amazes me that privileged people in Nigeria believe that doing nothing is an option."

"Don't you think I should at least try to get my father released?"

"If you stand with others. But on your own, you are nothing but another victim. Those men I begged at Shangisha, they could easily have harmed me."

"You managed to trick them."

"That doesn't make me a willing hero. Make no mistake, I am not about to be recognized posthumously, as they do over here, people forgetting you and nothing ever changing. I may not be able to write freely with the threat of treason over my head, but I cannot write if I'm dead, eh?"

"You still believe I should avoid Shangisha?"

"Yes."

"It is frustrating, just sitting around."

She reached for a sheet of paper on a side table and handed it to me.

"See. Maybe you would like to come. They've invited me to speak. They are a good group. They work with writers overseas to spread awareness of what is happening."

It was an invitation to an event in support of journalists in detention. Peter Mukoro was one of them.

"A reading," I said.

"There are people there who are involved in the campaign for democracy, human rights and civil liberty organizations. No one will expect you to be silent."

"Thank you," I said.

She smiled. "Hm, so you came here to see me?"

"Yes."

"Petrol shortage and all that?"

"Yes."

"*Na wa*, I'm flattered. It is nice to see your face again. You should come to the reading if you can. It will be good to have support. They say that great minds think alike, but in this country it is the stupid ones that have a consensus."

I decided to go to the reading. I wanted to be around people who had taken a stand against our government. At home, Niyi's silence was upsetting me, and I couldn't forget about my father's detention. I invited Dagogo and Alabi. They said they weren't wasting precious petrol, driving somewhere to listen to poems or whatever.

Looking back on the choice I made to go, I really wasn't interested in attending a literary event either. I never even realized writers in my country held readings, except within academic circles, or except when one retired senator, general, diplomat or the other, wrote his memoirs and threw a large party afterward to raise funds. I'd heard that there were published writers who had not yet seen a royalty, because publishers just didn't pay. My library at home was short on their books, because in an economy like ours books were scarce, if they were not banned by the government. If ever I did come across a book by an African author, it was in London, in a neighborhood where I'd gone to buy plantains, in a bookshop with kente cloth drapes. None of the books I encountered had characters as diverse as the people I knew. And African authors, it seemed, were always having to explain the smallest things to the rest of the world. To an African reader, these things could appear over-explained. Harmattan for instance. You already knew: a season, December–January, dust in the eyes, coughing, chilly mornings, by afternoon sweaty armpits. Whenever I read foreign books, they never explained the simplest things, like snow. How it crunched under your shoes, kissed your face both warm and cold. How you were driven to trample it, then loathed it after it became soiled. All these things! No one ever bothered to tell an African! This never occurred to me, until an English friend once commented on how my accent changed whenever I spoke to my Nigerian friends. That was my natural accent, I told her. If I spoke to her that way, she would never understand. She looked stunned. "I don't believe you," she said sincerely. "That is so polite."

After I'd come to terms with how polite I was being, I became incensed at a world that was impolite to me. Under-explained books, books that described a colonial Africa so exotic I would want to be there myself, in a safari suit, served by some silent and dignified Kikuyu, or some other silent and dignified tribesman. Or a dark dark Africa, with snakes and vines and ooga-booga dialects. My Africa was a light one, not a dark one: there was so much sun. And Africa was an onslaught of sensations, as I once tried to explain to a group of English work mates, like eating an orange. What single sensation could you take from an orange? Stringy, mushy, tangy, bitter, sweet. The pulp, seeds, segments, skin. The sting in your eyes. The long lasting smell on your fingers.

But people concentrated on certain aspects of our continent: poverty, or wars, or starvation; bush, tribes, or wildlife. They loved our animals more than they loved us. They took an interest in us only when we were clapping and singing, or half naked like the Maasai, who were always sophisticated enough to recognize a photo opportunity. And for the better informed: "How about that Idi Amin Dada fellow, eh?" That Mobutu Sese Seko fellow, that Jean-Bedel Bokassa fellow, as though those of us who just happened to be living in the same continent could vouch for the sanity of any of these fellows.

We had no sense of continent really, or of nation in a country like mine, until we traveled abroad; no sense of the Africa presented outside. In a world of East and West, there was nowhere to place us. In a graded world, there was a place for us, right there at the bottom: third, slowly slipping into fourth world. A noble people. A savage culture. Pop concert after pop concert for starving Africans. Entire books dedicated to the salvation of African women's genitals. If only the women themselves could read the books, critique them: this is right; this is incorrect; this is total nonsense. If only Africa could be saved by charity.

Niyi said it was as simple as economic prowess. Economic prowess equaled respect and love. If we had economic clout the rest of the world would love us; love us so much they might even want to mimic us. Why did I think England was beginning to resemble an American colony? Why did I think the most stylish people in the world were forcing themselves to eat sushi? He made sense, I had to admit.

The reading began at 7:00 P.M. but I arrived late, Lagos-style. It was held in a small hall that normally served as a venue for wedding receptions. The hall was the size of a school assembly hall, with folding doors, which, once fully pushed back, allowed air to flow freely from one side to another. Two white fans were suspended from the ceiling. There was a low wooden stage where I expected various brides and grooms had been set on display during their wedding receptions together with ribbons and balloons. The lighting was poor. I sat at the back, under a broken light by the door, wanting to observe. I hoped no one would notice me.

There were about forty or so people present. They were mostly men. One of them caught my eye because he was smoking a pipe. He looked about my father's age. Another, a skinny tall man, walked around with a serious expression. He was handing out leaflets. I saw Grace Ameh. She laughed and patted her chest. She was chatting with the man seated next to her. The skinny man got on the stage. He talked about activism and writing. His voice was so soft it made me wonder if he breathed. He spoke about a rally he had attended, where state security agents had arrested people. They arrived during the first speech and none of the speakers had been seen since. His friend, a writer and journalist, was one of them. He himself wrote poetry and he didn't believe that writers had any special obligation to be activists. "Why must I write about military tyranny?" he asked. "Why can't I write about love? Why can't I just write for the rest of my life about a stone if I want?"

The next reader was Grace Ameh. For a while people adjusted their chairs and she waited for the noise to die down. "In this state we're living in," she said, "where words are so easily expunged, from our constitution, from publications, public records, the act of writing is activism." The audience clapped.

She begged our forgiveness if she was out of touch, but she hadn't read the papers since her return. The news was so heavily censured and she hated to come across the words "socio-economic" and "socio-political," which were over-used by her colleagues in the media. This brought on jovial hisses from the audience. I was surprised Grace Ameh didn't talk about her arrest, only about her trip to South Africa. She said she felt like an honorary white, drinking South African wine and discussing literature. She feared the world would judge Winnie Mandela as a woman, not as the general she was in the war against apartheid.

Grace Ameh was an entertainer. She was also openly self-absorbed, as if she'd decided to crown herself because no one else would. She flirted and quoted from English poems and Zulu sayings. She dared to move daintily. After her, the man with the pipe read an excerpt from his short story about a surgeon with a missing finger, followed by another man who read a poem full of words like sweat and toil. I imagined it had something to do with the demise of farming in our country.

I was in awe of the people I was listening to, that they wrote without recognition or remuneration, and more so that they denounced injustices as a group, at the expense of their freedoms and lives. At the same time, I thought that none of them could be fully conscious of the implications of speaking out. They would have an awareness only; an awareness that manifested itself in whispers, omitted names, substitute names when people discussed politics at gatherings or over the phone. I had lived with the awareness so long, it had become normal. But what made a person cross the frontier of safety? It wasn't consciousness. Anger, I thought. Enough to blind.

The evening ended with a question-and-answer session. I would have stayed, but I was already feeling hungry. These days my hunger was as fierce as thirst. I took note of the next reading, slipped out of the back door. Outside, I hurried to my car in the dark. I'd parked by the gates because I expected to be boxed in. The grounds of the property were over an acre wide with a huge flame-of-the-forest tree in the front court. There were no lamps in the lot, so it took me a while to find my car keys. When I finally did, the headlights of three cars blinded me. I kept perfectly still, recognizing the familiar Peugeot shapes. One car stopped before me and the others carried on toward the hall. The back door of the car before me flew open. A man jumped out. I raised my hands. He was carrying a rifle.

"Don't move," he warned.

⌒

They threw us into a cell, Grace Ameh and I. They said we had disobeyed public orders.

The police stormed the reading and ordered people out at gun point. They arrested Grace Ameh; she was the one they came for. They arrested the four men who came to her rescue. I was arrested because I was the first person they saw.

"Why?" I asked the police officer.

"Inside de car," he said.

"Why?"

"Inside de car," he said, pushing me in.

Through the back window I saw the other policemen running into the hall. They aimed their rifles and shouted orders; I shut my eyes and blocked my ears. I thought they were about to shoot the people inside. I heard Grace Ameh screaming, "Don't touch me." They marched her into the car. I felt so ashamed; I wanted her to be quiet, but she wouldn't stop until we reached the police station, telling them what cowards they were.

There were twelve other women in the cell they threw us in; fourteen of us in a space intended for seven, with ventilation holes on an area the size of an air-conditioning unit. There was no air, no light. My pupils widened in the dark. Outside crickets chattered. Mosquitoes buzzed around my ears. The women lay on raffia mats, overlapping each other on the cold cement floor. One woman had been ordered to fan the others with a large cardboard sheet. Another sat by a shit-bucket in the corner, carrying on a conversation with herself: "Re Mi Re Do? Fa So La Ti Re. La Ti La Ti... "

Grace Ameh stood by the cell door. I was crouched behind her, as far away from the shit-bucket as possible. The smell was already in my nostrils, in my stomach, churning it over. My breath was coming in gasps.

"Get away from the grill," a loud voice said.

It was the woman who seemed to have assumed control of the others in the cell. She had been giving orders to the fanner: "Face north. Face south. Quicken up. Why are you slowing down? Are you crazy?"

Her voice was full of mucus. I was able to make out the roundness of her face, but not her exact expression.

"I stand where I want," Grace Ameh answered.

A woman of words, her voice had broken in her rage.

"I've told you, madam," the loud woman said. "Get away from that grill. You're disrupting everything inside here since you came, and I don't like disruptions."

"I'm not part of your little brigade," Grace Ameh answered.

She was spent from screaming. One or two people slapped mosquitoes from their legs. Someone coughed and swallowed. I gritted my teeth to control my nausea.

"You think because you're educated," came the woman's voice again. "You think you're better than me. I'm educated, too. I read books. I know things. You're no better than me. You and your butter-eating friend in the corner who can't take the smell of shit."

"Look at you, treating people so badly in here," Grace Ameh said.

"Don't speak to me like that," the woman shouted. "You're no better than me. Not in here. We sleep on the same floor, shit in the same bucket. I'll deal with you in a way you least expect if you insult me. Any of my girls here will deal with you in a way you least expect. Even Do-Re-Mi in the corner. Ask her. She kills people and can't even remember. Ask her. She'll tell you."

"How can she tell me if she can't remember?"

"Eh?"

"If she kills people and can't remember, how can she tell me that she's killed them?"

The woman was silent for a moment, then she laughed. "Madam, you know too much. More than God, even. Holding cell must be full again, otherwise I wouldn't have to deal with the likes of you."

She lay down and I shut my eyes. Who would know I was here? Who would think to look for me? All night here, by morning then what? I thought of Niyi at home, waiting.

Do-Re-Mi began to talk louder: "Fa So La. Ti Mi Re? La So La So... "

"Do-Re-Mi, keep the noise down," the loud woman ordered. "And you, fanner, face south again. The women over there need air."

The fanner did an about turn. She was moaning that her arms ached.

"What is wrong with her?" Grace Ameh asked.

"She's lazy," The loud woman answered. "She never wants to do her turn."

"Do-Re-Mi, I mean."

"She's a witch. She hears voices from the other world. They tell her what to do and she does it."

"Schizophrenia?"

"Only you knows, madam. Skipping-freenia. All I know is she's a witch."

Grace Ameh sighed. "I think you know."

"All right, all right!" the woman said. "She's sick in the head. What am I to do? Half of them in here are sick in the head. Listen. Who art thou?"

A voice answered. "I am that I am."

"I say who art thou?"

"I am that I am?" the voice mumbled.

The loud woman laughed. "*In nomine patris, et filii, et spiritus sancti.* I call that one Holy Ghost. She thinks she's God, quarter to her grave, from the day they brought her in, old as a rag, soon to be six feet under. Looks like she really suffered. I mean under Pontius Pilate. But she obeys, she obeys... "

Someone began to pee in the bucket. I heard her grunts, followed by a trickle. My stomach tightened.

"What are you here for?" Grace Ameh asked.

"What is your concern?" the loud woman answered.

"I only ask."

"Don't concern yourself with me. Concern yourself with yourself. We've all done something. Some of us don't even know what, because they haven't told us yet."

"They haven't?"

"Six years. Six hundred, even. Awaiting trial."

There was mumbling and more slapping. Someone complained about the smell from the woman who had gone. Tears welled in my eyes. I sank lower. If I had been made to lick a toilet bowl, I could not feel sicker. The bile twisted my insides, shot up to my temples. My eyes criss-crossed.

I reached for Grace Ameh's leg.

"The smell... I can't... "

She knelt beside me. "My dear, are you okay?"

"You think it smells of perfume here?" the loud woman said.

"She's pregnant," Grace Ameh said.

The woman sat up. "Eh? What are you saying? The butter-eater is pregnant? No wonder she can't stand the smell of shit."

"Try and keep calm," Grace Ameh said.

"I've had a miscarriage before," I whispered.

"Butter-eater," came the woman's voice again. "Who impregnated you?"

"Enough of that," Grace Ameh said to me.

"I thought you were too good for sex."

"Don't mind her," said Grace Ameh.

"What's going on over there?" came the loud woman's voice again.

"Nothing," Grace Ameh said.

The loud woman laughed. "Is your pregnancy still intact? I hope so, because I know you butter-eaters, small thing and babies start falling out of you, plop, plop."

In the dark, I despised her. Plop plop, she kept saying.

"Your baby dead," she said between laughs.

～

I vomited, wiped my mouth with the back of my hand and sat next to my mess. My head felt clearer. I used my sleeve to clean my tears.

The first protest came from the far corner. "You don't have to speak to her like that."

"Why not?" the loud woman asked.

"After all, she's expecting."

"Is she the first to expect?" the loud woman answered.

"It's not Christianly," came a whiny voice. "It's not Christianly. She doesn't deserve to be here, a pregnant woman."

"Do I deserve to be here? Do any of us, bloody dunces. Fanner!"

The fanner had slackened again.

"Do I have to tell you again? Or do you need a slap to remind you?"

The whiny voice continued. "It's not Christianly what you do. It's not Christianly. You blaspheme... " She sounded like a broken whistle.

The loud woman stood up. "Sharrap. Are we equals? Are we? I thought not. Christian it isn't, Shit-stian it is. Where are your best friends hallelu and hallelujah since you've been calling them? I don't see them here. On the day of judgment those who don't know will, so keep your trap shut until then. Thou shalt not speaketh unless you are speaketh to. Take that as your eleventh commandment and commit it to memory."

The whiny voice continued. "It's ungodly what you do. You treat us terribly, as if we don't have enough trouble. We are children of God."

The other women took up the chorus. Yes, they were children of God. They sounded wretched. Weak.

The loud woman stood up. "So. You have little loyalty to me in this place? Two new people and you begin to question me like this?" Her voice broke. "After everything I've done."

She began to weep. The women protested. They were not against her. They only wanted her to show some sympathy for the pregnant woman. She stopped and cleared her throat.

"Where is she even?"

She made her way toward Grace Ameh and I. The smell of stale urine was stronger than ever as she stood over us like a shadow. I stopped breathing.

"You're turning everyone against me," she said.

"She has a point," Grace Ameh said. "We are in here together."

"Born again? What does she know? Fertile and dumb. She has so many children she can't even count. Christian *ko*,

Shit-stian *ni*. Before she came in here what was she doing? Prostituting herself to feed her family. Half a dozen men a night. Stinking crotch. If she scrubbed it with limes, it still wouldn't be clean. Now she says she's born again."

She knelt.

"Butter-eater... "

Grace Ameh moved her hand over my belly. "Don't touch her."

Someone in the far corner shouted, "It's me and you if you touch that pregnant woman. You know you have little strength for fighting, only for talking."

The loud woman slapped her head. "Ah-ah? You think I would do something like that? Do I look like an evil person to you? Let me speak to her, that's all I want, woman to woman. I remember when I was expecting."

"You have children?" Grace Ameh asked.

"Twins," she said.

Her spit sprayed my face. She stroked my braids.

"Butter-eater, you ever had twins?"

I gritted my teeth. Her breath was like a bad egg.

She laughed. "It is like shitting yam tubers. This one is a real dunce. Doesn't say much..."

"You think you're speaking to a child?" Grace Ameh said. "She's a lawyer."

The woman's hand left my head. "A lawyer? And she's never seen the inside of a prison cell before? That's a focking lawyer." She laughed. "A very focking lawyer indeed. I used to work for a lawyer, just like you. A proper African-European. She spoke like she had a hot potato in her mouth: *fyuh, fyuh, fyuh*. She was always afraid: I'm afraid this, I'm afraid that. She was even afraid she couldn't take a telephone call, bloody dunce. Em, my Lord, if it em, pleases the court, can you tell me why, according to articles my left foot, and my right buttock, why 'whereas' a good woman like myself was living my life peacefully and 'whereas' my life story was straight, all of a sudden my life story got k-legs?"

I blinked once, twice. She expected an answer.

"Monday morning," she said, "my husband dies. Tuesday morning, they shave my head and say I must stay in a room. Alone. Naked. I can't touch my children. Twins. Twins, I had for that wretched family."

She began to cry again. The women begged her to be strong. She cleared her throat and continued.

"They say I can't see my twins. Instead they give me the water they used to bath my husband's corpse, to drink, to prove I didn't put a hex on him. I say I'm a secretary typist. Qualified 1988. I'm not going to drink it. They say I killed him."

"That's why you're here?" Grace Ameh asked.

"I didn't kill my husband. They said I did. The day I killed somebody, they said they were surprised. No one in their family ever did that."

She laughed and rocked. "I had not bathed for days after my husband died. I was walking around in one dress. One dress on my back and nowhere to go. No food to eat. They had sent me out and left me with nothing. I was walking the streets. One foolish man approached me. He called me Hey Baby. I said I'm not Hey Baby. I'm a secretary typist, qualified 1988. Maybe he thought I was a prostitute like Born Again over here, or a crazy like Do-Re-Mi. You know some of these men will go with the crazies to get rich, and some of these crazies will go with men. Crazy in the head but not so crazy in the crotch. The fool touched my breast, I slapped his face. He pushed me to the ground."

She cleared her throat. "I grabbed a stone, whacked his head. I couldn't stop whacking. He was shouting, 'Help! Help!' Before I knew it, he died there on top of me. The police came and carried me to prison."

"That is terrible," Grace Ameh said.

She used her wrapper to wipe her tears. "Yes. What was I supposed to do but kill him? Answer me that."

She reached for my braids again. Her hand felt rough.

"Doesn't this one speak?" she murmured." Or is she dumb?"

I cleared my throat and steadied my voice.

"I'm not," I said.

. "Eh? She speaks?"

"Yes, I do."

I sounded calm. My heart was beating fast.

"So tell me why, according to your law articles, this happened to me."

"You should not be awaiting trial this long," I said.

She stopped stroking my braids.

"And only a court can decide if you're guilty."

The woman started stroking my braids again. "That's very good," she said. "That's very very good, indeed. You're a Yoruba girl?"

"Yes," I said.

She began to speak in Yoruba. "A European one. I can tell. I never thought I'd see one of you in here. Smelling so clean, so clean... Your friend isn't Yoruba?"

"No," I confirmed.

"You keep answering in English. You are not a lost child of Oduduwa, I hope. You can speak the language?"

"Yes," I said in Yoruba.

"Tell me, since you've come in here, smelling so clean and speaking such good English, if I came to your office to see you, would you turn your nose the other way? Say that I smell? Ask someone to show me out? Would you drive past on the streets when I was walking and wonder? Had I eaten? Had I rested? Did I have a roof over my head?"

She tugged my braids.

"That is enough," Grace Ameh said.

"Would you?" she asked.

"You have to let me go," I said.

She released my braids.

"You see? You don't consider us your equals, you butter-eaters. You see us and you think we're no better than animals."

"That is not true," I said.

She turned to Grace Ameh. "You're saying this one is not a child? This one who can't even answer a simple question. Telling me only a court can decide and nonsense like that?"

Her saliva droplets hit my face again. I wiped them away. She got up and began to make her way over the bodies lying on the floor.

"You have not grown up," she said. "You're still a child."

"I am not responsible for your being here," I said.

"Shame on you. Shame. Bringing another child into the world."

"I did not arrest myself."

I tried to stand, but Grace Ameh's hand came down on my shoulder. "Don't listen to her. Can't you see? It is how she has control."

I stood up. It was not anger that propelled me, it was humiliation. She could be a client, and I would not allow her to ridicule me.

"What do you know about me?" I asked.

"I hope you're not trying to think you can follow me," she said. "I sincerely hope not. You dare not provoke me. I'm not nice when I'm provoked."

I climbed over another body. "I'm not scared of you."

She laughed. "Shaking like a fowl from the minute you walked in. Ooo, Ooo. Can't take the smell of shit. Will your baby's shit smell sweet? Your baby's shit won't smell sweet. That's what I know about you."

"You ask me a hundred questions. You don't even give me a chance to answer."

She began to rock back and forth, mimicking me. "O dearie me. O my goodness. O my goodness gracious."

"Ignore her," Grace Ameh said.

"No," I said.

She would bury me unless I faced up to her. I waited until her dance was over.

"You've finished?" I asked.

"You still have not answered my questions," she said.

I moved closer. "I answered one. You insulted me."

"Don't take a step forward," she shouted.

"Why not," I said.

"I will damage that precious pregnancy of yours."

"You will have to kill me afterward," I said. "Because if there is a heartbeat left in me, I will kill you."

It was a gamble. She was a bully, nothing more.

She was waving her arm in the air, breathing heavily. I heard women mumbling. Mother of Prisons. Wouldn't she ever stop?

"What have I done to you?" I asked.

"You talk too much," she said. "You should have shut up. You should have shut up, in the first place. Only a court can decide. You think this is a joke?" Her voice broke. "All these years I've been in here. The one thought that stopped me from becoming like these crazies, is that nothing, nothing, can be done for me."

She began to cry. This time she sounded genuine.

"This is the kind of hope you have?" I asked.

I looked around. A few of the women were sitting up. They thought we were about to fight. I heard some more grumbling. Mother of Prisons, she was always fighting, and she had no strength, only for talking.

But how could I have answered her question honestly? A government dedicated to eradicating opposition. A country without a constitution. A judicial system choking, even over commercial matters. Sluggish, sluggish as an old man's bowels.

"I'm sorry, " I said. "I should have been quiet."

"I have no quarrel with you," she said.

I took her arm. Her skin felt damp.

"S'all right!" she said.

We lay on the floor. Grace Ameh by my side, Mother of Prisons next to her. She said she was not sleeping next to any stinking people, and there were many in this cell. Someone protested. "Sharrap," she said. "Watch your step, butter-eater," she said to me, as we found places to lie. "Easy, easy now. We don't want any accidents. Don't worry, I will take care of you."

There was not enough space for us, unless our legs and arms touched. My eyes were wide open. I listened for every creak outside. Soon, someone would come in to free us. They would open the door and let us out.

No one came. I remembered the last time I was in a police station. It was during my national service year, when I worked for my father. A client called. Could he send one of his "boys" over to Awolowo Road station? One of his expatriate tenants was there with a hawker he'd caught trespassing.

I went with Dagogo, only for the drama. We arrived to find an Englishman drenched in his gray lightweight suit: Mr. Forest. His hair was wet with sweat and his nostrils flared. He reminded me of every impatient boss I'd worked with in England—I made a suggestion and they ignored it. I made a mistake and they told everyone. I cracked a joke, and they asked, "What on earth are you talking about?"

It was hard not to feel vengeful.

"D-dagoggle?" Mr. Forest asked, for confirmation, and Dagogo answered to the name. It turned out that the hawker had been trespassing on Mr. Forest's lawn, to see her cousin who lived in the servants' quarters in the house behind his. He had warned her, but she wouldn't stop. Every time he looked out of his window, there she was, trespassing again. I studied the police officer on duty, a rotund man with perfectly white teeth. He listened with a grave expression. I suspected he was daydreaming. Dagogo meanwhile questioned the woman. Why did she trespass? Didn't she know it was wrong to trespass? The woman, a popcorn and groundnut seller, looked as if she couldn't understand what was happening. I knew she would do it again and still look just as confused. We advised Mr. Forest to let her go, he'd scared her enough. "She's really, really sorry, Mr. Frosty," I said.

My legs began to itch from mosquito bites. The cement floor pressed into my shoulder. My stomach groaned. I was hungry; hungry enough to forget the nausea that seized me when I first entered the cell. I pulled dry skin from my lips and swallowed it until I tasted blood. My lips stung. I turned to relieve my shoulder.

"Can't you sleep?" Mother of Prisons asked.

"No," I said.

"Me too," she said.

The others were asleep. There was some snoring and two women were coughing incessantly. The rhythm was disturbing. Grace Ameh was awake, though she wasn't talking. She had confessed that this was her worst nightmare, to be locked up, and I was sure she could not hear our whispers.

Mother of Prisons said, "I can never sleep at night, only during the day. By evening, I'm fired up."

How long could people stay in a place like this before they broke down. One week? I thought. Two? How long before their minds broke down irreversibly? I felt the need to tell her.

"My father is in prison," I said.

"Eh?"

"My father is in prison."

"What did he do?"

"Nothing, nothing. Like you."

"Where is he? Kalakuta or Kirikiri maximum security?"

"No one knows."

He was a political prisoner, I explained. The new government was detaining people under a state security decree. I explained it to her in simple terms, wondering why

I felt the need to treat her like a child. She would know that a man like my father would never be in prison unless he was a political prisoner.

"I know nothing of our government," she said. "Or our president, or any African leaders for that matter. I don't care to know. They are the same. Short, fat, ugly. Not one ounce of sense in their heads. How long has your father been in detention?"

"Over a month," I said.

"He's done well," she said.

There was a loud snore. She sucked her teeth.

"Who was that? These women, worse than any drunken husband... "

"You must miss your husband," I said.

"No," she said. "Focking ass couldn't keep a job."

"But you... "

"But me no buts. My whole life was ruined by one but."

I smiled. "But you married him."

"Doesn't mean. You're a woman, aren't you? We marry anybody for marry sake, love anyone for love sake and once we love them, we forsake ourselves. Make the best of it, till they die or till we do. Look at me. Everything, everything, in that house I bought, and I was sending money to my parents in the village, sending money to his parents."

"You must have had a good job."

"A shipping company. Paspidospulus, or however they pronounce his name, these Greeks. You know white people, they pay well, unlike our people."

"He treated you well?"

"Paspidospulus? The kindest man ever. He gave me his wife's old clothes to maintain a professional appearance, though her trousers never fitted my ass."

"Goodness."

"Then like a fool I was telling everyone that it was my husband who was providing, you know, to boost him up.

Then he started telling everybody that, yes, he was taking care of the family, he was providing. Providing what? Five hundred extra mouths to feed? Ate like a focking elephant, that man. Greediness killed him, not me."

She began to laugh, and her laughter turned to grunts as she spoke.

"It's my children I miss. Not him. You eat like that, you bear the consequences, God rest his soul. He ate my food store empty. Buy a week's beans and he demolishes it. *Pfff!* A month's meat... "

"Please," I said, waving an arm. Her grunts were funny and my head was light from hunger.

"Gone in a day," she said. "Can eat fried ants if you put them on his plate. He won't know the difference. Paspidospulus couldn't have paid me enough... "

I felt laughter in my belly, and a sweet pain lower down. My bladder was full.

She kept on grunting. "Paspidospulus couldn't have paid me enough. I'm telling you, tomato. Tomato, I tell you. This was when tomato was becoming expensive. The focking ass... "

"Please," I said. "Stop, otherwise I will have to go."

"Huh?" she said. "Go where? Who released you yet?"

"To toilet."

"Piss in the bucket," she said. "What do you think?"

I could not let her down. She was enjoying our friendship, and I thought she might begin her tirade again. The bucket was available, she said. For whatever business I had to do. We were all women in this place. There was no reason to be proud. Worse things were happening here, worse than I could imagine. One woman was rotting away. Couldn't I smell it?

"What?" I asked.

"Her cancer," she said. "It's terminal."

I had not taken a step before the familiar wave forced me over again. The back of my neck tightened, bile rose from my stomach and singed my throat. I'd gotten up too fast.

"What's going on?" Mother of Prisons asked.

My mouth opened again, involuntarily. I crouched between two bodies, held my sides.

"Are you all right?" Grace Ameh asked, sitting up.

"She's miscarrying," Mother of Prisons said. "Help her."

The bile tasted bitter on my tongue. Nothing else came out. I was trying to say I was fine. The women rose in varying stages of alertness. They circled me, the sick and the mad with their sores and ringworm and tuberculosis. Their body heat enveloped me. I stretched one arm out, to prevent them from falling over me. I took shorter breaths, shut my eyes.

"Let her breathe. Let her breathe," Grace Ameh was saying.

They kept on pushing.

"She's miscarrying," Mother of Prisons said.

Do-Re-Mi began to talk to herself again. "La So Fa Mi. Ti Ti Re Mi... "

A whiny voice recited a psalm. *"He that dwelleth in the secret place of the most High shall abide under the shadow of the almigh-tee... "*

"Please, please let her breathe," Grace Ameh said above the noise. She sounded anxious. I was all right, I wanted to tell her.

"He shall deliver thee from the snare of the fowler, the noisome pestiii-lence... "

There were hands on my head. Someone kicked my back. I curled up.

"Thou shalt not be afraid of the terror by night. Nor for the arrow that flieth by day. Nor for the pestilence that walketh in darkness. Nor for the destruction that wasteth at noonday... "

They would suffocate me, I thought.

"A thousand shall fall at thy side. Ten thousand at thy right hand... "

There was loud banging on the door and shouting from outside.

"What is happening in there? What is happening?"

"Thine eyes shalt thou behold and see the reward of the wicked… "

The cell door creaked open. Light shone on our faces. The noise died to a few mumbles. The psalm stopped.

A stocky warder appeared. She was the one who had led us in. She spoke in a resigned voice. "Mother of Prisons, are you making trouble again?"

As the women dispersed, I finally saw her face, Mother of Prisons. Her hair was in patches. Sores had eaten into the corners of her mouth. She was shaking like an old woman. She was about my age.

"Trouble?" she said. "Which trouble? You see me making trouble here?"

The light made me squint.

"What are you doing with the new prisoners?" the warder asked.

"Me? It's you. You should be ashamed of yourself, locking up a pregnant woman. If she had miscarried, the blood of her child would be on your head. Right there on your head. It was I who looked after her. I alone. If not for the kindness in my heart, it would have been another k-legged story in this place."

She waddled back to her spot scratching her armpits. The others lay down. They looked like twisted tree branches. The warder walked between them.

"How is our sick prisoner today?"

"What do you think?" Mother of Prisons answered. "Why haven't her people come for her?"

"They say they can't afford the treatment."

"Take her to hospital. She hasn't opened her eyes for days."

The warder sighed. "Give her pain-killers."

"She won't take them."

"Crush them with your teeth and feed them to her. You did it before."

Mother of Prisons raised her fists. "Are you listening to me? I say she's nearly dead. How will she swallow? The whole womb is rotten now. We are choking on her smell."

The warder was silent for a moment.

"I've done my best," she said.

"Not enough," Mother of Prisons said.

The warder pointed to me and Grace Ameh. "You, you," she said, in a resigned voice. "Follow me."

I was prodding myself to check for wetness between my legs. I rose with my back bent over and breathed steadily to keep my nausea down.

"Better get a doctor inside here," Mother of Prisons said, as we walked out. "Before we have another wrongful death in this stinking place! If you think I will ever stop talking, you must be focking joking!"

The warder asked us to hurry back to the hall, "should-in case" armed robbers stole our cars, "plus-including" the men, we were free to go. She released us, no explanations given. She warned Grace Ameh not to participate in further political activities.

Grace Ameh's husband was waiting for us outside. We drove back to the hall and I occasionally caught his scowl in the rearview mirror. I did not know who he was angry with: me, his wife, or the people who had detained us. I did not care to know. I only wanted to get back home. I breathed in fresh air through the back window.

"I'm sorry I involved you in this," Grace Ameh said before we parted. "I suspected they were watching me but I didn't think they would go this far. Go home and stay home." She patted my shoulder and I had a feeling she'd left something of herself on me.

I arrived home at four in the morning. Niyi was waiting for me in the living room. He got up as I walked through the front door.

"What happened? I've been waiting five hours now. I thought you were dead."

I began to undress. My clothes fell to the floor as I told him.

"I can't believe this," he said.

"I swear."

"We were living normally, in this house, a few weeks ago. They were making political speeches. Why didn't you leave?"

I was in my underwear, surprised that this was what he couldn't believe. I mumbled, "One person. One person said something."

"What if they beat you up inside there?"

"They didn't."

"What if, I said."

"They didn't."

He raised his arms. "Come on. Wasn't it enough to be in prison?"

"I didn't ask them to arrest me."

"You're not hearing me. It's not just about you anymore."

"It's me they arrested. You weren't there."

"I'm talking about the baby."

I couldn't tell if he was holding back from slapping or hugging me.

"I'm sorry," I said.

"How are you?" he asked.

"Fine," I said.

"I don't know what else to tell you. I don't know what else to say. Your life means nothing to them. Can't you see? What will I tell people if something happens to you?"

"Please," I said. "Don't tell anyone."

He brushed past me to lock the front door. "You're confused, o-girl. It's not them I care about. It's you. You, and you're the one opening your mouth, not me."

I went upstairs to have a bath, then I lay on my bed in the spare room. I begged my child for a second chance. I could still smell the prison on me.

Niyi would never tell anyone about my arrest, and I would not tell anyone. I would take my time in prison and put it away. Do-Re-Mi, Mother of Prisons, Born Again, Holy Ghost, the woman with the rotting womb. Gone. Niyi went to the police station the next morning. They told him my arrest was an unfortunate incident. Two weeks later when I read in the papers that the hall had been fire-bombed and some of Sheri's customers complained because they would have to change venues for their wedding receptions, I said nothing. I didn't blame the police; I blamed myself for putting my child at risk for another miscarriage. No, they shouldn't have arrested me, and yes, people should be allowed to say what they want. But it was one thing to face an African community and tell them how to treat a woman like a person. It was entirely another to face an African dictatorship and tell them how to treat people like citizens.

I wasn't inviting trouble, that evening. Niyi knew, Grace Ameh knew, which was why she spoke to me with the sincerity of a mother telling her war-bound son, "Make sure you come back alive."

The day after my release, I saw my doctor for an unscheduled check-up, then I closed the office for a week after he cleared me. I went back to work the following week only because I knew my father's staff would have to earn their livings, even for as little as two hours a day, and also because I realized that wherever I was in Lagos, I was no longer safe. Like a joke, like a joke.

If February seemed long that year, March was beginning to feel longer. At work, jobs dried up as my father's clients shied from dealing with me; at home, Niyi's silence continued. I shuttled between the two locations feeling anesthetized. Only on occasion would I feel breathless for my father's safety and I would immediately fight the feeling down. I dared not think otherwise. Each moment carried me to the next and I no longer imagined prison cells because I'd seen the inside of one. I also promised myself that I would no longer speak for women in my country, because, quite simply, I didn't know them all.

One morning, I came in determined to tidy my father's drawers. His letters were in no order, and I was sure he kept them separate so his staff could not gain access to them. I sorted the bank letters first, then the letters from his accountants. The folder where I found salary details needed tidying, so I flicked through. I discovered my parents' divorce papers: *"Take notice that a petition has been presented to the above court by Victoria Arinola Taiwo instituting proceedings for a decree of dissolution of marriage and also seeking orders with respect to the custody of the one child…"*

My mother had given her reasons for falling out with my father: a neglectful and uncaring attitude; withheld housekeeping allowance; on several occasions did not return home and gave no reasonable answer as to his whereabouts; influenced her child to disregard her; disrespected her church family; made wicked and false allegations about her sanity; colluded with family members to alienate her; caused her much embarrassment and unhappiness. There was something about a car. I could not read on.

Peace came in.

"Someone to see you," she said.

"Who?" I asked.

"Your brother," she said.

I refused to allow my heart to jump. I had not done anything wrong. "Please tell him to come in," I said.

My brother looked like my father, although he was taller. He had big eyes and that wasn't from my father. He was wearing blue khaki trousers and a striped yellow shirt.

"Debayo," I said.

"Yes," he said.

He had a widow's peak. That was my father's.

"Uncle Fatai called me," he said. "I've been meaning to come."

I watched every move he made. He frowned at a spot on my father's desk, rubbed his thumb over the top of his lip. I held on to my pen with both hands. He did not know if he should come, but his mother would not forgive him if he didn't.

Outside the sound of sirens deafened us temporarily. It could have been a government official passing, a security van escorting money from the Central Bank, or a Black Maria van carrying prisoners.

"What kind of doctor are you?" I asked.

"Pathologist," he said.

"Eh? Why?"

"It's not so bad," he said.

"A doctor of dead bodies."

"I wanted to study law," he said.

"Why didn't you?"

"Two of us, in here. It would have been difficult."

He was smiling. Where he found the grace, I could not imagine.

"You have a right," I said.

He shrugged. "I'm over that now, wanting to work for Sunny. I had people pushing me in that direction. The way I see it, Sunny decided for me."

He called our father Sunny. He was not as cordial as he appeared.

"Debayo," I said. "I'm sorry, I don't know where he is, and the little I know, I don't know if it will put your mind at rest."

"What do you know?"

I told him. He gave me a telephone number and asked me to contact him if I heard anything else. He was visiting Uncle Fatai later that evening. He didn't seem worried and spoke as if he was relieved to have fulfilled his obligation to his mother. I walked with him to his car and we stood facing the road. His ears stuck out a little, and that was from my father. I shielded my eyes from the sun.

"Where are you staying?"

"Cousins," he said, and then he added. "My cousins."

"How is your mother taking the news?"

"My mother? They are not together anymore."

"No?"

"For many years now."

"I didn't know."

He turned to me. "You must know I'm the youngest in my family."

"I didn't."

"That I have three older sisters?"

"No."

"He didn't tell you anything about me?"

"A little. Did he tell you anything about me?"

"No," he said.

"You never even stayed with him?"

He smiled. "Once. Only once, one summer, when my mother caught me smoking, and it was lecture, lecture, lecture... "

"What were you smoking?"

"Cigarettes."

"Why didn't you tell him to leave you alone?"

"Him?" he said. "I was scared of him."

"You were?"

"Weren't you?"

"No," I said. "Not really."

He rubbed his thumb over his upper lip again. He was double-jointed. His fingernails were square and they reached his finger tips. That was my father.

It could have been different for a son. Debayo had not offered his help in any way, I thought, and I wouldn't either if I were him.

"You must be the only doctor left in Lagos," I said.

"No," he said, taking me literally. "We're many. Some of us don't want to go, even though the temptation is there. We keep hearing about those abroad, doing well, especially in America."

"Why do you stay?"

"Steady work."

"For goodness' sake," I said.

I sensed that he had delivered that line many times before, and I sensed he was enjoying my disapproval. My brother knew everyone in the office. He gave Dagogo and Alabi that manly handshake, before he left. *"Man mi,"* they called him. When I returned to the office I asked Alabi, "You know my brother this well?"

Alabi nodded. "He's our paddy."

"Our paddy-man," Dagogo said.

"I'm not your paddy-man?" I asked.

They laughed.

"Face like stone," Dagogo said.

"Worse than BS," Alabi said.

I recognized my father's initials. Bandele Sunday. In his office, I resumed my task. Some school bills caught my eye. They were not from schools I'd attended. I flicked through. There were school reports, letters from a principal. I read them. They were my brother's. He was an above-average student, played field hockey. He was good at math. Once he was in trouble for playing truant. My brother. It was a start.

∿

My mother's first thought was that he had come to do me harm. "What's he coming for?" she asked. "Suddenly he wants to see you? Don't take anything from him, you hear me? Whatever he gives you, straight into the bin. It's all well and good. If he wants to find out about his father, let him go to Uncle Fatai and find out what he needs to know there."

I was sitting next to her at her dining table. She slumped over it.

"No water no light," she said. "Now this. Ah, I'm tired."

"At least Sumbo is here to help," I said.

"Sumbo?" she said. "She's gone."

"Where?"

"She ran away. Two weeks, now."

"Back to her parents?"

"Those parents who sent her away in the first place? Who knows? I had to send word to them that she's disappeared. I woke up one morning and she wasn't there. I went everywhere searching for her. I even went to the police for that girl. Not a thing. These people, it's always something or the other with them. "

It was easy to distract her. My mother had bought a few baby rompers. She spread them on her dining table and held a yellow one up.

"I'll get some more," she promised.

"I've never seen you like this before, " I said. "Don't finish your money."

"Why not?" she said. "I spent money on my church and what thanks did I get? For the first time in how many years last month my tithes were low. They were complaining. I told them I had other obligations. They said I must put God first. I told them I am putting God first. He gave me a grandchild, and I must thank Him by preparing."

I smiled. "Why do you stay in that church?"

She raised her hand. "I didn't ask for your opinion."

I raised my hand, too, in surrender. I was tearful. The

rompers, the light in my mother's eyes. I worried about her as if she were a teetotaler with a glass of wine in her hand. It would have to be good this time. If not for me, for her.

As we talked and folded the rompers, my mother told me the story of a faith healing gone wrong. A man in her church, deaf from birth, claimed he could hear after going through cleansing. My mother spoke to the man afterward to congratulate him. "Couldn't hear one word," she said. "And I've asked Reverend Father before, 'You say that only those who love God will be healed from cleansing. Shouldn't a person who loves God be eager to die as quickly as possible in order to be with Him? Why would they want healing?' He couldn't give me a straight answer to that. 'As for me,' I told him, 'when my God calls, I'm ready to go.'"

My mother's analysis surprised me. No one satirized the people in her church as she did. Half of them were sinners, she said, and fault-finders, and they gave cheap gifts at Christmas. I couldn't fold from laughing. She was a total gossip. She asked me to return an aluminum bowl to her new tenant, Mrs. Williams, so that I could meet her. Mrs. Williams was a divorced woman who worked for a large fishing company. "She is high, high up in the company," my mother confided. "They say her husband drove her out because she was always going out: parties, Lioness meetings, this and that. You should see her, pretty thing and slim. Now they say she's found herself a boyfriend."

"That's good," I said, wiping tears from my eyes.

"Quick-quick, like that? It's not good."

"You should try it yourself."

She eyed me. "Don't be rude."

"Why not? It will keep you looking fresh. Just make sure he's young and... "

"Will you stop?"

Fresh, fresh, I kept saying to tease her. She eventually smacked my arm.

"Leave this house, Enitan."

As I walked to Mrs. Williams's house, I was thinking that I was due for another sex talk and this time I would be just as shy. At what age was a woman content to be celibate? No one ever said. If they caressed themselves, the pleasure they got, they would never say. The thought made me wince. I was twenty when I first saw my father kiss a woman. He did it properly, the way they did in films. He circled her waist with one hand, bent his knees, straightened up. I covered my eyes with my hands and screamed silently. Then I avoided him for the rest of the day, in case I smelled perfume on him or something. I had never seen my mother kiss a man; not even my father.

"You must be Enitan," Mrs. Williams said, unlocking her gate.

Her hair was weaved in intricate patterns that ended in a miniature crown of plaits on top of her head. She was wearing one of those up-and-downs, which dipped in at the waist and flared like a tutu. It made her look as slight as a teenager, but I was certain she was in her late forties. Her eyes were that composed.

"You're so pretty," I said.

"You," she said.

Her gate opened.

"I've heard a lot about you," she said.

"Good or bad?" I asked, walking in.

"Your mother and I are friends," she said, knowingly.

"She says thank you for the fish."

I placed the bowl over my stomach like a tortoise shell. She glanced at it.

"Would you like some? Come in and get some."

We walked to the back door that led into her kitchen.

"I'm with Universal Fisheries," she explained. "I'm sure

your mother told you. They give us senior officers frozen fish every holiday. But we've had light on and off for two days now and it will spoil if I don't give it away." She kicked a toy car by the kitchen door. "Watch out for that. I keep telling my children to put their toys away before they go out."

"They are not in?"

"They're with their father."

There was a collapsible iron table in Mrs. Williams' kitchen that took up most of the space. Behind it was a large freezer like mine. She removed a slab of frozen fish.

"See?" she said. "Melting already."

I stood back as she wrapped the slab in several sheets of newspaper and placed it in the bowl.

"Here," she said, handing it to me.

It was heavier than expected.

"This is your first?" she asked.

"Yes!"

"You should put that down," she said. "The fish. You should put it down if you're not ready to leave."

I placed it on the table next to her. "I saw your children. Your little girl, Shalewa, told me off for not calling her by her name. I think she was upset the boys were not playing with her."

"Don't be fooled. She bullies her brothers. The minute they touch her, she's going to tell her father. Even me she reports."

"She's so cute. Forgive her."

"Her? It's not her I have to forgive. But, you know, the day you've had enough, your legs just carry you... "

She was explaining her own circumstance, but I didn't mind listening. It was good to be reminded that everyone, smiling or not, had overcome adversity.

"I'm sorry to hear about your father," she said. "I hear you're the one running his practice."

"Yes."

"That must be hard."

"I try."

"It's all you can do," she said. "In this place. Look around you. Not one of us asked to be in the situation we're in. My children, they keep complaining, oh they want to go to their father's house, oh they want to play video games and watch cable. I told them, 'The children without video games and cable, you think they're from a different planet?' Before we moved here, they were always indoors, staring at a screen from morning till night. Now they're outside playing. They're getting fresh air."

"They won't want to hear that."

"I know, but sometimes I think the sooner they learn the better. The disappointment is less. There are no more ivory towers in Lagos. The waves just keep coming one after the other. When they do, you raise your head higher. If you don't, then what? I was used to my comforts. I'm used to being without them now."

I smiled. Yes, we were the city of broken survivors, children included.

"Condition," she said.

"Hm?"

"Condition make back of crawfish bend," she said.

During the week the government announced they'd uncovered a coup plot. The details in the press were sketchy and the latest issue of the *Oracle* barely dedicated a column to the story. I wondered why. Then the rumors started coming in, this really wasn't a coup; this was an excuse to arrest more government opponents. A former military ruler and his deputy were detained. There would be more.

The government had warned the newspaper editors not to speculate about the coup. People began to joke in that senseless way that a beaten people might: "You're speculating?

Why are you speculating? You've been warned not to speculate. I'm not speculating with you."

I buried my head in token stories and editorials meanwhile. A woman had been murdered by her house boy. He left her body indoors and used her car for taxi services. I couldn't get that image out of my mind. A cannibal was out on the loose, another story said. Was this a modern Dahmer-style murderer or a throwback to paganism, the editor speculated, since he could speculate on nothing else. Someone had accepted radioactive waste from overseas for a tidy sum and dumped it in his village. The villagers were placing their radios on trees, hoping that the radioactivity would recharge their batteries. More jokes about that.

I read the most disturbing stories to escape from my own life, and two visits surprised me at the office later that week. The first was from Uncle Fatai, who came in after lunch, just at the time I'd kicked my shoes off, because my feet were beginning to swell. When he walked in, I stood up. He waved me down and squeezed into the visitor's seat. For the first time, I noticed how much he wheezed as he talked.

"I'm traveling to London," he said. "For a check up."

"I hope... "

He waved. "Annual. It's nothing to worry about. Half my problems would go, if I wasn't so fat. Do you need anything?"

"No, thank you."

Nigerians still made pilgrimages to London like no man's business. Over there, only our money was welcome.

"Any developments about your father?" he asked.

"No."

Dimples appeared in his knuckles as he placed his palms together. "He will be out soon, Old Sunny... em, staff paid?"

"Yes," I said.

"That's very good," he said.

"What about his clients?"

"They don't call anymore."

"That is to be expected."

"Debayo came here, Uncle," I said.

I watched for a reaction. There was none.

"Yes," he said. "I saw him myself. And how is your husband?"

"He's fine," I said.

"Your mother too. I have not had time to visit."

"She's fine, thank you."

"That's good," he said.

Uncle Fatai was not used to extending more than the usual courtesies to me. He ran out of questions and ended up asking after my mother again and again. When he finally heaved himself up, I could easily have rushed to his rescue the way he was tottering. He brought out a handkerchief and wiped his forehead.

"You know, em, you're not a child anymore, Enitan. Your father, he em, always felt bad about your brother... that he wasn't there when your mother took him to church like that."

"Yes," I said.

"Sunny always treasured you. He never stopped seeing you as a child. That was his mistake. But you know, an African man cannot die without leaving a son."

I could hear my colleagues talking behind the door. I wanted to say that I didn't know how to think like an African woman. I only knew how to think for myself.

"Yes, Uncle," I said.

"It is time you met your brother," he said. "I always told Sunny to bring you two together from the start, but Sunny makes his own mind up."

"Yes, Uncle."

"Take care of yourself."

"Safe journey, Uncle," I said.

The next visit was from Grace Ameh, who came first thing in the morning. She smiled as she did the day I met her and I was relieved to see her.

"You're out and about already?" I said, hugging her.

She was wearing a dress again. This one was pale yellow with a pleated skirt, and she carried her brown portfolio. She patted my back like a comrade.

"My dear, I can't let them stop me."

"I hope they're not still monitoring your movements."

"They must be tired of me. I've been up and down."

"Wicked people."

She placed his portfolio on the table. "I've been meaning to speak to you."

"Yes?"

"I was wondering if you would be interested in joining a campaign, for Peter Mukoro and our friends who have been detained, your father included. There will be more detainees, I'm sure, after this latest coup fiasco."

"Yes."

"A group of wives will spearhead this one. I think they feel left out of the wider campaign. They're looking for someone, anyone, who can be their spokesperson. I think you will be an ideal candidate."

"Me?"

"You're the most qualified. The other lady is a bank clerk and she works full-time, and she has three young children. Bear in mind we're in the early stages. We don't have many members. Ten at most."

"They want me?"

"I know you had reservations the first time we spoke, but that must have changed by now."

I remembered Niyi's warning. "Yes, I want my father out of detention."

"You may need to do more than want now. If they're conjuring up coups, they can conjure up coup plotters."

"My father?"

"Any of the detainees. I've always said, men fight for land, and women fight for family."

I was unable to agree, but she was in journalist mode again, stirring me in a pro-democracy direction.

"I don't know," I said. "But let me be honest. I know your magazine's agenda, I read it regularly and I will not campaign for deposed politicians, if that is what you're really asking."

Her eyes flickered with impatience.

"I'm sorry," I said. "They don't care about democracy. They never have, only about power. My memory of them, throwing cash to villagers, rigging elections, setting opposition groups on fire, making themselves richer... "

"The military enrich themselves. They've always done."

"We didn't vote for them, but politicians, we do. The last elections, I voted only because there was an election. No other reason."

"Our elections were the fairest they've ever been. And no one is campaigning for politicians. It's the process we're interested in. Let the process begin. Good will will take care of itself."

"What happens if there's another coup? There's nothing to stop the army from coming in again."

She knew the facts better than I did. Coup after coup after coup, especially on the west coast of Africa. 1963, Slyvanus Olympio of Togo, killed. 1966, Tafawa Balewa, our first Prime Minister, killed. The same year, Kwame Nkrumah of Ghana. After that, it was non-stop. No one in the world recognized that African soldiers had fought against Hitler, but almost everyone was aware they spent time deposing their own rulers, heading civil wars from Somalia to Liberia, fueling civil unrest from Algeria to Angola.

She asked, "You're suggesting we never seek democratic rule because of the threat of military coups?"

"I'm saying we may never have a democratic government if we have an army."

"Every country needs an army, to protect its people."

"Evidently, in Africa we need armies to kill our people."

She smiled. "Your views are impractical. Politicians with pure intentions and a country with no army. *Na wa*, I hope you're never thinking of running for office."

"No."

"So, will you settle for our small campaign, instead?"

This time I was thinking of my time in prison.

"I have a child to think about in a few months," I said.

"I wouldn't put you in a compromising situation."

"Tell me. What situation are you putting me in?"

"Let me see, a group of wives, coming together once a month, in someone's house, doing what women do best. Gossiping." She winked.

"I've never passed up the opportunity to gossip."

She smiled.

"Please," I said. "Give me time."

"Of course," she said.

They, too, would need time, she said, to raise funds. Their aim was to increase local awareness about detentions. The wives felt that only important people were being spotlighted. Grace agreed. "Not all detainees are equal."

She would be out of Lagos, meanwhile, covering a story in the Delta. There had been more detentions following protests against oil companies. "Peter Mukoro is from those parts," she explained. "It was his story to tell. He's the son of an Urhobo farmer."

"Wasn't he in a family dispute over the farm?"

"No, his dispute was with an oil company. They destroyed his father's land. The irony of it is that Peter Mukoro was offered a scholarship by the same company. He rejected it and became a journalist."

"I didn't know."

"Not many people do. He's a true son of the soil."

"They say it's a wasteland in the Delta."

"You should see," she said. "Oil spills, barren farmland, villages burned down. They don't pray for rain anymore.

When it rains, it shrivels their plants."

"Oil."

"It's always been about the oil. The control of it. They tell us we can't get along, ethnic tensions, Africans not ready for democratic rule. We know exactly where we want to go in this country. A few greedy people won't let us get there."

I thought about Niyi again. "My husband says he can name five men in our country who can pay off our national debt, and a hundred companies overseas who earn a higher turnover than our oil revenues. I think that it will be better when the oil finally dries up. Maybe then we can have leaders who will get on with the business of running this country."

"Maybe. But meanwhile their greed is our problem. Here and in the rest of Africa."

Drought, famine, and disease. There was no greater disaster on our continent than the few who had control over our resources: oil, diamonds, human beings. They would sell anything and anyone to buyers overseas.

Grace Ameh reached for her portfolio.

"You have to go?" I asked.

"Yes," she said. "To be honest, I don't know how much longer we can continue. We hold editorial meetings in churches and mosques these days. The government has warned us not to speculate about the coup. You've heard?"

"I don't speculate."

"They will arrest anyone who does."

"What keeps you going?" I asked, escorting her to the door. "You have a family to think of, and yet you risk your life to tell a story."

She smiled. "Because they detain us and fire bomb our offices? You can't kill a testimony of a country and of a people. That's what we're fighting for, a chance to be heard. And the second thing is, I love my country. "

Did I? I believed I could live nowhere else. I hoped to be buried nowhere else. Was that enough to say that I loved my country? I barely knew the place. We had thirty-six geographical states, from the triad of North, West, East regions the British created before I was born. My father was from a town in the middle belt of Nigeria; my mother, from the West. They lived in Lagos. I was born here, raised here. Privilege never did blind my eyes, but there were parts of the city I'd never visited, parts I never needed to. Most of my country I had not seen, not even the Delta Grace Ameh spoke of. I only spoke one of our languages, Yoruba.

There were times I'd felt my hand leprous, bringing out my Nigerian passport, in case an immigration officer mistook me for one of those drug smugglers who were giving us a bad name around the world; other times I'd felt happy to wave a flag for women in my country; African women. Black women. What was the country I loved? The country I would fight for? Should it have borders?

Walking to the window, I caught a glimpse of Grace Ameh leaving our premises. She stopped to buy sugar cane from one of the women who sat across the road. The woman had been there from morning, would probably be there all day. Her ware couldn't be worth more than twenty naira. The cheap pen in my hand was worth more. "People are hungry," people liked to say, especially when the political debate heated up, "People are starving *out there!*" I'd heard it said, with some pride, that we didn't have the same type of hunger as other African countries where people died because their bodies eventually rejected food. Hunger in my country always looked like a child with a swollen belly, and I strongly believed that no one, except those who were hungry, should speak of it. The rest of us, unless we were prepared to give up half our food, were only entitled to shut up. But this woman selling sugar cane, would she eat better on the promise of a vote? And if her children were hungry, could she tear up her ballot to slip into their mouths? I was almost certain she didn't vote, but the result of the general election was considered to be the will of the people. Some brave people caught bullets in their chests defending this will. I was not one of them. I stayed at home that day. The government had warned us not to participate in the protest, and our mothers reiterated the message at home. What freedom was worth dying for? Soweto, Tiananmen Square. Remember.

~~~

I was lying on my bed. One arm was over my belly, the other was behind my head. Through the mosquito netting across my bedroom window I could see a huge satellite dish perched on the house across the road. It was the sort of afternoon that made me want to rip my clothes off. We had no electricity.

I was thinking of campaigns, military decrees, constitutional rights. In a democratic system, with a constitution in place, a citizen could challenge injustices, even if the system itself was flawed. With the military in power, without a constitution, there was no other recourse besides protest, peaceful or violent. I was thinking of my country, which I'd done nothing for. If she were a Lagos woman, she would be laughing right in my face. "Did you give me food to eat? Did you put clothes on my back? No. So, clear out of my sight, with your miserable face."

Downstairs my mother-in-law chatted to Niyi about *frajon*, a dish prepared for Good Friday. "Enitan can't make *frajon*?" she was saying. "I'm surprised. It is so easy to make. All she needs to do is soak the beans overnight, boil them till they're soft, then grind them with a blender, then stir in coconut milk, boil it with nutmeg. But she must wrap the nutmeg in muslin cloth. Remember how your uncle broke his tooth? You don't want that to happen, eh? So. When the *frajon* is boiled, then she can make the fish stew. You have fish? Not too bony fish, and I prefer not to fry mine, but that is her choice. *Frajon* is easy to make. In my day it was real work. We used to have to grind the beans and coconuts on slates, sift it... "

I turned over, imagining they had wrapped me in white muslin cloth and dipped me in scalding *frajon*. When I died, I would be called to give account of my time here on earth. What a pity if I said I cooked and cleaned. What a pity, even, if I couldn't give account of a little sin.

I imagined I marched downstairs to where they sat, banged my fist on the kitchen table and yelled, "Get out of my house!" Filled my lungs so our president could hear it in his presidential palace: "Get out of my country!"

I got up and stripped naked. The mirror on the dressing table was short so I could see my torso only. I liked the swell of my stomach; the roundness, tautness, softness of my hips; stretched nipples, darkened. I had not been touched in four months.

"Enitan?"

My mother-in-law stood in the doorway. I hurried over to my bed to retrieve my clothes. I was tripping and huddling over.

"Sit," she finally said.

She patted the bed, and I sat next to her, disheveled. She spoke without mixing her words. "Niyi has told me everything. I don't want you two to fight anymore. It's enough now."

"Yes, ma," I said.

She took my hand.

"I was not born into this family. I married into it. It was not easy for me as a young bride. I'd just finished nursing when I met Niyi's father. He was a difficult man. Difficult. The Franco men are difficult. But you know, my dear, when two rams meet head on, nothing can happen until one backs down."

"I know, ma."

"So. What you did for your father, that was right. But you

were wrong not to consult your husband first. He is the head of the house. He has a right to know. Now. What happened later, I think Niyi was wrong. To ignore your wife because she made a mistake like that. That was wrong, I told him, 'You cannot, cannot treat your wife that way. Say your piece to her, as a man and let it go.'"

"Yes, ma."

"You yourself, you must learn that a woman makes sacrifices in life. It shouldn't take anything out of you to indulge your husband for the sake of peace in your house."

"Yes, ma."

"So, let this be the end of it. You hear me? I don't want to lose another daughter."

She hugged me and I held my breath. I did not want to be that close. She drained me the way soft-hearted people did. Somehow I ended up deferring to her, as if to do otherwise would be taking advantage of her. She was fasting for Lent, she said, for the new baby.

"Thank you, ma," I said.

Niyi and I escorted her to her car. After she drove out of our home, we faced each other in our small driveway. "I'm sorry," he said. "I couldn't let you take a risk like that. I prefer that you hate me."

He twisted his soles on the gravel and stood up with his hands in his pockets. Four months separated us as if I'd licked my forefinger and drawn an indelible line in the air. Where would I begin?

"I don't hate you," I said.

I dreamed that night, in the spare room, clear as a prophesy. I was holding a newborn baby. "He's dead," my mother was saying. I tried to console her, but the more I did, the more her sorrow. I realized the baby was mine. I woke up in such pain. I waddled into our bedroom and switched on the bedside lamp.

"What's wrong?' Niyi asked.

"The baby," I said. "It's kicking."

He patted my side of the bed and I slid in. I moved close to him, to calm my heartbeat. He placed his arm over my belly.

"What's going on in here?"

My eyes were wide. "Is it normal?"

He patted my belly. "Yes, it is. Whoever you are, let your mother rest."

＊

On Good Friday I made *frajon* with my mother-in-law. She invited family members and I invited Sheri. Sheri and I sat at the kitchen table as Pierre washed dishes. Stacks of dirty plates surrounded him. We were surrounded by empty bottles of Star beer and Coca-Cola. We were tired. Sheri had brought her cousin's children, Wura and Sikiru. Sikiru, we banished to the living room. He sat there rocking himself in a persecuted manner. A more falling-down four-year-old I had not seen, with a head so long he could pass for Nefertiti. Outside, he'd collided with pots, grazed his knees, bumped his head on a washing line pole. "Sikiru! Sikiru!" we cried out every time we heard his yelps. After a while, we sounded like pigeons, or one of those old aunts we thought we'd never become. His sister, Wura, sat with us, a five-year-old with her hair pulled back like a rabbit's tail. She eyed my stomach until I got nervous and asked what she wanted.

"Coca-Cola," she said.

"I was not allowed to drink Coca-Cola at your age," I said.

"My mummy lets me. From when I had chicken pops."

"Chicken?"

"Yes. And my froat was paining me, that's why."

She held her neck.

"Throat," Sheri said.

"Troath," she said. "And my body was pops, pops, pops."

She pinched her forearm and wagged her forefinger. "But no scratching. No scratching, because that is the rules. And if you scratch, your pops will only grow bigger, like a balloon."

She stretched her arms wide and mistook my amazement for sympathy.

"It was terrible," she said, in a husky voice. "Now, can I have my Coca-Cola?"

I started breathing as if I'd gone into labor. When I served Wura *frajon*, it was, "Ee-yack, I don't like this Free John thing." "*Fray*-John," I corrected her. "Can I have fish?" she asked. I gave her some of the stew I made from Mrs. Williams's fish. "Ee-yack. Too much pepper in this fish," she said. "Aunty, do you have biscuits?"

I handed her a Coca-Cola. She drank it clean, burped, and went in search of her brother with caffeinated eyes. Dear Wura. "May I be askewed?" she asked. When I said yes, she said, "Fenks." I immediately forgave her.

"Are all children like this?" I asked Sheri.

"Be prepared," she said.

Pierre dropped cutlery in the sink. I placed my bowl aside. I had already had two helpings of *frajon* and some of her stewed crabs, so tasty I'd hidden them from everyone.

"I will be a terrible mother," I said.

Sheri stretched. "You're not looking forward to it?"

"I am. But I have not had time to think about it."

I did not feel comfortable discussing motherhood with her, but I was aware of a presence within me, as infinite as God. I did worry that I might spoil my child rotten.

"It's hard work," she said.

"I can see."

Niyi came through the door. "Pierre, water to drink. Quick."

He placed his hand on my shoulder and Sheri watched him the way she watched men, arching her brows and keeping her eyes on his midriff. Niyi rubbed my shoulder and left.

"Is he talking to you now?" Sheri asked.

"He is."

"You're not still angry with him."

"I need time."

Time really wasn't enough, I thought. Forgetting would be enough.

Sheri sat back in her chair. "It is good that you met your brother."

"I can get to like him."

"I hope so," she said.

"I don't have to like him, Sheri."

"I didn't say you did."

"But I know what you're thinking. In your family, everyone sticks together... "

"I never said we were perfect. We just happen to like each other, and thank God we do, because I don't know what would happen in the little village my father left."

"You're confessing something?"

"If they keep to one woman our lives would be simpler."

"Ah."

"But we, too, are just as guilty for what we do to each other. I've never met a man who had an affair with himself."

"No."

"So. The blame is on two sides then. I keep telling my sisters. Stop letting these boys treat you badly. They tell me, 'But we're not strong like you.' Strong. I don't even know what that word means. But look at the way we were raised, two women in one house, one man. Mama Kudi's turn to cook for Daddy. Mama Gani's turn to sleep with Daddy. A young girl shouldn't grow up seeing such things. But that is my family. I've accepted it."

We accepted the world we were born into, though we knew what felt right and wrong from the start. The protesting and detesting could come afterward with confirmation that our lives could have been better, but the acceptance was always there.

Pierre left the kitchen with a bottle of water and I dared to cross a line.

"Are you curious about your mother?"

"Hm." Her lips were thin.

"Enough to look for her?"

"Not like that."

"Why not?"

"What if she doesn't want to know me?"

"What if she's thinking what you're thinking?"

"I'm not ready. I'm not."

"I'll be behind you when you are."

I couldn't imagine being that estranged from my own mother. We listened to the Francos' chatter in the living room for a moment.

"Can you see yourself married?" I asked.

She shrugged. "If I meet someone with sense. But what I've seen so far: rich man wants to own your future, poor man wants to own your past. Some are just plain untidy, and you know me, I can't stand the mess. Some must have children, and, well... "

"Aren't you sometimes angry?"

"Why?"

"Looking back."

"I'm a today-tomorrow woman. I can't look back. I have my business, plenty of children around me. Someone will always chase me. I still have a pretty face. *Abi?*" She sucked her cheeks in. "It's other people who worry about me. Me, I have no worries, except when I die."

"Why then?"

"Because who will bury me?"

"I will," I said, poking my chest.

"What if you die before me?"

"Then my child will bury you," I said.

Sheri had two mothers. Why couldn't my child?

"What I really want," she said. "Really, really, *sha*, is to work for children. You know I practiced saying that for Miss World? I memorized a whole speech even, children are our future, all that. I didn't care about one word. I was annoyed the judges eliminated me before I had a chance to use it. Then one day I was thinking about the speech. Children beg on the streets here and people drive past them. Everyone is fed up. You open the papers and someone is asking for their child to get treatment abroad. Why not raise money for them? I started thinking... "

"About?"

"A charity. I'm good at asking for money, I know people and these photographers are always snapping me somewhere. Why not use them? The one thing that has stopped me is that I can't stand people knowing where I am and what I'm doing. But I think I can get used to that. It's a small price."

The work suited Sheri more than she thought. A charity. Her unfriendliness was an asset. People were intrigued by her. Those she approached would feel privileged. She would thrive.

"You have to do it," I said. "You will be so good and you'll be surprised how much you've missed being around. You're not a background person. What, you want to hide for the rest of your life because people talk? Let them talk. One day they will ask themselves what they're doing with their own lives. Any social event in this place, people will come whether or not they care about your cause. They will buy tickets, give money, so long as they're recognized. You have to do it, Sheri. If you had told me this before I would have sat on your back."

"I've been thinking seriously, end of this year hopefully. I need to find a name and trustees... "

"Put me. We will arrange the paper work for you at the office. You'll be the best charity in Lagos."

Her birth mother and motherhood taken away from her, and she wasn't thinking of tearing her clothes off and walking naked on the streets. She was stronger than any strong person I knew. The word strong usually meant that a person was being short-changed emotionally and physically and had to live with it. I had always been motivated by fear, of lowliness, of pessimism, of failure. I was not strong.

Sheri was planning to make the next pilgrimage to Mecca. I couldn't imagine her becoming an Alhaja. She would have to get a gold tooth, at least, to fit my image of a Lagos Alhaja. More guests arrived and she decided it was time for her to leave. I saw her to her car and when I returned to the kitchen, my mother-in-law was serving more *frajon* for them.

"I'll do that, ma," I said, reaching for the bowl.

"No no," she said. "You've done enough."

She tugged at the same time I did, and we found ourselves fighting over the bowl. I stood back as she bent over the pot. I thought she was searching for her life, the unborn child, who had given birth to everyone but herself. She too was strong; strong enough to live with a man who wouldn't even look at her when she spoke to him. She was a human shock-absorber.

Pierre walked in with more dirty plates and jiggled cutlery around in the sink.

I headed for the living room. Niyi was sitting on the floor by his Uncle Jacinto's feet. Uncle Jacinto was leaning over him, talking hush-hush as the Francos did. I imagined it was like sticking my nose into a petrol pump. Uncle Jacinto was a retired law professor and the reigning king of Latin phrases: *de jure, de facto, ex parte, ex post facto*. He enjoyed his spirits, though the word "drunk" had never been mentioned in relation to him.

Niyi nodded politely. If our friends were here, this was about the time he would be stirring up trouble, either on his own or in support of me, telling someone or the other I was the boss in the house. As soon as they left, it was Enitancanyou? With his family Enitancanyou began while they were around and I couldn't challenge him, because they would hate me for controlling him, he said. Watching him, I felt sorry. It was no lie, he was protecting me. I was protecting him too. I didn't want anyone to call him a weak man, even though I thought the sooner his family hated me the better. From then on I could do exactly as I pleased.

There were about twenty of them present and any family as large as that was bound to have the usual array of people: Uncle Funsho, who rubbed my bra straps whenever he hugged me; Aunty Doyin, the pretty one who locked herself in a room. She still wore wigs and pale pink lipstick of the early seventies. She wasn't so pretty anymore, because the man she had locked herself up for ended up punching her face whenever another man looked at her. There was Simi, her daughter, braids down to her butt, sassy as Brazilian Samba. Too cool to smile or be pleasant. What was it about this new generation? I loved their bad attitude. Simi walked around with a T-shirt and exposed her navel. After she pierced her nose the Francos said she would get pregnant, but she didn't. She was studying to be an accountant, though her university was closed after a student protest. There was Kola, her brother, who always looked weighed down because his family had called him a dullard for so long. "Won't learn a thing, keeps taking photographs and thinks that will suffice," they said. I knew he was dyslexic. And Rotimi his first cousin. Rotimi, whose voice was high. Niyi and his brothers tried to slap his manhood into his back, punch it into his skinny ribs. "Speak like a man! Speak like a man!" I warned them, "You'll kill this boy before he discovers his sexual preference." Now he had a girlfriend, and his voice was still high.

Gnarled and plump people, the Francos, I thought. The old and young. I could well be jealous of them. When did we ever have family in our home? My mother's family was her church. My father avoided his because they were always trying to extort money from him. "Big Foot," I said.

It was Niyi's youngest brother, the tallest and skinniest.

"Yep?" he answered.

"Gerrin here," I said.

He walked toward me looking like some sort of willow tree. Big Foot was my favorite—clumsy, and his feet were size fourteen.

"We need help in here," I said.

"Who needs help?"

"Your mother, who gave birth to you, needs help."

"Doing what?"

"Serving food."

He frowned. "I don't know how to do that."

"No one knows how to do that. They learn. So you better gerrin here or else those girls you keep bringing around here, trying to impress, I will start talking."

"You won't do that."

"Just ask your brother what a wicked woman I can be."

"You women's liberation-nalists," he mumbled.

He tackled his mother for the bowl. "Relax woman," he told her.

She sat by the kitchen table watching him. "Big Foot knows how to do this? Big Foot? You know how to do this? I thought you were useless, like the rest of my sons."

Big Foot spilled stew on his shirt and yelled.

～

That evening, I found a dress in my wardrobe. It was not one of mine. It was made from tie-dyed fabric and newly sewn. I thought I'd stumbled on infidelity.

"What is this?"

I held it up. Niyi was lying on our bed.

"I can't even have a girlfriend in this place," he muttered.

"Whose is it?"

"You were not supposed to see it. It's yours."

I lifted it. "Mine?"

"For Easter."

"You've never given me a present for Easter before. Who made it?"

I placed it against my body.

"Your seamstress," he said.

"You went to my seamstress?" I leaned forward. "You went to my seamstress?"

He nodded. "Now I know where our money goes. That woman has a bigger fan than ours in that shack of hers."

Niyi called me Jackie O. I ran to my seamstress more than any other woman he knew, for all my principles. Well, he was a big fat liar, but it was true that new clothes could make me salivate. I sniffed the dress. I could still smell the sweat of my seamstress' fingers on the cloth.

"Thank you," I said, using the dress as a shield.

"You too," he said. "You did a lot today."

"I know," I said.

I also clipped his toe nails before we slept. I always did because he wouldn't and he would end up scratching my legs. As I wrestled with three months' nail growth, I was finally able to tell him about meeting my brother.

"These men," he said. "I don't know how they do it. I didn't choose to have two families and most days I feel like half a man."

"Since when did you feel like half a man?"

"Watch what you're doing."

"What will I do with half a man? I want you to be double man. How many years now, and we've been fighting. I want you to be my greatest ally."

"I am."

"You're not."

"Here we go."

"Keep still," I said.

"Don't amputate my foot!"

He wasn't kicking me and I was cutting him up. We were talking again.

"My love for you is much," he said. "You just don't know."

⁓

Baba came to collect his monthly salary the next day. He was still tending my father's garden on Sundays, and on Saturdays worked at a house nearby.

"Compliments of the season," I said. "How are you?"

I spoke to him in Yoruba, addressing him by the formal you, because he was an elder. He responded with the same formality because I was his employer. Yoruba is a language that doesn't recognize gender—he the same as she, him the same as her—but respect is always important. "We are fine," he said. "Hope all is well with you. Have you heard from your father?"

"No word yet."

"I will be there to work tomorrow."

"Please excuse me," I said.

He waited by the kitchen door as I went to get his money. When I returned, I felt a slight breeze through the mosquito netting. I handed the money to him.

"It's cold," I said.

"It's going to rain," he said.

"Rain? So early? The rain is strange these days."

"Yes," he said.

"You'd better not get caught in it," I said.

"I will hurry."

I rubbed my arms as goose bumps appeared. Walking upstairs, I imagined Baba trudging to the nearest bus stop in the rain. He had withered so much, it was hard to believe he was the same person who had chased me round the garden when I was small. I told Niyi I would give him a lift, then visit my mother. "She hasn't been well," I said.

"Again?" he said.

"It's not her fault," I said. "She prefers to be well."

He, who listened to his father's self-praise without yawning. I'd asked him to stop finding every excuse to leave home whenever my mother visited. Mostly, he said he had to go to the office. She worried that he was overworked.

I found Baba by the gates of our estate, and drove him to the nearest bus stop. We passed a marketplace. The sky had turned gray and the market women were clearing up in anticipation of the rain. They placed plastic sheets over their wooden stalls and secured them with rocks. Children scurried with full trays perched on their heads. Some were giddier than the wind with excitement. Their trays were colorful with tomatoes, cherry peppers, purple onions, okras, and bananas. A sign post on a shack caught my eye.

We specialies in
Gonerea
Sifilis
AID
Watery sperm

"I didn't know you lived on the mainland," I said.

"I moved," Baba explained. "Ten years now. I used to live in Maroko. They drove us away and flattened our homes. Your father let me stay in the quarters, until we found a new place."

"I didn't know."

"You were with your mother. They came to us that day with coffins, and told us that if we didn't leave, we would end up inside them."

When Baba said "they," he meant anyone in uniform: the army, the police, traffic conductors. He would have seen different rulers under the British, First and Second Republics, and military governments.

I slowed for a group of hawker women to cross the road.

"Did you vote at the elections?"

"Yes. They told me to put an "X," I put an "X." Now they're telling me my "X" is nothing. I don't understand."

He said "hex" instead of "X."

"They're following their predecessors," I said.

"These ones?" he said. "They have surpassed their predecessors. For the first time, I'm looking at them, and saying, it is as if... "

Baba took time to finish his sentences. I waited until he was ready.

"It's as if they hate us," he said.

I dropped him at the bus stop. It began to rain as he boarded his bus. The rain coursed down on my windscreen; the wipers barely cleared my view. I drove slow and noticed the sign post on the shack again.

We specialies in
Gonerea
Sifilis
AID
Watery sperm

My face was wet and steamy. The gutter in front of my mother's house flowed like a muddy river. My mother didn't come to her door when I rang her bell, so I rushed to the back door to check if it was open. It was. I walked upstairs cleaning the rain from my arms, knocked on her bedroom door.

I smelled her death before I saw her.

"Mummy!" I screamed.

She was lying on the floor, before an empty candle holder. I reached for her shoulder and shook, bent to listen to her heart. There wasn't a sound. I ran out of her house and swallowed rain.

On the front porch of Mrs. Williams' house, Shalewa stuck her toe into a puddle. She took one look at me and froze.

I rattled the gate. "Shalewa, where is your mother?"

"Upstairs."

"Please. Open the gates."

Shalewa ran into the rain.

"Tell her it's Enitan from next door. Tell her I need to see her. Please."

She unlocked the gates and I followed her indoors.

Mrs. Williams didn't think it was wise to call an ambulance. "They may come, they may not come," she said as though discussing the month's profit margins. "We will have to carry her to hospital in my van. Shalewa?"

"Yes, Mummy."

"Get me my phone, my sweet."

"Yes, Mummy."

She'd been skirting around, trying to hear our whispers. As her mother made phone calls in the dining room, I sat in the living room with her. She moved a place mat around a side table, and sang a pop song; not one I recognized, "Treat me like a woman," occasionally peeping at me. She knew I'd been crying.

Mrs. Williams returned to the living room.

"I've found help," she said. "I'd better call the hospital now. You stay here and I will come for you when we're ready."

Who would carry my mother? I thought. Her arms, her legs. They would have to carry her with care, as if she were sleeping, as if she could wake.

Once her mother left, Shalewa resumed her game with the place mat. I wanted to tell her not to worry, but children knew when they were being lied to and she would think she was responsible for my sadness regardless. She continued her song. "Treat me like no other... "

Her mother returned.

"Shalewa," she said. "You want to go to Temisan's house?"

Shalewa nodded.

"That's my girl. Go upstairs and get your shoes. Her mummy is coming for you."

Shalewa ran upstairs, half-smiling. She tripped on a stair and exaggerated her limp.

"Will she be okay?" I asked.

Her mother nodded. "I'll explain to her later. We'd better go."

I noticed the mobile phone in her hand, but mine were shaking too hard to make a call. I asked her if she would.

On the way to the hospital, Mrs. Williams kept talking to herself, "I hope the police don't stop us. You know, these checkpoints... "

Her windscreen wipers hypnotized me. They tore the rain apart each time and I hugged myself, not because I was cold, but because my mother was lying in the back of her van, wrapped in white bed sheets. Above us the rain beat proverbs on the car roof:

Let our tears help us see clearer

He who denies his mother rest will not rest himself

Below us the rain beat the earth.

"I knew there was something," Mrs. Williams murmured. "There had to be something. The rain, pouring like this, coming so early."

~

My mother had been dead a day. Going through her medicines later, I discovered a batch which appeared to have been re-dated. I did not know where she'd purchased them, or how long they had expired. I imagined she'd bought them because they were cheaper.

Mrs. Williams washed her. The nurse's aide in the hospital would not.

"There are others," she said. "She will have to wait."

"But she's waited too long," Sheri said.

Sheri was anxious; Moslems buried within a day. The nurse's aide shrugged. Her eyes were like a dead fish's, sunken and gray. Too much, they were saying. I've seen too much, can't you see? Whatever your story is. I don't care.

"Is there someone else?" Sheri asked.

"Only me," the aide said. "Only me is here."

Irritation crept into her voice. She was shifting, wanting to resume her task. Who were these people? Coming down to the mortuary, getting in her way?

Sheri turned to Mrs. Williams. "What will we do?"

I stood by the door with Niyi. I'd been waiting upstairs for three hours. Niyi arrived first and Sheri after him.

"I can wash her, " Mrs. Williams said to me.

I felt Niyi's hand. He led me into the corridor outside.

A week later we buried my mother, in Ikoyi cemetery next to an angel with broken wings. The cemetery was filled with decapitated statues. Thickets grew higher than the head stones. It was where my brother was buried, but the plots next to his had been filled. I paid the local council for a plot by the entrance. During the funeral the pallbearers we'd hired to carry her casket refused to carry it further until we'd paid their money.

"You will burn in Hell for this," our priest told them.

"Reverend Father," said the stocky man who'd snatched the money from Niyi. "Hell and Lagos? Which is worse?"

He squinted as he counted the notes. One of his mates yawned and scratched his crotch.

For two days after my mother's funeral, I stopped eating. On the third day Niyi accompanied me to my pre-natal check up and at the end of it, the doctor told us, "I don't like what I'm seeing. This baby isn't growing properly."

"Enitan hasn't been eating," Niyi said.

"Why not?" the doctor asked.

"She's lost her appetite," Niyi said.

"How can we get it back?" the doctor asked. "Can't her mother cook her something nice?"

He was an old man and tended to talk to people as he pleased. Normally I didn't mind because he was also one of the best ob-gyns in Lagos. Niyi began to explain but I tapped his arm. I could barely form the words because my mouth was dry.

"My mother is dead," I said.

We arrived home and Niyi headed straight for the kitchen to cook a meal. I was lying in bed when he brought it to me. Fried plantain. They were golden brown and cooked right through, unlike the charred, half-raw pieces I usually handed to him. He picked one up and carried it to my mouth. He pried my lips open with his forefinger and thumb. The plantain slithered into my mouth, warm and sweet. I shut my eyes as it clung to the roof of my mouth, pulled it down with my tongue and began to chew.

As a child, whenever I had malaria, I would have a bitter taste in my mouth, after my fever broke. I hated that bitter taste. It tainted everything that went into my mouth, but the bitterness meant that I was cured: no more bouts of nausea, no more pounding headaches. I did not like the taste of the plantain in my mouth, but I began to eat from then on.

My daughter Yimika was born on the morning of August 3. Between the time crickets sleep and roosters wake, I tell her. After my water broke, I begged to be gutted like a fish. Then I saw her. I burst into tears.

"She's beautiful," I said.

Like a pearl. I could have licked her. I had only one wish for her, that she would not be disinherited in her lifetime. I chose Sheri as her godmother. She would understand. Following Yoruba tradition, Yimika could have been called "Yetunde," "mother has returned" to salute my mother's passing, but I decided against it. Everyone must walk their own path unencumbered. Hers wouldn't be easy, born in a motherland that treated her children like bastards, but it was hers. And I didn't worry that she wasn't born in a more fortunate place, like America, where people are so free they buy stars from the sky and name them after their children. If you own a star from the day you are born, what else is there to wish for?

My milk took me in a tackle, tugging on my shoulder, and tearing through my chest. I sat up in bed and unbuttoned my nightgown. Yimika's tiny mouth snatched my nipple and dragged. Bluish-white milk spurted from my free nipple. I covered it with a tissue from the box on my bedside table. The air-conditioner blasted cold air over my face; I lay back.

As my breast softened in her mouth, I eased it out and transferred her to the other. Yimika grabbed it with the same hungriness and I bit my lip to overcome the pain. Her palms traveled up my ribs. Her own ribs were separated from mine by her soft pink cotton romper. I wriggled her toes.

The night she was born, I was too tired to do anything but hold her. The day after, I was overwhelmed by visitors in my hospital room. The day after that, I braved my sutures and came home. "We won't need to press this one's head," my mother-in-law said. "It's round already."

She suggested that we wash her the traditional way, smothering her with shredded camwood and stretching her limbs. I refused and settled her in a crib by my bed; gave her a top and tail instead. Afterward, I checked her ears. They were as dark as my hands, which meant that she'd taken after me. I traced down her spine where Mongolian spots had left her skin black and blue. I dressed the mush on her navel, felt the pulse under her ribs. I imagined her heart pink and moist and throbbing. There was a tiny bald patch on her head, which worried me, though her doctor said it was nothing but a birth mark. I told him to be sure, because if anything happened to her, my faculties would close down and there would be no begging me out of that state.

I remembered my mother. There were times I still felt tearful, and I found that if I placed Yimika against me, she soothed me. She was tiny, but as heavy as a paper weight on my chest. I stared at her face for hours. She had taken her father's eyes, shaped like two halves of the moon. I knew she would shine.

Niyi shuffled in wearing his pajamas. He was sleeping in the spare room because Yimika was keeping him up at night. He scratched his shoulder. "How are you feeling?"

"It hurts," I said. "My whole body hurts, like she's sucking out my marrow."

"Why are you smiling then?"

I'd heard that some women cried for days after childbirth, because their bodies were out of control. But I had not shed a tear. If women cried, perhaps it was because we were overwhelmed by the power granted to us.

Niyi sat on the bed and began to stroke Yimika's head.

"She's tiny," he said.

"Too small," I said, opening her fingers one by one.

"Fatten her up for her debut."

I pressed her closer. It was four days to her naming ceremony. I touched his cheek. "I can't believe this is happening. We must make sure we behave ourselves from now on. We will be the best family."

For a while, he watched as if he were supervising.

"Is Sheri coming again?" he asked.

"Yes," I said.

"She's really helped."

"She's good with children."

"I feel so bad. The things I've said about her."

"Really?" I said.

He shook his head. "Nope."

He had to go to work. Sheri arrived when the hairdresser who had come to undo my braids was almost through with her task. She brought pounded yam and okra stew from her family's restaurant.

"Your hair has grown," she said.

The hairdresser pulled another braid and began to poke it loose with a comb. Her price had increased since the last time, but so had the price of food, she said. The veranda floor was littered with hair extensions. Yimika slept in a pram stationed next to Sheri. Sweat trickled down my back and I shook my gown down. I studied my reflection in the hand mirror and was surprised by how long my hair had grown, and by how much my face had changed. I had a shadow over my cheeks from where my skin had darkened.

The hairdresser loosened the last braid. I lifted my hand mirror to inspect her work.

"Oh-oh," I said.

Sheri edged forward. I lowered the mirror as she inspected my hair line.

"You have white hair," she confirmed.

"I'm only thirty-five."

"I've had mine since twenty-nine. Dye it."

"I won't dye it," I said. "Why should I?"

The hairdresser pulled my hair back. She hadn't said a word since she started her work, but it was obvious she was enjoying my discomfort.

I paid her and she left. Yimika cried in her pram and I hurried over to check her. She was still asleep, smiling too. I preferred to think she was having a good dream, but Sheri had told me that it was wind. There was sweat in her hair. I couldn't help but pick her up. Whenever she was sleeping, I missed her. Her arms flopped over my hands and her mouth opened.

"*Alaiye Baba*," I whispered. "Master of the earth."

She looked like one of those plump empresses who had slaves peeling grapes for them. I bent to kiss her. Her lashes unlocked.

"Our friend is awake," I said.

Sheri came over and eased her out of my arms. She made clucking sounds and began to rock her. We were standing by the bed of purple hearts and I surveyed them as though I'd just planted them. A red-head lizard slithered across the veranda floor. It slid between two pots of mother-in-law's tongue and disappeared into the garden.

"Congratulations, mummy."

I turned around to see who had said that. It was Grace Ameh.

From the moment she stepped into my home, her eyes were darting around. "I went to your office to look for you. Then they told me about your mother. My sincere condolences. I'm terribly, terribly sorry."

I felt shy now that she was on my turf. We were like strangers who'd been forced to use the same bathroom.

"I'm surprised you had time to find your way here," I said.

"We closed down last month. Our final issue."

"That's a shame," I said.

"Yes," she said, in her usual neutral manner. She down-played her struggles, so successfully one could almost believe she dismissed them.

"You must eat with us," I said.

It was a joy to watch her, the way she dipped and separated, and swallowed. She talked between gulps about journalists and activists who had been sentenced following the alleged coup in March. They were charged with being accessories after the fact of treason.

"It's a farce," she said.

I placed my fork down. "They say the Commonwealth ought to impose sanctions."

"Commonwealth," she huffed.

"Don't you think that will work?"

"Our problems are ours to solve, not anyone else's. I'm not one of those who believe in crying to the West. They still haven't got it right themselves. Freedom of speech, human rights, democracy. Democracy, some would say it's for sale. Besides, their leaders are constrained. They can't help us if helping us will hurt their constituents. We will always have to look within for our own solutions. I have faith in Africa, anyway. A continent that can produce a Mandela? I have faith."

Instead, she looked weary, and I did not entirely agree with her. Intellectuals like her resented foreign intervention. It was the same with the Nigerian elite and foreign aid, always complaining about how patronizing that was, when Nigerians who really needed help could not care less where it came from. Sheri was discovering just how hard it was to get money from wealthy Nigerians. They pledged their support to her charity and then they disappeared. I wasn't sure about the extent of foreign intervention in our local politics—CIA-backed coups and assassinations included—but was it too much to expect other countries to take an interest in our well being, if most of our stolen wealth was invested in their economies?

"Economic sanctions," Sheri said, "Let's be realistic. Who will they hurt—Brigadier Big Belly or Mama Market?"

"Exactly," Grace Ameh said.

"You know there are detainees who have nothing to do with politics," I said.

"I don't understand," she said.

"Half the people in prison," I explained.

"I know," she said. "Most of them are awaiting trial. Some of them die before they ever see a court room."

I thought I had badgered her enough.

"When do we start our campaign?" I asked.

"As soon as you're able."

My heart beat faster.

Grace Ameh stayed for a while after we finished eating. She wanted to avoid the lunchtime traffic. I cleared the table when she left as Sheri watched over Yimika.

"You never told me about this," she said.

"Ah, well," I said.

"What does Niyi think?"

I wiped the table using circular motions.

"He doesn't know."

"Will you tell him?"

"Today."

She laughed. "You're joining the ranks, *aburo?*"

I made my circles smaller and smaller.

"Small by small," I said.

~~⌒~~

I washed my hair and braided it into two, sat in a bowl of brine to heal my sutures. I had to shake my head to shift the fuzziness that plagued me since Yimika was born. By the time Niyi returned from work, I was ready.

I watched as he undressed in our bedroom. He hopped out of his trousers, placed them over a chair. As if he remembered I'd asked him not to, he took the trousers off the chair and laid them on the bed. The gesture made me sad. How caustic we were to each other, and we'd wasted time over what we didn't want, and what we didn't like. Was it simply that we knew not to ask for what we wouldn't receive? Our jokes saved our marriage, I realized. When we shared them we were within a safe zone. But we had no jokes to spare now, except the one about the man who had chosen the wrong women twice.

"Grace Ameh came here today," I said.

"Who?"

"Grace Ameh, the journalist from *Oracle* magazine."

"What did she want?"

"She wants me to chair a campaign for my father, Peter Mukoro, and others."

"What did you say?"

"It's a small one."

"What did you tell her?"

"I said that I will. That I want to. It's the chance I've been waiting for. I'm hoping we can meet once a month... " My voice trailed off.

He released his tie. "Not here I hope."

"We can meet at my mother's house. It doesn't really matter."

He walked toward the bed.

"We've talked about this already."

"No. We never talked. At least we never agreed. And nothing is safe around here, anyway. Robbers could break in as we speak. The police, the army, whether or not you are looking for trouble, they give it you. I've thought it through. We will appeal to the government. There are women and children involved. Yimika. You know I won't take chances with her."

He pulled his tie through his collar. Yimika whined in her crib. I could feel my milk in my chest. I rolled my shoulders. I was not ready to feed her.

Niyi undid his cufflinks.

"I care about my family," he said. "Only my family."

"So did I," I said. "Once. But that has changed now. I wasn't worried about my mother. Who are we fooling? The state our country is in affects everyone."

He didn't answer.

"Are you listening?" I asked.

"No," he said.

"No what?" I asked.

Yimika began to cry. My milk began to leak into my bra. It seemed to be dripping from my armpits.

"No, I can't allow that," he said. "I am sorry."

No one's "no" was more final than Niyi's, but I pressed further. I was not looking for a compromise. He had to change his mind. I was desperate enough to force him. From childhood, people had told me I couldn't do this or that, because no one would marry me and I would never become a mother. Now, I was a mother.

"I'm not the same," I said.

"What?"

"I'm not the same as I used to be. I want you to know."

I shook my blouse down. My milk had stained it.

I listened to many voices that night. One told me I would be dragged to one of those far-off prisons: Abakaliki, Yola, Sokoto, where harmattan winds would brittle my bones. I hushed that. Another told me I would never see Yimika again; that she would grow up, like Sheri, without a mother, Niyi would replace me and I would fall sick from heartbreak. I let that talk and talk before I hushed it. When the last hush was hushed, I listened.

I, alone, had beaten my thoughts down. No one else had done that. I, believer in infinite capabilities, up to a point; self-reliance, depending. It was internal sabotage, like military coups. Wherever the malice came from, it would have to go back. Yimika began to cry. I checked her but she wasn't wet. I rocked her back to sleep. My eyes grew heavy and I shut them. I could agree with Niyi; at least the tiredness would go away.

"Everyone has at least one choice," my father said, whenever I talked about women in home prisons. He was shocked. How could one make such a false and simplistic comparison? Likening a handful of kitchen martyrs to people confined in Nigerian prisons. Some prisoners set free would choose to stay on, I argued. My point was about a condition of the mind. Most days, I was as conscious of making choices as I was of breathing. "I raised you better," my father said. "You think," I said.

～⊃

Yimika was dressed in her white christening gown. Sheri cradled her. I offered a calabash of kola nuts to my father-in-law. He picked one, split it in half and took a bite. My mother-in-law sat next to him, also chewing. I was wearing traditional dress: a white lace blouse, and red wrapper tied from my waist down. Around my neck were coral beads and on my head was a scarlet head tie with gold embroidery.

Because of my mother's death, only family members were invited to Yimika's naming ceremony, but they filled our living room. I placed the calabash on an empty stool and bit my kola nut. It was a gesture of affirmation for our prayers. Initially, all I could taste was bitter caffeine, then I tasted a slight hint of sweetness at the back of my tongue.

A few china bowls were laid out on the dining table: honey and salt for sweetness in Yimika's life, water for calmness, peppercorns for fruitfulness, palm oil for joy. She had received four names: Oluyimika, God surrounds me; Omotanwa, The child we waited for; Ebun, Gift; Moyo, my middle name, I rejoice.

Niyi's grand aunt began to pray in Yoruba. She was the oldest in the family and the other family members responded, "*Amin*," each time. I joined the prayer for my daughter, then added a prayer for the place she'd arrived, that leaders would find their way to children, and our customs would become kinder. After our last amen, Niyi's grand aunt poured libation and raised a glass of Schnapps to her mouth, to salute her ancestors. Her lean body stiffened as the alcohol shot down her throat. She adjusted her head tie. It was time to eat.

In the kitchen, one of Sheri's cooks sat on a chair with a wooden mortar between her knees. She scooped lumps of pounded yam from it using a calabash quarter and wrapped them in cellophane. Blue bottle flies swarmed the sink where someone had knocked a can of mango juice over. A second cook served fried meat onto small plates. They worked together like big band players, rehearsed and indifferent.

"Are you ready?" I asked.

"It's done," the first cook said.

They were not ready. As I left the kitchen, my mother-in-law hurried toward me.

"What about the food?" she asked.

"They're almost finished, ma," I said.

"The guests are hungry."

"Don't worry, ma," I said.

"Where are you going?" she asked.

"Upstairs, ma," I said.

I could not wait. There were babies who stayed in their mother's wombs too long. By the time they were born, they were already dead. There were people who learned to talk on their death beds. When they opened their mouths to speak, they drew their last breaths.

The staircase in my house had never been a staircase. Often, I walked up imagining I was making an ascension, into heaven even. I was rising above a miscarriage, my mother's death, casting off malaria fever, rage, guilt. My mother-in-law's disapproval, I cast that off, too. My peace surpassed her understanding.

Niyi gave me a wave when I almost reached the top. He was making sure everyone had wine. I tried to steady my smile. What story would I tell him for making him less than half a man? That would be a k-legged story.

In my bedroom I removed my head tie and retired it among my jars of pomade and perfume. Along the parting between my braids, white hairs stood out.

Sheri walked in. "People are... what's happening here?"

I wondered how to tell her. Downstairs, the people began a thanksgiving song:

My joy overflows
I will give thanks every day
My joy overflows
I will rejoice every day
Will you?

～ಾ

The women arrived late for the first day of the meeting. Lagos was recovering from another petrol shortage and public transport had just resumed. Some sat on the edge of their seats; others as if this were their first opportunity to sit. One pregnant woman asked to put her feet up. There were seventeen of us now: wives, mothers, sisters of journalists.

We appointed a treasurer and a secretary. I took my place in the middle of the room and announced that those who had something to say should speak; those who had come to listen, should. The surprise visitor was Peter Mukoro's wife. The one who had exposed him to the tabloids. She asked us not to call her Aunty, Madam, or any of that nonsense. Her name was Clara, Clara Mukoro.

The others were quick to tire of Clara and her trouble. I tried to retaliate with kindness. One day, she said, "You. Don't you ever get angry?" I answered, "If we both are angry, Aunty Clara, where will we get?"

Clara and I soon became close, enough for me to ask why she would fight for a man who had humiliated her. She had a square-shaped face with eyes I only expected to see on a woman from the Far East, and whenever she talked, she narrowed them.

"I knew Peter from primary school," she told me. "My father was headmaster of our school, Peter was in my class. He helped me with my school books. I was there when his father's farm was ruined. I was there the day Peter turned down the scholarship. When he left for Lagos, I left with him. My father disowned me. It was Peter who supported me through university. That is the Peter I remember, not the Peter running around like a little boy in a sweet shop. He is still the father of my children. Besides, if anyone should be locking Peter up, it should be me."

We would write letters to our president, asking for the release of our relations, whether or not he read them. We would not stop until our relations were freed. There were other campaign groups like ours, and they often appeared in the press. Some were petitioning for the release of women journalists. We gained strength from their voices. The threat of state security agents hung over us, but surprisingly, they never came.

If we didn't try, we would never have known.

If we didn't try, we would never have known, I still say.

I was born in the year of my country's independence, and saw how it raged against itself. Freedom was never intended to be sweet. It was a responsibility from the onset, for a people, a person, to fight for, and to hold on to. In my new life, this meant that there were bills to pay alone; memories to rock and lay to rest; regrets to snatch and return; tears, which always did clear my eyes.

These days, I stretched. I spread my legs wide on my sofa, flung my arms wide over the back. I lay like animal hide on my bed, face up, face down. Niyi was so tall, I'd always thought he deserved more space. The shrinkage I experienced was never worth it. He came to see Yimika almost every day, and nearly always left slamming my front door which made me miss him less and less. But I didn't blame him. He was fighting as though we were vying for the same cylinder of air: the more I breathed, the less there was for him. I did not sit too long with his family members either, not even my brothers-in-law. It wasn't out of ill-will: I had little energy for that. But I knew that given half the chance, they would confuse me with their advice, and nothing would be left of my original thought.

One morning I found an old picture of my mother and me. She was carrying me and I was about six months old wearing a dress with puffy sleeves. She was wearing a mini dress and her legs were as skinny as mine. My mother once said she whispered words of guidance into my ear, when I was born. She never told me what she said. She said that I had remembered. I whispered into my daughter's ear like that, in my mother's house. I told her, "I love you. You have nothing to do but remember."

Sheri wouldn't stop nagging me about feeding her later that day. "This child is hungry! This child needs to eat right now!"

"You're driving me crazy," I finally told her. "She's my baby."

I was running around trying to prepare a feeding bottle. Yimika screamed loud enough to put us both in a state of panic. Sheri rocked her. It was no mistake that the smallest, weakest person in the room was in control.

"All you did was push," Sheri said.

"No praise for a mother."

"Someone mothered you."

"I praise my mother. I praise her from when I suffered labor pains."

"Stop exaggerating. You had only seven hours labor. Feed my child, please."

"Your child didn't want to be born, and I don't blame her. You hear me? I don't blame you, my baby. All you did was arrive here on earth. Henceforth a state of confusion. Can't even get milk on time."

"What confusion? She will know what there is to know. Hurry up with this bottle."

"Shit, I can't do the cap!"

When people speak of turning points in their lives it makes me wonder. I can't think of one moment that made me an advocate for women prisoners in my country. Before this, I had opportunities to take action, only to end up behaving in ways I was accustomed, courting the same old frustrations because I was sure of what I would feel: wronged, helpless, stuck in a day when I was fourteen years old. Here it is: changes came after I made them, each one small. I walked up a stair. Easy. I took off a head tie. Very easy. I packed a suitcase, carried it downstairs, put it in my car. When situations became trickier, my tasks became smaller. My husband asked why I was leaving him. "I have to," I replied. Three words; I could say them. "What kind of woman are you?" Not a word. "Wouldn't you have tried to stop me too?" he asked. Probably, but he wouldn't have had to leave me to do what he wanted. My old neighbor from Sunrise Estate, Busola, a smile for her when she confided, "Everyone is talking about you. They say you left for no reason. He never beat you, never chased. I know he's moody, but he went to work for God's sake. What would you do married to a lazy bugger like mine?" And Sheri had this to say: "You wait. You just wait. Your father will ask when he's out, 'Why did you leave your husband?'"

My husband, our home and small suburban community like a busybody extended family, I had these reasons to stay. But I was lucky to have survived what I believed I wouldn't, the smell of my mother's death. I couldn't remain as I was before, otherwise my memory of her would have been in vain, and my survival would certainly be pointless. Anyone who experienced such a trauma would understand. The aftermath could be a reincarnation. One life was gone and I could either mourn it or begin the next. How terrifying and how sublime to behave like a god with the power to revive myself. This was the option I chose.

It would be another two months before I heard from my father. He had been in detention for ten months and our country was at the center of an international uproar over the hanging of nine environmental activists from the Niger Delta, including the writer Ken Saro-Wiwa. Greenpeace, Friends of the Earth, Amnesty International were protesting their murders. Our government remained unrepentant meanwhile. I was beginning to despair. One family in our campaign was facing eviction; another had welcomed a new child without their father.

That afternoon, Shalewa from next door had been with me, helping to watch Yimika. I was tidying my mother's living room, relieved that Yimika had finally fallen asleep when my mobile phone rang. I dashed for it, but it was too late. Yimika began to cry again. I picked her up then reached for the phone.

"Enitan?"

It was my father.

"Daddy? Daddy, is that you?"

His voice cracked. "I'm out!"

Tears filled my eyes.

"They released me today. Mukoro and the others. I thought I must call you first. Is that the baby? Is it a boy or a girl? This one cries like a fog horn. How is everyone, your husband, your mother? Fatai? You must bring the baby over. Where are you? I have so much to tell you. Enitan? Enitan, you're not talking. Are you still there?"

"Yes," I said.

I wiped the tears from my eyes.

"Where are you?" he said. "What my eyes have seen, I will never be the same again."

"Me too," I said.

I had to tell someone. Sheri was the first person I thought of. It was a humid afternoon. My back was wet with sweat and my windscreen heavy with dust and dried gnat legs. The sun burned through it.

My brother told me, once we began to talk freely, how he saw people's insides before he saw anything else. If he met a smoker, he saw their black lungs. If he met a woman with a huge chest, while his friends were getting cross-eyed, he could see the yellow fat deposits under her skin. Whenever he saw children, he saw their hearts, pink. I thought it was a strange view he had of the world. He said he did not have an imagination. He did not dream either, and had a hard time understanding women, though he grew up in a house full of them. But he loved cars. Once when he asked how I was feeling, and I said that I felt as if someone had tailgated me for miles, driving me off course. Suddenly I lost them, now I was lost myself, but I was finding my way home, small by small. He said he understood.

My heart was bubbling. I needed to stop; the traffic was too slow. Nearing the junction of a residential road, I pulled over. A couple of "All right-sirs" who had been sitting on a bench thought I needed their assistance to park. They began to direct me with conflicting hand signals. "To the left. Right. Yes, yes, reverse, reverse, slowly, slowly. Halt."

They seemed to be swatting flies. I acted as if they were invisible. I had no money to give. A driver behind pressed on his horn. I wound down and saw he was driving one of those private transport vans we called *danfos*.

"What?" I shouted. "Can't somebody be happy in peace?"

He pressed on his horn again. I checked my mirror. He would have to wait. I wriggled in my seat. The first song that came to me was a Yoruba one: Never dance the *palongo*. It can make you go crazy.

I sang the words aloud. The van crawled to the side of my car. I could see the passengers inside. Their faces were shiny with sweat. The driver spread his fingers. "Get out of my way!"

I stepped out of my car and began to sing to him.

"Never dance the *palongo*. It can make you go crazy."

The passengers clapped their hands in disgust. "Sistah what's wrong with you?" "Behaving like this?" "On a hot afternoon." "Grown woman like you." "Acting like a child."

I raised my hand in a fist. "Our men are free," I said.

The van driver blinked. "What? What is she saying?"

Someone relayed my message. "Our men are too free with women."

"Nothing good will come to you!" the van driver said.

"Tell him," I said. "Tell him, *a da*. It will be good. Everything good will come to me."

She repeated my message, but the driver seemed to have heard. He hopped out of his van.

"Maybe she's mad," someone offered.

One man simply hung his head. Yet another delay.

"Are you mad?" the driver asked. "You're mocking me? Is your head correct? I said move your vehicle out of my way."

My hands went up. I wriggled lower, and sang again.

"Never dance the *palongo*. It can make you go crazy."

The "All right-sirs" stood with their mouths open. The van driver looked me up and down.

"You must be a very stupid woman," he said.

"Was," I said.

"Maybe you didn't hear me," he said, flexing his arms.

I heard him. I danced the *palongo*, fearing nothing for my sanity, or common sense. I added a few foreign steps to disorientate the discontented so-and-so: flamenco, can-can, Irish dancing from side to side. Nothing could take my joy away from me. The sun sent her blessings. My sweat baptized me.